I0817747

THE ART OF PULP HORROR

©66 FRAZETTA

THE ART OF PULP HORROR

AN ILLUSTRATED HISTORY

EDITED BY STEPHEN JONES

FOREWORD BY ROBERT SILVERBERG

FEATURED ARTISTS

Bill Alexander
Al Avison
Jill Bauman
Rob Birchfield
Robert Bonfils
Randy Broecker
Hablot K. Browne
Margaret Brundage
Harry Clarke
Joseph Clement Coll
Frederick Cooper
Steve Crisp
Cyrus (“Ciro”) Cuneo
Sara Deck
Vincent Di Fate
Reginald Easton
Les Edwards
Bob Eggleton
Lee Elias
Ed (“Emsh”) Emshwiller
Virgil Finlay
John Richard Flanagan
Christopher Franchi
Frank Frazetta
David Henry Friston
Jack Gaughan
Gary Gianni
Thomas Gianni
Karl Godwin
Basil Gogos
Edmond Good
Károly Grósz
HagCult
Graham Humphreys
Richard Wynn Keene
Warren Kremer
Alan Lee
Mark Maddox
Chevalier Fortunino Matania
Paul McCaffrey
Dave McKean
Mike Mignola
Rowena Morrill
Lee Moyer
Rudy Palais
Bruce Pennington
Richard M. Powers
Sanjulián
Norman Saunders
E.F. Skinner
Walter Velez
H.J. Ward
Michael Whelan
Bernie Wrightson

www.elephantbookcompany.com

Published in 2025 by Lyons Press
An imprint of The Globe Pequot Publishing Group, Inc.
64 South Main Street, Essex, Connecticut 06426

Editorial director: Will Steeds
Project manager: Adam Newell
Book design: Paul Palmer-Edwards
Picture researcher: Sally Claxton

Printed in China

Library of Congress Cataloging-in-Publication Data is available upon request

ISBN 978-1-5400-3297-3

www.globepequot.com

FRONT ENDPAPERS: Splash-panel detail by veteran American comic book artist Rudy (Rudolph) Palais (1912–2004) from the five-page horror story "Screaming City" in Harvey Comics' *Witches Tales Magazine* Vol. 1, No. 7, January 1952.

HALF-TITLE PAGE: *People of the Black Circle* (2003), pen and ink illustration by American artist Gary Gianni from *Robert E. Howard's Complete Conan of Cimmeria Volume Two* (1934) (Wandering Star, 2003) for the novella first serialized in *Weird Tales*.

FRONTISPIECE: *Dracula Meets the Wolfman* (1966), oil on academy board by Frank Frazetta for Warren Magazines' *Creepy* No. 7, (February 1966), based on a pencil rough by Roy Krenkel. "I always had a pretty good time," said the artist, "and I think it shows in the art."

PREVIOUS SPREAD: Original cover art illustrating "L'uomo porco" (The Pig Man) in issue No. 33 of the Italian *fumetto*, *Il Vampiro presenta* (September 1977). Published by Edifumetto, the title ran for 123 issues over four series, from April 1972 to August 1980.

BACKGROUND THIS SPREAD: Hungarian-born artist Károly Grósz's stylized portrait of Bela Lugosi as "Dr. Mirakle" for the one-sheet poster for Universal Pictures' *Murders in the Rue Morgue* (Dir: Robert Florey, 1932), inspired by Edgar Allan Poe's story.

CONTENTS

FOREWORD

THOSE GAUDY PULPS!

Robert Silverberg

"The trick is not becoming a writer. The trick is staying a writer."

Harlan Ellison

"There is something about the literary life that repels me, all this desperate building of castles on cobwebs, the long-drawn acrimonious struggle to make something important which we all know will be gone forever in a few years, the miasma of failure which is to me almost as offensive as the cheap gaudiness of popular success."

Raymond Chandler

WHEN I WAS about ten I discovered Jules Verne's *Twenty Thousand Leagues Under the Sea*, and then H.G. Wells's *The Time Machine*, and my reading took a science-fictional twist: Donald A. Wollheim's two anthologies, *The Pocket Book of Science-Fiction* and *The Portable Novels of Science*, and then the science fiction magazines themselves.

Oh, the science fiction magazines! How I loved those gaudy pulps! I would run to the newsstand and buy the latest issue of *Thrilling Wonder Stories* or *Amazing Stories* or *Astounding Science-Fiction* and read it from cover to cover and back again, not comprehending everything I was reading, but loving it all. When I grow up, I told myself, I will write for these magazines.

Reader, that's exactly what happened.

I wrote my first science fiction story when I was about 13, and then wrote some more, and sent them to the editors of my favorite magazines, and by the time I was 15 or so the editors were sending me encouraging letters, and within a few years they were sending checks. I was pretty much a full-time science fiction writer by my third year of college, attending classes, more or less, by day, and then ducking into a telephone booth, changing into my superhero costume, and emerging as Captain Science Fiction to write stories half the night long. By the time I was 19 I discovered that I could write quickly and efficiently and that the editors would buy whatever I wrote. I sold stories to the bottom rungs of pulp-adventure fiction magazines and to the more cerebral upper-level ones with equal facility. The adventure magazines usually paid a cent a word and the fancier ones three times as much, which meant that I turned out the pulp stuff just as fast as I could type, and did a little more revising for the stories aimed for top-bracket magazines like *Galaxy* and *Astounding*. A 20-page story for *Astounding* would earn me $150, and half a century ago that was a lot of money, enough to pay for a month's rent on a very fine Manhattan apartment.

In June of 1956 I got my college degree, I married my college girlfriend a couple of months later, and I set up shop that summer as a full-time writer. Thus writing became my job straight out of college. I had not wanted any other sort of employment, and I made no attempt to find one. But I was not going to be supported by indulgent parents, nor did I have a trust fund that some thoughtful ancestor had established for me. My livelihood would have to be generated by my typewriter. My wife had a decently paying job, yes, so I can't say I was completely on my own, but we could hardly have lived on her earnings alone if my writing had failed to bring in an income. Rent had to be paid; furniture for our new apartment had to be bought; the pantry had to be stocked with food; whatever medical expenses we might have came out of our own checkbooks, not out of any medical insurance plan, since such things were rarities then, especially for self-employed writers. Telephone bills, electricity, the cost of typewriter ribbons and typing paper, a haircut now and then, movie tickets, restaurants, subway fares (even back then it was madness

How I loved those gaudy pulps! I would run to the newsstand and buy the latest issue of *Thrilling Wonder Stories* or *Amazing Stories* or *Astounding Science-Fiction* and read it from cover to cover and back again, not comprehending everything I was reading, but loving it all.

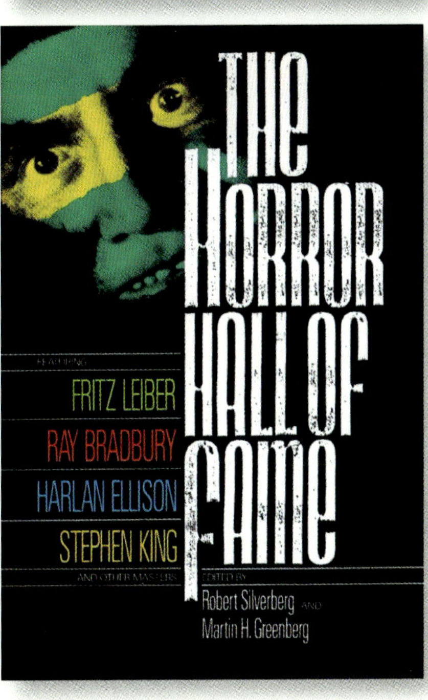

TOP LEFT: A number of fan letters by a teenage "Bob" Silverberg were published in the pulp magazines in the early 1950s, including one in the August 1950 issue of *Famous Fantastic Mysteries*, which had a striking cover by (Norman) Saunders.

ABOVE RIGHT: Robert Silverberg contributed a number of pseudonymous stories to M.J. Shapiro's monster magazines in the late 1950s, including two to the second issue of Magnum Publications' *Monster Parade* (November 1958).

TOP MIDDLE: Cover by "Emsh" (Ed Emshwiller) for the final issue of Headline Publications, Inc.'s digest magazine *Super-Science Fiction* (October 1959), a "Weird Monster Issue!" that included three stories by Robert Silverberg.

BOTTOM LEFT: The April 1974 edition of the Mercury Press, Inc.'s *The Magazine of Fantasy and Science Fiction* was a "Special Silverberg Issue" that featured three essays about the writer, a new novella, and another cover by Ed Emshwiller.

BOTTOM MIDDLE: Co-edited by Robert Silverberg, Martin H. Greenberg, and an uncredited Stefan Dziemianowicz, *The Horror Hall of Fame* (Carroll & Graf, 1991) collected 18 classic horror stories dating from 1839 to 1981.

to own a car in Manhattan), the occasional new pair of shoes—well, writers have expenses just like everyone else. What they don't have is regular paychecks.

What I had chosen for myself was the next-to-impossible task of earning my living as a full-time science fiction writer in an era when only two American publishers were regularly issuing science fiction novels and their total output was something like three or four titles a month, and an upheaval in magazine distribution had reduced the 30 or so science fiction magazines of 1953 to a mere handful of wobbly survivors. All of the greatest writers in science fiction, Alfred Bester, Isaac Asimov, Theodore Sturgeon, James Blish, Fritz Leiber, and a host of others, were in their primes and competing for the few available slots in the magazines that remained. I was a precociously skilled craftsman, and my stories all found ready markets, but there just weren't enough science fiction markets to absorb what I wrote, and though the magazines I wrote for paid very well, I had to sell them plenty of stories to cover the expenses of my new adult life. I wrote plenty of stories, all right. I wrote quickly, very quickly indeed, sometimes three or four stories a week. But I saw at once that I would have to look outside science fiction for much of my livelihood, because there simply weren't enough magazines left to absorb my vast output of work.

So I wrote all sorts of other things. I wrote Western stories, I wrote sports stories, I wrote vivid pseudo-fact articles about my adventures fighting giant crabs in the Caribbean or sinister Bedouins in the Sahara, and much, much more; a wildly varied output that amazes even me when I think about it now, 60 years later.

Coming straight out of college as I was, without any day job to see me through times of thin inspiration or editorial rejection and having no significant savings to draw on, there was no other option.

I didn't want to dilute my energies by putting in eight hours at some mundane job and trying to write science fiction in the evenings, as so many of my well-known colleagues did. I wanted to be a writer, not a public-relations man or a bookkeeper or a shoe salesman. But I wasn't of the sort of temperament that encouraged me to starve for the sake of my art, either. I have never been much into asceticism. I loved science fiction and yearned to write it as well as those of my predecessors whose work had given me such delight as a reader, but there was time to be an artist later, I reasoned: right now, if I wanted to make a go of it as a writer, I had to write whatever editors would be willing to pay me for.

Fiction magazines of all sorts began to experience difficulties in 1958, after a great upheaval in the magazine-distribution industry. When science fiction magazines seemed to be going out of fashion and monster movies were the rage in Hollywood, a good many magazines of horror fiction with "Monsters" in their titles were started then: among them *Monster Parade* and *Monsters and Things*, both of them edited by Larry T. Shaw, for whose science fiction magazines I had been a prolific contributor. When those magazines folded, Larry asked me to write some horror stories for the new magazines, and I turned in about a dozen of them over the next year, working under a host of pseudonyms.

I continued to write science fiction, of course. I suppose I believed that writing science fiction was what I had been put on Earth to do, and an astonishing number of stories about robots, spaceships, time machines, and the like flowed from my white-hot typewriter in that busy time 60 years ago. But nearly every month I wrote a crime story or two—or three, or four, or five—and took them downtown to turn them in at the office of W.W. Scott of two low-end crime-fiction magazines called *Trapped* and *Guilty*, along with my latest offerings for the science fiction magazine, *Super-Science Fiction*, that Harlan Ellison had talked him into publishing as well.

SF publishing was doing poorly then also, so I drifted into various other things, such as writing a series of books on archaeological and historical themes that for a decade became my main occupation. I did expand some of my longer stories into paperback novels in the mid-1960s.

I found real joy in writing at such great velocity, working with flying fingers and sweaty forehead—a 20-page story in a morning, a 40-page novelette in one six-hour working day.

I found real joy in writing at such great velocity, working with flying fingers and sweaty forehead—a 20-page story in a morning, a 40-page novelette in one six-hour working day. One draft was enough to do the job. I had the youthful energy to do that, day in and day out, throughout the year. And I loved the cognate fun of knowing that I had made myself part of a pulp-writer tradition that went back through such early SF favorites of mine as Henry Kuttner and Leigh Brackett and Poul Anderson and the rest to Edgar Rice Burroughs, Max Brand, Robert E. Howard, and the other famous high-volume writers of a pulp generation that had thrived before I was born.

I did, it must be said, learn a great deal about writing fiction from writing these stories: how to open a story in an interesting way and keep it moving, how to set a scene and sketch in a character (however roughly) without a lot of ponderous exposition, how to provide with a few quick touches a bit of color and inventiveness. And they allowed me to pay the bills regularly while I was getting ready to become the writer whose work brought me both critical praise and quite a decent income in the decades that followed. So as a writer I was born in the pulps, and though I traveled a long way from them in the years that followed, I look back on them and their era with warm nostalgic fondness.

OPPOSITE: *Spacerogue* (1958), acrylic on illustration board by American artist "Ed Emsh" (Edmund Alexander Emshwiller, 1925–90). The painting originally appeared on the cover of the November 1958 issue of the digest magazine *Infinity Science Fiction*, illustrating the novelette of the same name by "Webber Martin" (Robert Silverberg).

EMSH

INTRODUCTION
PULP FRICTION

Stephen Jones

"There is more than one way to burn a book. And the world is full of people running about with lit matches."

Ray Bradbury

FOR MOST CRITICS—especially those in the mainstream media—genre fiction has always been associated with "trash." And when it comes to the arts, then horror seems to be the trashiest genre of all.

As horror is already perceived by many to be a creative ghetto, then "pulp horror" must therefore be the lowest form of entertainment that could possibly exist.

Author and academic Clive Bloom has described horror as being "loud, brash, sexy, violent, passionate, and unlikely," which is about as good a description as any, while genre historian Mike Ashley noted that the pulp magazines "have received a great deal of bad press over the years and are still generally dismissed by many as of little merit. Whilst it is true that during the 1930s there were some appalling pulp magazines of dismal quality, that is not true of most pulps, and indeed in their early years, especially just before and after the First World War, the magazines carried much of interest and significance."

In fact, "pulp horror," as we know it today, grew out of the popularity of the cheaply produced penny dreadfuls, dime novels, and story papers that were produced in huge quantities during the late nineteenth and early twentieth centuries.

However, whereas the public has always been eager to consume gratuitous and gory tales of horror as a form of escapist entertainment, there have always been those who believed themselves to be morally superior to the masses and have done their best to curtail or ban such things.

It is worth remembering that back when it was first published, Mary Shelley's *Frankenstein; or, The Modern Prometheus* (1818)—a novel that the author did not originally attach her byline to because she was a woman—was described by *The Quarterly Review* as "a tissue of horrible and disgusting absurdity."

Bram Stoker's *Dracula* (1897) was dismissed upon publication by one reviewer as "more often grotesque than terrible," while even an author as well regarded as H.G. Wells was castigated for putting out "his talent to the most flagitious usury" and producing a volume "unworthy of restrained art" when he published *The Island of Doctor Moreau* in 1896.

From the earliest days of cinema, in America movies were often shown through what was known as the "states rights system," which meant that titles were sold directly—by territory—to a local distributor, who would then try to generate as much money from them as possible.

But state censorship boards could also insist on their own cuts, which meant that a number of US states objected to the scene where Boris Karloff's Monster innocently drowns the little girl in James Whale's *Frankenstein* (1931), or when Colin Clive's scientist blasphemously compares himself to God in the same film. Similarly, a number of sequences were excised from *King Kong* (1933)—including natives being trampled by Kong when he attacks a village, and the giant ape mistaking a sleeping woman for Ann Darrow and casually dropping her from a hotel window—while Tod Browning's *Freaks* (1932) was banned in some American states and cities, and also in the UK, where it was not released until 1963.

Whereas the public has always been eager to consume gratuitous and gory tales of horror as a form of escapist entertainment, there have always been those who believed themselves to be morally superior to the masses and have done their best to curtail or ban such things.

With growing political pressure over an "upsurge of violence and sexuality" in motion pictures, in 1930 the big Hollywood studios agreed to adopt a Catholic-influenced, self-regulated, "code of standards"—more popularly referred to as the "Hays Code" after Will H. Hays, who was president of the Motion Picture Producers and Distributors of America—as an alternative to the state-by-state film censorship boards that existed across America at that time. After July 1934, movies were additionally required to obtain a certificate of approval before they could be distributed.

TOP LEFT: William Reusswig's spooky cover for the first issue of Tower Magazine, Inc.'s bedsheet pulp *The Illustrated Detective Magazine* (December 1929) illustrated "Murder House" by Will Levinrew. It was sold exclusively in Woolworths and aimed at female readers.

BOTTOM LEFT: Free membership card for the Weird Tales Club, illustrated by Hannes Bok and signed by Martin Ware. Created in 1941 to help fans correspond or meet each other, the names and addresses of members were published in the letters column of *Weird Tales*.

TOP RIGHT: This typical newsstand in Omaha, Nebraska, photographed in November 1938 by John Vachon (1914–75) for the US government's Farm Security Administration, shows the wide range of pulp magazines that was available prior to World War II.

BOTTOM RIGHT: Herald for Universal Pictures' *The Old Dark House* (Dir: James Whale, 1932), which was based on a novel by J.B. Priestley. *Variety* called it "somewhat inane" and gave it a negative review, and the movie suffered from poor word of mouth.

Unfortunately, as with many movies reissued after the introduction of the Production Code, the studios had made cuts in the original camera negatives and the missing scenes were either lost or not rediscovered for decades.

Not only did they ban outright such films as *Island of Lost Souls* and *Freaks* in the UK, but in 1932, the British Board of Film Censors (BBFC) introduced the advisory "H" (for "horror") certification for films that included frightening or disturbing scenes, following an outcry led by the National Society for the Prevention of Cruelty to Children over the drowning of little Maria in *Frankenstein*. This restricted patrons to those aged 16 and over. With the outbreak of World War II, the British censor actually banned all "H" films in case they were considered too morbid and damaged public morale. The consequence of this was that many horror movies were not released in the UK until after 1945.

Following public concern over gory horror comic books being published for children, The Comics Magazine Association of America was formed in 1954 to create a Comics Code Authority, a self-policing "code of ethics and standards." Spurred on by Fredric Wertham's alarmist book *Seduction of the Innocent* (1954), and a Senate Subcommittee on Juvenile Delinquency that same year, the inevitable result was the cancellation of numerous titles and the collapse of such popular horror comics lines as EC and Harvey.

In Scotland, an outbreak of mass hysteria among schoolchildren led directly to the 1955 "Children and Young Persons (Harmful Publications) Act" being passed by Parliament. In September 1954 hundreds of children from the Hutchesontown district of Glasgow converged on the city's Victorian Southern Necropolis with stakes and penknives, searching for a seven-foot-tall "Gorbals Vampire"—a creature with iron teeth that they blamed for killing and eating two young boys.

Although initially linked to "Jenny wi' the Iron Teeth" —an urban legend about an old woman who supposedly haunted Glasgow Green in the early nineteenth century—an exceptional alliance of Christians, communists, and the National Union of Teachers blamed "lurid" imported American horror comic books for the panic, especially after it was discovered that a story called "The Vampire with the Iron Teeth" appeared in *Dark Mysteries* No. 15 (December 1953).

In the early 1980s, another association consisting of the popular press, religious organizations, and social commentators such as the self-appointed pressure group the National Viewers' and Listeners' Association, got together to lobby against the new videocassette industry in the UK. Due to a loophole in the law, video releases did not have to be reviewed by the British Board of Film Classification. As a result, there was a media-led outcry against these unregulated movies *possibly* being viewed by children. This ultimately led to Parliament passing the Video Recordings Act 1984, which imposed a stricter code of censorship on videos than was required for cinema releases.

Many horror films were (often wrongly) banned or randomly seized and confiscated by overzealous police forces as these so-called "video nasties" were blamed for an increase in violent crime among young people (including at least two totally unsubstantiated murder cases). Eventually, 39 films were successfully prosecuted under the Obscene Publications Act.

It is almost as if there is something subversive about "pulp horror"—something dangerous, challenging, radical—that the establishment doesn't want people to be influenced by.

Broadly speaking, the "pulp era" lasted from the late 1800s until the late 1900s. Over little more than a century it flourished in the underbelly of the creative arts, pushing the boundaries when it could, and challenging the status quo when it was needed. Writers, artists, and filmmakers toiled away in the cheapest, least appreciated markets to tell their tales or give form to their imaginations.

> In 1932, the British Board of Film Censors (BBFC) introduced the advisory "H" (for "horror") certification for films that included frightening or disturbing scenes . . . This restricted patrons to those aged 16 and over. With the outbreak of World War II, the British censor actually banned all "H" films in case they were considered too morbid and damaged public morale.

Ironically, it was probably Quentin Tarantino's 1994 movie *Pulp Fiction* which was partially responsible for starting to bring respectability to the term in the mainstream, and by the end of that decade true "pulp" was all but dead—superseded by knowingly self-referential or post-modern books and films that were merely cashing-in on their pulp origins rather than adding anything new to the genre. Possibly today, in our electronic age of political correctness, we consider ourselves too enlightened—or too sophisticated—for "pulp."

But for that century or so, pulp horror thrived—in periodicals, paperbacks, comic books, on television and in movies, and, of course, in the pulp magazines themselves.

During that period creators brought their garish, ghastly, and grotesque stories and images to a public that couldn't get enough of them, either on the newsstands or at the drive-ins, and this volume is a tribute to a time when there was a desire to push the limits of taste and creativity to new levels of acceptance.

And that, surely, is something that is always worth honoring and celebrating.

TOP MIDDLE: *The Case Against the Comics* was a 32-page pamphlet published in 1944 by the Catechetical Guild in St. Paul, Minnesota. Written by Gabriel Lynn, it firmly blamed comic books for fueling the rising tide of juvenile delinquency and immorality in America.

ABOVE LEFT: Trade advertisement from the April 2, 1953 edition of *Kinematograph Weekly* for the British re-release of *Dark Eyes of London* (aka *The Human Monster*, 1939) and *Dead Men Walk* (1943), which the BBFC reclassified with "X" certificates.

TOP RIGHT: Hy Fleishman's cover for Master Comics, Inc.'s pre-Code *Dark Mysteries* No. 15 (December 1953), which included the six-page story "The Vampire with Iron Teeth," supposedly the inspiration for Glasgow's "Gorbals Vampire" hysteria in September 1954.

BOTTOM MIDDLE: Hector Garrido's art for *The Little People* by John Christopher (Avon Books, 1968) is possibly the most "pulp" paperback cover ever, with its depiction of psychic Nazi "Gestapochauns" who enjoy a bit of S&M and prey on visitors to an Irish castle.

BOTTOM RIGHT: Refused a cinema certificate in 1972, Mario Bava's "slasher," *Ecologia del delitto* (aka *Blood Bath*/*A Bay of Blood*, 1971), was one of 72 films Britain's Director of Public Prosecutions deemed obscene when it was released on video.

ABOVE & RIGHT: *16th Annual Drive-Invasion* (2014), gouache on watercolor paper poster suggestive of beach, surf, and retro horror by British artist Graham Humphreys. "The client was happy for me to interpret the brief as I saw fit," recalls the artist. "I decided to turn the sea to blood by introducing a comical *Jaws*-themed attack, with spat-out surfer bones. Just to add to the fun, the monster selfie was a further reference to contemporary beach narcissism . . . as was the headless muscle man. The retro color palette was designed to signify the B-movie aesthetic."

Thomas Gianni '15

1

PENNY DREADFULS

SARAH CLEARY

You may imagine the horror and the consternation of those who entered the room to find her in the grasp of a fiend-like figure, whose teeth were fastened on her neck, and who was actually draining her veins of blood.

VARNEY THE VAMPIRE; OR, THE FEAST OF BLOOD (1845–47)

> "The amount of crime, treachery, murder and slow poisoning, and general infamy required [by my readers] . . . is something terrible."
>
> Mary Elizabeth Braddon (1835–1915)

> "There was an illustration to every number in which there was always a pool of blood, and at least one body."
>
> Charles Dickens (1812–70)

HAVING EXPERIENCED A myriad of changes during the twentieth century, one era in particular seemed to revolutionize and democratize the horror genre, not only the manner in which it was consumed, but the very audience it was consumed by. At the helm of this revolution was something very dreadful, very dreadful indeed . . .

Although an extremely popular (though contentious) genre associated with overindulgence and hyperbole, the Gothic literary tradition which emerged mid-eighteenth century with Horace Walpole's *The Castle of Otranto, A Gothic Story* (1764) provided something of a blueprint for genre fiction.

Emphasizing the Gothic's provocative dalliance with the more visceral and gruesome corners of our imagination, Matthew Lewis's controversial *The Monk: A Romance* (1796), along with countless other "maggot maladies" by authors such as Ann Radcliffe, Charlotte Dacre, and Wilkie Collins gave the reading public that escape and sense of danger they so desperately craved. However, while these novels were indeed popular, they were for the most part inaccessible to the majority of the British public due to widespread illiteracy and the fact that most editions were published as large, expensive, leather-bound books, at a cost far outside the spending remit of the lower classes.

One way to circumvent this cost was the publication of chapbooks, which flourished between 1770–1820. A means of publishing a broad spectrum of books—from Gothic romance, to adventure, to home improvement manuals in abridged periodical form—they were aimed mostly at an adult working-class audience. Produced in various sizes, depending upon the dimensions of the original sheet of paper, chapbooks consisted of multiple folds of paper sold as "street fiction." Falling out of vogue in the early nineteenth century, they underwent a transformation in terms of content, readership, and format and were reborn as "bloods," "penny dreadfuls," "shilling shockers," dime novels, pulp magazines, and, later still, comic books.

The popularity of the penny dreadful—or "penny blood" as they were originally known—cannot be underestimated, not only as a historical litmus recording the tastes of Victorian popular culture, but also a product of social and technological developments and advancements in nineteenth-century Britain.

After the Reform Bill of 1832, access to education was progressively expanded to include working-class children. Augmented in 1870 with the Forster Education Act, the government was now ultimately responsible for providing elementary schooling to the children of families who could ill-afford it otherwise. As a consequence of these reforms, literacy among the lower classes grew substantially.

The popularity of the penny dreadful—or "penny blood" as they were originally known—cannot be underestimated, not only as a historical litmus recording the tastes of Victorian popular culture, but also a product of social and technological developments and advancements in nineteenth-century Britain.

Faster methods of typesetting, machines manufacturing paper, and rotary steam presses able to churn out quarto and folio magazines, combined with an increased literacy, provided the perfect environment for the "blood" to flourish as a cheap form of entertainment. Typically issued on a weekly or bi-weekly basis, each "number" or "episode" was eight (or sometimes 16) pages, with an illustration filling half the front sheet and double columns of text for the remaining pages. Occasionally the text on the final page would end abruptly, often in mid-sentence if space ran out. The booklets were also trimmed down to weigh less than half an ounce, to further cut costs.

These cheap periodicals proved extremely popular with the public, and between 1830 and 1850 there were up to 100 publishers of penny-fiction. By the 1840s, even established publishing houses who produced more "highbrow" periodicals such as *The Calendar of Horrors* and *Terrific Tales* had to compete with a dominant penny dreadful market which dealt primarily in death, hardship, and misery—familiar themes to the majority of the readership.

Growth in escapist literature for the poorer classes coincided with one of the most horrific publications of the nineteenth century in which Sir Edwin Chadwick,

PREVIOUS SPREAD: ***The Adventure of the Sussex Vampire*** **(2015), oil on panel by American artist Thomas Gianni, based on Arthur Conan Doyle's Sherlock Holmes tale, first published in *The Strand*, January 1924. "I chose to paint this story," explains the artist, "not only because it is one of my favorites out of the Holmes canon, but because of its pulp-like quality and its suggestion of horror."**

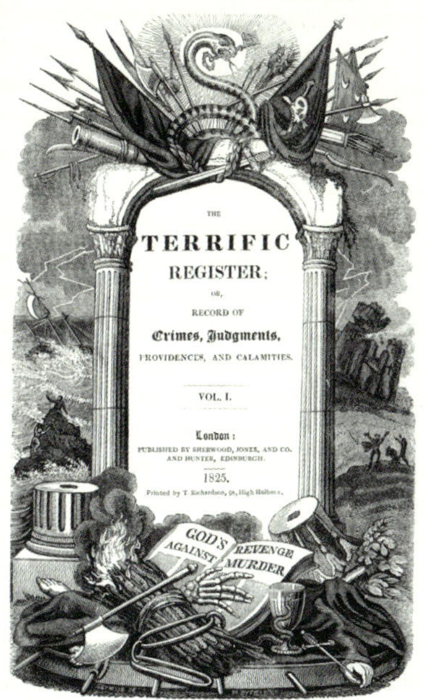

THE

TERRIFIC

REGISTER;

OR,

RECORD OF

Crimes, Judgments,

PROVIDENCES, AND CALAMITIES.

VOL. I.

London:

PUBLISHED BY SHERWOOD, JONES, AND CO.
AND HUNTER, EDINBURGH.

1825.

Printed by T. Richardson, 98, High Holborn.

THE STRING OF PEARLS. 225

"You know, Mrs. Ragg, the last you told me of him was that—that Mr. Todd had said he was mad, you know, and then you went to fetch somebody, and when you came back he was gone; and Mr. Todd told you the next day that poor Tobias ran off at great speed and disappeared. Has anything been heard of him since?"

THE MURDER OF THE USURER.

"Ah, my dear, alas! alas!"

"Why do you cry alas?—Have you any more sad news to tell me?"

"He was my only son—and all the world and his wife, as the saying is, can't tell how much I loved him."

Minna Gray clasped her hands, and, while the tears coursed down her young fair cheeks, she said—

"And I, too, loved him!"

No. 29.

No. II.] MAY, 1870. [Price One Shilling.

THE MYSTERY OF EDWIN DROOD. BY CHARLES DICKENS. WITH ILLUSTRATIONS.

LONDON: CHAPMAN & HALL, 193, PICCADILLY.

Advertisements to be sent to the Publishers, and ADAMS & FRANCIS, 59, Fleet Street, E.C.

[The right of Translation is reserved.]

On the tombstone, with upraised arms and rage in every feature, towered the terrific form of Spring-Heeled Jack. Freezer and Links stood transfixed; their ghastly burden slipped slowly to the grass, but they remained gaping, terror-struck. Vengeance had fallen!

ABOVE LEFT: Illustration entitled "The Vampyre's Midnight Visit" from the influential penny dreadful *Varney the Vampire; or, the Feast of Blood* (1845–47), attributed to writers James Malcolm Rymer (1814–84) and/or Thomas Preskett Prest (est. 1810–59).

TOP MIDDLE: A teenaged Charles Dickens had his "very wits" frightened out of his head by the gruesome "true life" wood engravings in Sherwood, Jones and Co.'s weekly *The Terrific Register; or, Record of Crimes, Judgments, Providences, and Calamities* (1823–25).

TOP RIGHT: An engraved illustration of "The Murder of the Usurer" by demon barber Sweeny Todd in the penny dreadful serial "The String of Pearls: A Romance" (1846–47), once again attributed to writers James Malcolm Rymer and/or Thomas Preskett Prest.

BOTTOM MIDDLE: The cover of the second issue (May 1870) of Chapman & Hall's shilling serial *The Mystery of Edwin Drood*, which remained uncompleted upon Charles Dickens's death on June 9, 1870, with only six of its intended 12 illustrated installments published.

BOTTOM RIGHT: Inspired by an urban myth based on sightings of a demonic figure, *Spring-Heeled Jack* was first turned into a popular penny dreadful in 1867. It was later adapted into a 12-part weekly serial in 1904 by "Charlton Lea" (Alfred Burrage) for the Aldine Publishing Co.

TOP LEFT: A collection of supernatural stories for Christmas, *Ghost Stories and Phantom Fancies* by [James] Hain Friswell (1825–78) was published at a cost of two shillings by Richard Bentley in 1858. Author and essayist Friswell strongly campaigned against the penny dreadfuls.

TOP MIDDLE: *The Whitechapel Murders; or, An American Detective in London* appeared as No. 21 (November 1888) of Laird & Lee Publishers' monthly *The Pinkerton Detective Series*, which featured highly fictionalized cases of the private detective agency.

BOTTOM LEFT: British author Bracebridge Hemyng's Young Jack Harkaway confronted a giant sea-serpent in *The Five Cent Wide Awake Library No. 1334* (August 27, 1897), published weekly by New York dime novel pioneer Frank Tousey (1853–1902).

BOTTOM MIDDLE: The January 4, 1905 edition of another of Frank Tousey's story papers, *Pluck and Luck: Complete Stories of Adventure* (No. 344). This weekly reprint became the longest-running dime novel series, lasting for 1,605 issues between 1898–1929.

ABOVE RIGHT: Frank Tousey was also the original publisher of *Mystery Magazine*, which featured "A Story of the Voodoo Worshippers" on the front cover of its first issue, dated November 15th, 1917. It lasted for seven years before finding a new publisher.

Commissioner for Public Health, produced a *Report on the Sanitary Condition of the Labouring Population of Great Britain*. His findings, which portrayed urban Britain as a dystopian landscape of open sewers spilling raw sewage onto public streets and pauper-graveyards literally bursting at the seams with the corpses of the poor, provided the perfect backdrop for Gothic tales of horror read by candlelight. Consequently, capitalizing on the popularity of earlier Gothic novels, blatant plagiarism was rife among penny dreadfuls.

In one example clearly influenced by Ann Radcliffe, *Angela, the Orphan; or, The Bandit Monk of Italy: A Romance* (1841) presented a mixture of elements from both *The Italian, or The Confessional of the Black Penitents, A Romance* (1797) and *The Mysteries of Udolpho, A Romance* (1794), as the heroine at the center of the narrative was packed off to a nunnery, locked up in a castle by an evil uncle, and finally rescued by a hero in disguise.

Seen as a corrupting influence among the poor, penny dreadfuls became a central player in a Victorian bourgeoisie anxiety pertaining to the contaminating effects of such literature upon the working classes.

Influenced heavily by Lewis's *The Monk*, another very popular late Gothic novel that was issued in penny parts was *The Black Monk; or, The Secret of the Grey Turret: A Romance* (1844), attributed to James Malcolm Rymer. Rymer, however, would become best known for his vampire periodical featuring a hapless, even camp, creature who inevitably grows more sympathetic as the narrative progresses throughout 200 chapters.

Varney the Vampire; or, the Feast of Blood first appeared in 1845–47, detailing the adventures of Sir Francis Varney and the trouble he inflicted upon the formerly well-to-do Bannerworths, disgraced by their recently deceased father. Credited with shaping much of the vampiric tropes we know today, *Varney the Vampire* heavily influenced the most famous of all vampire fictions by Irish writer Bram Stoker, half a century later. After more than 670,000 words, the melancholic Varney—unable to stay dead by conventional means as he was "revived by moonbeams"—finally achieved his end goal by throwing himself headlong into Mount Vesuvius!

A further source of inspiration for penny dreadfuls came from the news headlines themselves, with various versions of the *Newgate Calendar* frequently reprinted as penny dreadfuls featuring some of the most gruesome murders of the time. One of the earliest cases of true crime to find its way into penny issues was "Sawney Bean, the Man-Eater of Scotland." Traditionally linked to controversial London publisher Edward Lloyd, the narrative concerned a real-life fourteenth-century cave-dwelling cannibal who, together with his incestuous clan, murdered and ate passers-by. It ran for 104 parts in *The Terrific Register; or, Record of Crimes, Judgments, Providences, and Calamities* (1825). Signaling a tonal and stylistic shift from Gothic to horror, the emphasis on physical violence paved the way for a more brutal and visceral form of literature.

Making his debut appearance in "The String of Pearls: A Romance," the most enduring of penny dreadful characters —Sweeney Todd, the Demon Barber of Fleet Street— appeared over 18 weekly parts in Lloyd's *People's Periodical and Family Library* (1846–47). As a tale of pitch-black humor, *double entendres*, and extreme brutality—in which Todd and his co-conspirator Mrs. Lovett sold pies made from Todd's victims—it proved itself extremely popular.

A further monstrosity which, strangely enough, first appeared in actual news headlines in the 1830s, was a bearded creature by the name of "Spring-Heeled Jack." Like the Loch Ness Monster, flying saucers, and Bigfoot, Jack was an urban legend, who arrived in a storm and roll of thunder jumping across the rooftops of London with his "bat-like wings." By 1867 he had his own serial spanning more than 40 issues.

Seen as a corrupting influence among the poor, penny dreadfuls became a central player in a Victorian bourgeoisie anxiety pertaining to the contaminating effects of such literature upon the working classes. In 1874, journalist James Greenwood called the dreadfuls "penny packets of poison," while in a paper delivered to the Religious Tract Society in 1878, terrified that the masses had "infected" the upper classes with a fondness for "cheap filth," Lord Shaftesbury exclaimed that "it [penny dreadful fiction] is creeping not only into the houses of the poor, neglected and untaught, but into the largest mansions; penetrating into religious families, and astounding careful parents by its frightful issues."

Furthermore, these early periodicals shared many similarities with 1950s horror comics (which in turn grew out of the boys' magazines of the late nineteenth century). Printed on cheap pulp paper, and often tinged with the supernatural, the penny dreadfuls and their American cousin, the dime novel, were infamous for their lurid and graphic descriptions of murder and dismemberment. A century on, horror comics would also find themselves subject to severe condemnation, resulting in an informal ban after government investigations into their apparent ability to corrupt and deprave young boys and girls.

The popularity of the horror genre has always seemed to parallel social reform and upheaval, capturing the zeitgeist of the time and reproducing it as a manifestation of our contemporary anxieties and changing tastes. Without the penny dreadfuls and dime novels of the nineteenth and early twentieth centuries, we would never have had the pulp magazines, horror movies and comics, and paperback books that followed.

OPPOSITE: *Edgar Allan Pope 1809–49* (2015), pencil, Painter, and Photoshop portrait by American artist Lee Moyer. "He looked outward to the cosmos," says the artist, "but never forgot the fears and excesses of the earthbound. Poe was no saint, but he was one hell of a writer. *Amen.*"

ABOVE LEFT: *Ligeia* (1923), pen and ink, and watercolor by Irish artist Harry Clarke (1889–1931), done for the 1923 reprint of *Tales of Mystery and Imagination.* Edgar Allan Poe's story first appeared in *The American Museum of Science, Literature, and the Arts* (September 1838).

ABOVE RIGHT: *Murders in the Rue Morgue* (1976), oil on board by American artist Berni(e) Wrightson (1948–2017), done for *The Edgar Allan Poe Portfolio.* Poe's tale—considered the first detective story—originally appeared in the April 1841 issue of *Graham's Lady's and Gentleman's Magazine.*

TOP LEFT: Richard R. Montgomery's "Jack and I! or, The Secrets of King Pharaoh's Caves" appeared in issue No. 208 (May 28, 1902) of Frank Tousey's story paper *Pluck and Luck*. Boy inventor Jack Wright was created in 1891.

TOP MIDDLE: Proudly subtitled *An Interesting Weekly for Young America*, No. 220 of *Work and Win* (February 20, 1903) featured Hal Standish's dime novel "Fred Fearnot and the Haunted House! or, Unraveling a Great Mystery."

BOTTOM LEFT: "Buffalo Bill's Dead Drop or, Pawnee Bill Betrayed," by "the author of *Buffalo Bill*," was reprinted in No. 354 (June 21, 1919) of Street & Smith's dime novel series *New Buffalo Bill Weekly*, which ran from 1912–19.

BOTTOM MIDDLE: There were more ghosts of the Wild West in *The Boys' Friend* No. 654 (December 20, 1913) with "The Red Man's Ghost" by Andrew Gray. This boys' story paper was an attempt to put the penny dreadfuls out of business.

ABOVE RIGHT: Tom Merry and the juniors of St. Jim's school were on the trail of a mysterious hooded kidnapper in "The Hidden Hand!" by "Martin Clifford" (Charles Hamilton) in No. 1,505, of the Amalgamated Press's *The Gem* (December 19th, 1936).

Chillers for "Chums"

From the early 1900s through to the wartime paper shortage of the 1940s, many of the big newspaper publishers in Britain produced illustrated "story papers" aimed at boys (and sometimes girls). These usually weekly titles were predominantly intended for a young male readership (often referred to as "chums" in print) and would regularly feature stories or serials that combined ghosts, monsters, or dinosaurs with ripping school yarns and thrilling detective mysteries.

ABOVE LEFT & TOP RIGHT: Billy Bunter and his fellow pupils from Greyfriars investigated a skeletal ghost in "The Spectre of Hoad Castle!" by "Frank Richards" (Charles Hamilton again) in No. 1,335 of *The Magnet* (September 16th, 1933).

BOTTOM MIDDLE & RIGHT: The prolific British writer Edwy Searles Brooks (1889–1965) was a regular contributor of stories to Allied Newspapers' *Boys' Magazine*, which ran for a total of 627 issues (1922–34). This included "Vampires in Terrorland" (the first in the "Terrorland" series) in issue No. 522 (March 5, 1932) and "The Werewolf of Blackston Hall" in No. 580 (April 13, 1933), featuring his detective hero Bulldog Hamilton. Under his own name and others, Brooks wrote around 40 million words.

TOP LEFT: *The Black Guest of Drumgunniol* (1847), steel engraving by Hablot K. Browne (aka "Phiz") for the novel *The Fortunes of Colonel Torlogh O'Brien: A Tale of the Wars of King James* by J. Sheridan Le Fanu (1814–73), first serialized anonymously in the *Dublin University Magazine*.

BOTTOM LEFT: Electrotype after wood engraving by British illustrator David Henry Friston for the third (February 1872) of four installments of Irish author Joseph Sheridan Le Fanu's seminal vampire novella "Carmilla" to appear in *The Dark Blue* (December 1871–March 1872).

ABOVE RIGHT: George Brinsley Le Fanu (1854–1929) compiled and illustrated his father's posthumous collection *The Watcher and Other Weird Stories*, (Downey & Co., 1894). The book featured six stories, including the classic 1839 novelette "Strange Event in the Life of Schalken the Painter."

TOP LEFT: Founded in July 1877, *Journal des voyages: et des adventures de terre et de mer* (Journal of Journeys and Adventures of Land and Sea) was a weekly French travel/adventure story paper that lasted until 1949. George Conrad's cover for the May 5, 1907 issue (No. 544) depicted Russian zombies.

TOP MIDDLE: Spanish story paper apparently based on a series of comedic French silent movie shorts (1910–21) starring actor Georges Vinter as the eponymous "clever detective" of the title. *Nick Winter* No. 20 (circa 1910s) featured the anonymous story "La posada de la muerte" (The Inn of Death).

ABOVE RIGHT: Nazi artist Richard Klein's cover for the March 1921 edition of the German magazine *Der Orchideengarten: Phantastische Blätter* (The Orchid Garden: Fantastic Tales). Widely considered to be the world's first horror publication, it ran from 1919–21 (51 issues).

BOTTOM LEFT: With cover art by "Niel" (probably Daniel Masgoumiery i Pena), issue No. 36 of the Spanish "cloak and sword" story paper *Mascara Negra (El Vengador)* (Black Mask The Avenger, circa 1925), pitted its masked swordsman hero against a collection of fantastic apparitions.

BOTTOM MIDDLE: *Terkedilmiş Maden Ocaği* (Mystery of the Abandoned Mine), No. 7 (circa 1930) in the *Meshur Amerikan Polis Hafiyesi* (Great American Detective) series, published in Turkey by Güven Basimevi and featuring German "King of the Detectives" Nat Pinkerton.

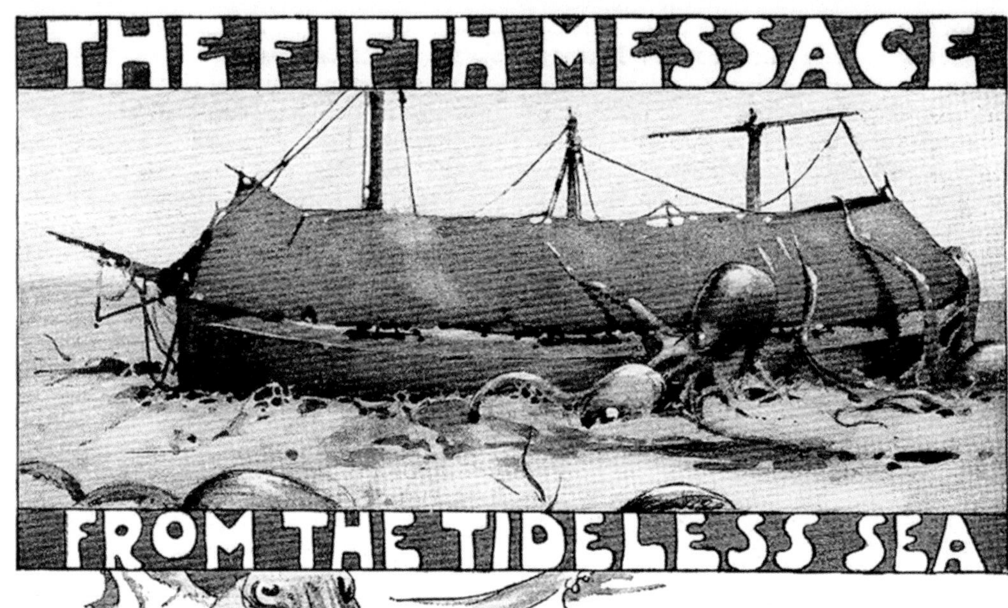

A Complete Short Story

By WILLIAM HOPE HODGSON

Illustrated by Lawson Wood

LEFT: "The Goddess of Death" was the first published story by British author William Hope Hodgson (1877–1918) [BOTTOM RIGHT]. It first appeared in the April 1904 issue of *The Royal Magazine* with this illustration by Italian-American artist Cyrus ("Ciro") Cuneo.

BOTTOM MIDDLE: E.F. Skinner's illustration for "From the Tideless Sea" in the April 1906 edition of the American periodical *The Monthly Story Magazine*. This was the first of William Hope Hodgson's series of "Sargasso Sea" stories, reprinted the following May in the UK.

TOP RIGHT: William Hope Hodgson's "The Fifth Message from the Tideless Sea" (aka "More News from the Homebird") was first published in 1907 and was reprinted in the May 1911 issue of *The London Magazine* with this heading illustration by Lawson Wood.

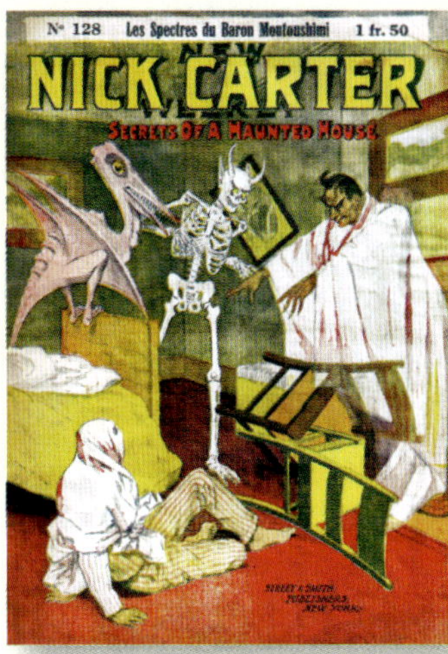

The Grand American Detective

Gentleman detective Nick Carter was created by Ormond G. Smith and John R. Coryell and made his debut in the September 18, 1886 issue of the story paper *New York Weekly*. The character soon got his own dime novel magazine from Street & Smith Publishers, *New Nick Carter Weekly*, which was published all over the world. The October 26, 1907 edition (No. 565) [ABOVE LEFT] featured the story "Secrets of a Haunted House" (probably written by Frederick Van Rensselaer Dey). The issue was subsequently reprinted in France [TOP RIGHT] with reworked cover art, Spain [MIDDLE RIGHT] with new cover art by Luis Palao, and Italy [BOTTOM RIGHT], again with new art. In later years the character was revived in pulp magazines, novels, comic books, movies, and a radio show. Prolific dime novel author Dey committed suicide in a New York hotel on April 25, 1922 when he thought that his literary career was drying up.

MARY AND HER MONSTER

"I was much amused, and it appeared to excite a breathless eagerness in the audience . . . all stayed till it was over."

Mary Wollstonecraft Shelley

"Do Not go to the Lyceum to see the monstrous Drama, founded on the improper work called *Frankenstein*—Do not take your wives and families—The novel itself is of a decidedly immoral tendency."

Leaflet issued by the London Society for the Prevention of Vice and Immorality (1823)

PART NIGHTMARE OF dead babies resurrected, part playful dare between friends, Mary Shelley's biotechnological anomaly was born out of an era of scientific skepticism and religious dogmatism. A response to philosopher Jean-Jacques Rousseau's "Theory of Man," no doubt influenced by the burgeoning "Vitalist Controversy," in *Frankenstein; or: The Modern Prometheus* Shelley explored both scientific and philosophical anxieties rife within post-Enlightenment society.

Published anonymously by small London publishing house Lackington, Hughes, Harding, Mavor, & Jones on January 1, 1818, the novel had a modest start with a small run of only 500 copies in three volumes. Considered by critics a godless text, *The Quarterly Review* described it—quite ironically given the subject matter—as a "tissue of horrible and disgusting absurdity." Arguably prompted by the popularity of Richard Brinsley Peake's musical melodrama *Presumption! or, the Fate of Frankenstein* on the stage in July 1823, which Shelley attended but once, sarcastically proclaiming that she had found herself famous, a second edition now including her name was published on August 11, 1823 in two volumes by G. and W.B. Whittaker.

Long before Colin Clive roared "It's alive!" on screen, theatrical productions of *Frankenstein* made significant contributions towards "constructing" and "deconstructing" the mythos of Shelley's Monster.

A testament to the intertextuality of these adaptations, Shelley's 1831 revision of the novel diluted the religious and moral complexities of her central characters in keeping with the highly popular appetite for dramatic yet simplistic stage adaptations, such as Peake's three-act *Presumption*.

Having created iconoclastic characters that challenged the shallow trappings of civility, for the most part these adaptations and revisions downplayed such indictments. Similarly lost in adaptation was one of the most significant themes of the novel: the doppelgänger, favoring instead the more burlesque stock characters of hero, villain, heroine, and clown in varying degrees of narrative fidelity.

Examples are numerous, but some of the most popular nineteenth-century adaptations included *Humgumption; or, Dr. Frankenstein and the Hobgoblin of Hoxton* (1823), *Presumption and the Blue Demon* (1823), *Another Piece of Presumption* (1823), and *Frank-in-Steam; or, The Modern Promise to Pay* (1824) by unknown dramatists. Also, Henry M. Milner's *Frankenstein; or, The Man and the Monster!* (1826), John Kerr's *The Monster and Magician; or, The Fate of Frankenstein* (1826), William and Robert Brough's *Frankenstein; or, The Model Man* (1849), and Richard Henry's *Frankenstein; or, The Vampire's Victim* (1887).

Shelley's revision of the original novel in 1831 diluted the religious and moral complexities of her central characters.

By 1910, when Mary's Monster made his cinematic debut, the complexity of interchangeability between man and creature—facilitated through a sustained emphasis on mirroring—would make a welcome return. Written and directed by J. Searle Dawley for the Edison Company, this self-described "liberal adaptation" bravely flirted with a renewed focus on re-humanizing the Monster. What's more, in a deliberate attempt to re-engage the doppelgänger, in the final moments of the film, staring at his master in what seems to be a doorway or frame, the Monster suddenly disappears, leaving only Frankenstein's reflection on a looking-glass.

Adapted time and time again, *Frankenstein* remains one of the most culturally ubiquitous texts of literary history. What has remained a constant, however, is an unceasing desire to displace and vex the very authority of the "original" narrative.

Enduring countless metamorphoses, destroyed only to be reborn again, *Frankenstein* reflects specific cultural appetites, yet remains quintessentially timeless. *SC*

Number 431. COMPLETE. One Penny.

DICKS' STANDARD PLAYS.

FRANKENSTEIN.

BY R. B. PEAKE.

ORIGINAL COMPLETE EDITION.—PRICE ONE PENNY.

*** THIS PLAY CAN BE PERFORMED WITHOUT RISK OF INFRINGING ANY RIGHTS.

LONDON: JOHN DICKS, 313, STRAND.

TOP LEFT: Posthumous miniature portrait (circa 1857) of Mary W. Shelley by Reginald Easton (1807–93), commissioned by Sir Percy and Lady Shelley and based upon a death-mask, following Mary's death on February 1, 1851 at the age of 53.

TOP MIDDLE: Mr. T. (Thomas) P. (Potter) Cooke (1786–1864) portrayed the unidentified Monster in the theatrical "Romance," *Presumption! or, the Fate of Frankenstein,* which opened at London's English Opera House in 1823.

BOTTOM LEFT: Cover of the one-penny Dicks' Standard Plays edition of *Presumption! or, the Fate of Frankenstein* by playwright R. (Richard) B. (Brinsley) Peake (1792–1847). Peake created the line "It lives!" and the character of the assistant "Fritz".

BOTTOM MIDDLE: Actor Thomas Potter Cooke recreated his role of the mute Monster in *Le Monstre et le magicien* by Jean-Toussaint Merle and Antoine-Nicolas Béraud, which opened at the Théâtre de le Porte Saint-Martin in Paris in 1826.

ABOVE RIGHT: Sketch by Richard Wynn Keene (aka designer "Dykwynkyn") of the British actor O. Smith (Richard John Smith, 1786–1855) as the Monster in the summer 1828 revival of *Presumption! or, the Fate of Frankenstein* at the Lyceum.

ABOVE LEFT: A gigantic caterpillar turned into an even more gigantic moth in "Winged Terror" by G.R. Malloch (*Pearson's Magazine*, February 1931), which was reprinted the same year in the June issue of *Weird Tales* as "Moth."

TOP MIDDLE: The anonymous story "The Channel Tunnel and—Dynamite" ran complete in issue No. 428 (May 17, 1930) of Allied Newspapers Ltd.'s weekly *Boys' Magazine*, which published 627 issues between 1922 and 1934.

BOTTOM MIDDLE & RIGHT: The weekly *The Nelson Lee Library* was launched by The Fleetway House (later The Amalgamated Press) in June 1915 and ran through four series (a total of 956 issues) until August 1933. Detective Nelson Lee, his assistant Nipper, and the schoolboys of St. Frank's had to deal with gigantic crustaceans in both "The Island of Ships" by S.B. Halstead (No. 25, July 12th, 1930) and "The Scarlet Death" by Edwy Searles Brooks (No. 144, October 22nd, 1932).

TOP RIGHT: The anonymously written "Monster of the Marsh" appeared in *Scoops* No. 3 (February 24), a weekly science fiction story paper launched by C. Arthur Pearson that ran for just 20 issues from February 10 to June 23, 1934.

TOP & BOTTOM LEFT: The pocket-sized *The Boys' Friend Library* was launched by Amalgamated Press in September 1906 and lasted until World War II paper shortages killed off the title in June 1940 (after a total of 1,440 issues over two series). Most of the fiction was reprinted from other story papers. *Gan Waga's Island!* (1922) by Sidney Drew (Edgar Joyce Murray) appeared in No. 691 (November 30, 1923) and *The Isle of Peril* (1928–29) by Stacey Blake was in the second series No. 256 (September 4, 1930).

ABOVE RIGHT: Interior illustration by Italian-born artist Chevalier Fortunino Matania (1881–1963) in *The Passing Show* (June 15, 1935) for the apocalyptic serial "The Thousandth Frog" by American author Wynant Davis Hubbard.

TOP MIDDLE: H. (Harry) Irving Hancock's Fu Manchu-like villain, Li Shoon, made his debut in "Under the Ban of Li Shoon" in Street & Smith's *Detective Story Magazine* Vol. 4, No. 3 (August 5, 1916). He was described as "A wonder at everything wicked."

ABOVE LEFT: H. Bedford-Jones's "Mr. Shen of Shensi" appeared in the October 1, 1919 issue of Street & Smith's *The Thrill Book*, widely regarded to be the first US horror and science fiction magazine. This cover was later reused on the April 1931 issue of *The Shadow*.

TOP RIGHT: Self-styled "King of the World," Lama Kwen Sun, was the Oriental villain of the serial "The Scarlet Scorpion!" by Arthur Brooks (Arthur C. Marshall), which began in Vol. III, No. 27 (July 14th, 1923) of the weekly British boys' paper *The Champion*.

BOTTOM MIDDLE: World-famous detective Ferrers Locke and his clever young assistant Jack Drake battled the eponymous villain in No. 31 (January 30, 1926) of *The Boys' Friend Library: The Yellow Claw!* by Hedley Scott (Hedley Percival Angelo O'Mant).

BOTTOM RIGHT: Edward Dalton Stevens's cover for Macfadden's *True Detective Mysteries* Vol. XIII, No. 5 (August 1930) illustrated "Tong War!" by Yee Kong, the notorious "Lone Wolf" of the Suey Sing Tong, who supposedly gave his thrilling story as he faced the gallows.

ABOVE RIGHT: *On the Bottom Step of the Stair, Facing Me, Stood Dr. Fu-Manchu!*, pen and ink illustration by American artist Joseph Clement Coll (1881–1921) from *Collier's* (June 28, 1913) for "The Knocking on the Door," part ten of *The Insidious Dr. Fu-Manchu.*

TOP LEFT: *Fu Manchu's Daughter*, pen and ink illustration by Australian-born artist John Richard Flanagan (1895–1964), who illustrated all Sax Rohmer's stories in *Collier's* from 1929 to 1935. This is from Chapter IX, which appeared in the May 3rd, 1930 issue.

BOTTOM LEFT: First published in *The Illustrated London News*, Christmas Number 1918, *The Golden Scorpion* by "Sax Rohmer" (Arthur Henry Sarsfield Ward) appeared in hardcover from Methuen & Co. Ltd. in 1919 with a cover by British artist Frank Wright.

BOTTOM MIDDLE: The cover by Polish-born artist W. (Wladyslaw) T. (Teodore) Benda (1873–1948) for the first part of Sax Rohmer's 12-part serial "The Mask of Fu Manchu" in *Collier's* (May 7, 1932) was adapted for the book cover, published by A.L. Burt the same year.

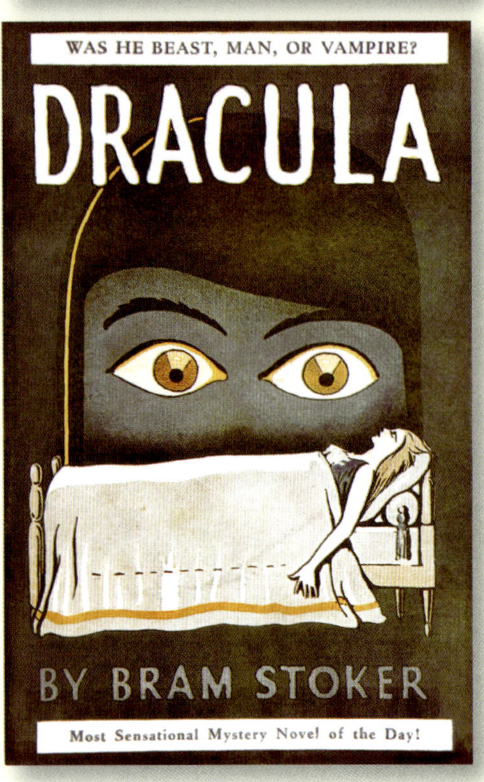

The HORROR OMNIBUS

Two Famous Novels of the Supernatural, Complete in One Volume

"DRACULA" by Bram Stoker

"FRANKENSTEIN" by Mary W. Shelley

SKRENDA

TOP LEFT: Handforth's dust jacket art for the posthumously published *Dracula's Guest and Other Weird Stories* by Bram Stoker (George Routledge & Sons, 1914), which collected a deleted chapter from the novel and eight other stories.

BOTTOM LEFT: This 1927 reprinting of Bram Stoker's *Dracula* from Grosset & Dunlap was a tie-in to John L. Balderston's stage play, which opened at the Fulton Theatre on Broadway in October that year and starred Hungarian actor Bela Lugosi.

ABOVE RIGHT: *The Horror Omnibus* (Grosset & Dunlap, 1939) reprinted the novels *Dracula* by Bram Stoker and *Frankenstein* by Mary W. "Skelley" (as misspelled on the title page!) with dust jacket art by Alfred G. Skrenda (1897–1978).

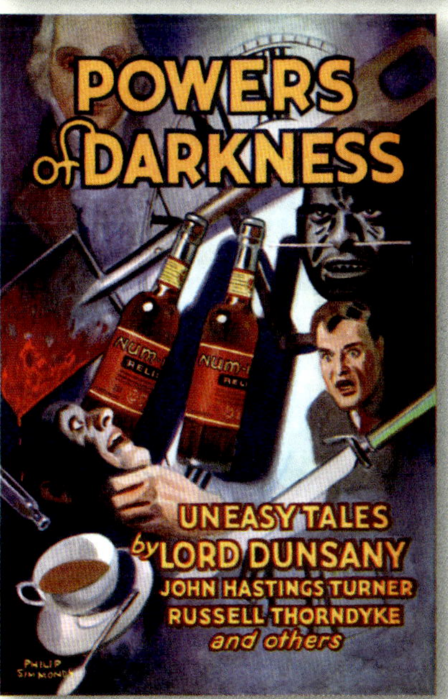

ABOVE LEFT: Seventh printing (April, 1927) of *Not at Night* (Selwyn & Blount, 1925), the first of a series of 12 British hardcover horror anthologies edited by Christine Campbell Thomson (1897–1985) that took its name from this volume.

TOP MIDDLE: The Creeps Library was published in hardcover in the UK by Philip Allan from 1932–37. The anthology *Shivers: A Third Collection of Uneasy Tales* (1932) featured a truly bizarre dust jacket painting by Nat Long.

TOP RIGHT: The 1921 collection *The Strange Papers of Dr. Blayre* by "Christopher Blayre" (Edward Heron-Allen) was reissued in 1932 with two variant dust jackets, this one reusing Nat Long's artwork for the initial *Creeps* (1932) anthology.

BOTTOM MIDDLE: The Creeps series was edited by writer Sir Charles Birkin (1907–85), who remained uncredited. *Powers of Darkness* (1934) had a cover by Philip Simmonds, illustrating Lord Dunsany's "The Two Bottles of Relish."

BOTTOM RIGHT: *Thrills* (1935) was the tenth in the popular Creeps anthology series and included stories by series regulars Tod Robbins, H. Russell Wakefield, and "Charles Lloyd" (editor Birkin himself), along with William F. Temple.

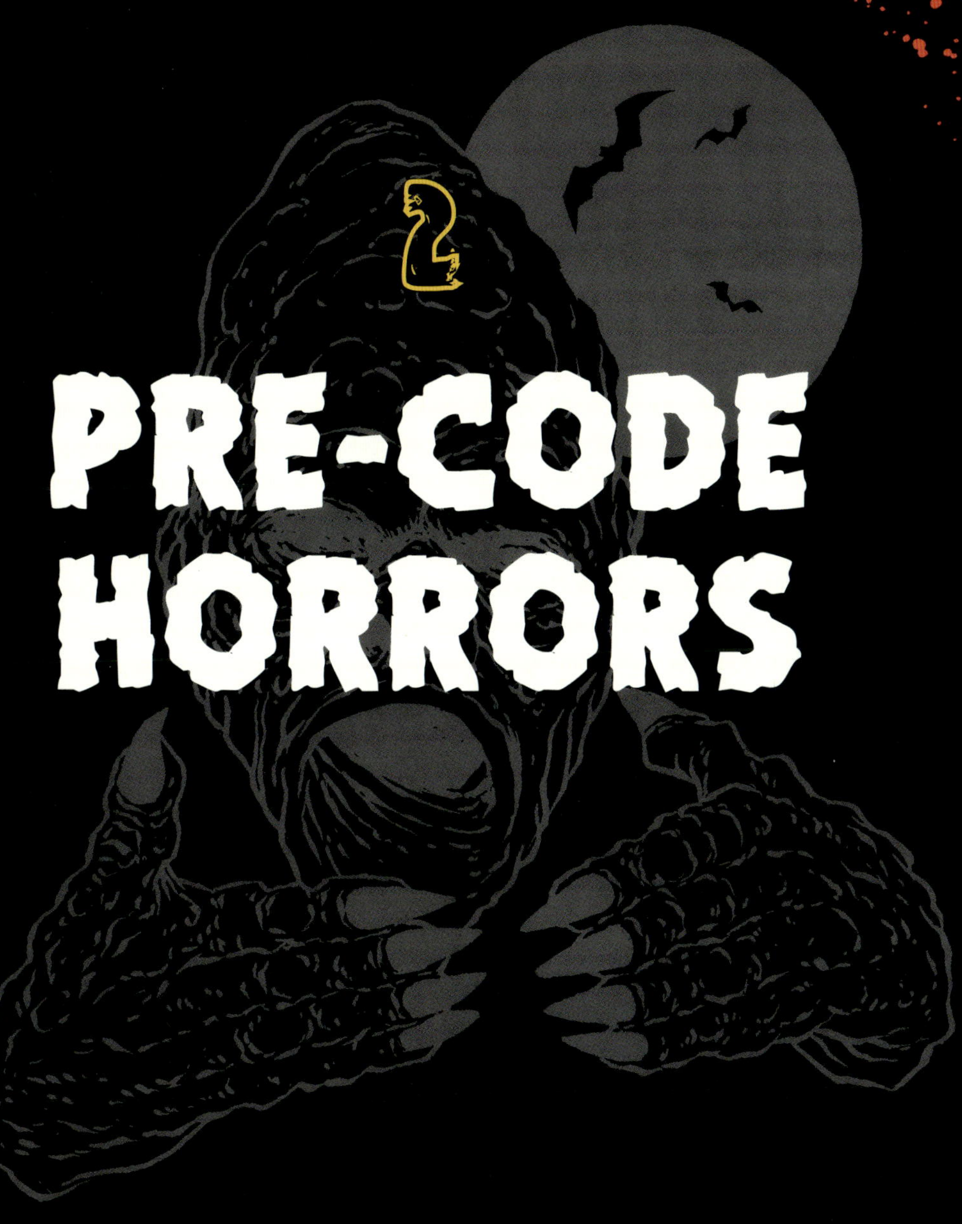

2 PRE-CODE HORRORS

RICHARD HARLAND SMITH

"What difference did it make if a few people had to die? Their flesh taught me how to manufacture arms, legs, faces that are human! I'll make a crippled world whole again!"

DR. WELLS (PRESTON FOSTER) IN *DOCTOR X* (1932)

"No picture shall be produced which will lower the moral standards of those who see it. Hence the sympathy of the audience should never be thrown on the side of crime, wrongdoing, evil or sin."

The Motion Picture Production Code (March 31, 1930)

"I wish to join the Legion of Decency, which condemns vile and unwholesome moving pictures. I unite with all who protest against them as a grave menace to youth, to home life, to country and to religion. I condemn absolutely those salacious motion pictures which, with other degrading agencies, are corrupting public morals and promoting a sex mania in our land."

Catholic Legion of Decency Pledge (1933)

ON MAY 7, 1934, American newspapers heralded the premiere of Universal Pictures' Edgar Allan Poe-inspired chiller *The Black Cat*, which would team for the first time on the silver screen newly minted "horror kings" Bela Lugosi and Boris Karloff. Those papers also ran, in some cases on the very same page, a related sidebar announcing "SCREEN WILL GET ITS FACE WASHED."

As fleetly forewarning as a political broadsheet, the notice proclaimed that "the laundry for Hollywood's motion picture productions, demanded by church organizations throughout the country for the past month, will open here on July 15th" and laid out the agenda for every picture due from the studio pipeline to "obtain a bill of cleanliness before being released."

Thus tolled the death knell for what would come to be called Hollywood's "pre-Code horrors."

The Motion Picture Production Code—a tick-list of cinematic subject matter and situations to avoid at all costs—had been on the film industry's negotiating table for years. Pushback from state censors and church groups began well before the advent of sound, sparked by a spate of scandals that tarnished the reputations (and in some cases claimed the lives) of several silent film stars.

To stave off legislature arising from decency laws and censorship bills damning movies as immoral, the major studios agreed to self-censor, but adherence to the Code was slow in coming.

It took Hollywood's first "horror cycle"—initiated by the release of Tod Browning's *Dracula* in February 1931 and James Whale's *Frankenstein* that November—to help turn the Code's guidelines into a playbook; but horror movies were not the sole focus of the crackdown: for a time, spook shows were able to get away with considerably more than murder.

Prior to 1931, the phrase "horror movies" could be applied to any film evoking a sensation of disgust and dread; thus, gangster pictures and those depicting the wages of war were considered horror movies, while morbid foreign imports such as Robert Wiene's *The Cabinet of Dr. Caligari* (1920) and F.W. Murnau's *Nosferatu* (1922) were deemed art pictures and examples of Germanic decadence.

American adaptations of literary classics such as *Dr. Jekyll and Mr. Hyde* (1920) and *The Phantom of the Opera* (1925) were marketed less for their Gothic blandishments

The Motion Picture Production Code—a tick-list of cinematic subject matter and situations to avoid at all costs—had been on the film industry's negotiating table for years.

than as showpieces for their chameleonic stars, John Barrymore and Lon Chaney. Adapted from Broadway plays, old dark house thrillers such as *The Bat* (1926) and *The Cat and the Canary* (1927) were cloaked in supernatural "blood and thunder," but revealed themselves by the final curtain to be mere tales of human greed operating behind the mask of monstrousness.

It took the success of Universal's *Dracula* to prove there was gold to be mined from genuine ghoulishness.

Profits from *Dracula* begat *Frankenstein* and transformed jobbing actors Bela Lugosi and Boris Karloff into *bona fide* horror movie stars. The pair subsequently brought branded legitimacy to *Murders in the Rue Morgue*, *The Mummy*, *The Old Dark House*, *White Zombie*, and *Island of Lost Souls* (all 1932). The latter, an adaptation of H.G. Wells's novel *The Island of Doctor Moreau*, was a bid by Universal's well-heeled rival, Paramount Pictures, to cash-in on the vogue for fright films.

A veritable flood of "weird chillers" followed from Universal (*The Invisible Man*, *WereWolf of London*) and Paramount (*Murders in the Zoo*, *Supernatural*), as well as

PREVIOUS SPREAD: *WereWolf of London* (2015), oils on canvas portrait of Henry Hull from Universal Pictures' 1935 movie by Sanjulián (Manuel Pérez Clemente). As the Spanish artist explains: "It was a real creative challenge for me to be able to convert the photo of the actor in black and white into color since I tried not to lose his strength."

TOP & BOTTOM LEFT: Front and back of the herald for Universal's alternate Spanish-language *Drácula* (Dir: George Melford, 1931), which is almost a half-hour longer than the American version that was filmed on the same sets during the day.

TOP RIGHT: *Vampyr* (2009), a paper collage created using acrylic, twigs and leaves, and texture paste, one of a continuing series of images re-imagining the extraordinary liminal images of early cinema by British artist Dave McKean.

RIGHT: French artist and typographist Raymond Gid (1905–2000) created this specially commissioned poster for *Vampyr* (Dir: Carl Theodor Dreyer, 1932) for the Art Deco art-house cinema Raspail 216, located in Montparnasse, Paris.

ABOVE: There is probably only one surviving example in existence of this three-sheet poster for Universal's *The Phantom of the Opera* (Dir: Rupert Julian, 1925).

LEFT: *A Night at the Opera* (2017), a digital portrait by American artist Rob Birchfield, who reveals: "I found it an interesting and fun challenge trying to come up with what I felt were the proper hues for Erik's deformed flesh."

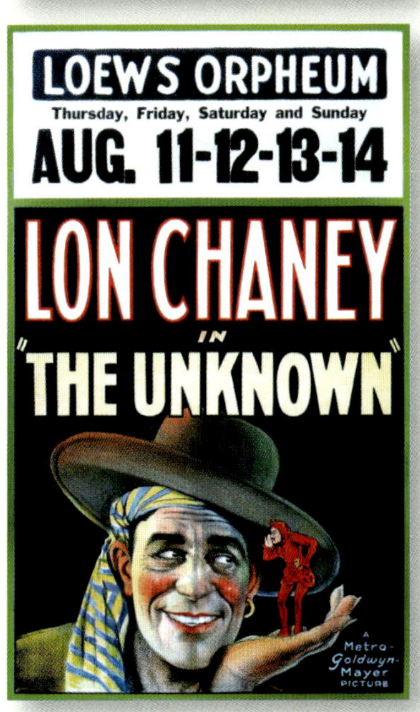

ABOVE RIGHT: Circa 1920s Argentinean "personality poster" of actor Leonidas Frank "Lon" Chaney, who was born in 1883 to deaf parents. He rose from bit actor to Hollywood star before his untimely death in 1930 at the age of 47.

TOP LEFT: German four-panel (6 x 9 foot) poster for Universal's *The Hunchback of Notre Dame* (Dir: Wallace Worsley, 1923), the studio's top-grossing silent picture, based on the 1831 novel by Victor Hugo. Lon Chaney starred as Quasimodo.

TOP MIDDLE: Advance Swedish stone litho poster for Universal's "coming" *The Phantom of the Opera* (Dir: Rupert Julian, 1925). Based on the 1910 novel by Gaston Leroux, it depicts Lon Chaney's Erik in his "Bal Masqué" costume.

BOTTOM LEFT: Window card for Metro-Goldwyn-Mayer's *The Unknown* (Dir: Tod Browning, 1927), in which Lon Chaney played "armless" carnival knife-thrower Alonzo, who fell in love with the assistant in his act (Joan Crawford).

BOTTOM MIDDLE: Window card for Lon Chaney's final film, *The Unholy Three* (Dir: Jack Conway, 1930), a "talkie" remake of Metro-Goldwyn-Mayer's 1925 version that also starred the actor as criminal ventriloquist Professor Echo.

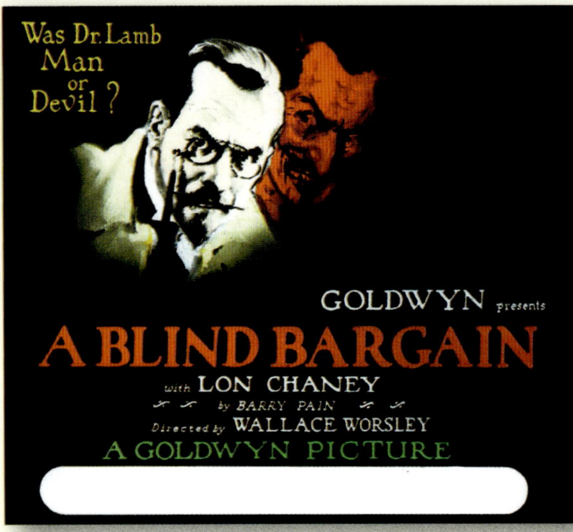

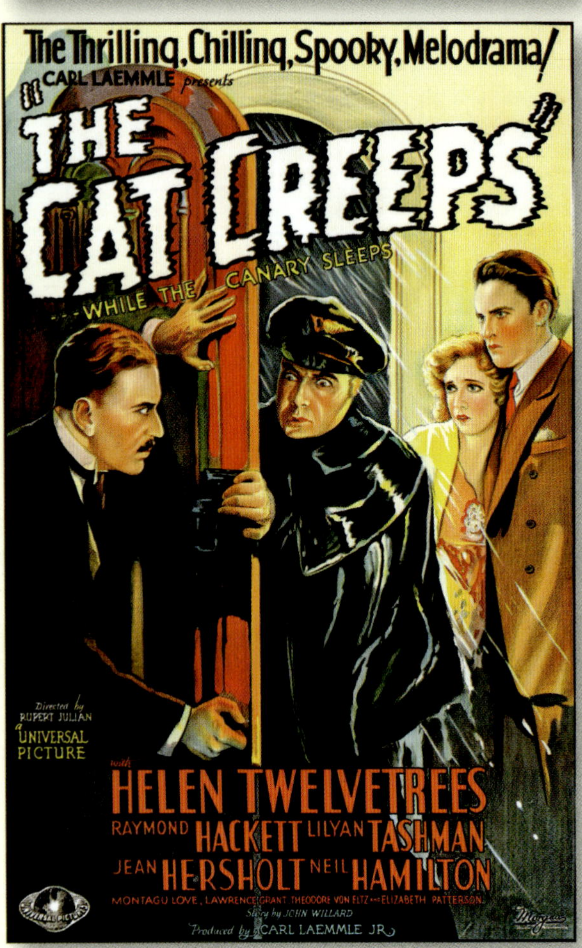

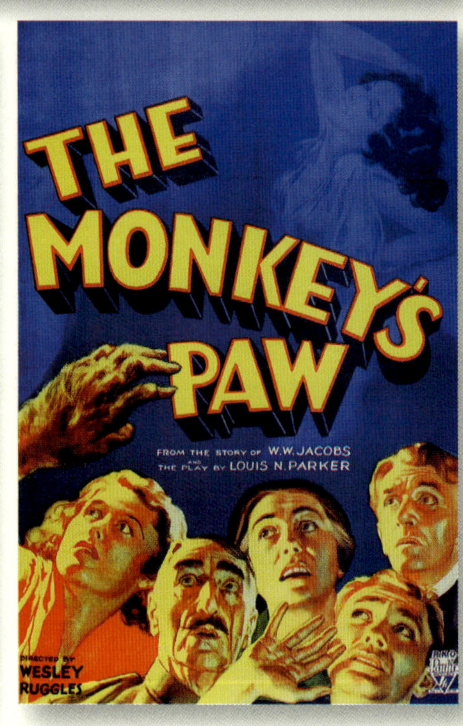

BOTTOM MIDDLE: Press advertisement from the March 24, 1917 issue of *Motion Picture News* for the Hawk Film Company's *The Monster of Fate*, the American re-titling of the mostly lost 1915 version of *Der Golem* (Dir: Henrik Galeen and Paul Wegener, who both also starred).

TOP LEFT: Glass slide for Goldwyn Pictures Corporation's lost horror movie *A Blind Bargain* (Dir: Wallace Worsley, 1922), in which Lon Chaney portrayed both the mad doctor and the ape man he created. The last print was in the same vault fire that also destroyed *London After Midnight*.

BOTTOM LEFT: The only known copy of the stone litho one-sheet for Universal's lost old dark house mystery *The Cat Creeps* (Dir: Rupert Julian, 1930). Based on the 1922 stage play *The Cat and the Canary*, only a few clips and the sound discs still survive. Even the Spanish-language version is lost.

TOP RIGHT: Lobby card for the mostly lost F.P. Pictures Corp. low-budget production *The Horror* (1932) from American writer/producer/director Bud Pollard (1886–1952). Possibly never given theatrical distribution, about half the picture exists in fragmentary form in The Library of Congress.

BOTTOM RIGHT: One-sheet poster for RKO Radio Pictures' *The Monkey's Paw* (Dir: Wesley Ruggles, 1933), a "lost" adaptation of the 1902 short story by W.W. Jacobs and the 1910 stage play by Louis N. Parker. A 1936 French copy (*La main de singe*) is now known to have survived.

TOP LEFT: US herald for Metro-Goldwyn-Mayer's lost *London After Midnight* (Dir: Tod Browning, 1927).

BOTTOM LEFT: Program flyer for the Lincoln Theatre, Los Angeles, February 1928.

RIGHT: Title lobby card for *London After Midnight*.

TOP RIGHT: *London After Midnight* (2018), oil painting by American artist Bob Eggleton. "This painting was done as a private commission for a friend," he recalls. "He is a big fan of the movie, or what we've seen of it as no surviving prints are known to exist. While I was researching the film, I was fascinated to learn that Lon Chaney would utilize excruciating, painful makeup devices such as fine wires to make his eyes look manic and pull up the corners of his mouth, and he had pointed wooden teeth. Since all the photos are black and white, I was free to use whatever skin colors I wanted."

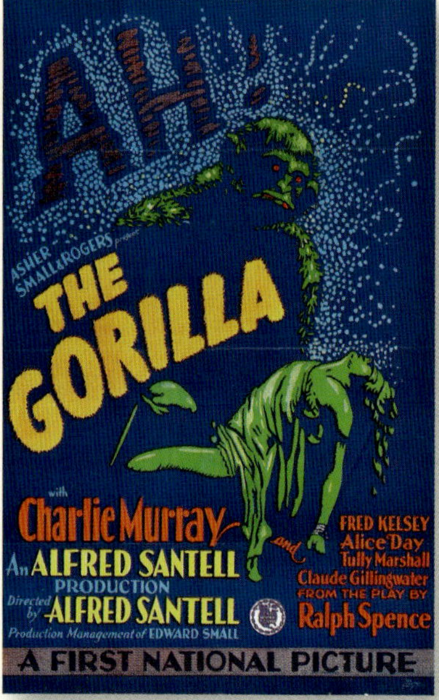

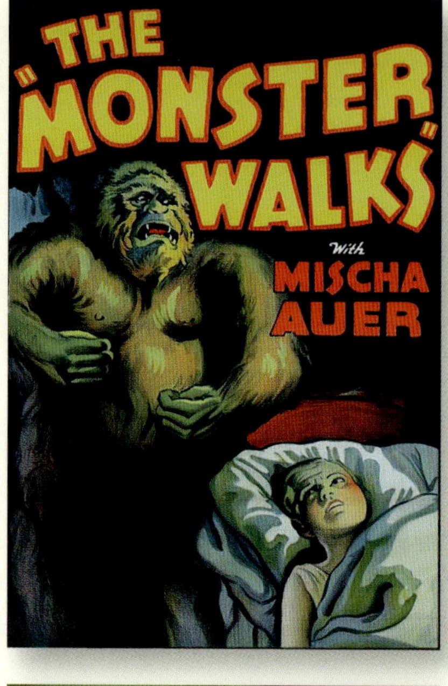

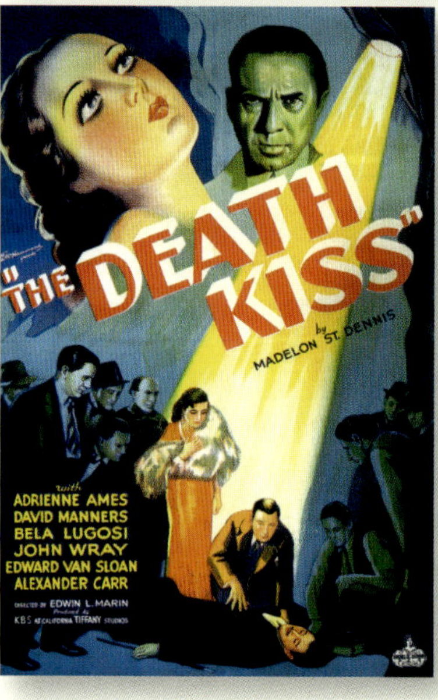

ABOVE LEFT: Stone litho six-sheet poster for the lost "all colored" Western/mystery *The Crimson Skull* (Dir: Richard E. Norman, 1922), produced by the Poverty Row Norman Film MFG. Co. studio of Jacksonville, Florida.

TOP MIDDLE: This one-sheet poster for First National Pictures' *The Gorilla* (Dir: Alfred Santell, 1927) features remarkably modern graphic design. Based on a 1925 play, this lost movie included an early appearance by future film star Walter Pidgeon.

TOP RIGHT: Stone litho reissue one-sheet for the Poverty Row mystery *The Monster Walks* (Dir: Frank Strayer, 1932), which was produced by Ralph M. Like Productions and distributed locally in America via the territorial states rights system.

BOTTOM MIDDLE: Based on the 1932 movie murder mystery novel by Madelon St. Dennis, World Wide Pictures' *The Death Kiss* (Dir: Edwin L. Marin, 1932) reunited three of the stars of Universal's *Dracula* from the previous year to little effect.

BOTTOM RIGHT: Swedish poster for Monogram Pictures' *The Sphinx* (Dir Phil Rosen, 1933), in which Lionel Atwill stars as an apparently deaf-mute suspect in a series of strangulation murders of investment stockbrokers.

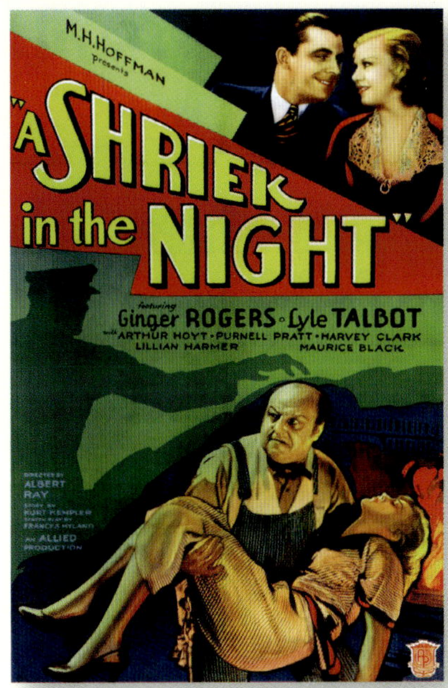

ABOVE RIGHT: American six-sheet for Majestic Pictures' low-budget *The Vampire Bat* (Dir: Frank Strayer, 1933), in which Lionel Atwill's mad doctor terrorizes a small European village with a series of "vampire" murders.

TOP LEFT: Ginger Rogers gives a sparky performance as an undercover newspaper reporter investigating a series of macabre murders in an apartment building in Allied Pictures' Poverty Row *A Shriek in the Night* (Dir: Albert Ray, 1933).

TOP MIDDLE: Based on the 1924 Edgar Wallace short story "The Ghost of John Holling" (which was also the film's UK title), Monogram Pictures' *Mystery Liner* (Dir: William Nigh, 1934) features a surprisingly futuristic radio remote-control device.

BOTTOM LEFT: A decent cast searches for a missing Indian diamond in Monogram Pictures' *The Moonstone* (Dir: Reginald Barker, 1934), a Poverty Row adaptation of Wilkie Collins's 1868 book, which is widely regarded as the first detective novel.

BOTTOM MIDDLE: When an eccentric millionaire gathers together his greedy relatives in order to divide up his estate, murder inevitably follows in Mascot Pictures' lively old dark house mystery *One Frightened Night* (Dir: Christy Cabanne, 1935).

TOP LEFT: Lobby card for United Artists' formative old dark house mystery *The Bat* (1926). Visionary director Roland West (1885–1952) remade the movie with sound just four years later as *The Bat Whispers*, before retiring the following year.

BOTTOM MIDDLE: Three-sheet poster for Universal's *The Cat and the Canary* (Dir: Paul Leni, 1927), another of the silent era's old dark house thrillers based on a Broadway play. Once again, the heirs to a fortune gathered for the reading of a will.

ABOVE RIGHT: Roland West remade his 1927 movie *The Bat* as *The Bat Whispers* (1930) for United Artists before he opened a restaurant and was implicated in the death of his mistress and business partner, Hollywood actress Thelma Todd.

BOTTOM LEFT: Three-sheet poster for Monogram Pictures' *The Thirteenth Guest* (Dir: Albert Ray, 1932). Re-titled *Lady Beware* in the UK, it was based on a 1929 novel by pulp author "Armitage Trail" (Maurice R. Coons), who wrote *Scarface*.

BOTTOM LEFT: One-sheet poster for RKO Radio Pictures' *The Phantom of Crestwood* (Dir: J. Walter Ruben, 1932). It was based on a radio serial that featured a contest where listeners could send in suggestions for the movie's ending.

TOP LEFT: Lobby card for Invincible Pictures' *The Ghost Walks* (Dir: Frank Strayer, 1934), which cleverly inverted the whole "old dark house" genre and involves an escaped maniac and a mad scientist who is trying to revive the dead.

BOTTOM MIDDLE: A young couple (Wallace Ford and Barbara Pepper) stumbles into a series of murders in Puritan Pictures' Poverty Row *The Rogues' Tavern* (Dir: Bob Hill, 1936), which was distributed through the states rights system.

ABOVE RIGHT: Insert poster for Warner Bros.' *The Invisible Menace* (Dir: John Farrow, 1938), which stars Boris Karloff as a murder suspect on an island military base. It was based on a flop 1937 Broadway play by Ralph Spencer Zink.

RIGHT: *The Old Dark House* (2018), gouache on watercolor poster by Graham Humphreys for the 1932 Universal movie directed by James Whale. "The art and composition focussed on the cast of incredible character actors known to all classic horror fans, in particular Boris Karloff," explains the British artist, who took a similar approach to that used on the rare 1939 reissue one-sheet poster [ABOVE]. "Respecting the integrity of the beautiful black-and-white photography, I kept the color palette simple with atmospheric hues and just a small detail of orange in the windows of the house. In the tradition of classic painted cinema posters, the visible brushwork is integral to the design."

FATHER OF FRANKENSTEIN

"While writing the adaptation of Shelley's story, my idea was to give the role of Dr. Frankenstein to Lugosi . . . I directed several sequences—about two reels—of the first *Frankenstein* script with Bela as the Monster."

Robert Florey

A WEEK BEFORE James Whale was announced by Universal Pictures in the summer of 1931 as the director of their forthcoming feature film adaptation of *Frankenstein*, the name above the title had been Robert Florey.

A pipe-smoking Parisian (born Robert Fuchs in 1900) and former film journalist/publicist, Florey learned the fundamentals of filmmaking as an assistant to silent serialist Louis Feuillade.

Emigrating to America, he impressed Hollywood with a handful of avant-garde shorts made between 1927–28 in collaboration with Hungarian expatriate Slavko Vorkapić (later a busy studio montage artist), among them *The Life and Death of 9413 a Hollywood Extra* (1928), which impressed Charlie Chaplin. Signing a contract with Paramount Pictures, that same year Florey directed Edward G. Robinson in his first go as a movie gangster, *The Hole in the Wall*, and with Joseph Santley guided the Marx Brothers through their first feature-length film, *The Cocoanuts* (1929).

With the success of *Dracula* (1931) pulling Universal out of an extended slump, studio head Carl Laemmle, Jr. tapped the up-and-coming Florey to adapt *Frankenstein*, due to his familiarity with German Expressionism and gift for the weirdly beautiful.

Although the studio had paid $20,000 for the rights to an existing stage adaptation of Mary Shelley's novel, Florey insisted he be allowed to write his own treatment. The resulting scenario went far afield of the original tale, favoring Frankenstein over his creation, who was etched as a brutish automaton rather than a sympathetic antihero. On sets still standing from production of Tod Browning's *Dracula*, Florey shot a (now presumed lost) 20-minute test for his vision of *Frankenstein*, cadging Browning's supporting actors, Edward Van Sloan and Dwight Frye, to play the humans in the room, and a reportedly grumpy Bela Lugosi as the Monster.

Florey had promised Lugosi the role of Dr. Frankenstein, a sympathetic man of science, but the studio put its foot down and insisted that their moneymaking Count Dracula play another monster. In later years, Van Sloan remembered Lugosi standing seven-feet tall in boot extensions and wearing a fright wig that made him look not unlike Paul Wegener in *The Golem* (1920).

Contradictory reports of Lugosi's response to his own appearance range from mortification to ebullience, but Laemmle, Jr.'s reaction ("I laughed like a hyena") doomed Florey's participation in *Frankenstein* to footnote status.

Studio head Carl Laemmle, Jr. tapped the up-and-coming Florey to adapt *Frankenstein*, due to his familiarity with German Expressionism and gift for the weirdly beautiful.

Enter James Whale, an English expat and a veteran of both the British stage and the First World War, who had just wrapped production on the Universal wartime romance *Waterloo Bridge* (1931). While Florey's script was largely remaindered, two elements were retained: that the Monster be given, unbeknownst to his creator, an abnormal brain, and a fiery finish in a burning windmill (in Florey's script, the location of Frankenstein's lab). As a consolation prize, Florey was assigned Universal's next horror film, *Murders in the Rue Morgue* (1932), whose expressionistic production design (influenced by the 1920 German silent *The Cabinet of Dr. Caligari*) hints at the *Frankenstein* that might have been.

In the following years, Florey directed programmers for the major studios (*The Face Behind the Mask*, *The Beast with Five Fingers*) and ended his 50-year career in television (*Alfred Hitchcock Presents*, *Thriller*, *The Twilight Zone*, *The Outer Limits*).

Outliving Whale, Lugosi, Karloff, and almost Laemmle, Jr., Florey died in May 1979. Although he had the final word on *Frankenstein* and received due credit for his contribution in his native France, cineastes will continue to debate who best deserves the title "Father of Frankenstein." *RHS*

Florey's French Frankensteins

French-born director and screenwriter Robert Florey (1900–79) was supposed to direct Universal's *Frankenstein* (1931). But after shooting a now lost test-reel with Bela Lugosi in Jack Pierce's early makeup design for the Monster, producer Carl Laemmle, Jr. replaced both Florey and Lugosi with James Whale and Boris Karloff, respectively. Having originally collaborated on the script with Garrett Fort, Florey was only credited on French versions of the poster.

ABOVE LEFT: This 1932 French *affiche* for *Frankenstein* (1931) by Roland Coudon (1897–1954) accentuated the relationship between Colin Clive's eponymous creator and his Monster (Boris Karloff).

TOP RIGHT: Roland Coudon also created this only surviving French double-panel *affiche* for *Frankenstein* (1931), which managed to misspell Mary Shelley, Garrett Fort, and James Whale's names.

BOTTOM RIGHT: Jacques Faria (1898–1956) illustrated this French billboard *affiche* for Universal's *Frankenstein* (1931) which, like the other posters in that country, credited Robert Florey as co-screenwriter.

ABOVE LEFT: One-sheet poster for *The Man Who Reclaimed His Head* (Dir: Edward Ludwig, 1934), one of the "lesser" Universal horrors of the period, despite co-starring Claude Rains (who was in the original stage play) and Lionel Atwill.

TOP MIDDLE: Swedish poster signed "Från" for Universal's *Mystery of Edwin Drood* (Dir: Stuart Walker, 1935), which starred Claude Rains in an adaptation of Charles Dickens's unfinished 1870 novel about murder and drug-induced madness.

TOP RIGHT: French *affiche* for Universal's *The Invisible Ray* (Dir: Lambert Hillyer, 1936), which marked the studio's third major teaming of its horror stars Boris Karloff and Bela Lugosi and is often cited as an early science fiction movie.

BOTTOM MIDDLE: Boris Karloff's appearance in the movie was nothing like as sinister as he was depicted on this one-sheet poster for Universal's *Night Key* (Dir: Lloyd Corrigan, 1937), which revolved around a new burglar alarm system.

BOTTOM RIGHT: One-sheet poster for Universal's "forgotten" horror-comedy *The Missing Guest* (Dir: John Rawlins, 1938), which was the second of the studio's three versions of the 1931 German movie *Geheimnis des Blauen Zimmers*.

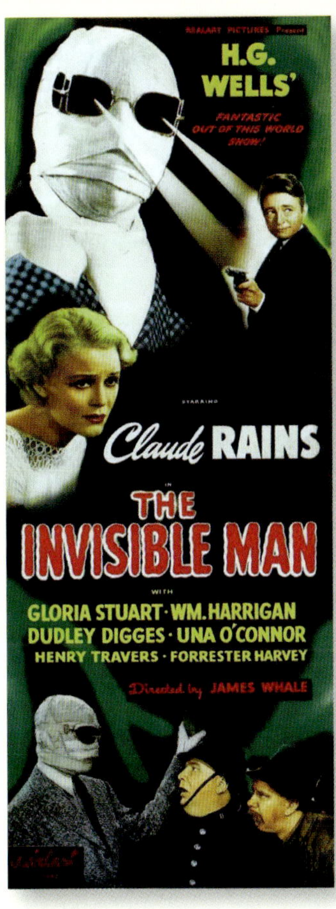

RIGHT: *The Invisible Man* (2016), an acrylic and paper collage private commission by British artist Dave McKean, inspired by the 1933 Universal movie [ABOVE] that starred Claude Rains and was based on the 1897 novel by H.G. Wells (1866–1946).

TOP LEFT & MIDDLE: Released in both silent and sound versions, Paramount Pictures' *The Mysterious Dr. Fu Manchu* (Dir: Rowland V. Lee, 1929) starred Swedish-born actor Warner Oland as Sax Rohmer's insidious Oriental villain.

BOTTOM LEFT: Trolly card for Metro-Goldwyn-Mayer's *The Mask of Fu Manchu* (Dir: Charles Brabin, 1932), which starred Boris Karloff as Sax Rohmer's evil genius and Myrna Loy as his seductive and equally villainous daughter.

ABOVE RIGHT: Once again starring Warner Oland in the title role, Paramount's sequel, *The Return of Dr. Fu Manchu* (Dir: Rowland V. Lee, 1930), was advertised in some US markets under the title *The New Adventures of Dr. Fu Manchu*.

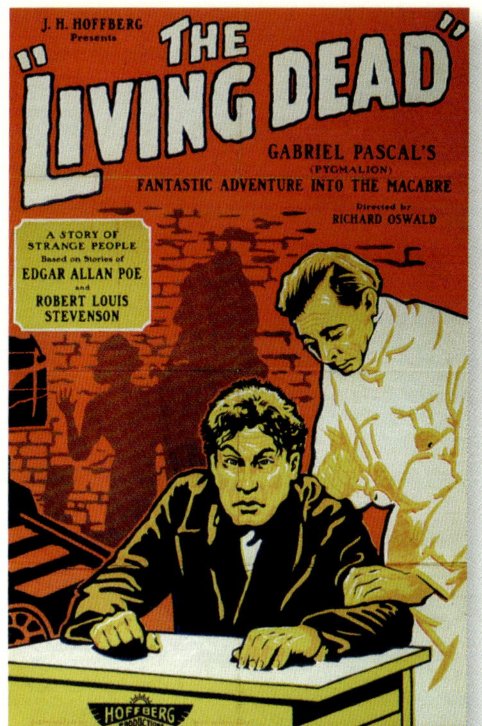

ABOVE LEFT: 1948 three-sheet for the reissue of Universal's Edgar Allan Poe adaptation *Murders in the Rue Morgue* (1932), which was the studio's compensation to director Robert Florey and star Bela Lugosi for not doing *Frankenstein* (1931).

TOP MIDDLE: 1940 US one-sheet poster for *The Living Dead*, a re-edited version of the German movie *Unheimliche Geschichten* (Dir: Richard Oswald, 1932), which was based on stories by Edgar Allan Poe and Robert Louis Stevenson.

TOP RIGHT: Swedish poster for Universal Pictures' *The Black Cat* (Dir: Edgar G. Ulmer, 1934). A *conte cruel* loosely based on the 1843 story by Edgar Allan Poe, it marked the studio's first teaming of horror stars Boris Karloff and Bela Lugosi.

BOTTOM MIDDLE: Belgian stone litho poster for Universal's *The Raven* (Dir: Louis Friedlander, 1935). The studio's second major teaming of Boris Karloff and Bela Lugosi, it was inspired by Edgar Allan Poe's 1845 narrative poem.

BOTTOM RIGHT: Suggested by Edgar Allan Poe's 1844 short story "The Premature Burial," Liberty Pictures' Poverty Row *The Crime of Doctor Crespi* (Dir: John H. Auer, 1935) starred Erich von Stroheim as a crazed scientist who buries his rival alive.

TOP LEFT: Based on an unpublished story by Jo (Joseph) Swerling and filmed a year earlier, Columbia Pictures' crime thriller *Behind the Mask* (Dir: John Francis Dillon, 1932) was sold as a horror movie due to Boris Karloff's involvement.

TOP MIDDLE: When released in America in 1935 by First Division Pictures, the British-made *The Scotland Yard Mystery* (Dir: Thomas Bentley, 1934) was re-titled *The Living Dead* to play up its criminal doctor's pseudo-scientific activities.

BOTTOM LEFT: Despite a plot revolving around a mythical dragon living in a pool, First National Pictures' *The Dragon Murder Case* (Dir: H. Bruce Humberstone, 1934) was based on one of author S.S. Van Dine's "Philo Vance" novels.

BOTTOM MIDDLE: Although the poster art makes it look like a horror movie, Warner Bros.' murder mystery *The Case of the Black Cat* (Dir: William McGann, 1936) was based on a 1935 "Perry Mason" novel by Erle Stanley Gardner.

ABOVE RIGHT: American three-sheet poster for J.H. Productions' British crime movie *Juggernaut* (Dir: Henry Edwards, 1936), in which Boris Karloff's dying doctor was forced to turn to murder so that he could complete his experiments.

THIS PAGE: From the early twentieth century onwards, studios and movie theaters would distribute copies of inexpensive advertising flyers known as a "heralds" to announce forthcoming productions or presentations directly to the public.

BOTTOM MIDDLE: Cover of the Spanish herald promoting Universal Pictures' *Murders in the Rue Morgue* (Dir: Robert Florey, 1932). Due to studio concerns, the movie was restructured and heavily cut during the editing process.

BOTTOM RIGHT: Cover of the July 1934 program from Warner Bros.' Clementon Theatre in New Jersey promoting the British-made *The Ghoul* (Dir: T. Hayes Hunter, 1933), supported by a Moe Howard comedy short and a Disney cartoon.

TOP RIGHT: Most heralds were usually a folded sheet of paper printed on both sides. As this effective interior spread illustrates, the herald for Metro-Goldwyn-Mayer's *Mark of the Vampire* (Dir: Tod Browning, 1935) was printed in two colors.

ABOVE LEFT: Cover of the October 1936 British program for London's Paramount Theatre advertising the first presentation of Universal's vampire sequel *Dracula's Daughter* (Dir: Lambert Hillyer, 1936).

THIS SPREAD: Almost since the inception of cinema itself, there have been book and magazine adaptations of movies. Those that include stills from the films are called "photoplays," while those that just use a cover image are known as "tie-ins."

BOTTOM LEFT: No. 272 of the 16-page French newsprint magazine *Le Film Complet* (August 29, 1926) featured an illustrated adaptation of Metro-Goldwyn-Mayer's *The Monster* (1925) by "Maurice Aubyn" (screenwriter René Pujol, 1887–1942).

BOTTOM MIDDLE: This paperback photoplay of MGM's *London After Midnight* (1927) by Lucien Boisyvon (1886–1967) was published in France in 1929 by J. Ferenczi et Fils, Éditeurs as part of the "Ciné-Volume" series.

TOP LEFT: This cheap British hardcover edition of *The Cat and the Canary* by playwright John Willard (1885–1942) from The Readers Library Publishing Co. Ltd. has a wraparound dust jacket that ties it into Universal's 1927 movie.

ABOVE RIGHT: This cheap American paperback edition of Victor Hugo's *The Man Who Laughs* from Jacobsen-Hodgkinson-Corporation includes stills from the 1927 movie and was adapted by Universal's director of publicity, Paul Gulick.

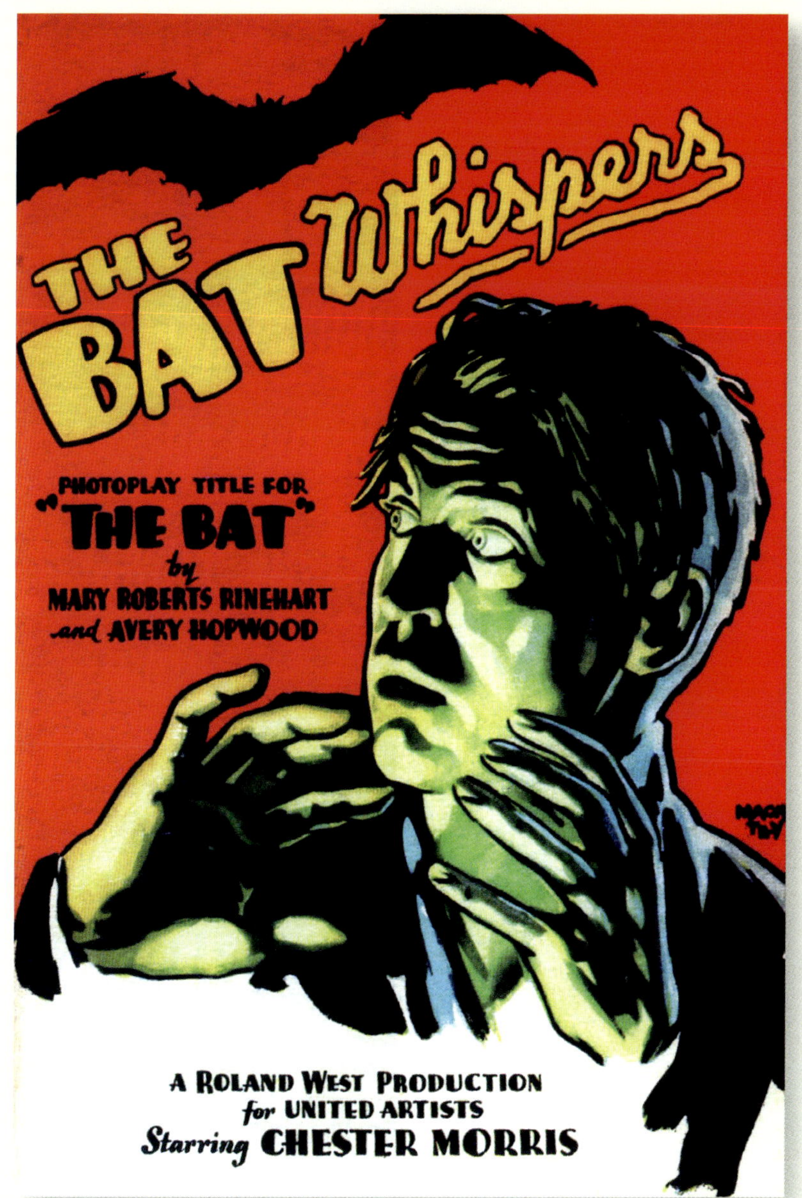

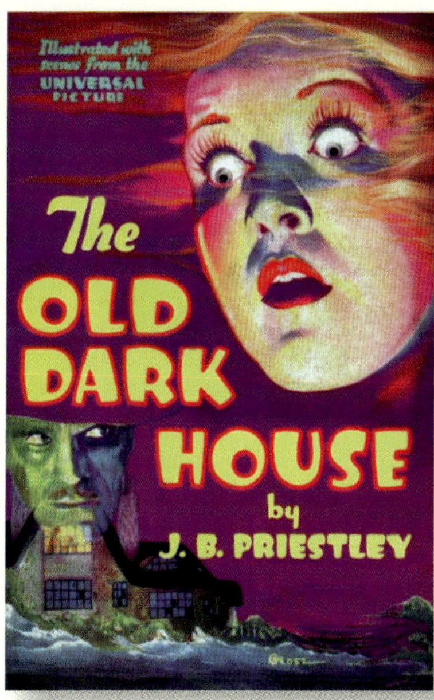

ABOVE LEFT: Dust jacket art by "Mach Tey" (Nathan Machtey, 1907–86) for *The Bat Whispers*, Grosset & Dunlap's photoplay reprinting of the original 1926 novel *The Bat* with eight glossy stills from United Artists' 1930 movie.

TOP MIDDLE: Grosset & Dunlap used Károly Grósz's art for Universal's trade advertisement on the dust jacket of *The Old Dark House* (1932), a photoplay of the 1928 novel *Benighted* by J. (John) B. (Boynton) Priestley (1894–1984).

TOP RIGHT: This cheap British hardcover of the classic mystery novel *The Moonstone* (1868) by Wilkie Collins (1824–89), published by The Literary Press Ltd., features a dust jacket that ties in to the 1934 Poverty Row Monogram movie.

BOTTOM MIDDLE: Cheap British hardcover of *The* (sic) *Bride of Frankenstein* (1935) from The Readers Library Publishing Company Ltd. It was written in just three weeks by author "Michael Egremont" (Maurice Desmond Rohan, 1907–91).

BOTTOM RIGHT: This Spanish softcover adaptation of Universal's *The Black Room* (1935), published as part of the "Ediciones Biblioteca Films" series from Editorial "Alas," includes a glossy six-page insert of photographs from the movie.

3

THE SHUDDER PULPS

MIKE ASHLEY

His hands slid lasciviously over her nude, helpless body, bestowing unspeakable caresses. "It's a pity such beauty must be destroyed, my dear," he murmured. "Soon I shall have to open your white skin and let your bright blood flow away."

"MONSTER OF HIS MAKING" BY HENRY TREAT SPERRY (*DIME MYSTERY MAGAZINE*, APRIL 1938)

> "In *Dime Mystery*, we demand a convincing motivation for the villain's actions. He may be mentally unbalanced, may be suffering from a complex, but he should be fiendishly clever, should have a sound reason for his villainy."
>
> Rogers Terrill, editor of *Dime Mystery Magazine*

> "Up to the day the first issue of *Weird Tales* was placed on the stands, stories of the sort you read between these covers each month were taboo in the publishing world."
>
> From "Why Weird Tales?" (attributed to Otis Adelbert Kline), *Weird Tales* May–July 1924

FICTION HAS ALWAYS had its divide between the "literary" and the "sensational," and at the start of the twentieth century the successor to the lurid penny dreadfuls and dime novels was the pulp magazine. Published on cheap wood pulp and selling for ten or 15 cents apiece, they proved immensely popular and promoted the more action-oriented adventure stories with few literary pretensions.

The earliest US pulps—*The Argosy*, *All-Story*, and *The Popular*—ran all forms of fiction, and the first to specialize in supernatural horror was *Weird Tales*, which ran from 1923 to 1954, with several more recent revivals. After an inauspicious first year under editor Edwin Baird (1886–1954), it flourished under Farnsworth Wright (1888–1940). Not only did the magazine develop the Cthulhu stories by H.P. Lovecraft and Robert E. Howard's adventures of Conan the Barbarian, it ran the Jules de Grandin occult detective series by Seabury Quinn, the exotic fantasies of Clark Ashton Smith and, by the late 1930s and early '40s, the early works of Robert Bloch and Ray Bradbury.

Weird Tales became notorious not just for its fiction but also for its covers. Those by C.C. Senf and Hugh (Doak) Rankin invariably portrayed women being grotesquely threatened or abused. J. Allen St. John, famed for his illustrations for Edgar Rice Burroughs's stories in the general pulps, brought his action style to the magazine and gave it its distinctive title logo in the 1930s. But the most famous artist was Margaret Brundage, whose portrayal of often highly erotic nudes boosted sales and has made those issues very collectible. Later cover artists, who are much revered today, included Hannes Bok and Virgil Finlay.

The sales of *Weird Tales* were never high, but it still outlived its competitors. *Ghost Stories* (1926–31), which catered for a readership interested in spiritualism and often presented its stories as true, was not a serious rival. Similarly, *Tales of Magic and Mystery* (1927–28) presented itself as publishing stories of eastern magic and the esoteric, and saw only five issues. Were it not that the fourth issue ran a story by H.P. Lovecraft, it would be of little interest today. *Mystic Magazine* (1930–31) also saw five issues and concentrated on palmistry and the occult. Surprisingly, it was edited by future horror author August Derleth. Of greater merit was *Strange Tales* (1931–33), which closely imitated *Weird Tales* and boasted some of the same writers, notably Hugh B. Cave, Clark Ashton Smith, and Henry S. Whitehead. Its covers by Hans Wessolowski were equally as lurid and dramatic, and that for Jack Williamson's "Wolves of Darkness" (January 1932) remains a classic. Alas, it saw only seven issues.

It was running stories where victims (usually women) were menaced by every conceivable type of horror—from mad scientists to the mentally unstable or physically challenged. Political correctness never entered the equation.

The short-lived nature of these magazines no longer encouraged others, but there was a shift from supernatural horror to weird terror. Popular Publications, Inc. had successfully launched *Dime Detective* in 1931 and began a companion title, *Dime Mystery Magazine*, the following year. By October 1933 it was running stories where victims (usually women) were menaced by every conceivable type of horror—from mad scientists to the mentally unstable or physically challenged. Political correctness never entered the equation. Popular soon launched two companions, *Terror Tales* (1934–41) and *Horror Stories* (1935–41). All three pulps reeked of the same pit of doom and featured the same authors (Wyatt Blassingame, Hugh B. Cave, John H. Knox, and Arthur Leo Zagat, among others) and artists (Walter M. Baumhofer and John Newton Howett being the most prolific).

Unlike *Weird Tales*, these magazines sold well, and inevitably rivals appeared such as *Thrilling Mystery* (1935–51) and *Ace Mystery* (1936–37). The main competition was from the "Spicy" series from Culture Publications, Inc., which included *Spicy-Adventure Stories* and *Spicy Mystery Stories* (both 1934–46) with cover art by H.J. Ward.

PREVIOUS SPREAD: Margaret Brundage's *risqué* pastel and mixed media on board cover for the January 1936 issue of *Weird Tales* illustrated "A Rival from the Grave" by Seabury Quinn. "They always wanted the ones with the scantiest clad girls," recalled the artist. "I drew what they wanted."

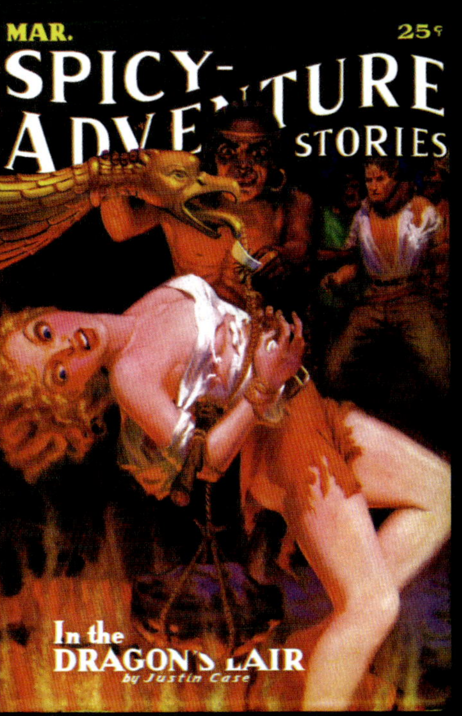

ABOVE LEFT: *Tales of Magic and Mystery* lasted for five issues from December 1927 to April 1928. Edited by an uncredited Walter B. Gibson (aka "Maxwell Grant"), this fourth issue (March 1928) featured a story by H.P. Lovecraft.

TOP MIDDLE: Cover by Harry Fisk for the second issue of Fawcett Publications' *Mystic Magazine* (December 1930), which ran for five issues from November 1930 to April 1931. The title was unofficially edited by author August W. Derleth.

TOP RIGHT: Striking cover art by "H.W. Wesso" (Hans Wessolowski) for Jack Williamson's novella "Wolves of Darkness" in the January 1932 issue of The Clayton Magazines, Inc.'s *Strange Tales*, which ran for just seven issues.

BOTTOM MIDDLE: "In the Dragon's Lair" by "Justin Case" (Hugh B. Cave) appeared in the March 1936 issue of Culture Publications, Inc.'s *Spicy-Adventure Stories*, which ran for nine years before it was re-titled *Speed Adventure Stories*.

BOTTOM RIGHT: Cover by Rafael M. DeSoto for the third and final issue of Periodical House, Inc.'s bi-monthly *Ace Mystery Magazine* (September 1936). The title was changed to *Detective Romances* for a further two issues.

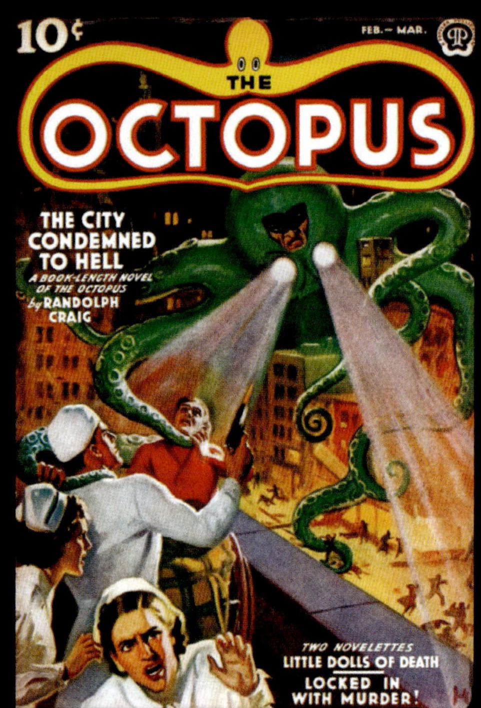

TOP LEFT: Creepy cover by Walter M. Baumhofer for the January 1934 issue of Street & Smith Publications, Inc.'s *Doc Savage Magazine*, which introduced the hero's cousin, Pat Savage, in "Brand of the Werewolf" by "Kenneth Robeson" (Lester Dent).

ABOVE RIGHT: Rudolph Zirn's cover for the first issue of Dell Publishing Company's *Doctor Death* (February 1935), illustrating the short novel "12 Must Die" by "Zorro" (Harold Ward). The villain pulp only ran for three monthly issues.

TOP MIDDLE: John Howitt's cover for the first and only issue of the Popular Publications, Inc.'s villain pulp *The Octopus* (February–March 1939) featuring the novel "A City Condemned to Death" by "Randolph Craig" (Norvell W. Page).

BOTTOM LEFT: The same cover artist, publisher, and editors (Ejler and Edith Jakobsson) tried again with another one-off villain pulp, *The Scorpion* (April–May 1939), which featured "The Corroding Death" by Wyatt Blassingame.

BOTTOM MIDDLE: Classic George Rozen cover for the January 15, 1942 issue of Street & Smith Publications, Inc.'s twice-monthly hero pulp, *The Shadow*, illustrating the novel "The Book of Death" by "Maxwell Grant" (Walter B. Gibson).

These magazines all featured covers with scantily clad women invariably clamped into some instrument of torture. So close did some of the covers and stories come to pornography that between 1935 and 1937 the *Spicy* titles issued both an uncensored and censored version (identified by a star on the cover).

The "weird menace" or "shudder" magazines also influenced the superhero pulps, which had started with *The Shadow* in 1931 and included *Doc Savage* (1933–49) and *The Spider* (1933–43). Alongside these emerged the super villains in *Doctor Death* (1935) with covers by Rudolph Zirm, *Dr. Yen Sin* (1936) with covers by Jerome Rozen, and *The Octopus* (later *The Scorpion*, both 1939) with covers by John Newton Howett. The hero and villain pulps were soon superseded by their comic book equivalents, and by the 1940s the weird menace pulps had toned down and reverted to more standard crime fiction.

Wartime paper rationing brought an end to many British magazines, and it was not until the 1950s that anything like regular weird-fiction magazine publishing arrived.

During this period the contents of *Weird Tales* sometimes reflected the weird menace pulps with Seabury Quinn's Jules de Grandin mysteries and the stories of Ascott Keane versus Dr. Satan by Paul Ernst. The deaths of Robert E. Howard and H.P. Lovecraft (in 1936 and 1937, respectively) inevitably had an effect upon the magazine, and even more so following a change of publisher and editor by 1940. At that time the magazine had seen some short-lived rivals, notably *Strange Stories* (1939–41) which, despite the weird menace covers, had stories closer in style to *Weird Tales*.

Popular Publications. Inc., which took over *Argosy*, plundered the archives—especially to *All-Story* and *Cavalier*—for a magazine of pure nostalgia, *Famous Fantastic Mysteries* (1939–53). With stunning covers by Virgil Finlay and Lawrence (Sterne Stevens), this title reprinted hard-to-find stories of the unusual, as well as longer works by A. Merritt, Ray Cummings, J.U. Giesy, and other American authors, and such British writers as William Hope Hodgson, H. Rider Haggard, and Warwick Deeping.

Its most influential rival was *Unknown* (1939–43) edited by John W. Campbell, Jr., who was at that time revolutionizing science fiction in *Astounding*. The emphasis in *Unknown* was on fantasy, but it also ran many horror stories such as "Fear" by L. Ron Hubbard and "It" by Theodore Sturgeon.

Weird Tales outlasted *Unknown* and, if anything, became more sophisticated in the 1940s under the editorial control of Dorothy McIlwraith (1891–1976). Alongside stories by Ray Bradbury, Manly Wade Wellman, and die-hards Edmond Hamilton, Robert Bloch, August Derleth, and Seabury Quinn, was new fiction by Algernon Blackwood and H. Russell Wakefield. Brundage's erotic covers gave way to more macabre, sinister covers by Matt Fox, Lee Brown Coye, and Boris Dolgov. At the start of the 1950s, however, as the pulp magazine scene faded with competition from comic books, television, and paperbacks, even *Weird Tales* had to submit, and ceased publication after 279 issues.

During World War II pulp imports were restricted, and Canada printed its own edition of *Weird Tales*. It initially ran new covers by Canadian artists, and issues switched around contents with authors sometimes listed under pseudonyms. At one point H.P. Lovecraft became "J.H. Brownlow," Robert Bloch was listed as "R.J. Comber," and Manly Wade Wellman was "T.K. Whiteley." These changes added to the magazine's idiosyncratic nature.

There were also attempts at new Canadian pulp magazines, of which *Uncanny Tales* (1940–43) was the longest running. However, apart from new material—mostly by Thomas P. Kelley under various pseudonyms—the best stories were reprints from American magazines.

British horror magazines did not fare much better. Between the wars many American pulps were imported, including *Weird Tales*, and there were limited attempts to create a British edition. The first homegrown British horror magazine was *Hutchinson's Mystery-Story Magazine* (1923–27), and although early issues contained many reprints from US pulps, over time British writers became the mainstay. These included the enigmatic G.G. Pendarves (Gladys Gordon Trenery) and Arlton Eadie (Leopold Leonard Eady), both of whom were also contributors to *Weird Tales*, Francis Grierson (Benjamin Henry Jesse Francis Shepard), and E. Charles Vivian (Charles Henry Cannell), who edited the magazine for the first two years.

Starting in 1933, World's Work began the pulp-style Master Thriller Series of anthologies, each issue covering a different genre, with most contents being reprints. Taking on separate identities from the series were *Mystery and Detection* (1934–35), *Tales of the Uncanny* (1936), and *Mystery Stories* (1936–42). All of these are now extremely rare, and while they did publish some new material, they never established a solid base for British weird fiction.

Wartime paper rationing brought an end to many British magazines, and it was not until the 1950s that anything like regular weird-fiction magazine publishing arrived with titles like *Phantom* and *Science Fantasy*.

In the United States the death of the pulps did not mark the end of the horror magazine. They metamorphosed into smaller digests, starting with the dazzling *Avon Fantasy Reader* (1947–52), which kept the pulp tradition alive.

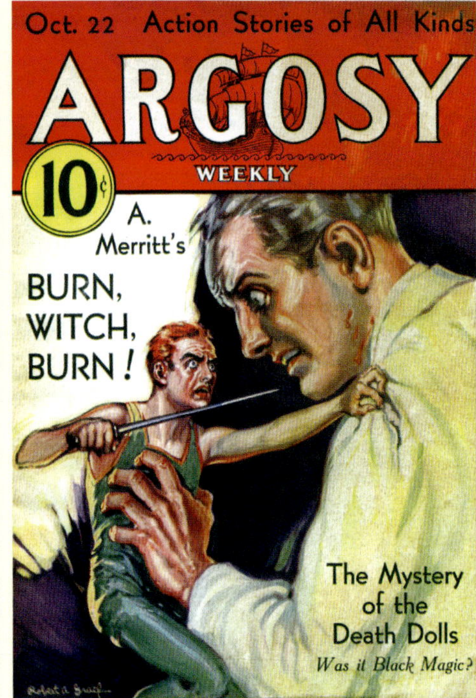

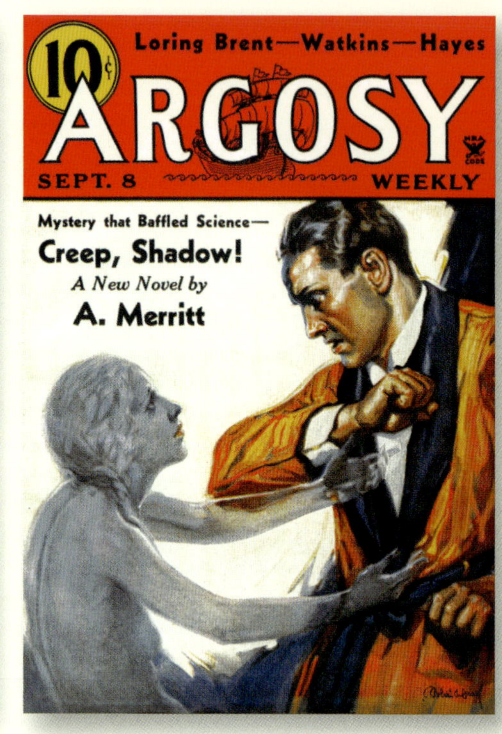

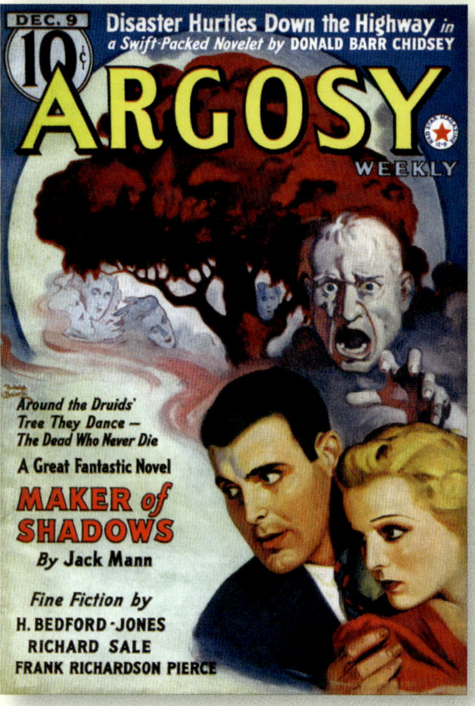

ABOVE LEFT: *Argosy Weekly* is widely regarded as America's first general fiction pulp magazine. Paul Stahr's cover for the May 10, 1930 issue illustrated the six-part, New Orleans-set serial "Voodoo'd" by Kenneth Perkins.

TOP MIDDLE: A. (Abraham) Merritt was a regular contributor to *Argosy Weekly*, and the October 22, 1932 issue featured the first part of his six-part serial "Burn, Witch, Burn!" with a cover by Robert A. Graef.

TOP RIGHT: Graef also provided the cover for the first part of Merritt's seven-part serial "Creep, Shadow!" in the September 8, 1934 issue of *Argosy Weekly*, published by The Frank A. Munsey Company.

BOTTOM MIDDLE: V. (Virgil) E. (Evans) Pyles's cover for Theodore Roscoe's "Z is for Zombie" appeared on the February 6, 1937 *Argosy Weekly*. Under various incarnations, the magazine ran from 1882 until 1978.

BOTTOM RIGHT: Pulp veteran Rudolph Belarski supplied the creepy cover for the five-part serial "Maker of Shadows" by "Jack Mann" (Charles Cannell) on the December 9, 1939 issue of *Argosy Weekly*.

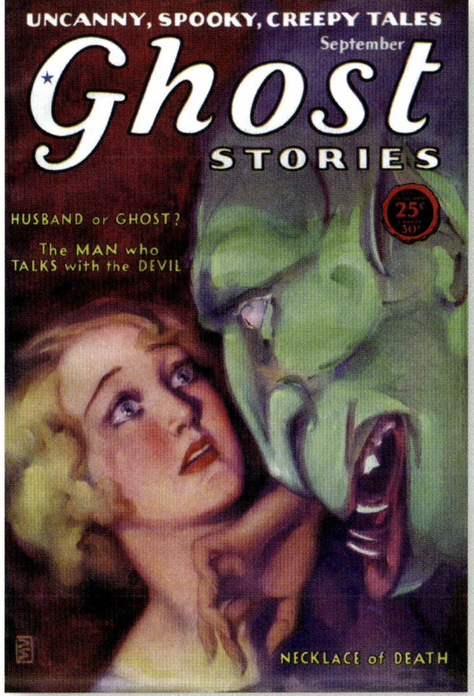

TOP MIDDLE: 64 issues of *Ghost Stories* were published between July 1926 and January 1932, the majority by Macfadden Publications, Inc. The October 1927 issue included a reprint of a H.G. Wells story from 1895.

ABOVE LEFT: *Ghost Stories* was one of the earliest competitors to *Weird Tales* and presented its stories as "true confessions." This cover for the November 1927 edition is one of the best they ever published.

TOP RIGHT: The June 1929 issue of *Ghost Stories* featured one of a number of covers Jean Oldham did for the large-format magazine, and included stories by Theodore Dreiser, Paul Ernst, and Nathaniel Hawthorne.

BOTTOM MIDDLE: *Ghost Stories* reverted to a standard pulp size for the second time at the beginning of 1930. This issue from March that year featured a cover by Dalton Stevens and an article by Sir Arthur Conan Doyle.

BOTTOM RIGHT: Dalton Stevens also painted this outlandish cover for the September 1930 edition of *Ghost Stories*. Early issues were printed on slick paper and used fake photographs for greater verisimilitude.

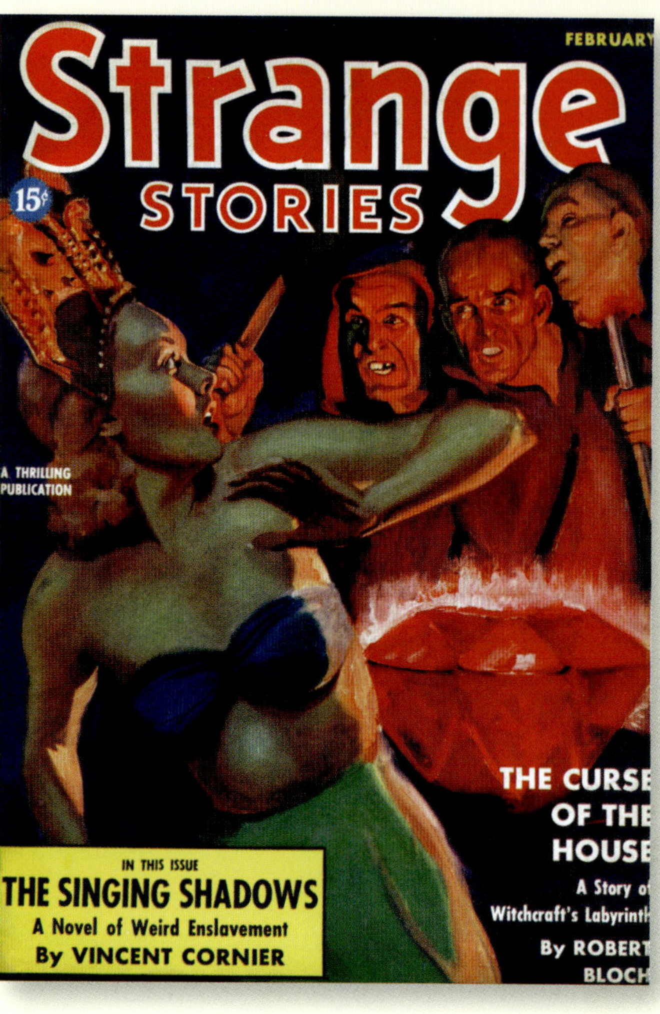

TOP LEFT: Edited by Harry Bates (1900–81), *Strange Tales* was launched in 1931 as a direct rival to *Weird Tales*. The cover by "Wesso" (Hans Wessolowski) for the October 1932 issue illustrated a Clark Ashton Smith story.

TOP MIDDLE: The December 1936 edition of *Weird Tales*, "The Unique Magazine" that was founded by J.C. Henneberger and J.M. Lansinger and ran for 279 issues between March 1923 and September 1954.

BOTTOM LEFT: Published by the Popular Fiction Publishing Co., *Weird Tales* for April 1938 not only included a cover story by Clark Ashton Smith, but also verse by H.P. Lovecraft and Robert E. Howard.

BOTTOM MIDDLE: Editor Farnsworth Wright (1888–1940) was coming to the end of his tenure with the July 1939 issue of *Weird Tales*, which featured an impressive line-up of big name writers, including H.P. Lovecraft.

ABOVE RIGHT: Although *Strange Stories* was the closest rival to *Weird Tales*, the cover for the first issue (February 1939) was more indicative of the "shudder pulps." It only ran for 13 bi-monthly issues.

ABOVE LEFT: Oil painting by Chicago artist J. (James) Allen St. John (1872–1957) for the cover of the December 1936 *Weird Tales*, illustrating the novelette "The Fire of Asshurbanipal" by Robert E. Howard.

TOP RIGHT: Cover painting by American artist Virgil Finlay (1914–71) for the April 1938 edition of *Weird Tales*, illustrating "The Garden of Adompha," one of Clark Ashton Smith's story cycle about "Zothique."

BOTTOM RIGHT: Watercolor on board rough by Virgil Finlay for the cover of the July 1939 issue of *Weird Tales*, which was a bumper 160-page edition. The art was inspired by Robert Barbour Johnson's story "Far Below."

BRUNDAGE'S BONDAGE BABES

> "They would always pick the one that showed a girl with the least amount of clothing. They felt that those pictures were best for the covers."
>
> Margaret Brundage

> "I have no objection to the nude in art . . . But I don't see what the hell Mrs. Brundage's undressed ladies have to do with weird fiction."
>
> H.P. Lovecraft in a letter to Willis Conover, September 1, 1936

IN LATE AUTUMN, 1931, a 30-year-old mother walked into the editorial offices of *Weird Tales* on North Michigan Avenue, Chicago, looking for work. She was Margaret Brundage. She had a four-year-old son and was barely supported by her husband, who was rarely at home. She was a qualified artist and had been working for fashion magazines, but needed further income and the chance of doing more varied work.

Among her art samples was a picture of an oriental dancer. She had no idea that *Weird Tales* had a companion magazine, *Oriental Stories*. Editor Farnsworth Wright was impressed by her work and asked to see more. Before long she was commissioned to provide covers for *Oriental Stories*, starting with the Spring 1932 issue.

That first cover, depicting a near-naked dancing girl, gave some idea of what was to come. Though her covers for *Oriental Stories* (and its continuation as *The Magic Carpet Magazine*) were relatively modest, they nevertheless showed Brundage's skill at depicting the female form. She soon provided covers for *Weird Tales*, starting with the September 1932 issue. The following month saw her illustrate her first Jules de Grandin story, "The Heart of Siva," but her cover for March 1933, depicting another de Grandin story, was her first full nude, showing a beautiful girl with flaming-red hair running with a pack of wolves.

Brundage's favorite author was Robert E. Howard, and her cover for the June 1933 issue with Howard's "Black Colossus" was one of the author's own favorites. For Howard's "The Slithering Shadow" in the September 1933 issue, Brundage depicted a naked, chained girl being whipped by a near-naked woman. Apparently that issue sold out, almost solely because of the cover, as new purchasers thought it dealt with flagellation.

There was long the belief that Brundage used her two daughters as models, but she had no daughters. Although she did occasionally use a cousin as a model, her inspiration came mostly from the pin-up and nudist magazines of the period.

She produced 66 covers for *Weird Tales* between 1932 and 1945, plus a further eight for *Oriental Stories/Magic Carpet Magazine* and *Golden Fleece*, a historical adventure pulp. Although she did some interior black-and-white illustrations, it is for her covers that she is remembered, many of which feature the most beautiful artwork ever to adorn a pulp magazine. Perhaps her most iconic cover

Brundage depicted a naked, chained girl being whipped by a near-naked woman. Apparently that issue sold out, almost solely because of the cover, as new purchasers thought it dealt with flagellation.

was for the October 1933 issue of *Weird Tales*, portraying the bat-masked female in Edmond Hamilton's "The Vampire Master"—surprisingly not a nude.

She worked in pastels, which meant that the original artwork, produced on a board usually twice the size of the final cover, was fragile, as the delicate chalks could be disturbed. This worked all the time she could deliver the pictures by hand to *Weird Tales* in Chicago, but it became a problem when the offices moved to New York in 1938. The artwork would often be damaged in the mail. Brundage switched to working in oils, but the pictures lost their vibrancy. She received fewer commissions, and these ceased at the end of 1944. The era of the "Queen of the Pulps" was over.

Margaret Brundage continued to work—including contributing to the civil rights movement—and lived until 1976, already a legend in her lifetime. *MA*

Risqué Business

Former fashion artist Margaret Brundage's first pastel chalk on paper cover for the pulp magazine *Weird Tales* was for the September 1932 issue, illustrating "The Altar of Melek Taos" by G.G. Pendarves [ABOVE LEFT]. It was also one of her best. The artist also used chalk on paper for the cover of the September 1935 issue of "The Unique Magazine," which featured one of her signature nudes to illustrate "a weird mystery story" by John Scott Douglas, "The Blue Woman" [TOP RIGHT]. Perhaps one of Brundage's most (in) famous "bondage" covers was her pastel on board illustration for "The Albino Deaths" by Ronal Kayser in the March 1936 issue of *Weird Tales* [BOTTOM RIGHT], which depicted "weird tortures in a ghastly abode of horrors." She was paid a flat fee of $90 per cover.

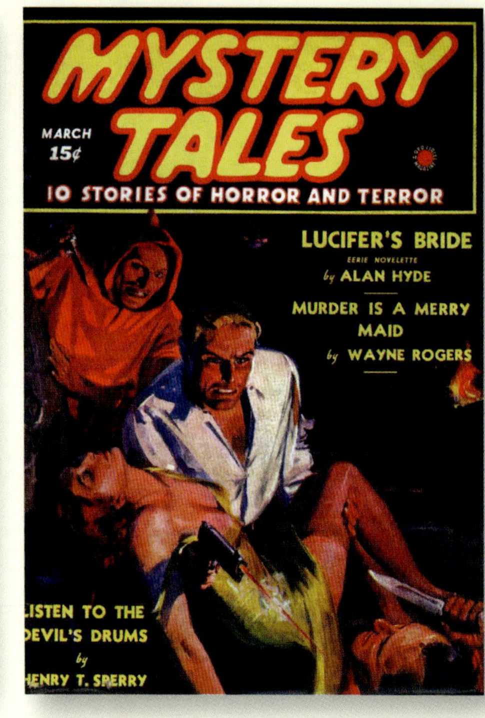

TOP MIDDLE: Fred Craft's cover for the June 1928 issue of The Priscilla Company's *Mystery Stories* illustrated the vampire story "Dead Men of the Mountains," by "O'Connor Stacy" (William Rollins, Jr.).

TOP RIGHT: The uncredited artist for the first edition of Western Fiction Publishing Co., Inc.'s *Mystery Tales* (March 1938) used a familiar pose for his hero and heroine. The title ran for nine issues, until May 1940.

BOTTOM MIDDLE: Emery Clarke's cover for the only issue of *Thrilling Mysteries*, published by Popular Publications, Inc. in January 1939 and featuring stories by Hugh B. Cave, Paul Ernst, and Arthur J. Burks.

ABOVE LEFT: The December 1939 issue of Double-Action Magazines, Inc.'s "weird menace" title *Mystery Novels and Short Stories*, which ran for six issues between September 1939 and September 1941.

BOTTOM RIGHT: The first of only two issues of Western Fiction Publishing Co., Inc's *Real Mystery Magazine* (April 1940), which was set up to reprint fiction from *Uncanny Tales* and *Mystery Tales* under new titles.

ABOVE RIGHT: This pulp from Nickel Publications had three different titles before it changed its name to *Strange Detective Stories* in 1933 and ran for four monthly issues. The January 1934 cover was by Clifford Benton.

TOP LEFT: Based on a radio show with a similar name, the first issue of Carwood Publishing Company's *The Witch's Tales* appeared in November 1936 with a cover by Elmer C. Stoner. It lasted for just one more edition.

TOP MIDDLE: The one and only issue of Magazine Publishers, Inc.'s *Eerie Stories* was dated August 1937. With a cover by Norman Saunders and subtitled "Startling Adventures of Chilling Horror," most of the stories were pseudonymous.

BOTTOM LEFT: The same publisher issued a companion title, *Eerie Mysteries* (August 1938), again with a cover by Norman Saunders. The title ran for four issues and although no artist is credited, all the covers are thought to be by Saunders.

BOTTOM MIDDLE: A continuation of *Star Detective Magazine* (1935–38), Manvis Publications' *Uncanny Tales* debuted with the April–May 1939 edition. Only five more issues appeared in just over a year.

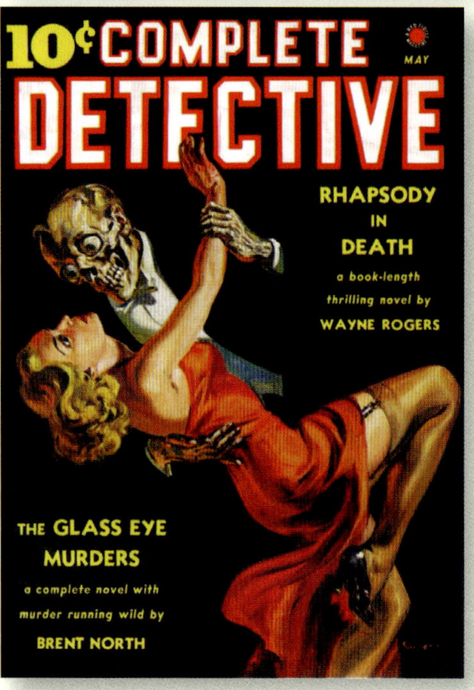

ABOVE LEFT: The October 1930 edition of Hugo Gernsback's *Amazing Detective Tales* (originally *Scientific Detective Monthly*) featured a cover by Howard V. Brown and a story by Clark Ashton Smith. The oversized "bedsheet" pulp only ran for five issues under this new title.

TOP MIDDLE: The villain portrayed by artist J. (Jerry) George Janes on the cover of the January 1934 issue of Magazine Publishers, Inc.'s *Ten Detective Aces* was undoubtedly modeled after Lon Chaney's Phantom of the Opera. Universal Pictures reportedly threatened to sue.

TOP RIGHT: Norman Saunders's striking cover for the last issue of Dell Publishing Co., Inc.'s *All Detective Magazine* (January 1935) illustrated the novella "The Sign of the Serpent" by prolific British-born pulp author Hugh B. Cave.

BOTTOM MIDDLE: John Fleming Gould's cover for the May 1938 edition of Popular Publications, Inc.'s long-running (274 issues, 1931–53) *Dime Detective Magazine*. This issue featured a short story by Cornell Woolrich.

BOTTOM RIGHT: Norman Saunders's suitably gruesome cover adorned the first issue of Western Fiction Publishing Co., Inc.'s short-lived pulp *Complete Detective* (May 1938), which lasted for just six issues, until October 1939.

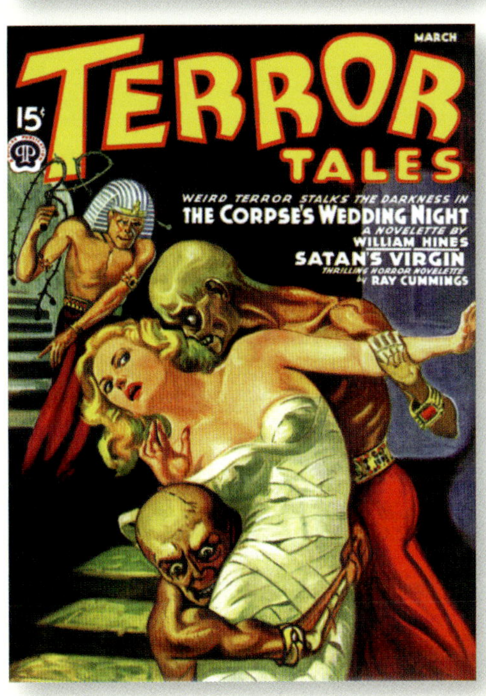

TOP LEFT: Charles L. Wren's cover for Popular Publications, Inc.'s March 1935 edition of *Horror Stories*, one of the most infamous "weird menace" pulps, which began publishing in January that year and ran for 47 issues.

TOP MIDDLE: Popular Publications' co-founder, Harry Steeger (1903–90), created the "weird menace" genre in October 1933 with *Dime Mystery Magazine*. Walter M. Baumhofer's November 1935 cover was typical of the magazine.

TOP RIGHT: A particularly gruesome cover for Better Publications, Inc.'s *Thrilling Mystery* (January 1939).

BOTTOM LEFT: John Drew's cover for the March 1940 issue of *Terror Tales*, a companion to *Horror Stories*.

BOTTOM MIDDLE: John Newton Howitt's cover for the April 1940 edition of Fictioneers, Inc.'s *Startling Mystery Magazine* (the second of only two monthly issues) was previously used on the October 1935 edition of *Horror Stories*.

BOTTOM RIGHT: John Drew's cover painting for the third and final issue (May 1940) of Fictioneers, Inc.'s *Sinister Stories*, one of the last of the "shudder" pulps, originally appeared on the November–December 1937 edition of *Terror Tales*.

Spice Girls

American pulp artist H. (Hugh) J. (Joseph) Ward (1909–45) was a prolific illustrator of pulp covers, but he is best remembered for his *risqué* oil-on-canvas artwork for Culture Publications' line of "Spicy" titles. His cover for the novelette "The Evil Flame" by "Justin Case" (Hugh B. Cave) [TOP LEFT] appeared on the August 1936 issue of *Spicy Mystery Stories* and sold at auction in 2010 for a record-breaking $143,400. Ward's cover for the August 1938 *Spicy Mystery Stories* [ABOVE RIGHT] illustrated another novelette, "Doll of Death" by "Larry Dunn" (Laurence Donovan), while his cover on the February 1940 issue of the pulp magazine [BOTTOM LEFT] illustrated the short story "Through Fire" by Robert Leslie Bellem. H.J. Ward also produced the first painting of Superman before he tragically died of lung cancer at the age of 35.

Although there had been "girlie" magazines since the early 1900s, it was in April 1934, with the launch of *Spicy Detective Tales*, that Harry Donenfeld's Culture Publications changed the pulp field by combining different types of genre fiction with "a very strong sex element." In July the same year they added *Spicy Mystery Stories* and *Spicy-Adventure Stories* to the line, while *Spicy Western Stories* followed in November 1936. Frank Armer was editor-in-chief of all four.

TOP LEFT: The second issue of *Spicy Detective Stories* (June 1934) featured a cover painting by H. (Harry) L. (Lemon) Parkhurst. Norman A. Daniels's short story "Do the Dead Live?" was wrongly titled "The Dead Live Again" on the cover.

BOTTOM LEFT: A typically provocative H.J. Ward cover graced the second issue of *Spicy-Adventure Stories* (November 1934). Some "Spicy" titles were self-censored by the publisher. These were identified with a star in a box on the cover.

ABOVE RIGHT: H.J. Ward also painted this cover for the February 1936 issue of *Spicy Mystery Stories* which, like its companion titles, lasted until December 1942, when a public outcry over "sex" pulps led to the word "Spicy" being replaced with "Speed."

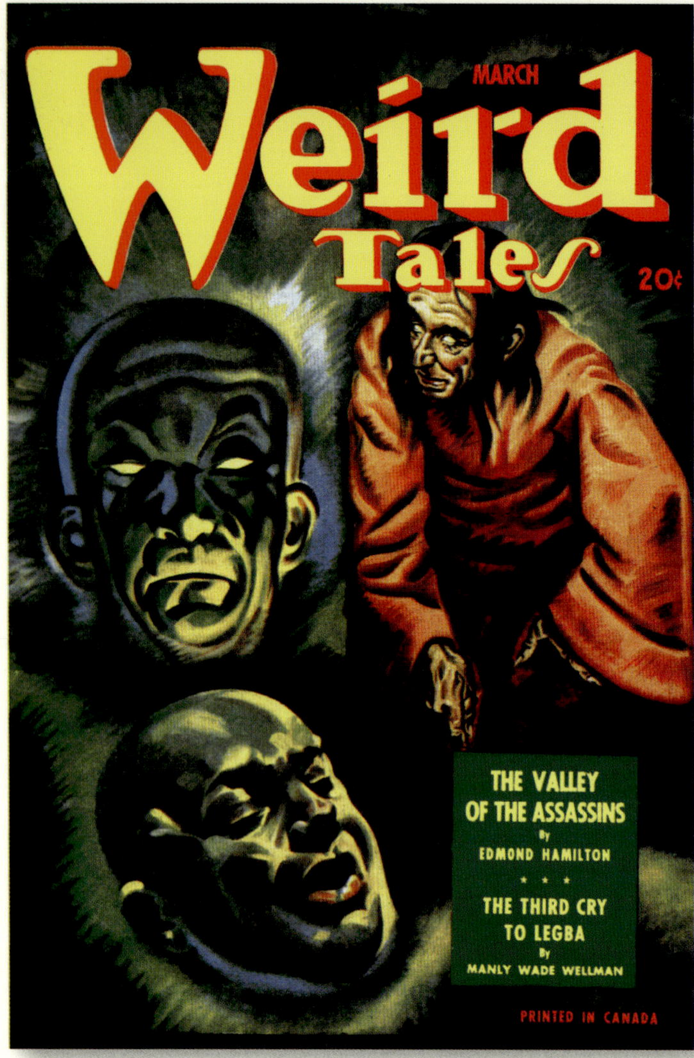

TOP MIDDLE: The first series of Canadian reprints of *Weird Tales* ran monthly from June 1935 to July 1936. The contents and covers were almost identical to the corresponding American editions but, as this February 1936 issue shows, they added "Printed in Canada."

TOP RIGHT: The second series of Canadian *Weird Tales* reprints began in May 1942 and ran bi-monthly until November 1951. The first 17 issues featured revised contents and original illustrations and cover art, as seen on this November 1942 issue.

BOTTOM MIDDLE: This March 1943 issue of the Canadian *Weird Tales* had a better cover than the American edition for Robert Bloch's story "Nursemaid to Nightmares." Unfortunately, as with most of these editions, the artist was not credited.

ABOVE LEFT: There was also no artist credited for the cover of the March 1944 Canadian *Weird Tales*, which illustrated "The Valley of Assassins" by Edmond Hamilton. This issue mostly reprinted the contents of November 1943 American edition.

BOTTOM RIGHT: The January 1945 issue was the last of the Canadian *Weird Tales* to feature original interior and cover art. After wartime restrictions were lifted, the magazine reverted to being a delayed reprint of the American edition.

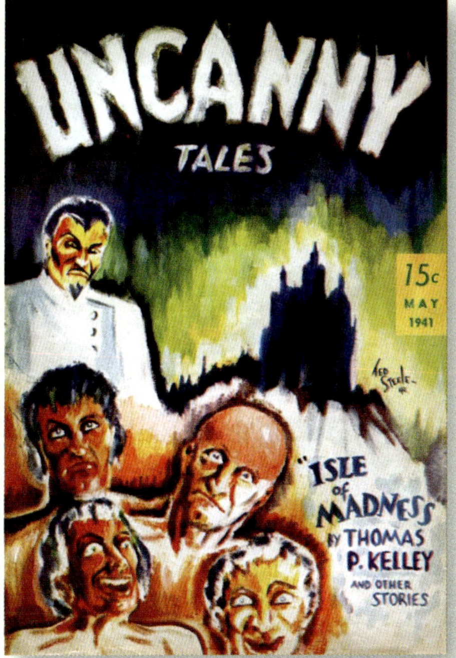

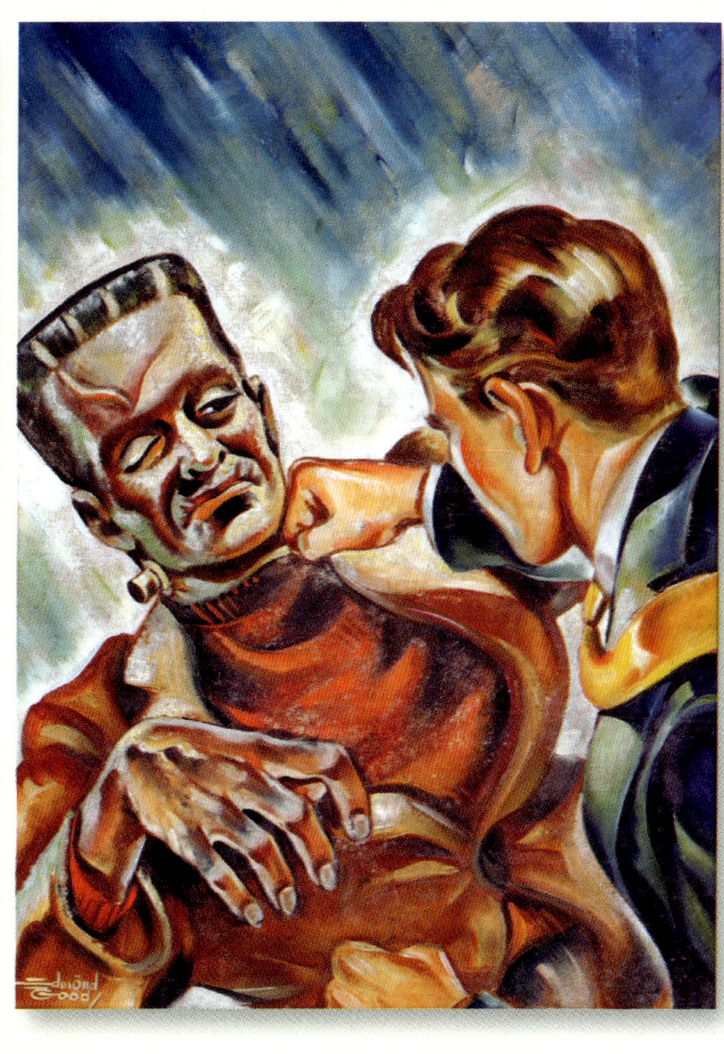

TOP LEFT: Having started out as a digest in November 1940, the Canadian *Uncanny Tales* moved to a pulp format with this May 1941 edition. It contained three stories by Thomas P. Kelley and the cover was by Ted (Theodore Arthur) Steele, who also supplied the interior art.

TOP MIDDLE: The January 1942 *Uncanny Tales* included a reprint each from *Weird Tales* and *Cosmic Stories* (along with the latter's Hannes Bok illustration). This issue featured the only known cover by an artist who signed themselves simply as "Bick."

BOTTOM LEFT: Hannes Bok had five illustrations reprinted in the December 1942 *Uncanny Tales*, but the striking cover was by regular artist K.P. Ainsworth. After a gap of nine months, the magazine finally folded with the September–October 1943 issue.

BOTTOM MIDDLE: Most of the one and only issue of Canada's *Eerie Tales* (July, 1941) was probably written by prolific Canadian author Thomas P. Kelley. American cover artist John K. Hilkert was disappointed, describing his poorly engraved pulp debut as an "abomination."

ABOVE RIGHT: American-born comics artist Edmond [Elbridge] Good produced a number of Canadian pulp covers during the 1940s. This oils on unstretched canvas painting was apparently intended as a *Short Stories* cover, although it is unclear if it was ever used.

ABOVE LEFT: The July 1923 edition of *Hutchinson's Mystery-Story Magazine*, which ran from February that year until June 1929. The monthly British periodical reprinted fiction from many American pulps, especially *Ghost Stories*.

TOP RIGHT: Although also issued by World's Work, a UK subsidiary of American publisher Doubleday, unlike two other magazines with the same title, the Mid-winter 1936 *Tales of the Uncanny* was not part of the publisher's "Master Thriller Series."

BOTTOM RIGHT: The December 1939 edition (No. 32) of World's Work's *Master Thriller: Tales of Ghosts and Haunted Houses* was the final issue in the pulp magazine anthology series that featured separate titles in different genres.

ABOVE RIGHT: The first of three unnumbered and undated UK issues of *Weird Tales*, published in 1942 by Gerald G. Swan Ltd. It was an abridged reprint of the September 1940 edition, and reused the cover art from that issue by Ray Quigley.

TOP LEFT & MIDDLE: British author and ghost hunter R. (Robert) Thurston Hopkins (1884–1958) had three collections of new and reprint stories published in digest format in 1945 by Mitre Press. Two of the booklets, *Horror Parade* and *Uncanny Tales*, featured cover art by H.W. Perl (Hyman Woolf Perlzweig), who also contributed the replacement cover for the first selection of the British *Strange Tales*. *Horror Parade* was also widely distributed in America.

BOTTOM LEFT & MIDDLE: Utopian Publications Ltd. produced two "selections" of *Strange Tales* in early 1946, as Britain's post-war paper shortage did not apply to the launch of new anthologies. Both featured covers by American artist Alva Rogers, although the original art on the first issue had to be replaced because it depicted a topless woman. Edited by an uncredited Walter Gillings (1912–79), both digest-sized issues featured reprint fiction from Ray Bradbury, H.P. Lovecraft, and others.

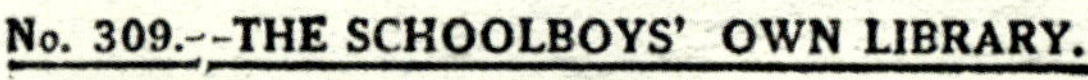

THIS PAGE: The Amalgamated Press, Ltd.'s pocket-sized pulp *Schoolboys' Own Library* ran for 411 bi- and thrice-monthly issues from 1925 to 1940, before it became another casualty of the wartime paper shortage (the final three intended issues were never published). It reprinted cut-down versions of earlier stories and serials from such boys' papers such as *The Magnet*, *The Gem*, etc. and the original author would receive a small honorarium payment. Edwy Searles Brooks's stories about detective-turned-housemaster Nelson Lee and the boys of St. Frank's School were originally published in *The Nelson Lee Library* and often featured fantastic elements—including lost worlds and supposed ghosts. Brooks wrote more than 100 novels and 2,000 stories under various pseudonyms.

TOP LEFT & RIGHT: No. 309 *The Lost Land!* (August 5, 1937) first appeared in *The Nelson Lee Library* [*TNLL*] Nos. 268–270 (1920).

BOTTOM LEFT: No. 372 *Yellow Menace!* (May 4, 1939) was originally published in *TNLL* Nos. 360–362 (1922).

BOTTOM MIDDLE: No. 387 *The Secret World!* (October 5, 1939) came from *TNLL* Nos. 375–377 (1922).

BOTTOM RIGHT: No. 393 *The Ghost of Somerton Abbey!* (December 7, 1939) was reprinted from *TNLL* Nos. 392, 394–395 (1922).

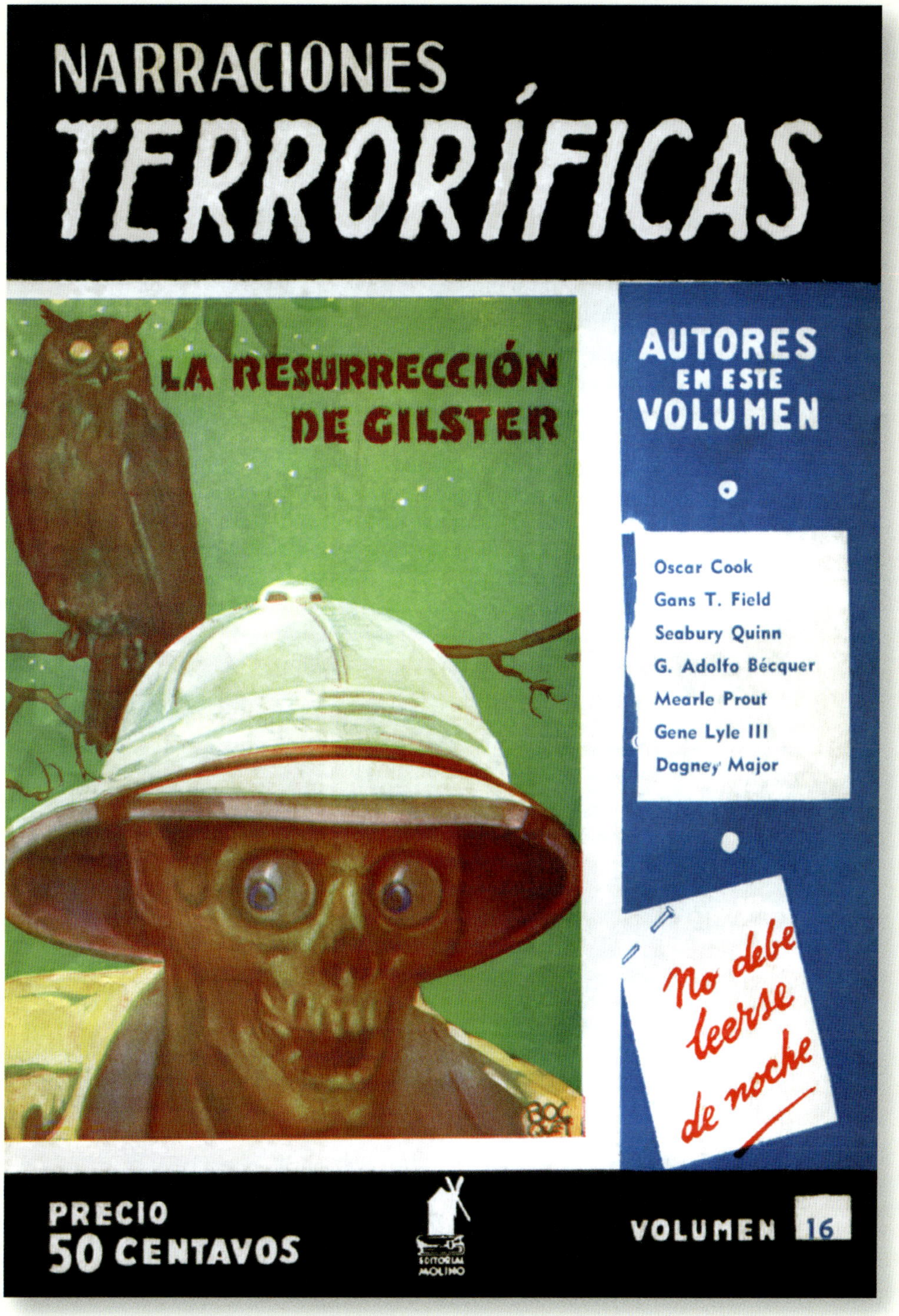

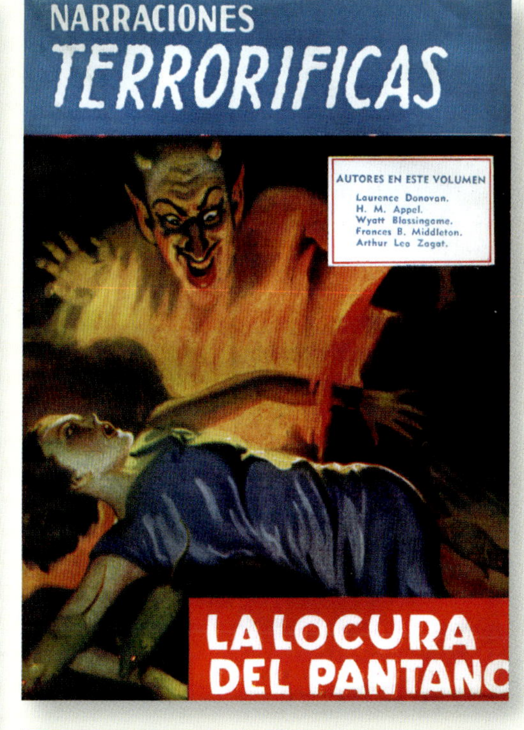

Hispanic Horrors

The Spanish-language pulp magazine *Narraciones Terroríficas* was edited by José Mallorquí Figuerola and published by Editorial Molino in Argentina. The title lasted for 76 issues, from mid-1939–March 1952, and many of the covers were the work of Spanish artist Joan Pau Bocquet (1904–66). Published by Mexico's Editorial Enigma, *Los Cuentos Fantasticos* ran for 44 issues from July 1948 to May 1953 and mostly translated (usually without permission) fiction from *Famous Fantastic Mysteries* and other American pulps.

ABOVE LEFT: *Narraciones Terroríficas* No. 16 (1940), with a cover by Joan Pau Bocquet. This issue reprinted fiction from *Weird Tales* by Oscar Cook, "Gans T. Field" (Manly Wade Wellman), Seabury Quinn, Mearle Prout, and Gene Lyle III, along with other stories.

TOP RIGHT: *Narraciones Terroríficas* No. 66 (June 1947) not only reused John Howitt's cover art from the December 1934 *Terror Tales*, but also five stories from that US "weird menace" pulp by Wyatt Blassingame, Arthur Leo Zagret, Laurence Donovan, and others.

BOTTOM RIGHT: Edited by Antonio Mejia, the Mexican pulp *Los Cuentos Fantasticos* also used reprint art, although this cover on No. 23 (December 1949) was an original signed "Fojeno." It featured reprint stories by A. Merritt, Stanley Mullen, E. Everett Evans, and others.

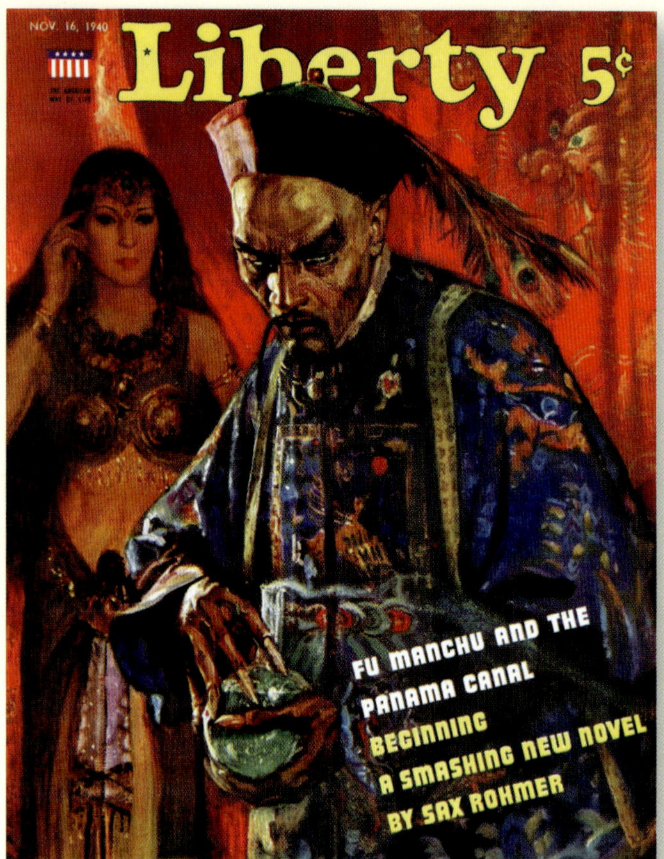

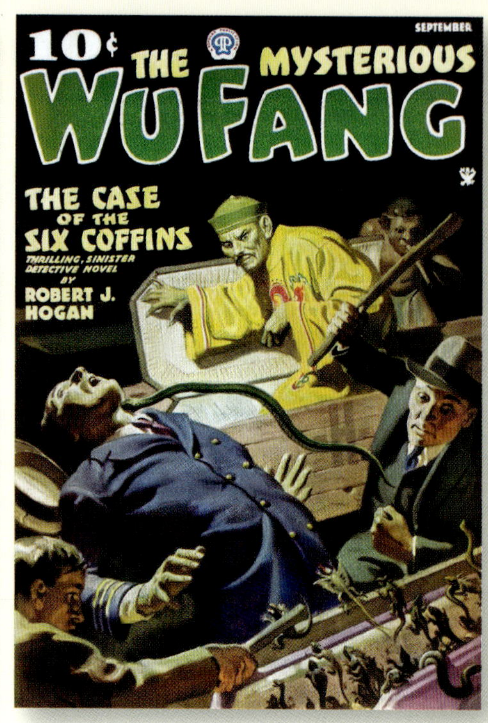

TOP MIDDLE: Artist George Goss obviously swiped the image of Boris Karloff from *The Mask of Fu Manchu* (1932) for his cover painting on the September 1935 edition of Winford Publication, Inc.'s *Mystery Novels Magazine*.

TOP RIGHT: Jerome Rozen's cover for the first issue of the Fu Manchu-inspired *The Mysterious Wu Fang* (September 1935) from Popular Publications, Inc. Created by Robert J. Hogan, it ran for just seven monthly issues.

BOTTOM MIDDLE: Jerome Rozen's cover for the premiere issue of *Dr. Yen Sin* (May–June 1936), the follow-up title from Popular Publications, Inc. Created by Donald E. Keyhoe, it only lasted for three bi-monthly issues.

BOTTOM RIGHT: Cover signed "Marchini" for *Alerta!* No. 69 (April 6, 1936), published in Santiago, Chile. It reprinted Sax Rohmer's *El Diabolico Fú-Manchú* (possibly a cut-down of *The Devil Doctor*, aka *The Return of Dr. Fu-Manchu*, 1916).

ABOVE LEFT: Arnold Freberg's cover for the first installment of the 12-part Sax Rohmer serial "Fu Manchu and the Panama Canal" in the weekly *Liberty* (November 16, 1940). It was published in book form as *The Island of Fu Manchu* (1941).

BOTTOM LEFT: Window card for *The Witch's Tale* half-hour radio series, which ran from 1931–38 on WOR-Mutual, New York, and in syndication. It features the show's host, "Old Nancy, the Witch of Salem" (originally played by stage actress Adelaide Fitz-Allen) and her black cat "Satan." The pioneering horror radio show was created, written, and directed by Alonzo Deen Cole (1897–1971), who also edited a tie-in pulp magazine, which lasted for just two "bedsheet" issues in 1936.

TOP LEFT: One of a number of promotional 1940s ink blotters from Blue Coal ("America's Finest Anthracite"), the sponsor of *The Shadow* radio show. The pulp character was originally conceived in 1930 as the host of *Detective Story Hour*.

BOTTOM MIDDLE: Based on a mystery novel imprint from Simon & Schuster and the 1941–52 radio show, the movie *Inner Sanctum* (Dir: Lew Landers, 1948) featured character actor Fritz Leiber, the father of pulp magazine author Fritz Leiber, Jr.

ABOVE RIGHT: *Weird Tales* artist Boris Dolgov illustrated this advert in the pulp for Neblett Radio Productions' *Stay Tuned for Terror*. First broadcast on WMAQ Chicago in 1945, Robert Bloch scripted and supervised all 39 episodes.

4 POVERTY ROW

GREGORY WILLIAM MANK

"Just picture gentlemen: An army of wolf men. Fearless! Raging! Every man a snarling animal! My serum will make it possible to unloose millions of such animal men. Men who are governed by one collective thought: the animal lust to kill!"

DR. LORENZO CAMERON (GEORGE ZUCCO) IN *THE MAD MONSTER* (1942)

"No matter how hokum or highly melodramatic the horror part may be, you must believe in it while you are playing it."

Bela Lugosi

"Poor old Bela, it was a strange thing. He was really a shy, sensitive, talented man who had a fine career on the classical stage in Europe, but he made a fatal mistake. He never took the trouble to learn our language. He had real problems with his speech and difficulty interpreting lines."

Boris Karloff

HOLLYWOOD, YULETIDE, 1942. Bela Lugosi is at Monogram Studios, starring in what will be his most notorious "Poverty Row" horror film, *The Ape Man.* He plays a mad doctor, whose experiments have made him a bitter, understandably abashed part-simian. Come the climax, leggy leading lady Louise Currie attacks Lugosi with a whip. Shortly thereafter, Emil Van Horn—who's played the gorilla as if he believes the role is Oscar-worthy—mauls Lugosi to death.

William "One Shot" Beaudine directs, living up to his posthumous nickname. Edward Kay scores the film in the style of Big Top "thrill" music. Meanwhile, Sam Katzman, who produces this opus, has a *soubriquet* for films such as *The Ape Man.*

He calls them "moron pictures."

Yet, when *The Ape Man* opens at the 475-seat Colony Theatre on Hollywood Boulevard on March 18, 1943, on a double-bill with *Kid Dynamite* starring the East Side Kids, it comes with a dash of pride. The Colony, expecting a winner, ups the ticket price to 55 cents. Lugosi, who's revealed no shame in portraying his Ape Man role ("I think it intrigued him," Louise Currie will recall), agrees to a personal appearance during the run's second week. The film's poster art, featuring the hirsute star, the blonde leading lady, and the uproarious man-in-the-ape-suit, evokes the splashy cover of a pulp horror magazine.

In fact, horror films such as *The Ape Man* were the pulps of Poverty Row.

In 1940s Hollywood, Universal Studios boasted Frankenstein's Monster, Dracula, the Wolf Man, and other prized goblins. RKO Studios heralded Val Lewton, who produced the quirky *Cat People* (1942) and followed up with a nightmarish pride parade of zombies and devil-worshippers. The Poverty Row studios—the most legendary of which were Monogram and PRC (Producers Releasing Corporation)—had to originate their own monsters with what they could afford.

Fortunately, "affordable" were several of the finest and most underrated actors in the business. Boris Karloff headlines Monogram's 1940 *The Ape*, skinning an escaped circus gorilla, donning its pelt as he kills victims; Bela Lugosi stars in PRC's *The Devil Bat* the same year, vengefully unleashing the title creature. Both stars act with gusto, but *The Ape* will be Karloff's only foray into

The Poverty Row studios—the most legendary of which were Monogram and PRC (Producers Releasing Corporation)—had to originate their own monsters with what they could afford. Fortunately, "affordable" were several of the finest and most underrated actors in the business.

Monogram horror—he heads to Broadway to star in the historic stage hit, *Arsenic and Old Lace.*

Lon Chaney, Jr. is the new horror star at Universal, which now gives Lugosi only featured billing. Monogram will be more generous to Lugosi with both billing and screen time; in all, the studio will star him in nine films.

A gruesome example: *The Corpse Vanishes* (1942). The unsavory plot: Lugosi kidnaps brides, tapping their youthful glands and hormones to keep "the Countess"—his evil crone of a wife—attractive and supple. A cartoonist would have delighted not only in Lugosi's leers, but in the cat-faced Elizabeth Russell, who, as the Countess, sleeps in a coffin, makes what appears to be a sapphic pass at the heroine and later slaps her face, and even calls dwarf Angelo Rossitto a "gargoyle." Shortly thereafter, Elizabeth Russell will become Val Lewton's choice as the original "Cat Woman," who greets Simone Simon on her snowy wedding night in RKO's mega-hit, *Cat People.*

Meanwhile, PRC competes with Monogram like two midnight sideshows playing the same small towns. Stately Britisher George Zucco is in especially bravura form in the studio's *The Mad Monster* (1942), hoping to create an army of werewolves to attack the Axis powers. Playing Petro, his prototype, is six-foot-four-inch Glenn Strange, soon to assume the role of Universal's Frankenstein Monster.

PREVIOUS SPREAD: Glenn Strange as the Monster in *Abbott and Costello Meet Frankenstein* (1996), acrylics on board by American artist Basil Gogos. "I preferred to work with a black-and-white photograph," recalled the artist. "And the way it worked for me was that I stared into it for a long time, and suddenly it started to change. In my mind's eye, it started to change to color, pure color, and the interesting part of it was, when that painting was finished, it was exactly the way I envisioned it." This painting was used on the cover of *Monsterscene* No. 9, Fall 1996.

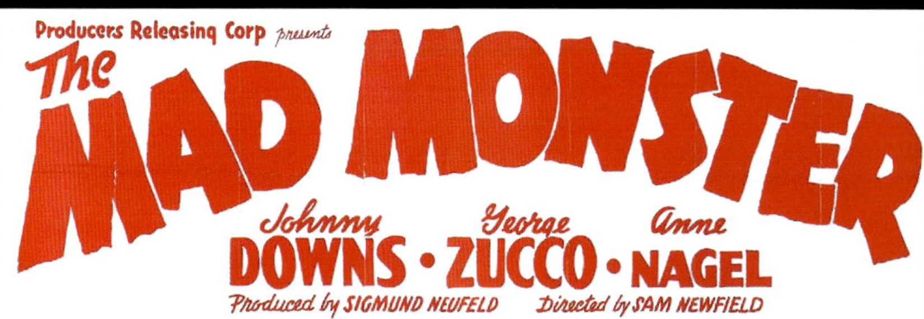

TOP LEFT: Pre-release trade advertisement for *The Ape* (Dir: William Nigh, 1940) from Monogram Pictures' spiral-bound 1940–41 exhibitor's book. It was the final film in Boris Karloff's six-picture contract with the Poverty Row studio.

BOTTOM LEFT: Italian *foglio* for RKO Radio Pictures' *Cat People* (Dir: Jacques Tourneur, 1942) by Giorgio Olivetti (1908–??). Producer Val Lewton created a mini-masterpiece with just a $150,000 budget and an 18-day shooting schedule.

TOP RIGHT: Six-sheet poster for Producers Releasing Corporation's *The Mad Monster* (Dir: Sam Newfield, 1942), in which George Zucco's mad scientist turns a simple-minded handyman (Glenn Strange) into a lupine super-soldier.

BOTTOM MIDDLE: Argentinean poster for Monogram's *The Ape Man* (Dir: William Beaudine, 1943). Bela Lugosi's mad doctor needs recently obtained human spinal fluid to prevent him from changing into a hairy ape-man.

BOTTOM RIGHT: Banner for Universal Pictures' *House of Dracula* (Dir: Erle C. Kenton, 1945). John Carradine's Dracula decides he doesn't want to be "cured" and instead turns sympathetic Dr. Edelmann (Onslow Stevens) into a vampire.

BOTTOM MIDDLE: Window card for Universal Pictures' multi-monster *House of Frankenstein* (Dir: Erle C. Kenton, 1944) featuring the Wolf Man, Frankenstein's Monster, Dracula, the hunchback, and the mad doctor.

BOTTOM RIGHT: Italian *foglio* for Universal's *House of Dracula* (1945) by Angelo Cesselon (1922–92), who became a renowned portrait artist. In 1955 he received the Spiga Cambellotti award for Italy's best cinematographic painter of the year.

TOP LEFT: Lurid six-sheet poster for Producers Releasing Corporation's *Strangler of the Swamp* (1946), German director Frank Wisbar's American Poverty Row remake of his own *Fährmann Maria* (Ferryman Maria, 1936).

TOP RIGHT: Half-sheet poster for Monogram Pictures' *Master Minds* (Dir: Jean Yarbrough, 1949), one of the better "Bowery Boys" horror-comedies, featuring Glenn Strange as a monstrous ape-man created by Alan Napier's mad doctor.

BOTTOM LEFT: Half-sheet for *Robot Monster* (Dir: Phil Tucker, 1953), a bargain basement 3-D release from Astor Pictures Corporation that was reportedly shot in four days and featured stock footage (including dinosaurs) from several other movies.

Zucco carries on in *Dead Men Walk* (1943), in a dual role for PRC as the vampire and the vampire's brother. Playing the vampire's hunchbacked minion: Dwight Frye, whose role seems a homage to his fly-eating Renfield in *Dracula* and deformed Fritz in *Frankenstein* (both 1931). The ailing actor, heartbroken by typecasting, dies a year later at the age of 44.

John Carradine, hoping to raise money for his own Shakespearean repertory company, joins the fold. He stars as a Nazi doctor who unleashes Monogram's *Revenge of the Zombies* (1943). Carradine's lean and hungry look, of course, would delight a pulp artist.

Inevitably, the Monogram and PRC chillers appall critics (e.g. "It lowers the average of all hands," snipes *Motion Picture Herald* of *The Ape Man*). Do these distinguished actors have any pride? One eventually does.

The mania comes to a climax in October of 1943, via Monogram's *Voodoo Man*. Bela Lugosi, in the title role, sports a goatee and wizard's robe as he tries to keep his 22-years-dead wife in a semblance of life. John Carradine, as Lugosi's mentally enfeebled minion, soulfully beats a bongo at the voodoo ceremony.

Monogram launches *Return of the Ape Man* (1944), in which Lugosi and Carradine thaw a cave man (*not* an ape man, despite the title) out of cellophane ice. Zucco is the cave man, in woolly beard, frizzy wig, and raggedy costume that reveals his legs. He lasts a day, appears in at least one scene, then becomes "sick." Asked about this situation 50 years later, Zucco's widow admits, "Until his stroke [in 1951], I don't remember George being sick a day in his life!" Frank Moran, an ex-boxer, assumes the cave man/ape man part.

The mania comes to a climax in October of 1943, via Monogram's *Voodoo Man*. Bela Lugosi, in the title role, sports a goatee and wizard's robe as he tries to keep his 22-years-dead wife in a semblance of life. John Carradine, as Lugosi's mentally enfeebled minion, soulfully beats a bongo at the voodoo ceremony. "Pride," apparently, didn't keep George Zucco from returning to Monogram to assume the role of the cult's high priest, wearing war paint and a headdress with feathers, as he fervently chants to "Ramboona."

William Beaudine shoots *Voodoo Man* (1944) so quickly that, six days after it starts, Carradine is in San Francisco, 400 miles up the Pacific Coast, for his opening night as Hamlet. Lugosi and Zucco continue on the film a while longer. On October 30, 1943, *Showman's Trade Review* writes, "Most intriguing sight of the week at Monogram was Bela Lugosi and George Zucco . . . taking jitterbug lessons from a group of youngsters working on an adjoining stage in jive scenes for the child delinquency drama, *Where Are Your Children?*"

In 1944, it's PRC who produces Poverty Row horror's finest film: *Bluebeard*. John Carradine, whose Shakespearean company has folded and who's just played Dracula in Universal's *House of Frankenstein*, portrays Bluebeard with sensitivity and a dash of classical tragedy. Edgar G. Ulmer directs with flair and stylistics, miraculously capturing nineteenth-century Paris on a Santa Monica Boulevard soundstage. The surviving paperwork belies the perennial rumors that this film (and others from Poverty Row) was shot for peanuts and in six days: *Bluebeard* cost $167,567.42, and took 19 days to shoot.

It's too daunting for Poverty Row to challenge Universal, who toss Dracula, the Wolf Man, and Frankenstein's Monster ("All together!") into *House of Frankenstein*, all let loose by Karloff for a Christmas 1944 release. Universal throws them together again (but without Karloff, who thumbs-downs the offer) into *House of Dracula*, that braves Broadway during Yuletide of 1945. Nor can Monogram or PRC vie with RKO, which offers Karloff and Lugosi in Robert Louis Stevenson's *The Body Snatcher* (1945), reaping the biggest worldwide rental of any Val Lewton horror film.

Carradine goes east to devote himself to the theater and escape alimony contempt charges. PRC stars Zucco in *Fog Island* (1945, with an equally slumming Lionel Atwill) and *The Flying Serpent* (1946), and goes "artsy" with *Strangler of the Swamp* (1946), which has no horror stars but boasts Miss America of 1941, Rosemary La Planche, and Frank Wisbar's expressionistic direction. The Atomic Bomb has changed the meaning of horror. So has Universal-International's 1948 box office smash, *Abbott and Costello Meet Frankenstein*. Cavorting with the comedy team are Chaney, Jr.'s Wolf Man, Glenn Strange's Monster, and Lugosi's Dracula.

As the Cold War chills, a horror film occasionally ekes its way out of a Poverty Row lot—e.g., mad doctor Alan Napier and towering Glenn Strange meet the Bowery Boys in Monogram's *Master Minds* (1949). Hollywood and the World, however, are changing. Come the early 1950s, Monogram becomes Allied Artists, PRC becomes Eagle-Lion, and science fiction largely displaces horror. A company called Three Dimension Pictures unleashes *Robot Monster* (1953), the title character resembling a gorilla wearing a diver's helmet . . . a perfect image for a comic book cover.

When filmmaker Alex Gordon comes to Allied Artists with a concept entitled *House of Terror*—a new horror film to co-star Karloff, Lugosi, and even Lon Chaney, Jr.—the studio rejects the offer.

The next notorious step down, although only Lugosi takes it, is working with Edward D. Wood, Jr.

TOP LEFT: Australian poster for *Sherlock Holmes and the Secret Weapon* (Dir: Roy William Neill, 1942). Lionel Atwill's Professor Moriarty joins forces with the Nazis for the second in Universal's wartime series about Basil Rathbone's master detective.

TOP MIDDLE: A Nazi fifth columnist hampers the war effort by using the legend of a headless ghost to terrorize the superstitious inhabitants of a Cornish mining village in Warner Bros.' *The Mysterious Doctor* (Dir: Benjamin Stoloff, 1943).

BOTTOM LEFT: Paul Cavanagh and John Abbott's private sanatorium on the English coast is a front for a ring of Nazi spies in *The Gorilla Man* (Dir: D. Ross Lederman, 1943), which was marketed as a horror movie by Warner Bros.

BOTTOM MIDDLE: John Abbott's patriotic tobacconist uses the cover of the Blitz to hunt down the members of a Nazi spy ring in Republic Pictures' *London Blackout Murders* (Dir: George Sherman, 1943), scripted by Curt Siodmak.

ABOVE RIGHT: Insert poster for Columbia Pictures' *The Return of the Vampire* (Dir: Lew Landers, 1943). Bela Lugosi's undead Armand Tesla and his werewolf assistant (Matt Willis) use the cover of the Blitz to stalk their victims through London.

Keeping the War at Bey

Born in Vienna, Austria, exotic-looking actor Turhan Bey (Turhan Gilbert Selahattin Sahultavy, 1922–2012) made his Hollywood debut in 1941 and was quickly signed as a contract player by Universal Pictures. Unlike many other actors in America, because Bey was a Turkish citizen he could not be drafted into the army until 1945. As a result, he soon found himself top-billed in such wartime movies as *The Mad Ghoul* (1943) and *The Climax* (1944). He returned to acting in the 1990s.

ABOVE LEFT: Three-sheet poster for Eagle-Lion Films' *The Amazing Mr. X* (aka *The Spiritualist*; Dir: Bernard Vorhaus, 1948), in which Lynn Bari's wealthy widow falls under the spell of Turhan Bey's suave spiritualist.

ABOVE RIGHT: *The Amazing Mr. X* (1994), acrylic on illustration board by Vincent Di Fate. "This painting was created for the cover of the Lumivision Corporation's laserdisc edition of a movie that starred Turhan Bey as a fake spiritualist," explains the American artist. "The movie is a hybrid of *film noir* and *horror noir*, along the lines of the famous horror titles that Val Lewton made for RKO Radio Pictures earlier that same decade."

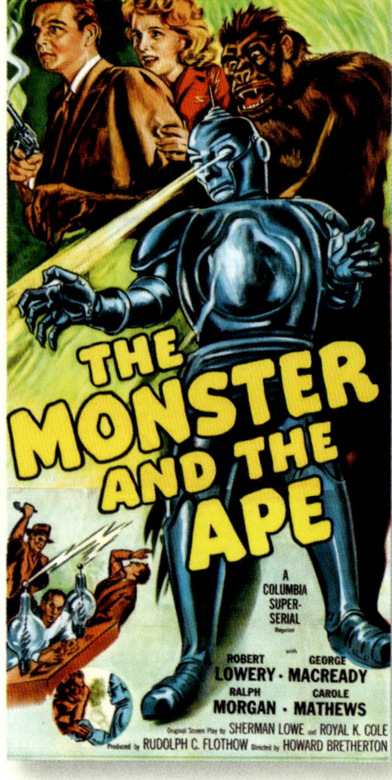

ABOVE LEFT: Three-sheet poster for 20th Century-Fox's *The Gorilla* (Dir: Allan Dwan, 1939), which featured the comedy trio The Ritz Brothers (Jimmy, Harry, and Al) along with Lionel Atwill, Bela Lugosi, and Poe the Gorilla (Art Miles).

TOP RIGHT: Half-sheet poster for Monogram Pictures' *The Ape* (Dir: William Nigh, 1940). Boris Karloff's misguided scientist dresses up as a killer ape (Ray "Crash" Corrigan) to get the spinal fluid he needs for his serum to cure polio.

BOTTOM MIDDLE: George Zucco's mad scientist transplants a dead man's brain into the skull of a gorilla (Charles Gemora) so that he can get revenge in Paramount Pictures' *The Monster and the Girl* (Dir: Stuart Heisler, 1941).

BOTTOM RIGHT: 1956 re-release three-sheet poster for Columbia Pictures' 15-chapter serial *The Monster and the Ape* (Dir: Howard Bretherton, 1945), which featured Willie Best as comedy relief and Ray Corrigan in the ape suit.

TOP LEFT: 1946 Italian *quattro-foglio* for Paramount Pictures' old dark house comedy *The Cat and the Canary* (Dir: Elliott Nugent, 1939) by Dante Manno (1900–??). Bob Hope and Paulette Goddard are stalked by a homicidal maniac.

BOTTOM LEFT: Window card for Warner Bros.' creepy comedy *The Smiling Ghost* (Dir: Lewis Seiler, 1941). Wayne Morris's bankrupt hero pretends to be engaged to a wealthy heiress whose previous three fiancés met untimely deaths.

TOP RIGHT: Title lobby card for Metro-Goldwyn-Mayer's *Whistling in the Dark* (Dir: S. Sylvan Simon, 1941). Red Skelton's radio sleuth gets involved with Conrad Veidt's fake moon cult. Two further "Whistling" movies followed.

BOTTOM MIDDLE: Three-sheet poster for Paramount Pictures' *One Body Too Many* (Dir: Frank McDonald, 1944), in which Jack Haley's insurance salesman gets mixed up with a missing body and murder. Bela Lugosi's butler is a suspect.

BOTTOM RIGHT: Insert poster for RKO Radio Pictures' *Zombies on Broadway* (Dir: Gordon Douglas, 1945). Comedy team Wally Brown and Alan Carney encounter Bela Lugosi's mad professor while trying to find a zombie.

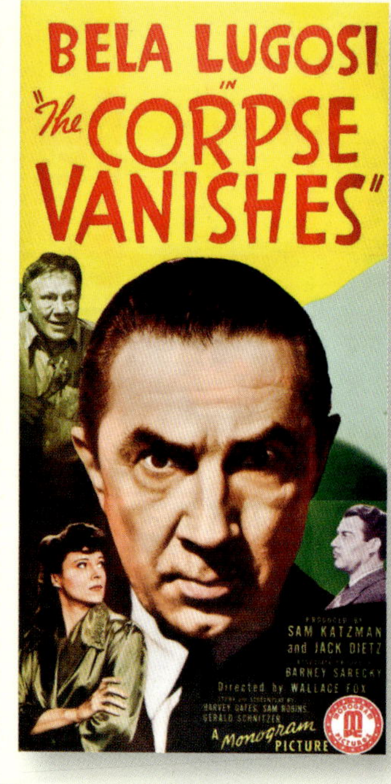

ABOVE LEFT: Stone litho one-sheet poster from Astor Pictures Corp.'s 1949 re-release of Monogram Pictures' *Invisible Ghost* (Dir: Joseph H. Lewis, 1941), starring Bela Lugosi as a somnambulist strangler driven mad by grief.

TOP, MIDDLE LEFT: Stone litho three-sheet for Monogram's *Black Dragons* (Dir: William Nigh, 1942). Bela Lugosi's Nazi plastic surgeon hunts down and murders a group of Japanese spies that he had previously transformed into American fifth columnists.

TOP, MIDDLE RIGHT: Three-sheet poster for Monogram's *The Corpse Vanishes* (aka *The Case of the Missing Brides*; Dir: Wallace Fox, 1942). Bela Lugosi's mad doctor extracts the glandular fluid of young brides to keep his wife (Elizabeth Russell) young.

TOP RIGHT: Insert poster for Monogram's *Bowery at Midnight* (Dir: Wallace Fox, 1942). Bela Lugosi's criminal mastermind uses a mad scientist to turn his victims into a zombie-like state and hide them in the basement of a soup kitchen.

BOTTOM MIDDLE: Three-sheet poster for Monogram's *Voodoo Man* (Dir: William Beaudine, 1944).

BOTTOM RIGHT: Belgian poster for Monogram's *Return of the Ape Man* (Dir: Philip Rosen, 1944).

POSTERS and LOBBIES

Also Sets of 11 x 14's and Colored Slides

PRODUCERS RELEASING CORPORATION OF AMERICA

TOP LEFT: Belgian poster for Producers Releasing Corporation's *The Devil Bat* (aka *Killer Bats*; Dir: Jean Yarborough, 1940). Bela Lugosi's mad doctor uses an aftershave lotion to attract the giant bat he sends out to kill those who wronged him.

TOP RIGHT: Stone litho six-sheet for PRC's *The Black Raven* (Dir: Sam Newfield, 1943), which revolved around strange happenings at the mysterious border inn of the title.

BOTTOM RIGHT: *The Black Raven* pressbook.

TOP MIDDLE: Three-sheet poster for PRC's *Bluebeard* (Dir: Edgar G. Ulmer, 1944). John Carradine (in his own favorite performance) starred as a crazed Parisian artist who strangles his models once he has finished painting their portraits.

BOTTOM LEFT: Italian *duo-foglio* for PRC's *The Monster Maker* (Dir: Sam Newfield, 1944) by Rinaldo Geleng (1920–2003). J. Carroll Naish's mad scientist uses his acromegaly serum to dispose of his enemies, aided by Glenn Strange's brute.

BOTTOM MIDDLE: Three-sheet poster for PRC's *Devil Bat's Daughter* (Dir: Frank Wisbar, 1946). Rosemary La Planche starred as the daughter of Bela Lugosi's mad doctor from *The Devil Bat*, accused of murder in this sequel-of-sorts.

"ONE SHOT" BEAUDINE

"Director William Beaudine, in spite of the tight shooting schedule, was a real pro—excellent and understanding."

Louise Currie

"Long ago I quit thinking that every picture I did was going to be an Academy Award contender. I'm a commercial director. I know how to save money and get something on the screen."

William Beaudine

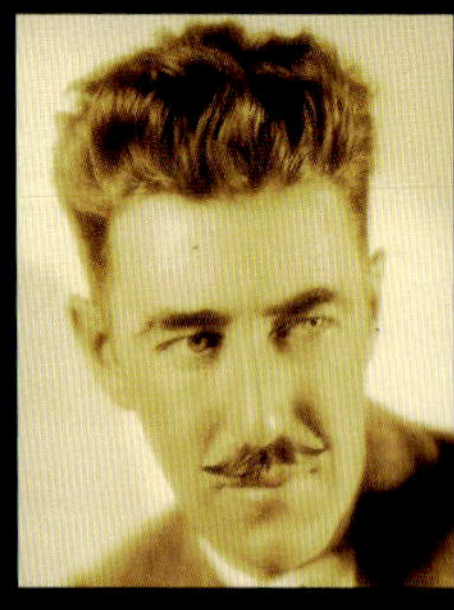

DURING HIS REMARKABLY prolific Hollywood career, no one referred to William [Washington] Beaudine as "One Shot" Beaudine. The nickname only came after his death, when historians, marveling at his staggering film and TV output, imagined he only racked up so many credits by shooting single takes.

An "artiste?" Probably not. But he made up for it with his wildfire energy, even-keel temperament, and madcap humor that made things go—and got movies made.

Born in New York City on January 15, 1892, Beaudine broke into the business working for D.W. Griffith. "I painted the properties and cleaned the cuspidors," said Beaudine alliteratively. "All for $10 a week." He was an assistant to Griffith on *The Birth of a Nation* (1915) and *Intolerance* (1916), learning from the master and soon directing pictures himself. He looked the part—tall, mustached, with a head-full of black hair. A famous credit: *Sparrows* (1926), in which Mary Pickford flees into a Gothic swamp, saving orphans from evil Gustav von Seyffertitz. Beaudine battled with superstar Pickford so vehemently that he developed a facial paralysis. His assistant, Tom McNamara, completed *Sparrows*.

Beaudine decided that, thereafter, moviemaking would be fun and brisk.

By the time Beaudine hit his prime at Monogram in the World War II years, he was a master at staying on schedule and budget, and perhaps more importantly, keeping a relaxed set. Bela Lugosi likely found him sympathetic when he showed up in his hirsute makeup for *The Ape Man* (1943), protective when he joined the East Side Kids in *Ghosts on the Loose* (1943), and complimentary when Lugosi got pathos into his performance as the *Voodoo Man* (1944). John Carradine undoubtedly found him agreeable when the actor decided to get thoroughly creepy as the mentally challenged "Toby" of *Voodoo Man*. Beaudine probably stayed poker-faced when George Zucco reported to the set of the same picture adorned in voodoo high priest feathers.

In 1945, Beaudine directed the sex hygiene film, *Mom and Dad*. Produced for $65,000, the exploitation quickie reportedly earned over $34.8 million!

He was a master at staying on schedule and budget, and perhaps more importantly, keeping a relaxed set.

In 1952, he was director of the remarkably titled *Bela Lugosi Meets a Brooklyn Gorilla*, co-starring the horror legend with an imitation Martin and Lewis team.

The late Elena Verdugo remembered, "William Beaudine directed me at Monogram in *Tuna Clipper* (1949) and *Jet Job* (1952); he had this waxed mustache and a twinkle in his eye, tall and lanky. He was fun, he was crazy, and he was 'Papa'—with a big family of children who all loved him."

He was a natural for the fast-paced world of television. Among the shows he helmed was *Lassie*, starting in 1960. Beaudine good-naturedly ribbed Lassie's trainer, Rudd Weatherwax, by referring to the canine luminary as "the meat-hound," but went on to direct 79 episodes.

Late in his career, Beaudine directed *Billy the Kid vs. Dracula* (1966). John Carradine, who played Dracula in the movie, alternated in calling *Voodoo Man* and *Billy the Kid vs. Dracula* the worst films of his lengthy career. Both were Beaudine pictures. If Carradine's judgment got back to him, the director probably laughed.

William Beaudine died March 18, 1970 in Canoga Park, California. He left memories for many actors of a gallant director, twirling his mustache, standing on a Poverty Row soundstage like a ringmaster in a Big Top circus ring, keeping the show fast, fun, and lightning-paced. GWM

TOP LEFT: Six-sheet poster for *Ghosts on the Loose* (1943), the second Monogram Pictures horror-comedy to team The East Side Kids with Bela Lugosi. Future star Ava Gardner received her first screen credit as Huntz Hall's sister.

TOP RIGHT: Lobby card for Monogram's *Spook Busters* (1946), in which the former East Side Kids (now renamed The Bowery Boys) encounter a mad scientist intent on transplanting Huntz Hall's brain into the body of a gorilla.

BOTTOM LEFT: Half-sheet poster for Monogram's *The Face of Marble* (1946), in which John Carradine's mad scientist attempts to revive the dead, much to the consternation of his cheating wife (Claudia Drake) and comedy relief Willie Best.

BOTTOM MIDDLE: Monogram's penultimate Charlie Chan mystery, *The Feathered Serpent* (1948), involved the detective (Roland Winters) and both his Number #1 and #2 sons in the hunt for a lost Aztec treasure in Mexico.

BOTTOM RIGHT: Realart Pictures, Inc.'s *Bela Lugosi Meets a Brooklyn Gorilla* (1952) starred the comedy duo of Duke Mitchell and Sammy Petrillo, whose act was such a blatant imitation of Dean Martin and Jerry Lewis that the latter sued.

ABOVE LEFT: *The Seventh Victim* (2015), digital poster by Sara Deck. "*The Seventh Victim* (1943) was produced by one of my favorites in the horror genre—Val Lewton," explains the artist. "It is a wonderfully suspenseful film and has some incredibly bleak imagery."

TOP MIDDLE: Pre-release trade advertisement for Val Lewton's production of *I Walked with a Zombie* (Dir: Jacques Tourneur, 1943) from the *RKO Radio Pictures 1942–1943* exhibitor book. The movie was inspired by an article by Inez Wallace in *The American Weekly*.

BOTTOM RIGHT: The only known six-sheet poster to exist for RKO Radio Pictures' *The Leopard Man* (Dir: Jacques Tourneur, 1943), a psychological thriller that was one of the most subtle and atmospheric of Val Lewton's movies for the studio.

TOP RIGHT: Three-sheet poster for RKO's *The Curse of the Cat People* (1944), producer Val Lewton's lyrical semi-sequel to *Cat People* (1942). When first-time feature director Gunther von Fritsch fell behind schedule, the studio replaced him with editor Robert Wise.

TOP LEFT: Although it wasn't produced by Val Lewton, RKO Radio Pictures' *The Falcon and the Co-Eds* (Dir: William Clemens, 1943)—the seventh in the detective series—shared the poetic and downbeat atmosphere of the studio's horror movies.

TOP MIDDLE: RKO's *Gildersleeve's Ghost* (Dir: Gordon Douglas, 1944) was the fourth and final movie in the comedy series based around Harold Peary's radio character "Throckmorton P. Gildersleeve." It featured ghosts, an ape, an invisible woman, and a mad scientist.

ABOVE RIGHT: Three-sheet poster for RKO Radio Pictures' atmospheric serial-killer mystery *The Spiral Staircase* (Dir: Robert Siodmak, 1945), loosely based on the 1933 novel *Some Must Watch* by British author Ethel Lina White (1876–1944).

BOTTOM LEFT: Previously filmed by the studio as *The Most Dangerous Game* (1932), RKO's *A Game of Death* (Dir: Robert Wise, 1945) was the second movie adaptation of Richard Connell's human-hunting short story, first published in *Collier's* (January 19, 1924).

BOTTOM MIDDLE: RKO's answer to Abbott and Costello, Wally Brown and Alan Carney, portrayed radio detectives on the hunt for a master criminal called "The Cobra" in *Genius at Work* (Dir: Leslie Goodwins, 1946), their eighth and final teaming for the studio.

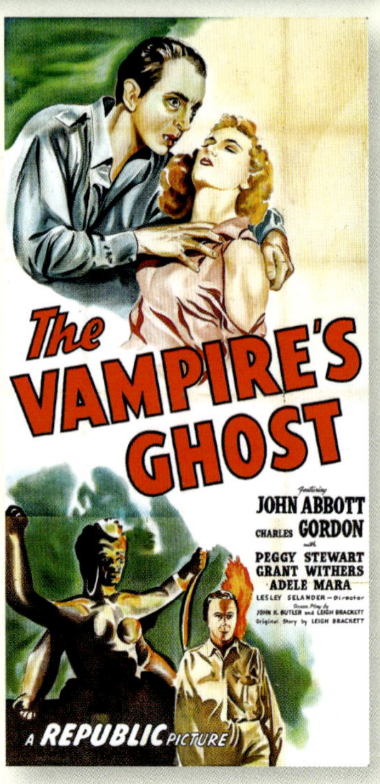

TOP LEFT: Lugubrious American character actor Milton Parsons (1904–80) is the real star of Warner Bros.' *The Hidden Hand* (Dir: Benjamin Stoloff, 1942). He plays an escaped lunatic posing as a butler in this old dark house mystery that was based on a 1934 stage play.

TOP MIDDLE: Creepy insert poster for Columbia Pictures' *The Soul of a Monster* (Dir: Will Jason, 1944), in which Rose Hobart's Satanic seductress mysteriously appears and prevents George Macready's famous surgeon from dying. But there is always a price to pay . . .

TOP RIGHT: Columbia Pictures' second attempt at a Val Lewton-style horror movie, *Cry of the Werewolf* (Dir: Henry Levin, 1944) starred Nina Foch as a gypsy werewolf, along with dependable support from John Abbott, Fritz Leiber, and Milton Parsons.

BOTTOM LEFT: Italian *duo-foglio* for *The Lady and the Monster* (aka *The Tiger Man*; Dir: George Sherman, 1944), Republic Pictures' version of Curt Siodmak's 1942 novel *Donovan's Brain*. Artwork by Averardo Ciriello (1918–2016), who later illustrated *fumetti* comics.

BOTTOM MIDDLE: The vengeful spirit of an executed murderer (Tom Powers) enters into the body of Stanley Ridges's kindly doctor and takes over control of his body and mind in Republic Pictures' *The Phantom Speaks* (Dir: John English, 1945).

OPPOSITE, BOTTOM RIGHT: Republic Pictures' *The Vampire's Ghost* (Dir: Lesley Selander, 1945), which allowed character actor John Abbott (1905–96) a rare opportunity to shine as a world-weary vampire. The screenplay was co-written by pulp author Leigh Brackett.

TOP LEFT: Italian post-war *duo-foglio* for Warner Bros.' sequel-in-name-only *The Return of Doctor X* (Dir: Vincent Sherman, 1939).

BOTTOM LEFT: *The Return of Doctor X* promotional envelope containing smelling salts for the faint-hearted.

BOTTOM MIDDLE: *Duo-foglio* for Warner Bros.' *The Beast with Five Fingers* (Dir: Robert Florey, 1946) by Luigi Martinati (1893–1983) who, along with fellow Italian artists Anselmo Ballester and Alfredo Capitani, co-founded the movie poster company BCM.

TOP RIGHT: Double-page pre-production trade advertisement for the double-bill release of *Valley of the Zombies* (Dir: Philip Ford, 1946) and *The Catman of Paris* (Dir: Lesley Selander, 1946) from the *Republic Pictures 1945–1946* exhibitor book.

BOTTOM RIGHT: Luigi Martinati's *duo-foglio* for Warner Bros.' *The Woman in White* (Dir: Peter Godfrey, 1948), based on the influential 1859 Gothic mystery by Wilkie Collins and featuring Sydney Greenstreet as the scheming villain, Count Fosco.

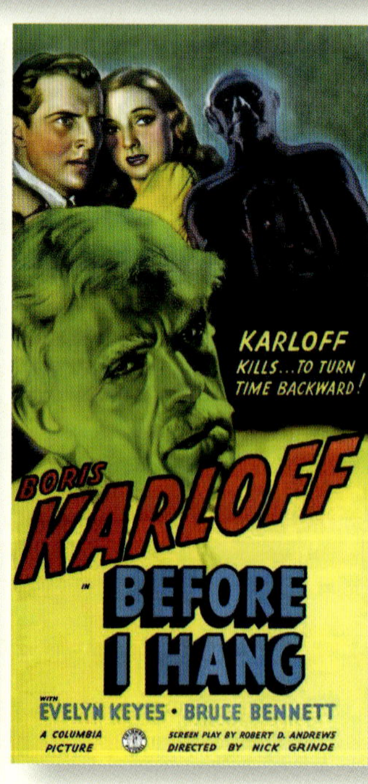

BOTTOM, MIDDLE LEFT: After Boris Karloff's Dr. Henryk Savaard is unjustly hanged for murder, he returns from the dead for revenge in *The Man They Could Not Hang* (Dir: Nick Grindé, 1939), the first of a quintet of "Mad Doctor" movies the actor made for Columbia Pictures.

TOP LEFT: Danish one-sheet poster for the 1947 reissue of Columbia Pictures' *The Man with Nine Lives* (Dir: Nick Grindé, 1940).

BOTTOM LEFT: Belgian poster for the same movie, featuring Boris Karloff's vengeful Dr. Leon Kravaal.

BOTTOM, MIDDLE RIGHT: Three-sheet poster for Columbia's *Before I Hang* (Dir: Nick Grindé, 1940). This time, Boris Karloff's Dr. John Garth experiments on a serum using criminals' blood. When he tests it on himself, he is rejuvenated but also turns into a murderer.

TOP RIGHT: Pre-release advertisement for *The Devil Commands* (Dir: Edward Dmytryk, 1941) from the *Columbia Pictures 1940–1941* exhibitor book. Boris Karloff's obsessed Dr. Julian Blair uses science in his attempts to communicate with his dead wife's soul.

BOTTOM RIGHT: For his final "Mad Doctor" film for the studio, Columbia teamed Boris Karloff with Peter Lorre for *The Boogie Man Will Get You* (Dir: Lew Landers, 1942), a horror-comedy that was very reminiscent of *Arsenic and Old Lace* (1941).

ABOVE LEFT: Insert poster for Columbia Pictures' old dark house comedy *The Ghost That Walks Alone* (Dir: Lew Landers, 1944), which doesn't feature any ghosts! A newly married couple (Arthur Lake and Lynne Roberts) discover a corpse in their honeymoon suite.

TOP RIGHT: Half-sheet poster for Paramount Pictures' *The Ghost Breakers* (Dir: George Marshall, 1940). Bob Hope and Paulette Goddard re-teamed from *The Cat and the Canary* (1939) and encountered Noble Johnson's zombie in a "haunted" Cuban castle.

BOTTOM MIDDLE: French *grande affiche* by Russian-born artist Boris Grinsson (1907–99) for Paramount Pictures' *The Uninvited* (Dir: Lewis Allen, 1944). Author Dodie Smith co-wrote the screenplay, based on the 1941 novel *Uneasy Freehold* by Dorothy Macardle.

BOTTOM RIGHT: Australian one-sheet poster for *The Unseen* (1945). Following *The Uninvited* (1944), Paramount reunited director Lewis Allen and star Gail Russell for this mystery-thriller based on the 1942 novel *Her Heart in Her Throat* (aka *Midnight House*) by Ethel Lina White.

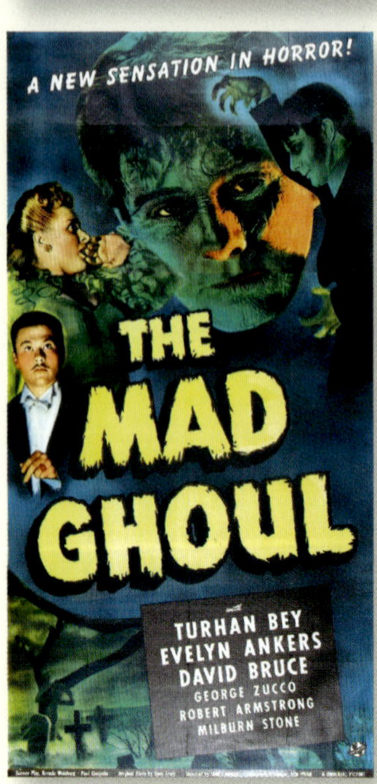

BOTTOM MIDDLE: Dick Foran's dubious boat captain organizes a treasure hunt to an offshore Caribbean castle "haunted" by a mysterious figure known as "The Phantom" (Foy Van Dolson) in Universal Pictures' B-movie *Horror Island* (Dir: George Waggner, 1941).

TOP LEFT: Lionel Atwill receives rare top billing on this Australian daybill for Universal Pictures' *The Mad Doctor of Market Street* (Dir: Joseph H. Lewis, 1942). The actor portrays a mad scientist who washes up on a tropical island and continues his reanimation experiments.

TOP MIDDLE: Based on an 1842 story by Edgar Allan Poe, a sequel to "The Murders in the Rue Morgue," Universal Pictures' *The Mystery of Marie Roget* (aka *Phantom of Paris*; Dir: Phil Rosen, 1942) starred Patric Knowles as scientist-sleuth Dr. Paul Dupin.

BOTTOM LEFT: Three-sheet poster for Universal Pictures' *The Mad Ghoul* (Dir: James Hogan, 1943), in which George Zucco's mad doctor uses a Mayan poison gas to turn a young student (David Bruce) into a living zombie who needs stolen hearts to reverse the process.

TOP RIGHT: Six-sheet poster for *The Climax* (Dir: George Waggner, 1944), Universal's Technicolor follow-up to *Phantom of the Opera* (1943), in which Boris Karloff's mad theater physician keeps a shrine to the embalmed body of his murdered sweetheart.

OPPOSITE, BOTTOM RIGHT: Six-sheet poster for *She-Wolf of London* (aka *The Curse of the Allenbys*; Dir: Jean Yarbrough, 1946). Coming toward the end of Universal's 1940s horror cycle, a cursed young woman (June Lockhart) is a suspect in a series of wolf murders.

TOP: Key promotional art for Universal Pictures' sequel *Frankenstein Meets the Wolf Man* (Dir: Roy William Neill, 1943), attributed to Canadian-born artist Karl Godwin (1893–1962).

BOTTOM LEFT & MIDDLE: Fox movie theater marquee, St. Louis, Missouri.

BOTTOM RIGHT: Artist Paolo Tarquini (1918–2011), who usually worked in pastels on colored paper, reworked Karl Godwin's original concept for this colorful *duo-foglio* for the 1949 Italian release of Universal's *Frankenstein Meets the Wolf Man*.

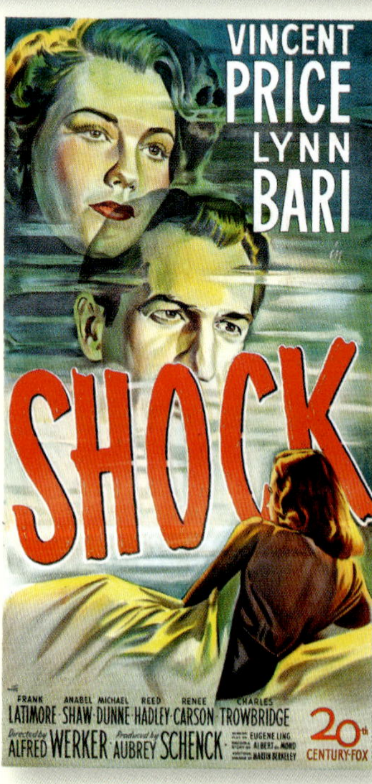

BOTTOM LEFT: Peter Lorre starred in RKO's *Stranger on the Third Floor* (Dir: Boris Ingster, 1940), which is often cited as the first *film noir*.

BOTTOM, MIDDLE LEFT: Australian daybill for Columbia's *The Face Behind the Mask* (Dir: Robert Florey, 1941), in which Lorre starred as a horribly scarred criminal.

TOP LEFT: French *affiche* by Russian-born artist Boris Grinsson for Metro-Goldwyn-Mayer's *Gaslight* (Dir: George Cukor, 1944), based on the 1938 psychological stage play by Patrick Hamilton. MGM tried to destroy all prints of the 1940 British film adaptation, but due to a mislabeling error it survived.

BOTTOM, MIDDLE RIGHT: Suffering from memory loss after a blow to the head during the Blitz, John Loder's actor Reginald Parker comes to believe that he really is Edward Grey, the crazed strangler he portrays on the stage, in RKO Radio Pictures' *The Brighton Strangler* (Dir: Max Nosseck, 1945).

BOTTOM RIGHT: Three-sheet poster for 20th Century-Fox's *Shock* (Dir: Alfred Werker, 1946), in which Anabel Shaw's psychologically disturbed patient witnesses Vincent Price's psychiatrist murder his wife, but she is then committed to a sanitarium under his care when nobody believes her story.

TOP RIGHT: Suffering from a psychological breakdown after becoming immersed in his role, Ronald Coleman's actor Anthony John comes to believe that he really is Shakespeare's Othello, the jealous murderer he portrays on the stage, in Universal-International's *A Double Life* (Dir: George Cukor, 1947).

The Melancholy Menace

American actor [Samuel] Laird Cregar (1913–44) began his short screen career as an extra in 1940. After appearing as a suave Satan in the romantic comedy *Heaven Can Wait* (1943), he played an obsessive serial killer in *The Lodger* (1944) and a mad pianist in *Hangover Square* (1945). Obsessed with his weight and tired of being typecast, both literally and figuratively, as one of Hollywood's top "heavies," the 300-pound Cregar went on an unsupervised crash diet for his role in *The Lodger* and he died of a heart attack at the age of 31, two months before his final film was released. Cregar's former co-star Vincent Price delivered the eulogy at his funeral.

ABOVE LEFT: Three-sheet poster for 20th Century-Fox's *The Lodger* (Dir: John Brahm, 1944), based on the 1913 novel by British author Marie Belloc Lowndes.

BOTTOM RIGHT: Title lobby card for 20th Century-Fox's *Hangover Square* (Dir: John Brahm, 1945), an adaptation of Patrick Hamilton's novel.

TOP RIGHT: *Laird Cregar* (2016), oils on board portrait by Les Edwards. "Laird Cregar's somewhat soft features might not seem to lend themselves to horror movies," explains the artist, "but he makes an absolutely splendid Jack the Ripper in *The Lodger*. His face seems very malleable, so capturing a likeness was tricky."

ABOVE LEFT: Three-sheet poster for Republic Pictures' superior 15-chapter serial *Drums of Fu Manchu* (Dir: John English and William Witney, 1940), in which Henry Brandon's devil-doctor searches for the tomb of Genghis Khan.

BOTTOM MIDDLE: Australian daybill for 20th Century-Fox's *Charlie Chan at the Wax Museum* (Dir: Lynn Shores, 1940). Charlie (Sidney Toler) gets involved with spooky goings-on in the twenty-fourth, and one of the best, in the series.

BOTTOM RIGHT: Charlie Chan's #1 son, Asian actor Keye Luke, took over from Boris Karloff to star as detective James Lee Wong in *Phantom of Chinatown* (Dir: Phil Rosen, 1940), the sixth and final movie in the Monogram series.

TOP RIGHT: One of two posters created by author, artist, and poet Mervyn Peake (1911–68) for the UK release of Monogram Pictures' third Charlie Chan movie, *Black Magic* (aka *Meeting at Midnight*; Dir: Phil Rosen, 1944), about the occult.

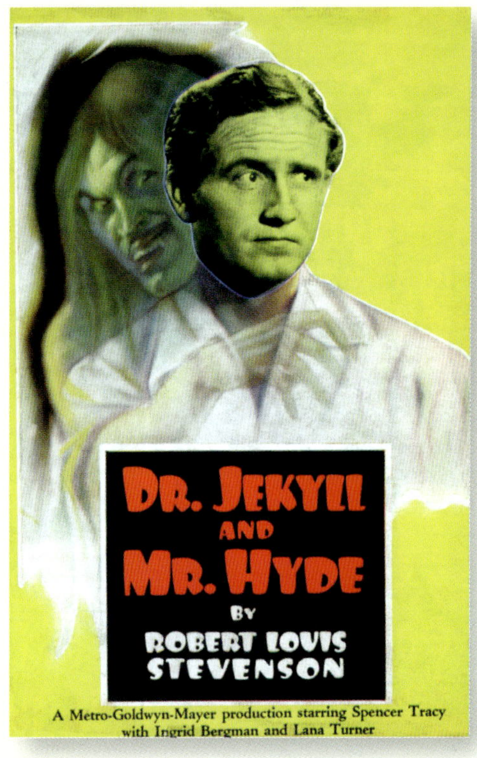

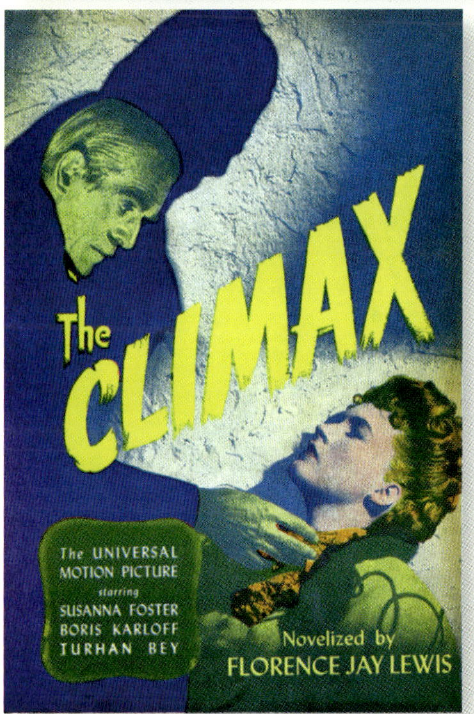

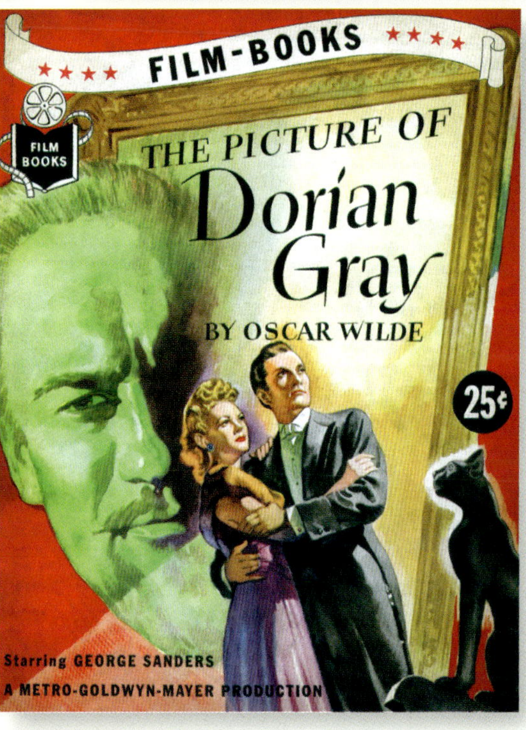

TOP LEFT: Spanish magazine novelization (one of Ediciones Bistagne's "Ediciones Especiales Cinematográficas" series) of RKO Radio Pictures' *You'll Find Out* (1940). The cover features facsimiles of the actors' actual signatures.

TOP MIDDLE: For its hardcover reprint tie-in to Metro-Goldwyn-Mayer's *Dr. Jekyll and Mr. Hyde* (1941), publisher Grosset & Dunlap just slapped star Spencer Tracy's head over the cover painting the publisher had used on its 1932 photoplay.

BOTTOM LEFT: Canadian-born playwright Florence Jay Lewis novelized Universal Pictures' *The Climax* (1944) for this "Midnight Mystery" hardcover from Books, Inc. that featured stars Boris Karloff and Susanna Foster on the dust jacket.

BOTTOM MIDDLE: Large-format magazine novelization in Caxton House, Inc.'s "Film-Books" series of Metro-Goldwyn-Mayer's *The Picture of Dorian Gray* (1945), adapted from the screenplay by C.P. Chadsey and illustrated with stills.

ABOVE RIGHT: For this hardcover reprint of Anya Seton's ghostly 1944 historical novel *Dragonwyck*, publisher Triangle Books added the stars of the 1946 20th Century-Fox movie, Vincent Price and Gene Tierney, to the cover design.

Norm Saunders

5

SEDUCTION OF THE INNOCENT

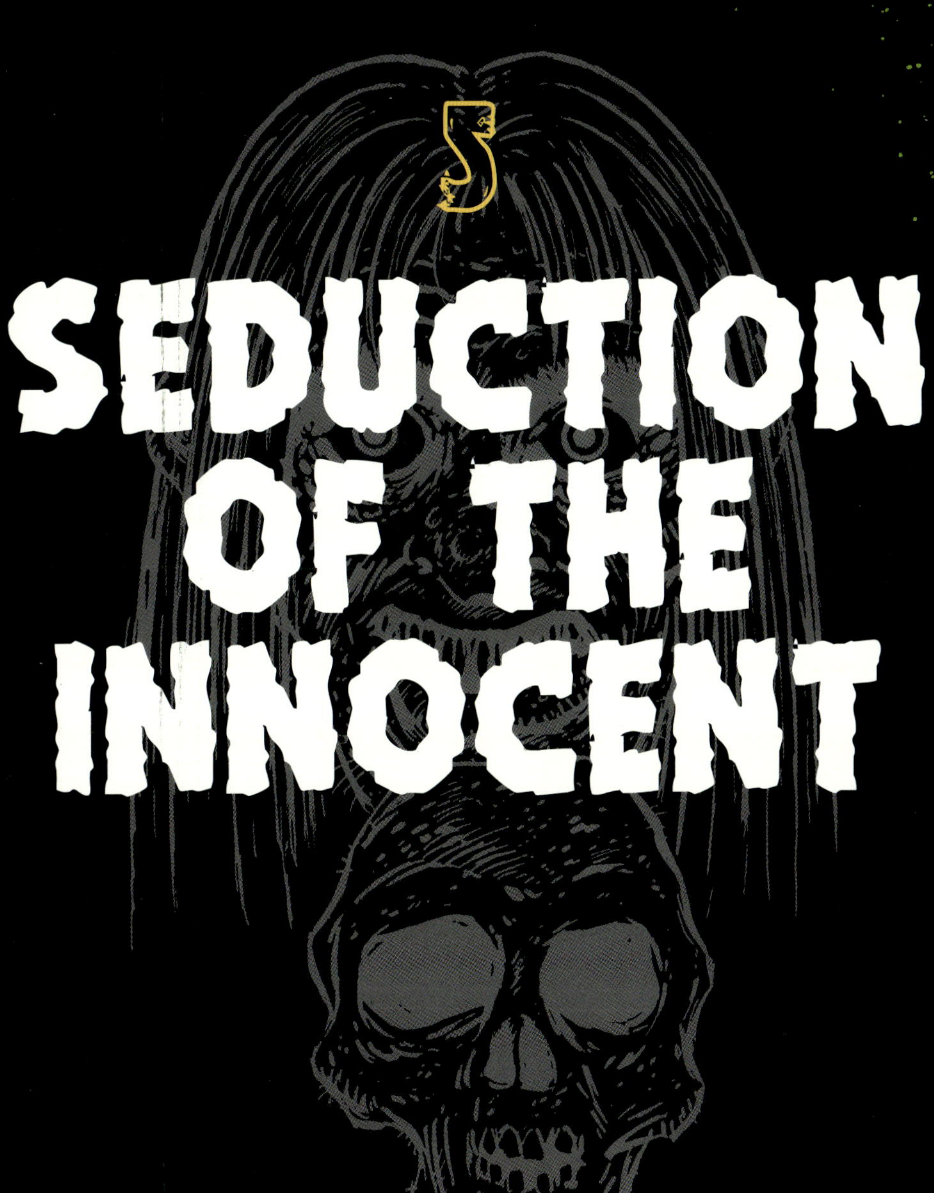

BARRY FORSHAW

"Heh, heh! Got a collector's item for you friends! Got a real great chiller-diller! Give the man your grimy little dime if you haven't done so already, and come into The Crypt of Terror! This is The Crypt-Keeper, ready with another of my tales of horror!"

"LOWER BERTH!" BY AL FELDSTEIN (*TALES FROM THE CRYPT* NO. 33, DECEMBER–JANUARY 1953)

“No comic magazine shall use the word ‘horror’ or ‘terror’ in its title . . . all scenes of horror, excessive bloodshed, gory or gruesome crimes, depravity, lust, sadism, masochism shall not be permitted.”

Code of the Comics Magazine Association of America, Inc. 1954

WHAT DO SUCH 1940s American magazines as *True Crime* (with its endless parade of buxom blondes, skirts hoisted around their thighs, menaced by brutal gun-wielding thugs) have in common with such notorious 1950s horror comics as *Menace* (with the thugs now supplanted by gruesome ambulant corpses, flesh peeling spectacularly from their faces)?

The answer is the publisher, Martin Goodman (the first employer of comics legend Stan Lee), who—like so many of his buck-chasing contemporaries—moved from the pulp magazines to comics in the early 1950s, reflecting the changing taste of readers. The post-war boom in American dime novels was transformed in the early 1950s into the brief but lucrative horror comics boom (which lasted until the establishment of the censorious Comics Code in the mid-1950s, echoing Hollywood's censorship decades earlier and banning anything remotely macabre).

In the UK, the lurid pulp magazines enjoyed wide circulation (often coming over as ballast on ships), while the American horror comics bonanza never quite happened on British soil—as the hysteria over the genre broke in the United States (whipped up by self-serving psychiatrist Fredric Wertham's 1954 book *Seduction of the Innocent*), reprints of such material were only just starting to appear in the UK and were torpedoed by similar censorship initiatives.

Some horror comics intermittently reached the UK in the late 1950s, such as the Atlas title *Adventures into Weird Worlds*, which dealt with everything from vampires rapacious for blood to killer robots, with illustrations far more grotesque and unsettling than the post-Code superhero material that was available at the time.

Contrary to popular belief, the horror comics phenomenon did not start with William M. Gaines's EC imprint (which stood for “Entertainment Comics”), even though they were to be the finest flowering in terms of artistry and writing in the genre. After an undistinguished one-shot comic published in 1947 by Avon, *Eerie* (not to be confused with the later books of that title), it was to be another bijou-sized publisher who was to come up with the first continuously running horror title.

Best remembered today for its melancholy post-Code fantasy tales with Ogden Whitney's covers or its humorous *Herbie* series, the American Comics Group (ACG) originally made its mark as a custodian of the horrific, producing the very first continuous horror comic in 1948, *Adventures Into the Unknown*. Editor/writer Richard E. Hughes (Leo Rosenbaum, 1909–74) was a one-man band, penning most of the material himself under a variety of pseudonyms. When post-Code readers later pleaded for zombies, werewolves, and vampires of the kind ACG had once produced, Hughes would assume a “schoolmarm” tone and claim that “such themes have been done to death.”

Hughes had written much horror material throughout the pre-Code era however, and his early efforts amply demonstrate his teeming imagination. Look at the third issue of *Forbidden Worlds* (1951)—such stories as “Lair of the Vampire” work primarily because their writer, subtly out of tune with the horror genre, tries to fashion new “wrinkles” to liven up his narrative.

The horror comics phenomenon did not start with William M. Gaines's EC imprint (which stood for “Entertainment Comics”), even though they were to be the finest flowering in terms of artistry and writing in the genre.

The company that created the most seismic effect in the field was, of course, the legendary EC, whose books boasted sophisticated and literate scripts along with wonderfully atmospheric artwork. Having initially specialized in educational and religious-themed titles, the company changed direction after the accidental death of its founder, Max Gaines, in 1947. His son William (1922–92) inherited the company, and soon the New York City-based publisher was churning out a stream of monthly horror (*Tales from the Crypt*, *The Vault of Horror*, and *The Haunt of Fear*), science fiction (*Weird Fantasy* and *Weird Science*), crime (*Shock SuspenStories* and *Crime SuspenStories*), and war (*Frontline Combat* and *Two-Fisted Tales*) titles.

Under editors Al Feldstein (1925–2014) and Harvey Kurtzman (1924–93), who were writers and artists themselves, EC achieved its justified reputation through its use of accomplished freelance artists—the splendidly eccentric covers of Jack Davis; the baroque Graham Ingels, who signed his work “Ghastly” and specialized in atmospheric images of rotting swamps and equally rotting corpses; the classically styled illustrations of one of the doyens of the field, Reed Crandall, and the exquisitely clean and uncluttered work of Johnny Craig and George Evans, both usually given contemporary urban stories to illustrate—and the distinctly adult-themed story lines with their trademark “twist” endings.

PREVIOUS SPREAD: ***Frankenstein*** **(1958), oils on canvas by American pulp artist Norman Saunders (1907–89) for the eighth printing of the** ***Classics Illustrated*** **comics adaptation (September 1958). As the artist explained: “If you do something from life, something that is really true that you see, the truthfulness and honesty in the picture comes through.”**

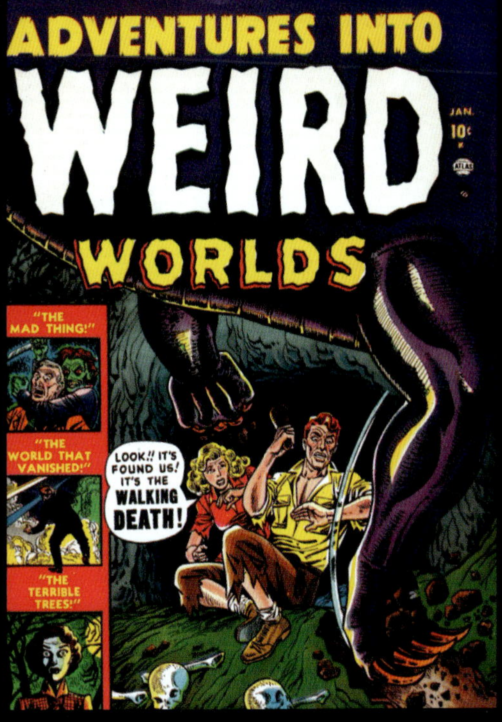

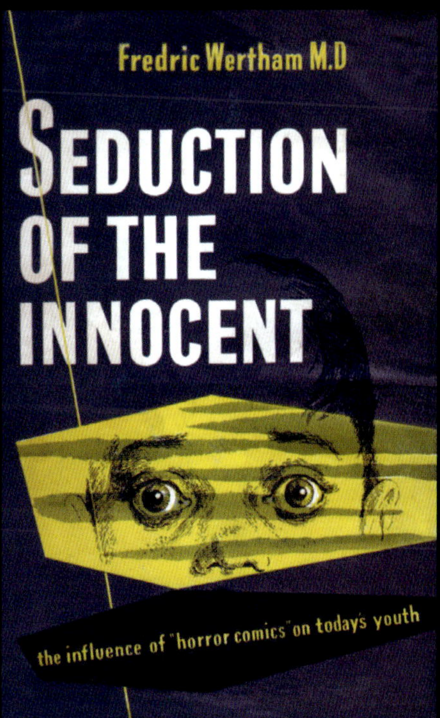

ABOVE LEFT: Widely regarded as ushering in the horror comics boom of the 1950s, the one-shot *Eerie Comics* was published by Avon Periodicals in January 1947 with a cover by Bob Fujitani (b. 1920). A regular series followed in 1951.

TOP MIDDLE: Cover art by Edvard Mortiz for the premier issue of the first ongoing horror comic, *Adventures Into the Unknown!* (American Comics Group, Fall 1948). The title survived for 174 issues until August 1967.

TOP RIGHT: *Forbidden Worlds* No. 3 (ACG, November–December 1951) featured a cover by Ken Bald (b. 1920) and included "Skull of the Sorcerer" illustrated by Al Williamson (with help from Wally Wood, Frank Frazetta, and Joe Orlando).

BOTTOM MIDDLE: The first issue of *Adventures Into Weird Worlds* (Atlas Comics, January 1952) with a cover by the great Joe Maneely (1926–58), who died in a tragic train accident at the age of 32. The comic ran for 30 issues, until June 1954.

BOTTOM RIGHT: The first UK edition of *Seduction of the Innocent* (Museum Press, 1955) by German-American psychiatrist Fredric Wertham, M.D. (1895–1981), that claimed that comic books were harmful to children and led to juvenile delinquency.

TOP LEFT: *Adventures Into Terror* No. 1 (November 1950) was actually numbered No. 43 after Atlas suddenly changed the title and format from the comedic *Joker Comics* to cash-in on the horror boom. Russ Heath (1926–2018) supplied the cover art.

TOP MIDDLE: Published by Fiction House, *Ghost Comics* No. 10 (March 1954) featured a typical cover by former pulp artist Maurice Whitman (1922–83). The comic lasted for just one more issue, which appeared in June 1954.

ABOVE RIGHT: Splash page for the eight-page "Ghost of the Gorgon" strip illustrated by John Belcastro (as "John Bell") in *Ghost Comics* No. 10. The crew of a relief ship encounters a seductive Medusa released by an earthquake on a Greek Island.

BOTTOM LEFT: Issue No. 18 of Charlton's *This Magazine is Haunted* (July 1954) boasted a cover by Steve Ditko (1927–2018) featuring the bi-monthly title's regular horror host "Dr. Death." The artist illustrated a different story inside the comic.

BOTTOM MIDDLE: The rare "ashcan" issue of Warren Publishing's *Eerie* No. 1 (September 1966), hastily produced in an edition of just 200 limited-circulation copies to trademark the title. Cover by veteran EC artist Jack Davis (1924–2016).

In the now-famous story "Judgment Day!" (*Weird Fantasy* No. 18, March–April 1953), written by Al Feldstein and illustrated by Joe Orlando, the space-helmeted galactic peace-maker was revealed in the final frame to be a black man—much to the delight of readers. However, when Gaines wanted to reprint the strip just three years later, he was (unsuccessfully) pressured by an administrator of the Comics Code Authority to change the color of the astronaut.

After a somewhat rocky start, when the company plagiarized two of his stories, even the renowned fantasy author Ray Bradbury ended up working with EC. "My thanks and gratitude for the really fine adaptations and beautiful artwork you are doing on my stories," he wrote to Gaines after the two became friends. "This is an entirely new experience to me, and I cannot tell you enough how much I appreciate the painstaking detail and thought you are putting into your efforts."

Those only familiar with 1960s kiddie-friendly Harvey Comics such as *Casper the Friendly Ghost* may be surprised by the company's grisly fare from a decade earlier.

For EC's three influential horror titles, readers were introduced to their gruesome contents by a trio of cackling "horror hosts"—the Crypt-Keeper in *Tales from the Crypt*, the Vault-Keeper in *The Vault of Horror*, and the Old Witch in *The Haunt of Fear*.

The co-creator of Spider-Man and the Avengers, workhorse editor/writer Stan Lee (1922–2018), downplayed his earlier involvement in the despised field of horror comics (before his employer Atlas changed its name to Marvel), but he in fact produced a greater quantity of titles in the genre than any of his contemporaries, including *Mystic*, *Menace*, *Journey Into Unknown Worlds*, *Spellbound*, and *Strange Tales*.

As Lee later revealed: "To admit in the 1950s that you wrote for comic books was totally unacceptable in most social circles (akin to child corruption)—and if such disapproval even fell on Superman and Batman, think just how close to the chest you'd keep the fact that you were the editor of a magazine called *Adventures Into Terror*!"

One of Lee's best titles was *Adventures Into Weird Worlds*. In issue No. 26 (February 1954), "Good-bye Earth" (drawn by Paul Reinman) had a genuine sense of loss as a man is forced to leave his family for his alien destiny. But the real kicker of the story lay in the face of the otherworldly creature who informs the hero of his true nature—by removing his own rubber face to reveal a heaving green protoplasmic mass. Unlike writers such as Al Feldstein and others over at EC, Lee and his fellow scribblers for Atlas made up in sheer gusto what they lacked in finesse.

Those only familiar with 1960s kiddie-friendly Harvey Comics such as *Casper the Friendly Ghost* may be surprised by the company's grisly fare from a decade earlier: *Tomb of Terror*, *Black Cat Mystery*, *Chamber of Chills*, and *Witches Tales*. Harvey was highly successful, boasting such assets as the massively talented illustrator Bob Powell. Powell was easily the equal of any of the skillful cadre of artists employed at EC, and could even match the latter company's team in terms of his frequently surrealistic invention. Harvey, with its oceans of blood and ripped bodies, was comfortably among the most unbuttoned in the genre.

The sticking point with Harvey (the fiefdom of Alfred, Robert, and Leon Harvey), however, is the often maladroit writing, which simply couldn't match the elegance and skill of Feldstein's work at EC, but instead substituted a wildly chaotic (and sometimes incoherent) quality that made the reader feel that they were entering a strange and disturbing world. The splendidly horrific covers for Harvey were mostly by Lee Elias, the company's other top illustrator.

Other companies had boundary-pushing gems hidden among the dross that typified their output. Take, for instance, Bob Powell's "The Wall of Flesh!" from Fawcett's *This Magazine is Haunted* No. 12 (August 1953), which had a nurse being drawn into a quivering tumorous mass that teasingly removed her clothes. Or *Ghost Comics* No. 10 (Fiction House, 1954), with "Ghost of the Gorgon": in a bat-haunted cave, two sailors shrink back from a snake-headed Medusa figure, seen from the side, clearly naked beneath a scarlet cloak. The tale was drawn by "John Bell" (actually John Belcastro), and Bell's panel of a grinning Perseus holding up Medusa's severed head was stronger stuff than ever graced the pages of *Batman*. But what really shocked was the pulchritudinous nude body of the Gorgon herself—despite her fanged, horned countenance and claw-like feet, Bell had clearly lavished carnality on that naked green body, which in several panels was even seen topless.

After the censorship axe fell in the mid-1950s, comics became a horror-free zone—until an Indian summer in the 1960s. James Warren, publisher of *Famous Monsters of Filmland*, inaugurated a trio of large-format black-and-white horror magazines, *Creepy*, *Eerie*, and *Vampirella*, with the canny notion of employing the EC master illustrators (notably Reed Crandall and Johnny Craig). The result was some of the most beautifully drawn, Code-free horror since the glory days of EC.

Many other countries have also had popular horror comics series, including Mexico, Germany, and—perhaps most notably—Italy, with digest-sized, erotic horror *fumetti* such as *Oltretomba* (a typical cover has a helpless naked woman being clutched by several skeletal hands). Horror comics weren't ready to fade away yet—as revivals in later decades were to prove.

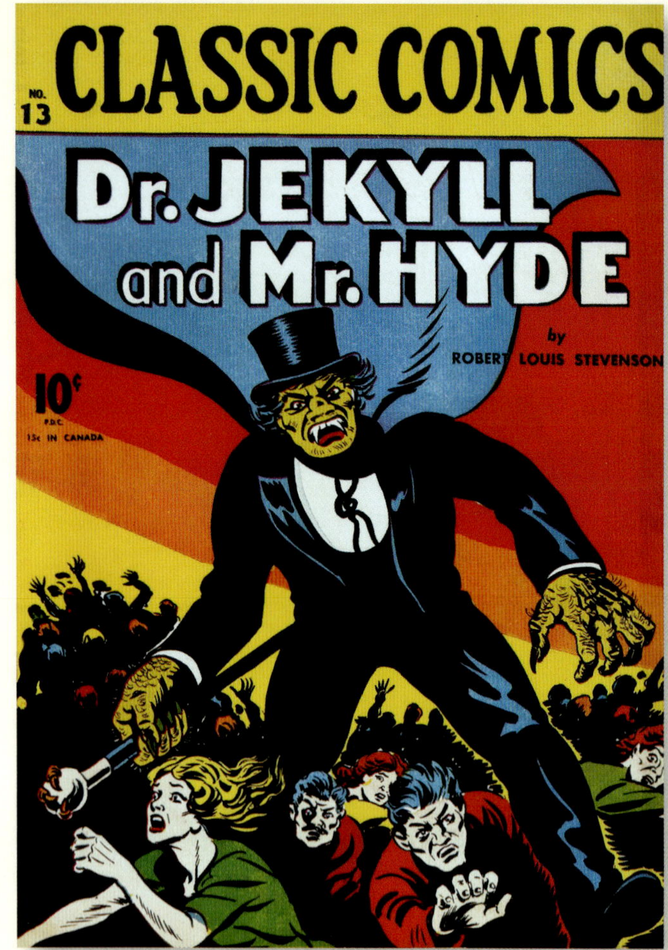

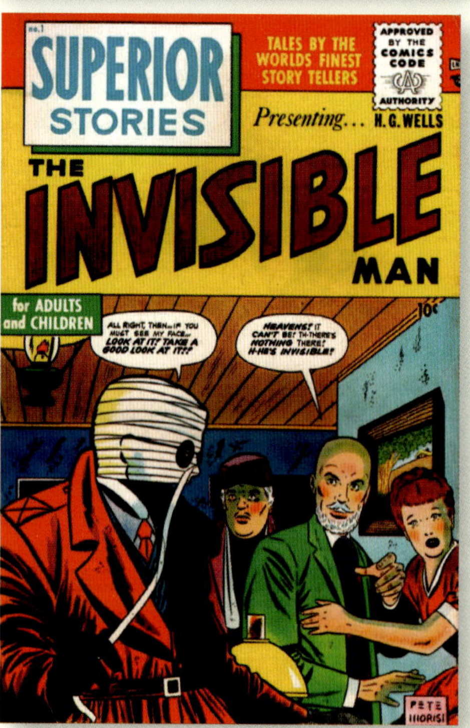

ABOVE LEFT: Arnold Hicks's cover for the Gilberton Company, Inc.'s *Classic Comics* No. 13 (August 1943). This Robert Louis Stevenson adaptation is widely considered to be the first horror comic.

TOP MIDDLE: Wally Wood (1927–81) provided the cover and interior art for Avon Periodicals, Inc.'s one-off publication *The Mask of Dr. Fu Manchu* (1951). Original creator Sax Rohmer wasn't even mentioned!

TOP RIGHT: The Summer 1952 issue of Feature Publications, Inc.'s *Frankenstein*. Creator Richard "Dick" Briefer (1915–80) had returned the character to his horror roots in the previous issue.

BOTTOM MIDDLE: The first comics adaptation of Bram Stoker's *Dracula* (with added exclamation mark!) in Avon Periodicals, Inc.'s *Eerie* No. 12 (August 1953), illustrated by Gene Fawcette and Vince Alascia.

BOTTOM RIGHT: The first of only four issues of Nesbit Publishers, Inc.'s bi-monthly *Superior Stories* (May–June 1955) featured an adaptation of H.G. Wells's *The Invisible Man* illustrated by Pete Morisi (1928–2003).

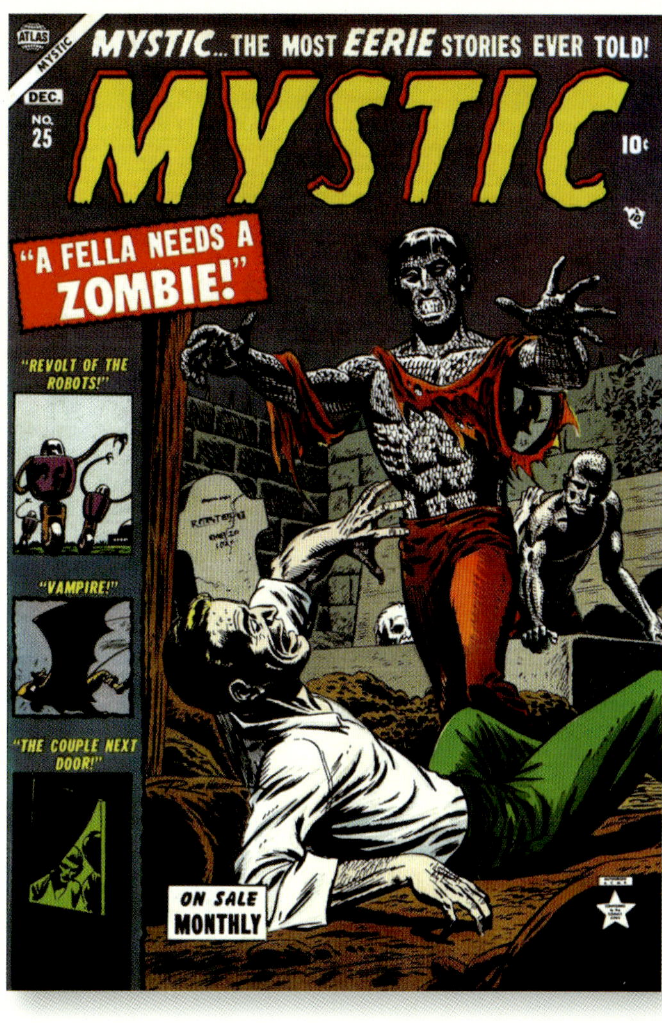

TOP LEFT: Editor Stan Lee (1922–2018) launched a range of horror comics for publisher Martin Goodman's Atlas imprint in the early 1950s. One of these titles was *Mystery Tales*, which debuted in March 1952.

TOP MIDDLE: Not only did Stan Lee edit all these titles, but he also wrote strips for them, as in this first issue of *Uncanny Tales* (June 1952). Atlas was the successor to Timely Comics, founded in 1939 by pulp publisher Martin Goodman.

BOTTOM LEFT: Russ Heath produced the cover for the first issue of *Journey Into Mystery* (June 1952). Goodman decided to increase his Atlas line of horror titles after noticing the success EC was having with the genre.

BOTTOM MIDDLE: The Stan Lee-edited *Suspense* No. 19 (June 1952) also featured a cover by Russ Heath. Despite flooding the market with cheaply produced product, Atlas had some of the most talented artists.

ABOVE RIGHT: The cover of *Mystic* No. 25 (December 1953) was also by Russ Heath. The Atlas imprint disappeared in 1957 due to distribution problems, and four years later it became Marvel Comics.

TOP LEFT: After publishing a one-off edition in 1947, Avon revived its *Eerie* title for 17 issues with yet another No. 1 (May–June 1951), which included a story from the earlier incarnation under a different title.

ABOVE RIGHT: *City of the Living Dead!* (1952) was a one-shot title from Avon Periodicals, Inc. with a cover by A. (Alvin) C. (Carl) Hollingsworth (1928–2000), one of the first black American comics artists.

TOP MIDDLE: A.C. Hollingsworth, who went on to become a fine art painter, also did the cover for *Diary of Horror!* (1952) which, despite being designated Vol. 1, No. 1, was another one-shot publication from Avon.

BOTTOM LEFT: *The Phantom Witch Doctor* (1952) was also an Avon one-shot title. It featured a striking cover by former pulp artist and Presidential portrait painter Everett Raymond Kinstler (1926–2019).

BOTTOM MIDDLE: Avon's *Witchcraft* No. 5 (December–January 1952–53) was the penultimate edition of the title and sported a painted cover by (Frank) Kelly Freas, who also did work for the publisher's paperback line.

ABOVE LEFT: *Adventures Into the Unknown!* from American Comics Group (ACG) was the first continuous horror-comics title. Issue No. 3 (February–March 1949) featured a cover by Edvard Moritz.

TOP RIGHT: *Out of the Night* No. 2 (April–May 1952) featured a cover by Ken Bald. The most overtly horror of all ACG's titles, it ran for 17 bi-monthly issues until killed off by the Comics Code in late 1954.

BOTTOM RIGHT: Ken Bald also contributed the cover to ACG's *Forbidden Worlds* No. 11 (November 1952). The company survived the Senate subcommittee hearings and continued to publish until August 1967.

TOP LEFT: The cover of Harvey Comics' *Witches Tales Magazine* No. 1 (January 1951) is attributed to Bob Powell. While the US edition lasted for 28 issues (1951–54), a Mexican reprint edition, *Cuentos de Brujas*, ran for 185 issues until 1964.

TOP MIDDLE: Lee Elias's cover for Harvey Comics' *Chamber of Chills* No. 23 (May 1954) was possibly inked over pencils by Warren Kremer. Oddly, the title was a continuation of *Blondie Comics* and lasted for 26 bi-monthly issues (1951–54).

BOTTOM LEFT: One of Lee Elias's more extreme covers appeared on the penultimate issue of Harvey Comics' *Tomb of Terror* No. 15 (May 1954). The title ran from 1952–54, before it ceased publication due to the Senate Subcommittee hearings.

BOTTOM MIDDLE: Lee Elias's cover for *Black Cat Mystery* No. 50 (August 1954), which began in 1946 as a crime-fighter comic. It became a Harvey horror title in October 1951 and survived under the Comics Code until March 1958.

ABOVE RIGHT: Original pen and ink on Bristol board cover for Harvey Comics' *Black Cat Mystery* No. 34 (April 1952) by American artist Al Avison (1920–84). It includes a section along the left-hand side that did not appear on the comic book.

ABOVE LEFT: Original pen and ink cover illustration for Harvey Comics' bi-monthly pre-Code horror comic *Chamber of Chills* No. 18 (July 1953) by British-born American comics artist Lee Elias (1920–98). The title logo is a replacement.

TOP & BOTTOM RIGHT: Two ink and colored pencil on vellum preliminary cover concept sketches for *Chamber of Chills* No. 18 (July 1953) by former pulp illustrator Warren Kremer (1921–2003), who created the character Richie Rich.

TOP LEFT: Original ink over pencil on Bristol board art for the cover of Harvey Comics' *Tomb of Terror* No. 12 (November 1953) by Lee Elias, with lettering by Joe Rosen. The title ran for 16 bi-monthly issues from 1952 to 1954.

TOP RIGHT: Warren Kremer's preliminary pen and ink on bond paper concept sketch for the cover of Ace Magazines' *The Beyond* No. 2 (January 1951). The pre-Code comic ran for 30 bi-monthly issues from 1950 to 1955.

BOTTOM RIGHT: Warren Kremer's ink, watercolor, and colored pencil on vellum preliminary sketch for Lee Elias's cover of Harvey Comics' *Chamber of Chills* (No. 19, September 1953), which ran for 26 bi-monthly issues from 1951 to 1954.

ABOVE RIGHT: The second of three black-and-white British issues of *Eerie* (circa 1952) from Thorpe & Porter Ltd./ Hermitage Publications Ltd., featured a cover by Wally Wood and reprinted the US Avon edition (August–September 1951).

TOP LEFT: The second of five British issues of Dick Briefer's *Frankenstein* published by The Arnold Book Company (circa 1954) reprinted No. 27 of Prize Group's US edition (October–November 1953) in black and white.

BOTTOM LEFT: Jack Kirby's cover for the penultimate edition of The Arnold Book Company's black-and-white British reprint of *Black Magic Magazine* (No. 15, circa 1954), which reprinted No. 24 of Prize Group's US edition (May 1953).

ELIMINATING THE GRUESOME

"The truth is that delinquency is the product of the real environment in which the child lives and not of the fiction he reads."

William M. Gaines

"Without all this splendid mediocrity, this sublime and wondrous trash in my background, I don't think I would be any sort of writer today."

Ray Bradbury

"SCENES OF EXCESSIVE violence shall be prohibited. Scenes of brutal torture, excessive and unnecessary knife and gunplay, physical agony, gory and gruesome crime shall be eliminated."

These are the words of the "Code of the Comics Magazine Association of America, Inc. 1954," which made Tennessee Senator Estes Kefauver and the German-American psychologist Fredric Wertham very happy—they had won a battle. The draconian Code decisively signaled the end of horror comics and (supposedly) the end of juvenile delinquency in America that was—Kefauver and Wertham maintained—the result of such magazines. EC publisher William M. Gaines's spirited argument in defense of the genre had fallen on deaf ears.

With reprints galore, it's hard today to remember when uncensored horror comics were difficult to come by. The hysteria that had engendered the Code had neutered the industry in America, and its UK equivalent (with questions even asked in the Houses of Parliament) similarly made such material in Britain—what little there was—impossible to find. While comics readers growing up in the UK in the late 1950s and early '60s enjoyed the Code-approved material that was available in British and Australian black-and-white reprint form, the rare appearance of horror fare from Atlas or EC was a source of rejoicing, and the cause of much frantic bartering in the school playground.

The Arnold Book Company's product was often cited by campaigners against horror comics in the UK (the campaigners were a strange mélange of moral guardians, librarians, and Communist groups with an antipathy towards any American material). Arnold's notorious reputation as a purveyor of "unacceptable material" was a contributory factor in the parliamentary inauguration of the "Children and Young Persons (Harmful Publications) Act 1955," with such august figures on the side of a ban as the then-Prime Minister, Winston Churchill. The horror comic in Britain was doomed, but at least two issues from Arnold of a UK reprint of *Tales from the Crypt* (along with a single issue of *The Haunt of Fear*) appeared before the metaphorical axe fell.

But was there, in fact, a fourth British reprint of an EC horror title? Did the much-sought-after UK *Vault of Horror* No. 1 ever exist? This title—which no living British comics expert has ever managed to track down—has been much discussed over the years, and possibly never appeared—or did it? There is one slender clue to the possible existence of this fabled book.

The draconian Code decisively signaled the end of horror comics and (supposedly) the end of juvenile delinquency in America that was the result of such magazines.

In the parliamentary debate that preceded the introduction of the Act mentioned above, there was cross-party agreement concerning the perceived evil of horror comics—and an urgent necessity to protect the youth of Britain against this material (the notion that such books might be read by adults was given short shrift). Frank Soskice (Baron Stow Hill) was a Labour MP who is said to have brandished a copy of *Vault of Horror*, against which he fulminated (according to parliamentary records of the day) that the book was designed to "appeal to the instincts of sadism and every excitation of one's most brutish inclinations, taste, and feelings."

There is, of course, the possibility that an American copy of the book had found its way into the MP's hands, and certainly no parliamentarian of the day would be likely to differentiate between an American comic and its British reprint.

We will never know. *BF*

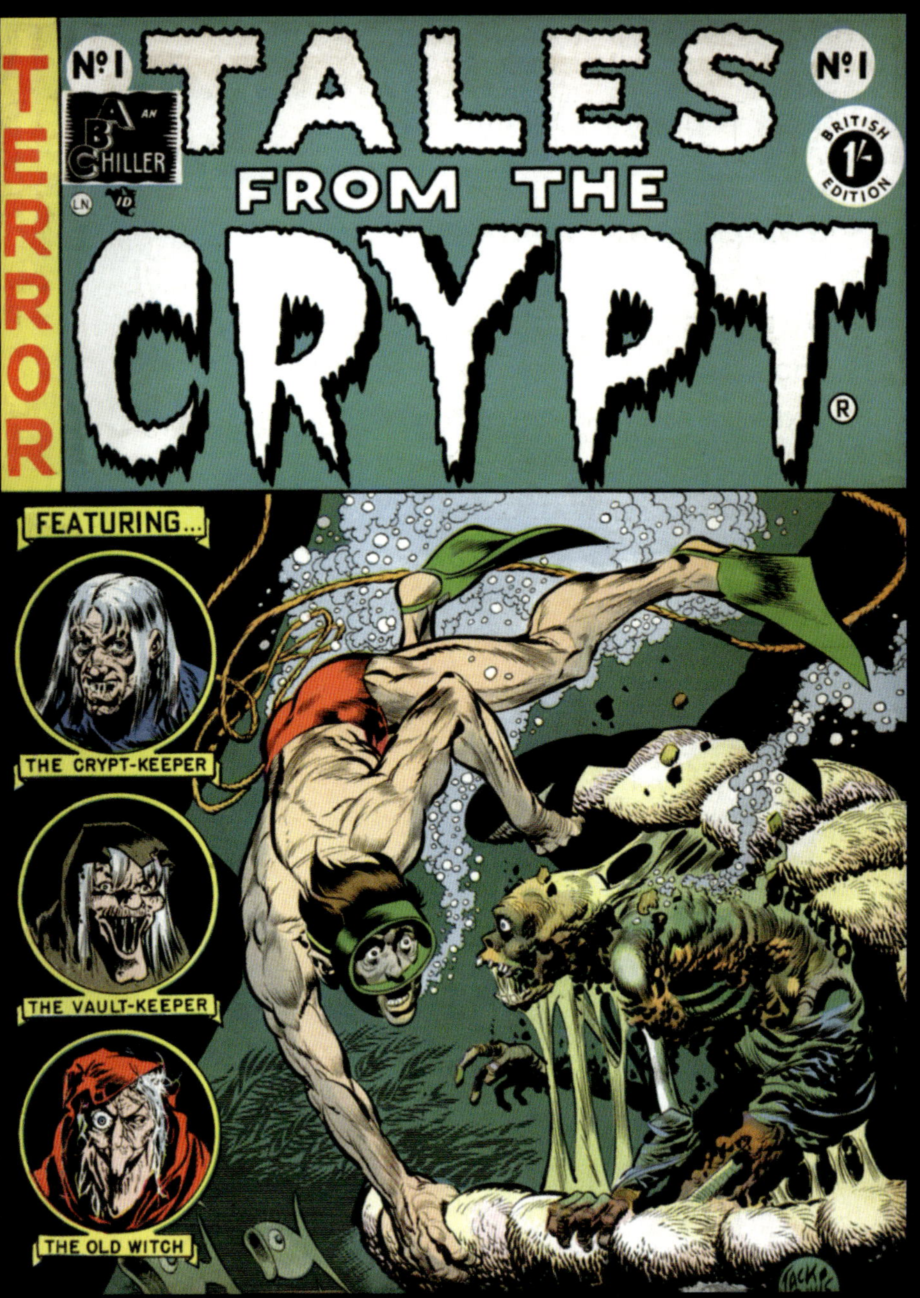

EC's Shilling Shockers!
Founded by Arnold Miller in the late 1940s, The Arnold Book Company Ltd. was run out of an apartment above a newsagents in Lower James Street, London. Circa 1954 they published the EC reprints *Tales from the Crypt* No. 1 and No. 2 (actually issues No. 24 and No. 41 of the American series, with covers by Jack Davis) and *The Haunt of Fear* No. 1 (originally issue No. 23, cover by Graham Ingels) [ALL THIS PAGE], which led to questions being asked in Britain's Houses of Parliament and the creation of the "Children and Young Persons (Harmful Publications) Act 1955," which was finally repealed in 1969. An advertisement in *Tales from the Crypt* No. 1 boasted they contained "68 big pages" of black-and-white strips (with bonus material drawn from other publishers) and sold for one shilling apiece.

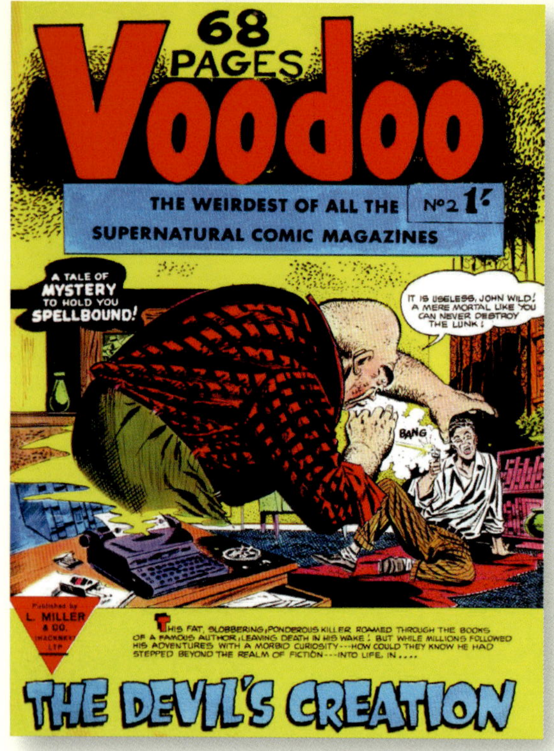

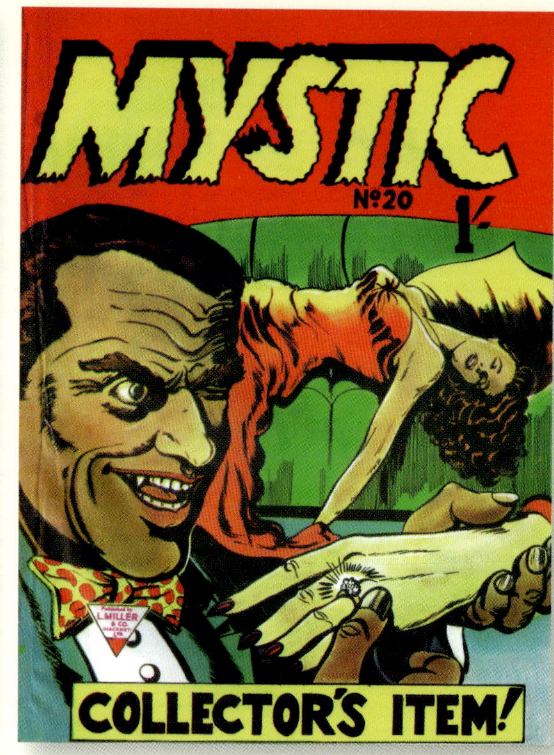

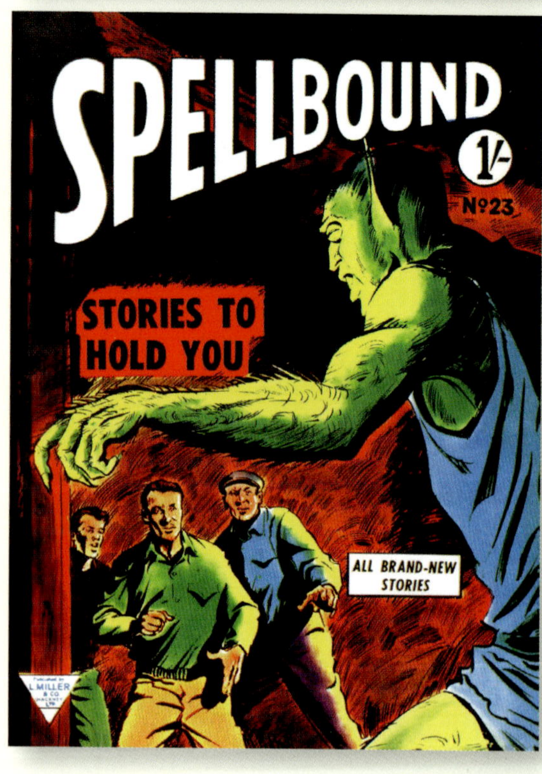

THIS PAGE: From 1943–66, L. Miller & Co. (Hackney) Ltd. published black-and-white reprints of American comic strips. During the early 1960s these included many pre-Code horrors in defiance of Britain's 1955 "Harmful Publications" Act.

TOP MIDDLE & RIGHT: *Mystic* No. 12 (circa 1960) and No. 20 (1962) both featured original cover illustrations by uncredited artists for reprints of 1950s strips from pre-Code Atlas and Marvel titles. The series ran for 66 monthly issues.

TOP LEFT: Miller's *Voodoo* No. 2 (circa 1961) featured a cover by Mike Sekowsky that was taken from the splash page of the story's previous publication in Fawcett's *Beware! Terror Tales* No. 2 (July 1952). The series lasted just nine issues.

BOTTOM LEFT: Leonard Frank's cover on Miller's *Zombie* No. 8 (circa 1961), the title's penultimate issue, was also the original splash panel lifted from that story's first publication in Fawcett's *Worlds of Fear* No. 9 (April 1953).

BOTTOM MIDDLE & RIGHT: *Spellbound* No. 19 and No. 23 (both 1962) also had cover art by unknown illustrators and included reprints from pre-Code Atlas, Ziff-Davis, and Farrell titles. This series also ran for 66 issues, until 1966.

FREE FANGS WITH THIS No1 ISSUE!

24th March 1984
Every Monday
22p

SCREAM!

Just when you thought it was safe to sleep in the dark...

NOT FOR THE NERVOUS!

We're waiting for you inside...

FREE! YOUR DRACULA FANGS!

JOIN US IF YOU DARE!

Australia 55c. New Zealand 55c. Malaysia $1.45. Transylvania 2 Marks.

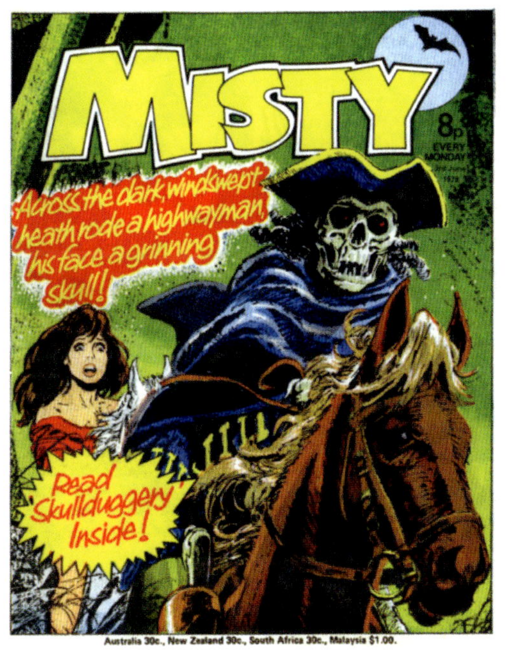

TOP LEFT: Cover-dated September 25, 1976, British publisher D.C. Thomson & Co., Ltd. launched the first issue of *Spellbound*, "the super new mystery story paper for girls." It ran for 69 weekly issues until it was merged into *Debbie* in 1978.

BOTTOM LEFT: Spanish artist Jaime Rumeu's cover for *Misty* No. 18 (June 3, 1978), IPC Magazines Ltd.'s rival newsprint "mystery paper" aimed at teenage girls. It ran for 101 weekly issues until it was incorporated into *Tammy* in 1980.

TOP & BOTTOM RIGHT: The first issue of IPC Magazines Ltd.'s *Scream!* (March 24, 1984), which was firmly aimed at younger readers. The newsprint weekly lasted for only 15 issues before it was merged with IPC's revived *Eagle*.

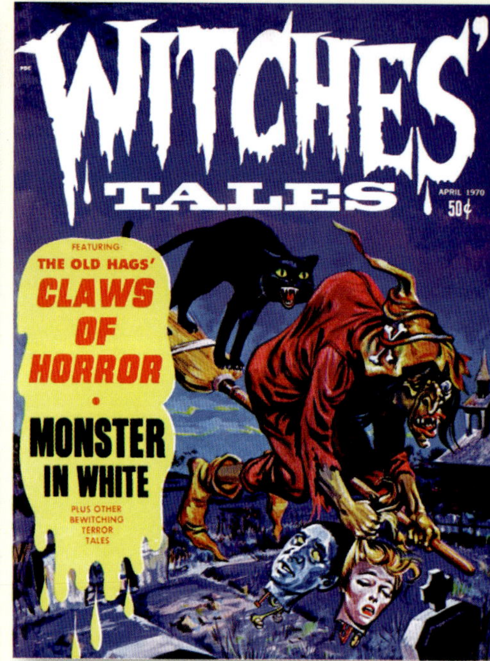

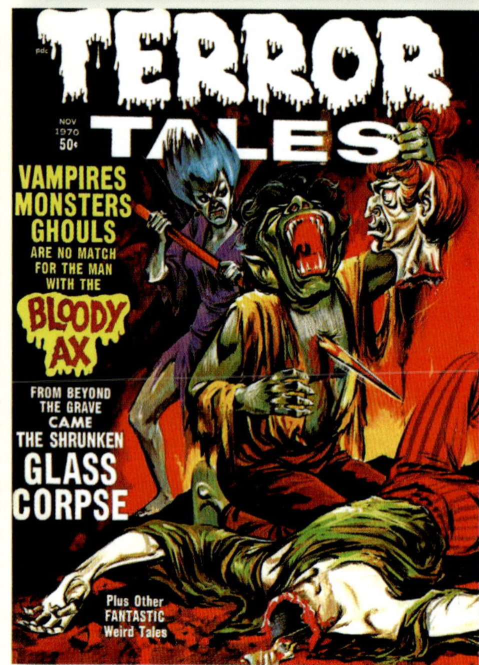

A Glut of the Gruesome

The low-rent American imprint Eerie Publications (1966–81) was co-founded by former comic book artist turned mercurial New York publishing mogul Myron Fass (1926–2006). The magazine-sized periodicals were able to skirt the restrictions imposed by the Comics Code Authority and contained gruesome black-and-white horror strips that were either rewritten or reprinted from 1950s pre-Code comics (with the art often altered to make it even gorier). However, what made the Eerie titles stand out on the newsstands from rivals such as Stanley Publications were their eye-popping (sometimes literally!) covers depicting grisly scenes of sadism in lurid color and detail.

TOP LEFT & MIDDLE: Veteran comics writer and artist "Carl Burgos" (Max Finkelstein, 1916–84) edited the Eerie line and painted the July 1968 covers for both the one-shot *Tales from the Crypt* plus *Weird Tales of Shock, Terror, Suspense*.

TOP RIGHT: Bill Alexander did the cover for the April 1970 issue of *Witches' Tales*.

BOTTOM LEFT: The March 1972 edition of *Horror Tales* featured a cover by Spanish comics artist Fernando Fernández (1940–2010).

BOTTOM MIDDLE & RIGHT: Typically garish and gory paintings by the enigmatic African-American artist Bill Alexander graced the covers of the November 1970 issue of *Terror Tales* and the October 1972 edition of *Tales of Voodoo*.

RIGHT: Acrylic on illustration board painting for the cover of *Terror Tales* (April 1973) [ABOVE] by American artist Bill Alexander, who also produced sleaze and bondage paperback covers for various publishers during the 1960s and '70s.

ABOVE LEFT: When American publisher James Warren realized that he could circumnavigate the Comics Code Authority by publishing black-and-white horror strips in a magazine format, he launched *Creepy* in late 1964 with a cover by former EC artist Jack Davis.

TOP RIGHT: Edited by comics writer Archie Goodwin (1937–98), Warren Publishing Co.'s *Eerie* No. 2 (1966) was the first issue widely distributed through newsstands after an "ashcan" issue was used to secure the rights to the title. Cover by the great Frank Frazetta.

BOTTOM RIGHT: Manuel Sanjulián's cover for the first UK edition of IPC Magazines Ltd.'s four-issue run of *Vampirella* (1975). The alien vampire and comic strip horror hostess was created for Warren Publishing in 1969 by Forrest J Ackerman and artist Trina Robbins.

ABOVE LEFT: *"Vampirella," "Cousin Eerie," and "Uncle Creepy"* (2002) pencil and ink on art paper by American artist Mike Mignola. This was a private commission portraying the Warren Publishing Co.'s terrible triumvirate of horror hosts.

RIGHT: *Uncle Creepy* (2013) pen and ink portrait of the Warren Publishing Co.'s first magazine horror host by Mike Mignola, published as the frontispiece of issue #12 (May, 2013) of Dark Horse Comics' revival of *Creepy*, which ran for 24 issues from July 2009 to June 2016.

TOP LEFT: In the late 1960s the major publishers began to challenge the Comics Code Authority. One of the first to do so was DC Comics with EC veteran Joe Orlando's reprint issue of *House of Mystery* No. 174 (June 1968).

TOP MIDDLE: Nick Cardy created the cover for the first issue of DC's all-new horror comic *The Witching Hour* (March 1969), edited by Dick Giordano. The title lasted for 85 monthly issues, until October 1978.

BOTTOM LEFT: DC's *The House of Secrets* No. 92 (July 1971) introduced readers to the character of Swamp Thing, created by writer Len Wein and illustrated by artist Berni(e) Wrightson, who also did the cover.

BOTTOM MIDDLE: DC Comics revived Prize's pre-Code comic *Black Magic* with No. 1 (November 1973). All the stories in the first issue were 1950 reprints illustrated by original editors Joe Simon and Jack Kirby.

ABOVE RIGHT: In 1971 the Comics Code Authority relaxed some of its rules, and the Marvel Comics Group returned to publishing horror. Frank Brunner did the Poe-inspired cover for *Chamber of Chills* No. 4 (May 1973).

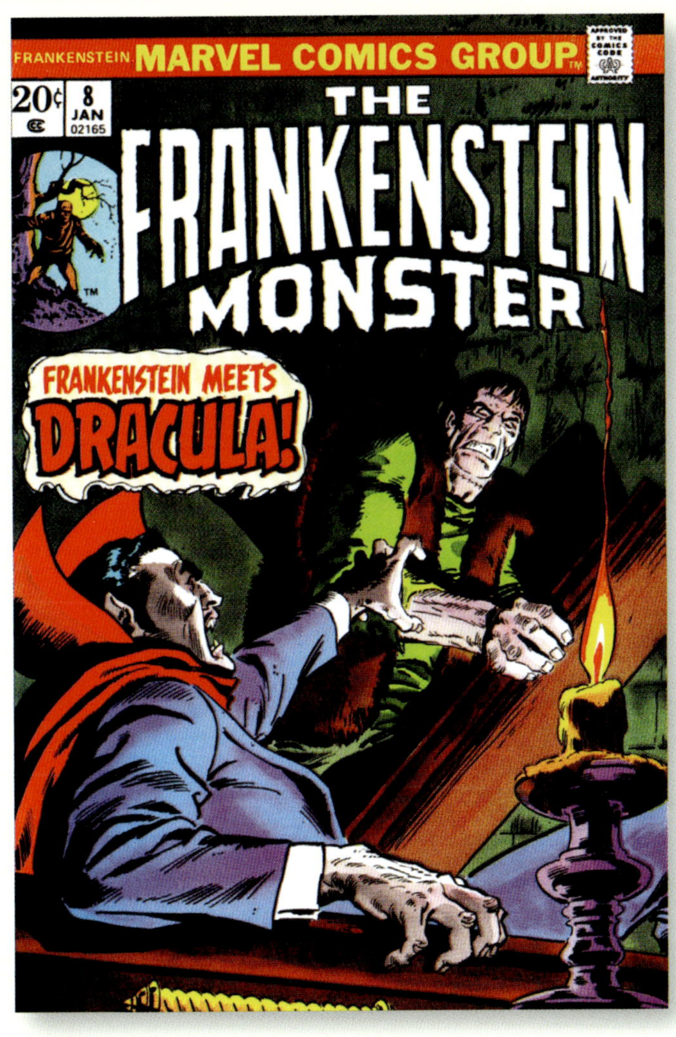

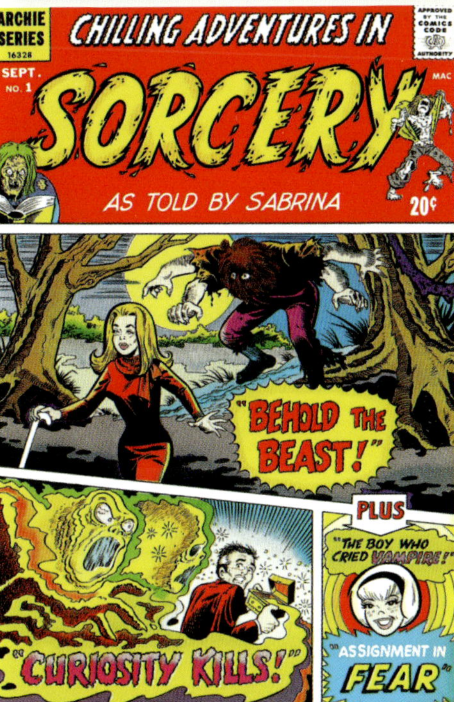

ABOVE LEFT: In 1972 Marvel revived Dracula as a villain in his own comic and some of its other titles. John Buscema's cover for *The Frankenstein Monster* No. 8 (January 1974) depicted an inevitable confrontation.

TOP MIDDLE: John Romita's cover for Marvel's *Supernatural Thrillers* No. 7 (June 1974). The 15-issue run featured a number of literary adaptations before settling on the exploits of N'Kantu, The Living Mummy.

TOP RIGHT: Penciller Ed Hannigan and inker Mike Esposito's cover for *Vault of Evil* No. 17 (February 1975). Until November that same year, the title reprinted strips from Marvel's pre-Code horror comics over 23 issues.

BOTTOM MIDDLE: The usually wholesome Archie Comics jumped on the horror bandwagon in the early 1970s with the all-new first issue of *Chilling Adventures in Sorcery as Told by Sabrina* (September 1972).

BOTTOM RIGHT: Gray Morrow's cover for *Mad House* No. 95 (September 1974) published under Archie's short-lived Red Circle Comics imprint. By the mid-1970s the popularity of horror comics was once again waning.

TOP LEFT: Cover by Pat Boyette for the first issue of Charlton Comics' *The Many Ghosts of Doctor Graves* (May 1967). The exploits of Ernie Bache's ghost-buster Dr. M.T. Graves lasted for 72 issues, until May 1982.

BOTTOM LEFT: Jesse Santos cover for Gold Key's *The Occult Files of Doctor Spektor* No. 1 (April 1973), which introduced Don Glut's Dr. Adam Spektor, Lakota Rainflower, and vampire Baron Tibor.

ABOVE RIGHT: Having started out under the Gold Key imprint in 1962 as a tie-in to the NBC-TV series *Thriller*, after the show was cancelled the Western Publishing Company, Inc. changed the title to *Boris Karloff Tales of Mystery* with the third issue. Hosted by Karloff, the anthology series survived the actor's death and ran for 97 issues, until February 1980. This painted cover for No. 32 (November 1970) is by George Wilson (1921–1999).

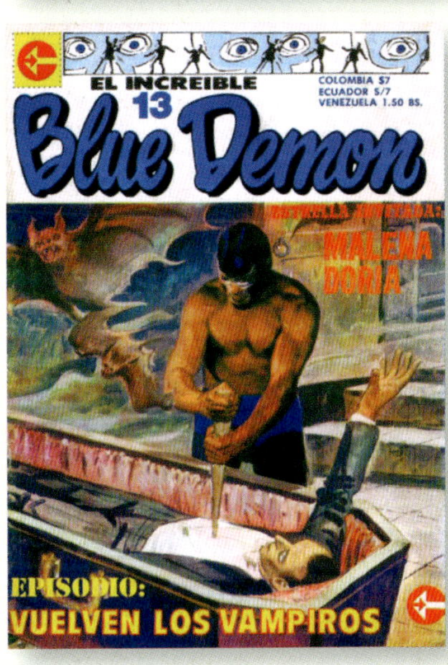

A Feast of *fumetti*

The word "*fumetto*" literally means "little puffs of smoke" in Italian, referring to the word balloons in comics. It has also come to describe pocket-sized books of (often violent and sexual) black-and-white horror strips. The most infamous of these was Italy's increasingly explicit *Oltretomba* (Beyond the Tomb), which lasted for 300 issues from 1971–86. Also from Italy, the erotic *Jacula* (1969–82) was reprinted in Greece from 1977 as *Zakoula*. Like his rival *luchador*, Santo, Mexico's El Increìble Blue Demon also enjoyed his own series of *foto-novelas* during the 1960s and '70s. *Gespenster Geschichten* (Ghost Stories) from Bastei Verlag was one of the most successful comic series ever in Germany, publishing 1,654 mostly weekly issues between 1974–2006. Australian publisher Gredown produced many reprint horror titles in the mid-1970s, including the series *Strange Experience*. The original Hindi horror series *Jinda Mar Jaa* (Forever Dead) appeared from New Delhi's Raj Comics, while Turkey's *Süper Korku* (Super Fear) reprinted horror strips from American comics.

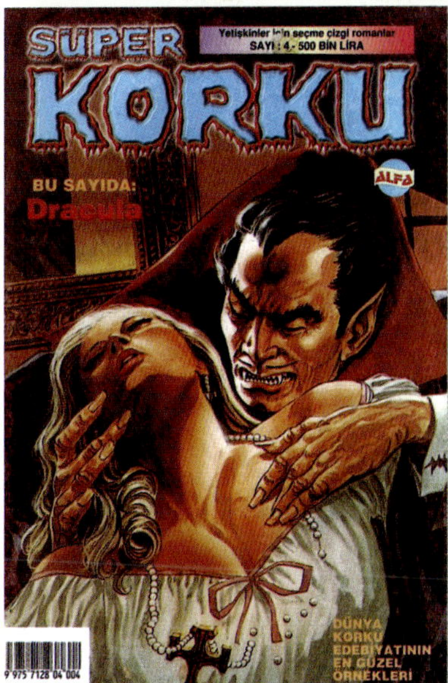

Maddox

6

DRIVE-IN DELINQUENTS

LISA MORTON

"Speak. I know you have a civil tongue in your head because I sewed it back myself."

PROF. FRANKENSTEIN (WHIT BISSELL) IN *I WAS A TEENAGE FRANKENSTEIN* (1957)

"In science fiction films, the monster should always be bigger than the leading lady."

Roger Corman

"What elements made these AIP films shlock classics? They were simple, shot in a hurry, and so amateurish that one can see the shadow of a boom mike in the shot or catch the gleam of an air tank inside the monster suit of an underwater creature (as in *Attack of the Giant Leeches*)."

Stephen King, *Danse Macabre* (1981)

ON JUNE 15, 1948, something momentous in the history of horror movies happened. It's not that a major classic was released that day, or something new and innovative. Far from it, in fact, for that date saw the release of Universal-International's *Abbott and Costello Meet Frankenstein*, the film that drove a stake through the collective heart of the monsters that had made up horror cinema for two decades. Thanks to sequels, copycats, and mash-ups, Frankenstein, Dracula, the Wolf Man, the Invisible Man, and all the rest had run their course and were now reduced to serving as sight gags for a pair of vaudevillian comedians.

It wasn't just horror that was in a state of flux, though. America and her allies had won a world war and inaugurated a new age of prosperity, but there were strains of dread bubbling just underneath the shiny, suburban surface. Fears of nuclear devastation instituted a new Cold War, an anxious multinational standoff that came with a side helping of the Space Race. As teenagers became anxious, exploitation films lured them away from their new TVs with fast-paced stories about hot rods and rockabillies. Drive-ins, first introduced in the 1930s, caught on, creating a ready-made market for the kind of films that caused teenage girls to grab onto their boyfriends in shock. And those shock films turned away from tired supernatural terrors to more provocative and relevant nightmares that focused on science run amok.

While the major studios were producing bigger-budget fare like *The Thing from Another World* (1951), *Creature from the Black Lagoon* (1954), and *Invasion of the Body Snatchers* (1956), a new kind of Hollywood *auteur* was emerging to fill the demand for low-budget scares. These new producers specialized in fast, cheap thrills; their movies were often sold on the basis of either a terrifying poster or a gimmick.

Surely the king of the low-budget horror maestros was Roger Corman (b. 1926). After starting out working in studio mailrooms and as an assistant to an agent, he produced his first film in 1954, *Monster from the Ocean Floor*, on a budget of just $12,000. Corman hooked up with James H. Nicholson and Samuel Z. Arkoff's American Releasing Company—later known as American International Pictures (AIP)—and turned to directing such films as *It Conquered the World* (1956), *The Undead* (1957), *Not of This Earth* (1957), *Attack of the Crab Monsters* (1957), *Teenage Cave Man* (1958), *A Bucket of Blood* (1959), and *The Wasp Woman* (1959).

These new producers specialized in fast, cheap thrills; their movies were often sold on the basis of either a terrifying poster or a gimmick.

However, Corman soon sensed a decline in the market for cheap, black-and-white thrillers, so in 1960 he directed the color feature *House of Usher*, starring Vincent Price and written by Richard Matheson. *House of Usher* was a hit, inaugurating a cycle of Corman-directed or produced Edgar Allan Poe films that included *Pit and the Pendulum* (1961), *Premature Burial* (1962), *Tales of Terror* (1962), *The Raven* (1963), *The Masque of the Red Death* (1964), and *The Tomb of Ligeia* (1964).

Like Corman, William Castle (1914–77) was another entrepreneur whose low-budget, black-and-white 1950s shockers would lead to a higher profile project in the 1960s. Castle's filmography included a string of B-movies headlining such established stars as Vincent Price, Joan Crawford, Robert Taylor, and Barbara Stanwyck, which he promoted using over-hyped gimmicks. Then, in 1968 he produced one of the finest horror films of the decade: *Rosemary's Baby*, directed by Roman Polanski and based on the book by Ira Levin.

Not all of the schlock *auteurs* were as successful as Corman and Castle, either financially or artistically. Bert I. Gordon (b. 1922)—nicknamed "Mr. B.I.G."—worked for various studios, producing movies that often dealt with mutated giants: *King Dinosaur* (1955), *Beginning of the End* (1957), *The Cyclops* (1957), *The Amazing Colossal Man* (1957),

PREVIOUS SPREAD: ***The Revenge of Frankenstein*** **(2013), pencil and digital cover for Bruce G. Hallenbeck's *British Cult Cinema: The Hammer Frankenstein* (Hemlock Books, 2013) by Mark Maddox. "It is an enormous pleasure to illustrate Peter Cushing whenever possible," reveals the American artist. "His talent is an inspiration."**

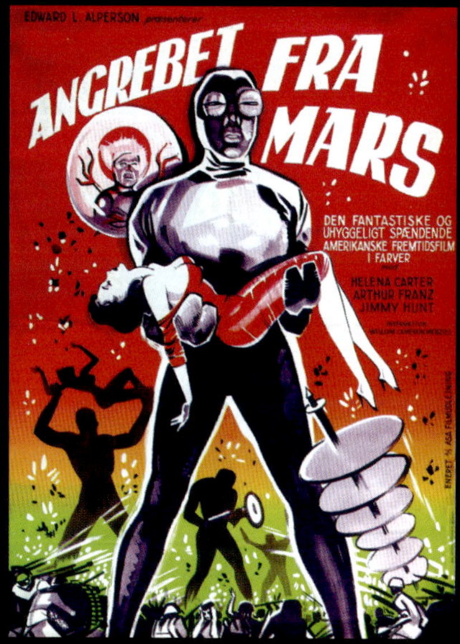

ABOVE LEFT: This 1950 Danish poster for Universal-International's monster mash-up *Abbott and Costello Meet Frankenstein* (Dir: Charles Barton, 1948) not only caricatured the two comedians, but also Count Dracula, the Wolf Man, and the Frankenstein Monster.

TOP MIDDLE: This colorful Danish poster for 20th Century-Fox's *Invaders from Mars* (Dir: William Cameron Menzies, 1953) would probably have given children as many nightmares as the surreal sci-fi movie did. Some sources claim it was supposed to be shot in 3-D.

TOP RIGHT: This one-sheet poster for *Beginning of the End* (Dir: Bert I. Gordon, 1957) certainly anthropomorphized the movie's radioactive giant grasshoppers attacking Chicago, which were actually real insects superimposed over stock footage.

BOTTOM MIDDLE: The one-sheet poster for Metro-Goldwyn-Mayer's British-made *Fiend Without a Face* (Dir: Arthur Crabtree, 1958) emphasized the movie's stop-motion "brain monsters." It was based on a 1930s *Weird Tales* story by Amelia Reynolds Long.

BOTTOM RIGHT: Despite his success with *House of Usher*, Roger Corman still hadn't left his low-budget roots behind by 1961, as this one-sheet poster for *Creature from the Haunted Sea* shows. Filmed in Puerto Rico, it co-starred future Oscar-winning screenwriter Robert Towne.

ABOVE LEFT: This Japanese poster for the 1956 American version of Ishirô Honda's influential *kaiju* ("giant monster") movie, *Gojira* (1954), released in the US as *Godzilla, King of the Monsters!*, features actor Raymond Burr (bottom left), who appeared in new scenes.

TOP RIGHT: Mexican lobby card for Fernando Méndez's *El ataúd del Vampiro* (aka *The Vampire's Coffin*, 1958). For the 1964 US release, the movie was "Recommended by Young America Horror Club," an organization dreamed up by distributor K. Gordon Murray.

BOTTOM MIDDLE: This Japanese poster for Hammer Films' *The Mummy* (Dir: Terence Fisher, 1959) reworked Bill Wiggins's original UK poster art, which had inspired the scene where Peter Cushing's archaeologist drives a harpoon through Christopher Lee's mummy.

BOTTOM RIGHT: Italian *duo-foglio* for Mario Bava's iconic Gothic vampire movie *La maschera del demonio* (aka *Black Sunday*, 1960) by artist Giuliano Nistri (b. 1929). British-born Barbara Steele starred as the resurrected witch, Princess Vajda, seeking revenge.

War of the Colossal Beast (1958), *Earth vs. the Spider* (1958), and *Village of the Giants* (1965).

The 1950s also saw the release of a number of unusual low-budget independent horror/science fiction films, some of which approached surrealism. The 1958 British film *Fiend Without a Face* used stop-motion animation to depict creatures made up of stolen brains dragging spinal cords like long tails. *The Monolith Monsters* (1957) focused on an invasion of giant rocks. The eponymous robotic invader in *Kronos* (1957, directed by Kurt Neumann, who would direct *The Fly* a year later) looked like a Bauhaus nightmare. *Invaders from Mars* (1953)—one of the few color films among the independents—featured a dreamlike plot and an alien commander who was a gold, tentacle-laden head floating in a bubble.

If it seemed like the old monsters were destined to appear only in comedies or teenaged renditions (*I Was a Teenage Frankenstein* and *I Was a Teenage Werewolf*, both 1957), it took a British studio called Hammer Films to prove that there was still (undead) life in the old boys yet. In 1957 the company unleashed *The Curse of Frankenstein*, a color film with a decent budget, a fine cast (led by Christopher Lee as the Monster and Peter Cushing as his creator), and an extraordinary amount (for the time) of gore. The next year, Hammer followed up with *Dracula* (known as *Horror of Dracula* in the US) and, in 1959, *The Mummy*. The Hammer formula of color, solid scripts, gifted actors, frank sexuality, and boatloads of blood and guts proved profitable around the globe, and as they moved into the 1960s Hammer not only continued their Dracula and Frankenstein franchises, but offered such superb stand-alone films as *The Curse of the Werewolf* (1961), *The Kiss of the Vampire* (1963), *The Gorgon* (1964), *The Plague of the Zombies* (1966), and *The Devil Rides Out* (aka *The Devil's Bride*, 1968).

Hammer, however, wasn't alone in seeking to resurrect the old monsters. In 1957, an actor and producer named Abel Salazar (1917–95) brought bloodsuckers to Mexico with *El vampiro* (aka *The Vampire*), which not only updated the Gothic design of the Universal horror classics by adding a Latin American flavor, it also became one of the first films to show a vampire with long fangs. After *El vampiro* and its sequel, *El ataúd del Vampiro* (aka *The Vampire's Coffin*, 1958), Salazar's work as producer/actor included *La maldición de la Llorona* (aka *The Curse of the Crying Woman*, 1963), based on the Mexican legend of the ghostly La Llorona, and *El barón del terror* (aka *The Brainiac*, 1962), an ultra-low-budget campfest featuring an alien creature that sucks human brains with a long, forked tongue. By the 1960s, Salazar's Mexican Gothics had given way to a series of wrestling movies in which *luchadores*—often the legendary silver-masked Santo—fought such menaces as Aztec mummies, mad scientists, zombies, and Martian invaders.

On the other side of the globe, however, was a film industry obsessed (rightfully, given the real-life horrors of Hiroshima) with giant monsters caused by atomic radiation. With *Gojira* (aka *Godzilla*, 1954), Toho Studios gave birth to the *kaiju*, or "giant monster" film.

Classic monsters were still popular in other parts of the world, too. In 1968, actor/screenwriter Paul Naschy (1934–2009) inaugurated a series of Spanish monster films with *La marca del Hombre Lobo* (aka *Frankenstein's Bloody Terror*). Also from Spain, Jesús "Jess" Franco (1930–2013) took on mad doctors with *Gritos en la noche* (aka *The Awful Dr. Orlof*, 1962), although far better is his *El conde Drácula* (aka *Count Dracula*, 1970), with Christopher Lee as the vampire and Klaus Kinski as Renfield. In France, Jean Rollin (1938–2010) introduced heavy eroticism into the vampire film with *Le viol du vampire* (aka *The Rape of the Vampire*, 1968).

It was Italy, though, that produced one of the decade's most interesting horror *auteurs*: Mario Bava (1914–80). After working his way up through the Italian film industry, in 1960 Bava directed British actress Barbara Steele in *La maschera del demonio* (aka *Black Sunday*), a film drenched in European Gothicism. Bava followed that modern classic with two films that jump-started the *giallo* subgenre: *La ragazza che sapeva troppo* (aka *Evil Eye*, 1963) and *6 donne per l'assassino* (aka *Blood and Black Lace*, 1964). His *Terrore nello spazio* (aka *Planet of the Vampires*, 1965) is a clear influence on Ridley Scott's *Alien* (1979), while his *Operazione paura* (aka *Kill, Baby . . . Kill!*, 1966) is widely considered to have inspired Federico Fellini's "Toby Dammit" segment in *Histories extraordinaires* (aka *Spirits of the Dead*, 1968).

On the other side of the globe, however, was a film industry obsessed (rightfully, given the real-life horrors of Hiroshima) with giant monsters caused by atomic radiation. With *Gojira* (aka *Godzilla*, 1954), directed by Ishirô Honda (1911–93), Toho Studios gave birth to the *kaiju*, or "giant monster" film. Over the next two decades, English-dubbed versions of movies featuring Godzilla, Mothra, Ghidorah, Rodan, Gamera, and a pair of furry Gargantuas filled American theaters and TV screens.

Just as one movie had dictated the end of an era in 1948, so a film 20 years later would pave the way for the future of low-budget horror thrillers. In 1968, an independent filmmaker in Pittsburgh named George A. Romero (1940–2017) took $114,000 and made *Night of the Living Dead*. The movie, which became one of the biggest hits in the history of independent film, introduced audiences to flesh-eating zombie hordes shambling their way through a plot couched in counter-culture sentiment, and drive-ins would never be the same again.

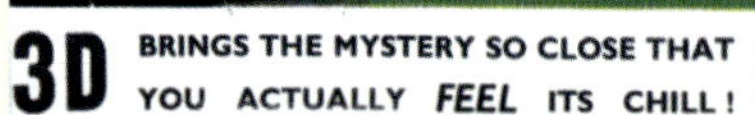

TOP LEFT: Nicola Piovano's Italian *duo-foglio* poster for the 1960 reissue of Warner Bros.' *House of Wax* (Dir: André de Toth, 1953), a remake of *Mystery of the Wax Museum* (1933) and one of the first major studio movies shot in 3-D.

BOTTOM LEFT: American 24-sheet poster for *House of Wax* (1953).

TOP MIDDLE: British trade advertisement from the August 27, 1953 issue of *Kinematograph Weekly* for Allied Artists' 3-D *The Maze* (Dir: William Cameron Menzies, 1953).

TOP RIGHT: Belgian poster for Warner Bros.' 3-D Edgar Allan Poe adaptation, *Phantom of the Rue Morgue* (Dir: Roy Del Ruth, 1954).

BOTTOM MIDDLE: Window card for 20th Century-Fox's *Gorilla at Large* (Dir: Harmon Jones, 1954), which was shown on US TV in the 1980s in 3-D.

BOTTOM RIGHT: Japanese poster for Warner Bros.' *The Mask* (aka *Eyes of Hell*; Dir: Julian Roffman, 1961), the first horror movie made in Canada.

OPPOSITE: *Creature from the Black Lagoon* (2014), pencil, acrylics, gouache, Prismacolor pencils, and Photoshop by American artist Christopher Franchi. "I feel the Creature is the most amazing 'man-in-a-suit' design of all time," says the artist. "I wanted to do this piece for many years, and I felt the 60th anniversary was a prime excuse."

AMAZING!
STARTLING!
SHOCKING!
RITA
Universal International
PRESENTS
CREATURE FROM THE BLACK LAGOON
IN 3-DIMENSION
RICHARD CARLSON - JULIA ADAMS
RICHARD DENNING - ANTONIO MORENO - NESTOR PAIVA - WHIT BISSELL
DIRECTED BY Jack Arnold SCREENPLAY BY Harry Essex and Arthur Ross PRODUCED BY William Alland A Universal International RELEASE

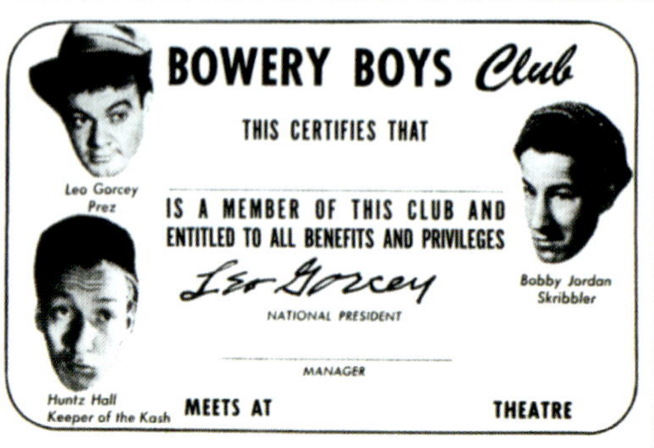

BOWERY BOYS Club

THIS CERTIFIES THAT

IS A MEMBER OF THIS CLUB AND ENTITLED TO ALL BENEFITS AND PRIVILEGES

Leo Gorcey

NATIONAL PRESIDENT

MANAGER

MEETS AT THEATRE

Leo Gorcey Prez

Bobby Jordan Skribbler

Huntz Hall Keeper of the Kash

TOP RIGHT: American half-sheet poster for Monogram Pictures' haunted house comedy *Ghost Chasers* (Dir: William Beaudine, 1951) starring Leo Gorcey and The Bowery Boys, and featuring Lloyd Corrigan as a real ghost who helps them out.

TOP LEFT: Belgian poster for Paramount Pictures' comedy *Scared Stiff* (1953), a remake of *The Ghost Breakers* (1940).

BOTTOM LEFT: The Bowery Boys Club card was issued to patrons by movie theaters in the 1940s and '50s.

BOTTOM, MIDDLE LEFT: Insert poster for Universal-International Pictures' *Abbott and Costello Meet the Invisible Man* (Dir: Charles Lamont, 1951), in which the comedy duo help Arthur Franz's boxer clear himself of a murder charge.

BOTTOM, MIDDLE RIGHT: Insert for Universal-International Pictures' *Abbott and Costello Meet Dr. Jekyll and Mr. Hyde* (Dir: Charles Lamont, 1953), in which Bud and Lou have to deal with both Boris Karloff's Dr. Jekyll and Eddie Parker's Mr. Hyde.

BOTTOM RIGHT: US insert for Universal-International Pictures' *Abbott and Costello Meet the Mummy* (Dir: Charles Lamont, 1955), the final entry in the series. Stuntman-actor Eddie (Edwin) Parker portrayed Klaris, the mummy.

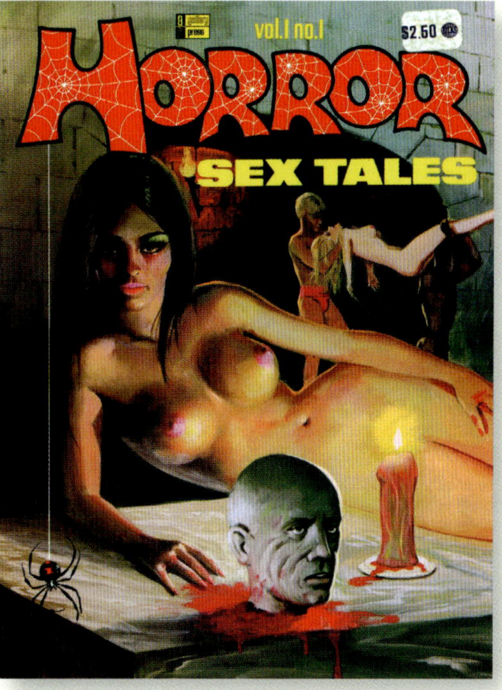

TOP LEFT: German poster for Banner Productions' *Bride of the Monster* (aka *Bride of the Atom*, 1955), written and directed by Edward D. Wood, Jr. (1924–78) and starring his friend Bela Lugosi in his last major movie role as yet another mad scientist.

ABOVE RIGHT: Insert poster for Allied Artists Pictures' *The Bride and the Beast* (Dir: Adrian Weiss, 1958), which was scripted by Ed Wood. Under hypnosis, Charlotte Austin's new bride is revealed to be the Queen of the Gorillas in a former life.

TOP MIDDLE: Ed Wood's most (in)famous movie was DCA's *Plan 9 from Outer Space* (aka *Graverobbers from Outer Space*, 1958), which featured some silent footage of Bela Lugosi shot circa 1955, prior to his death the following year at the age of 73.

BOTTOM LEFT: Ed Wood wrote the script and the tie-in novel for Astra Films' *Orgy of the Dead* (Dir: "A.C. Stephen" [Stephen C. Apostolof], 1965), a nudie burlesque featuring a mummy, a wolfman, and various seductive creatures of the night.

BOTTOM MIDDLE: In 1972, desperate for money, Ed Wood edited and wrote porno fiction (under his own name and pseudonyms) for four illustrated magazines published by Gallery Press, including *Monster Sex Tales* and *Horror Sex Tales*.

KING OF THE GIMMICKS

"It has always amazed and baffled me that audiences will wait patiently in line and pay money to have the wits scared out of them."

William Castle, from his autobiography *Step Right Up! . . . I'm Gonna Scare the Pants Off America* (1976)

WILLIAM CASTLE'S CAREER as a horror *auteur* began at the age of nine, when he discovered that he could scare the other kids at summer camp by bending his double-jointed body into a human spider. At 15, Castle dropped out of high school to become an assistant stage manager for the touring company of *Dracula*, starring Bela Lugosi (who Castle had met when Lugosi was starring on Broadway). The show's producers soon found that the young man's promotional ideas—like putting a coffin in the lobby—were worth their weight in gold.

After working a variety of jobs in the film business, Castle—inspired by the success of Henri-Georges Clouzot's *Les diaboliques* (aka *Diabolique*, 1955)—decided it was time for him to make his own thriller. In 1958, he mortgaged his house, bought the rights to a book called *The Marble Forest* by Anthony Boucher and 11 other mystery authors writing as "Theo Durrant," re-titled it *Macabre*, and shot it in nine days. To promote the film, Castle came up with the idea of insuring anyone who died of fright during a showing for $1,000, and he sold the picture to Allied Artists. After *Macabre* became a hit, Castle hired Vincent Price to star in his next film, *The House on Haunted Hill* (1959); this time the gimmick was "EMERGO," which involved a plastic skeleton being flown on a wire over the audience.

Castle carried on the string of promotional gimmicks for his next films: *The Tingler* (1959) used "PERCEPTO," electric buzzers installed under the seats; *13 Ghosts* (1960) was filmed in "ILLUSION-O," which required audiences to put on cardboard "ghost viewers" to see the film's apparitions; *Homicidal* (1961) employed the "Fright Break," which stopped the film just before the ending and informed audiences that if they were too frightened to continue they had 45 seconds to leave the theater and receive a full refund; and *Mr. Sardonicus* (1961) offered audiences the "Punishment Poll," in which they (apparently) got to vote on the title character's fate. For *Strait-Jacket* (1964), Castle traded in the gimmicks for a Hollywood legend: Joan Crawford, fresh from the success of *What Ever Happened to Baby Jane?* (1962).

A few years later, Castle acquired an advance copy of Ira Levin's novel *Rosemary's Baby*. He immediately dubbed it "one of the most powerful books I've ever read" and

After working a variety of jobs in the film business, Castle—inspired by the success of Henri-Georges Clouzot's *Les diaboliques* (aka *Diabolique*, 1955)—decided it was time for him to make his own thriller . . . To promote the film, Castle came up with the idea of insuring anyone who died of fright during a showing for $1,000.

snagged the rights. Although he intended to both produce and direct, Paramount expressed interest in making the film if Roman Polanski directed. Castle reluctantly agreed to meet the young director, but was won over.

For the first time, Castle was attached to a film that was both a hit *and* a critical success: *Rosemary's Baby* (1968) received an Academy Award nomination for Polanski's screenplay, an Academy Award for Ruth Gordon, and Castle was nominated by the Producers Guild for Producer of the Year. Unfortunately, shortly after he completed *Rosemary's Baby*, Castle fell ill and his career never fully recovered. In 1974 he directed *Shanks*, a zombie film starring French mime Marcel Marceau, and the following year he produced *Bug*, for which he came up with one final gimmick: he insured his lead cockroach for $1,000,000.

Castle passed away in 1977 from a heart attack at the age of 63. *LM*

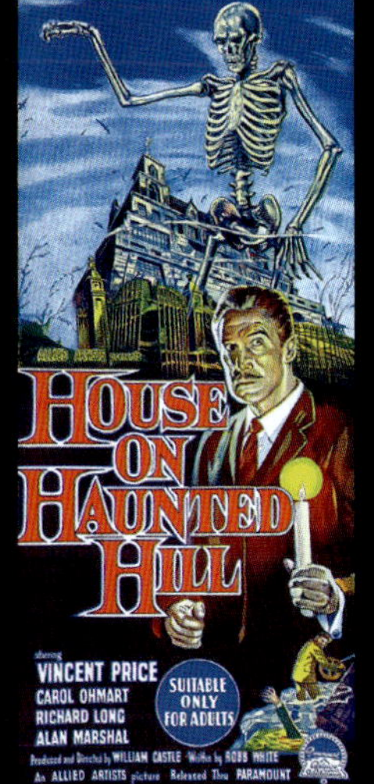

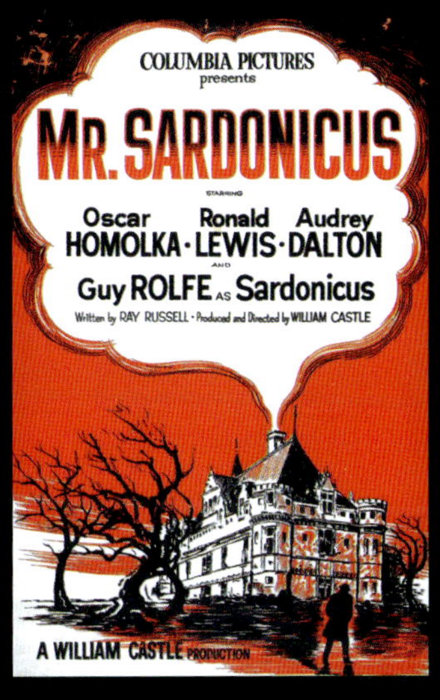

TOP LEFT: Roy Besser's half-sheet poster for William Castle's first horror movie, *Macabre* (1958), which had its own insurance policy from Lloyd's of London offering $1,000 against death by fright of any audience member. So far as we know, nobody ever claimed the money.

BOTTOM LEFT: This Australian daybill for *The House on Haunted Hill* (1958) censored the images of a hanging woman and a severed head. During the movie's initial theatrical engagements, a plastic skeleton would swoop down above the audience.

BOTTOM, MIDDLE LEFT: William Castle told audiences to scream to protect themselves when the titular creature broke loose in the movie theater in *The Tingler* (1959). Meanwhile, a few unlucky patrons discovered that their seats had been wired with electric buzzers!

BOTTOM, MIDDLE RIGHT: William Castle popped up on screen at the end of *Mr. Sardonicus* (1961) to ask the audience to vote on the fate of the eponymous Baron. All known prints have the "No Mercy!" ending, although Castle claimed to have also shot a "Merciful!" resolution.

ABOVE RIGHT: Reynold Brown's one-sheet poster for William Castle's *The Night Walker* (1964) was obviously inspired by Henry Fuseli's 1781 painting, *The Nightmare*, although studio bosses at Universal Pictures still censored the artist's original version.

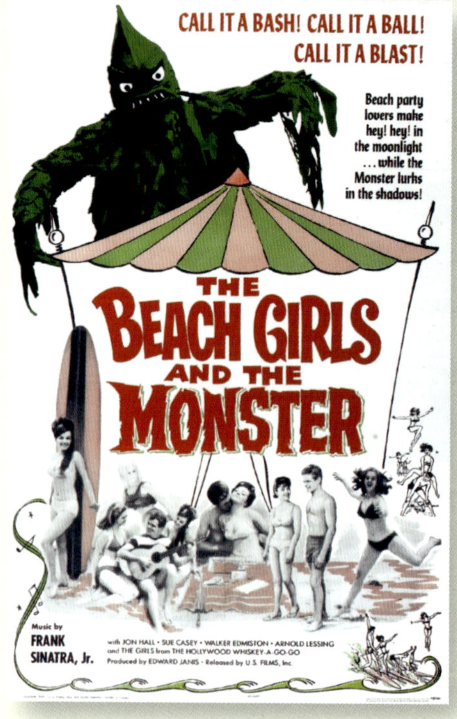

TOP RIGHT: Belgian poster for American International Pictures' *I Was a Teenage Frankenstein* (aka *Teenage Frankenstein*; Dir: Herbert L. Strock, 1957), one of the first 1950s movies to combine traditional horror motifs with rebellious teenagers.

TOP LEFT: Reynold Brown's impressive one-sheet poster for American International Pictures' US release of the British-made teen comedy *The Headless Ghost* (1959), which was shot in just three weeks on the same sets as *Horrors of the Black Museum* (1959).

BOTTOM LEFT: Half-sheet poster for American International Pictures' hot-rod comedy *The Ghost of Dragstrip Hollow* (Dir: William Hole, 1959), in which low-rent monster-maker Paul Blaisdell (1927–83) is unmasked at a teen Halloween dance before a real ghost shows up!

BOTTOM RIGHT: The teen "Beach Party" craze of the mid-1960s resulted in a few horror-themed entries, such as U.S. Films' *The Beach Girls and the Monster* (1964), directed by and starring veteran actor Jon Hall. Frank Sinatra, Jr. supplied the theme tune.

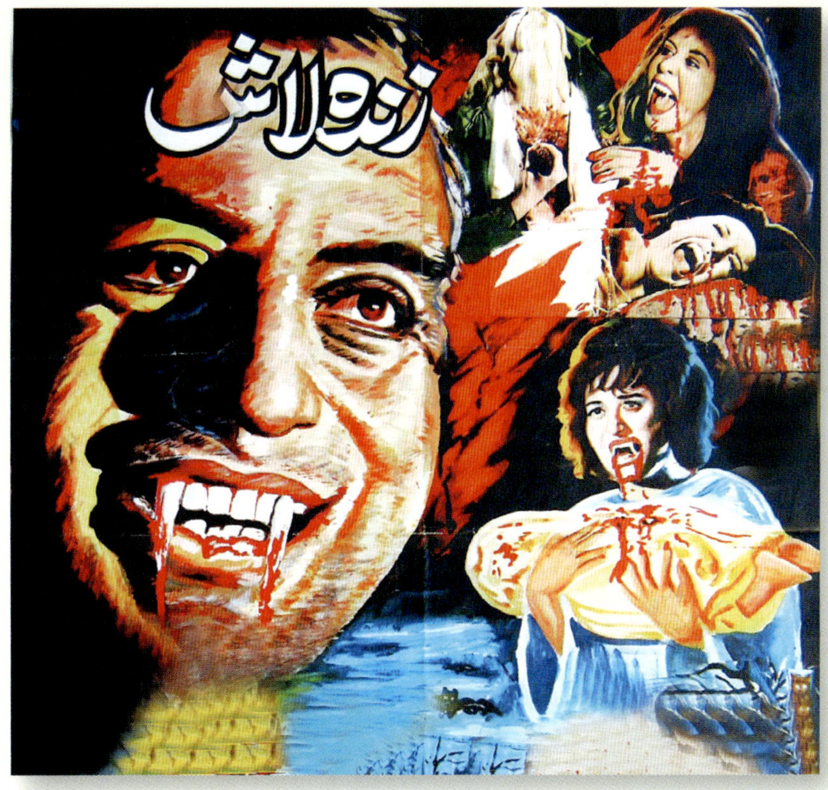

TOP RIGHT: Poster for the Egyptian horror-comedy *Haram Aleyk* (Have Mercy; Dir: Isa Karamah, 1953), which was basically a remake of *Abbott and Costello Meet Frankenstein* (1948) and featured a vampire, a werewolf, and a Frankenstein Monster-like "mummy."

BOTTOM RIGHT: Poster for the Turkish vampire movie *Drakula Istanbul'da* (Dracula in Istanbul; Dir: Mehmet Muhtar, 1953), which was surprisingly faithful to Bram Stoker's uncredited novel. Bald-headed Atif Kaptan became the first screen Dracula to sport fangs.

TOP & BOTTOM LEFT: Pakistani posters for *Zinda Laash* (The Living Corpse; Dir: Khwaja Sarfraz, 1967), an Urdu version of Bram Stoker's novel that is virtually a shot-for-shot remake of Hammer's *Dracula* (1958), with added singing and dancing!

TOP RIGHT: British quad poster for Eros Films' *Womaneater* (Dir: Charles Saunders, 1957), in which George Coulouris's sleazy mad doctor sacrifices his hypnotized female victims to a flesh-eating plant so that he can extract a serum that will revive the dead.

TOP LEFT: American six-sheet poster by artist Joseph "Joe" Smith (1912–2003) for Eros Films' *Blood of the Vampire* (Dir: Henry Cass, 1958), which stars stage actor-manager Sir Donald Wolfit as an undead doctor experimenting on the inmates of an insane asylum.

BOTTOM LEFT: Dynamic Belgian poster for Anglo Amalgamated's *Horrors of the Black Museum* (Dir: Arthur Crabtree, 1959), in which Michael Gough's crazed crime author hypnotizes his assistant to commit the gruesome murders he writes about.

BOTTOM RIGHT: French *grande affiche* for Anglo Amalgamated's lurid British film *Circus of Horrors* (Dir: Sidney Hayers, 1960) by artist Gilbert Allard (aka "Georges"). Anton Diffring plays a mad plastic surgeon who runs a circus as a cover for his surgical operations.

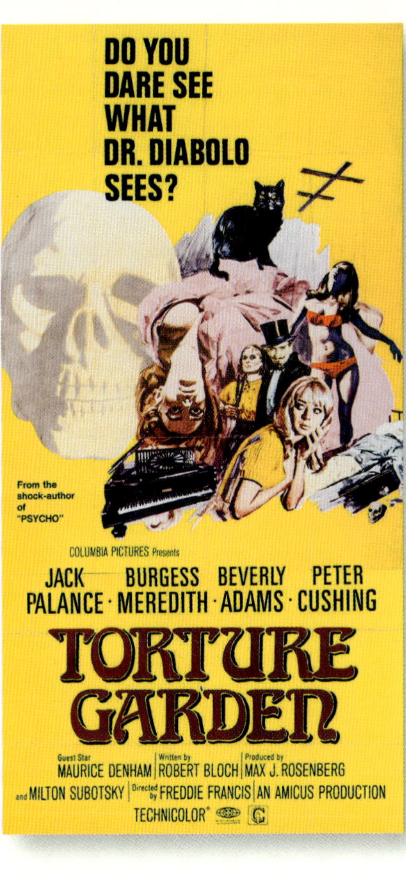

RIGHT: *Torture Garden* (2019), marker and pencil on Bristol board by American artist Frederick Cooper. "I love the Amicus anthology flicks," says the artist, "and the 1967 film *Torture Garden* [ABOVE] has long been an obsession. Burgess Meredith's depiction of Dr. Diabolo is absolutely wicked."

LEFT & OPPOSITE: *Oakley Court* (2018 and 2019), gouache on watercolor paper posters by Graham Humphreys. Built in 1859, the Victorian Gothic manor in Berkshire was the home of Hammer Films in 1949 before the company moved to an adjacent property, which would become Bray Studios.

Hammer still used Oakley Court, most notably in *Brides of Dracula* (1960) [OPPOSITE TOP RIGHT] and *The Reptile* [ABOVE] and *The Plague of the Zombies* (both 1966). It continued to be a film location into the 1970s, most notably in *The Rocky Horror Picture Show* (1975), before being turned into a hotel.

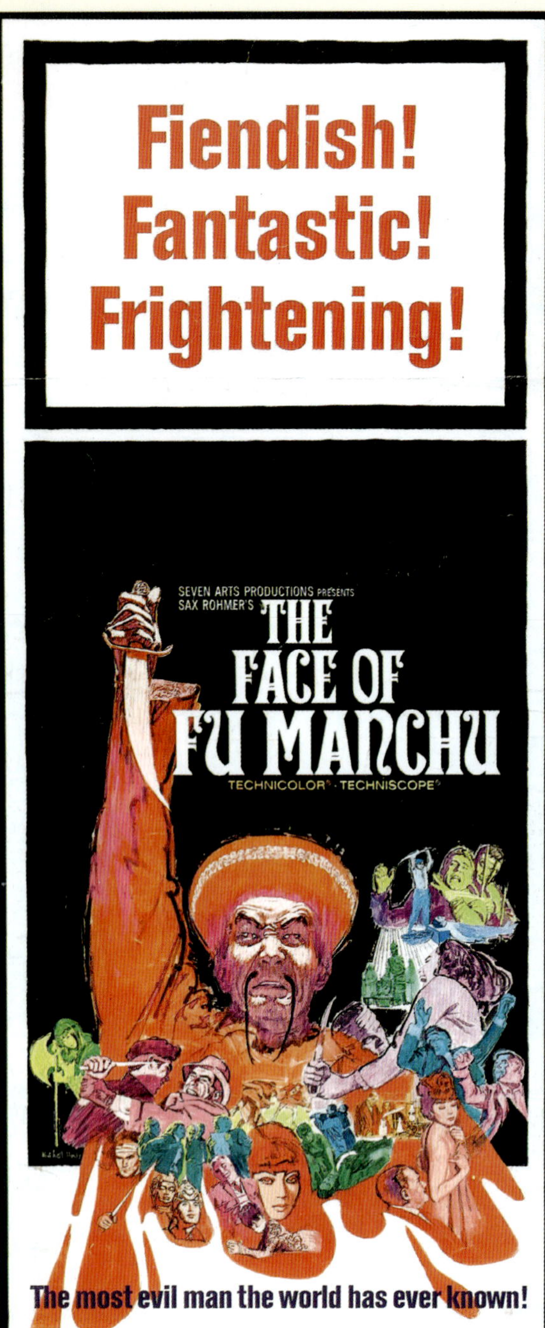

The World Shall Hear from Him Again

Christopher Lee starred as Sax Rohmer's Fu Manchu in five international co-productions produced by Harry Alan Towers (1920–2009), who also scripted them under his regular pseudonym "Peter Welbeck." Aided by his daughter Lin Tang (Tsai Chin), the Oriental devil-doctor was pursued around the world by Nayland Smith of Scotland Yard (Nigel Green, Douglas Wilmer, or Richard Greene) and his faithful sidekick Dr. Petrie (Howard Marion-Crawford). *The Face of Fu Manchu* (Dir: Don Sharp, 1965) [ABOVE LEFT] was filmed in Ireland, and *The Brides of Fu Manchu* (Dir: Don Sharp, 1966) [TOP MIDDLE] was shot in England. *The Vengeance of Fu Manchu* (Dir: Jeremy Summers, 1967) [TOP RIGHT] moved the action to Hong Kong, while both *The Blood of Fu Manchu* (aka *Kiss and Kill*, 1968) [BOTTOM MIDDLE] and *The Castle of Fu Manchu* (1969) [BOTTOM RIGHT] were made on much smaller budgets and filmed on locations in Spain, Brazil, and Turkey by director Jess (Jesús) Franco.

ABOVE LEFT: French *grande affiche* by Italian-born artist Jean Mascii (1926–2003) for Georges Franju's influential mad doctor movie *Les yeux sans visage* (aka *Eyes Without a Face/The Horror Chamber of Dr. Faustus*, 1960), based on the novel by Jean Redon.

TOP MIDDLE: Striking Spanish poster for the Italian/French co-production *Il mulino delle donne di pietra* (aka *Mill of the Stone Women/Drops of Blood*; Dir: Giorgio Ferroni, 1960), about a crazed Dutch sculptor (Wolfgang Preiss) who petrifies his victims.

TOP RIGHT: French reissue *affiche* for the West German *Ein Toter hing im Netz* (aka *Horrors of Spider Island/It's Hot in Paradise*; Dir: Fritz Böttger, 1960), in which the voluptuous survivors of a plane crash are menaced on a remote island by spiders with a transformative bite.

BOTTOM MIDDLE: French *affiche* for the Spanish/French co-production *Gritos en la noche* (aka *The Awful Dr. Orlof/The Demon Doctor*; Dir: Jesús Franco, 1962), the first in a long-running series starring Swiss-born actor "Howard Vernon" (Mario Lippert).

BOTTOM RIGHT: French *grande affiche* by Ukrainian-born artist Constantin Bélinsky (1904–99) for the Italian *Lo spettro* (aka *The Ghost/The Spectre*, 1963), which was sold as a sequel-of-sorts to an earlier film also starring Barbara Steele and directed by Riccardo Freda.

ABOVE LEFT: Italian *maestro* Mario Bava (1914–80) was originally employed as the cinematographer, but stepped in to finish directing *I Vampiri* (aka *Lust of the Vampire*/*The Devil's Commandment*, 1957) when credited director Riccardo Freda left the project after arguing with the producers.

TOP RIGHT: Mario Bava's *I tre volti della paura* (aka *Black Sabbath*, 1963) starred Boris Karloff as a vampire and freely adapted three stories by Anton Chekhov, Aleksei Tolstoy, and Guy de Maupassant. The American version from American International Pictures was re-edited and re-scored.

BOTTOM RIGHT: In his second and final movie with the director, Christopher Lee starred as the ghost of a sadistic nobleman who haunted his masochistic lover (Daliah Lavi) in Mario Bava's stylish and sexy Gothic, *La frusta e il corpo* (aka *The Whip and the Body*/*What*/*Night is the Phantom*, 1963).

IN THE NAME OF SATAN I PLACE A CURSE UPON YOU!

RIGHT: *In the Name of Satan* (2014), silkscreen print by "HagCult" (M. Fersner). "This piece was a tribute to the inimitable Barbara Steele," explains the American artist. "It was inspired by her character in Mario Bava's *La maschera del demonio* (aka *Black Sunday*, 1960) [ABOVE]."

TOP LEFT: 1960 poster for the dubbed Italian release of Mexico's first major horror movie, *El monstruo resucitado* (Dir: Chano Urueta, 1953), in which a horribly disfigured mad doctor uses a revived corpse to get his revenge.

BOTTOM LEFT: *Échenme al vampiro* (aka *Bring Me the Vampire*; Dir: Alfredo B. Crevenna, 1961) was a Mexican old dark house comedy that featured the comedian "Mantequilla" (Fernando Soto) as a fake vampire.

ABOVE RIGHT: "Mantequilla" (Fernando Soto) also turned up as the comedy-relief in the Hammer Films-inspired Mexican horror movie *La invasión de los vampiros* (aka *The Invasion of the Vampires*; Dir: Miguel Morayta, 1961).

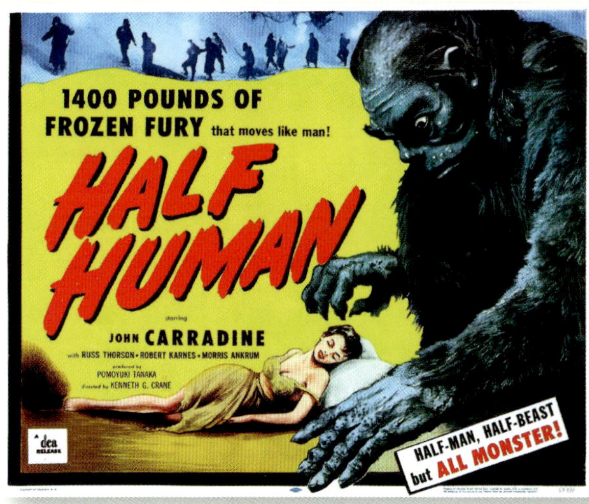

ABOVE LEFT: Japanese STB ("STanding Board poster") for the Toho Company's rarely seen *Jû jin yuki otoko* (Dir: Ishirô Honda, 1955), a *tokusatsu* ("special effects") movie in which a yeti monster attacks an expedition in the Japanese Alps.

TOP MIDDLE: American half-sheet for DCA's *Half Human The Story of the Abominable Snowman* (Dir: Kenneth G. Crane and Inoshiro Honda, 1957), a heavily edited version of *Jû jin yuki otoko* incorporating new footage.

BOTTOM MIDDLE: An American newspaper reporter is the subject of a mad doctor's experiments in United Artists' *The Manster* (aka *The Split*; Dir: George Breakston and Kenneth G. Crane, 1959), which was filmed in Japan.

ABOVE RIGHT: Japanese STB or *tatekan* signboard poster for Toho's *Matango* (aka *Attack of the Mushroom People*; Dir: Ishirô Honda, 1963), loosely inspired by William Hope Hodgson's 1907 short story "The Voice in the Night."

TOP & BOTTOM LEFT: This pair of 1965 British quad posters from Anglo Amalgamated/Warner-Pathé for American International Pictures' *The Tomb of Ligeia* (1964) and *Black Sabbath* (1963), and *Monster of Terror* (aka *Die, Monster, Die!*, 1965) and *The Haunted Palace* (1963), were illustrated by the prolific Tom Chantrell (1916–2001), who reworked Reynold Brown's original US poster designs and is best remembered for his work for Hammer Films and the *Carry On* comedy series.

TOP RIGHT: This 1966 "Shockorama" double-bill from Embassy Pictures featured the final two movies directed by Poverty Row veteran William Beaudine, *Billy the Kid vs. Dracula* and *Jesse James Meets Frankenstein's Daughter*.

BOTTOM RIGHT: This 1972 one-sheet poster for the "Orgy of the Living Dead" triple-bill was conceived and illustrated by film writer/director Alan Ormsby (b. 1943). It consisted of three re-titled, but unrelated, Italian horror movies.

Reel Horrors

During the 1960s, the only way that horror fans could watch their favorite films when they wanted to was through 8mm home movies—200-feet cut-downs of classic titles issued by New York's Castle Films and other companies (such as Ken Films Distributors of New Jersey). In the late 1940s, Castle Films had become a subsidiary of Universal Pictures, which led to the company issuing Universal's library of horror films from 1959 onwards. Available in camera shops, department stores, and through mail-order advertisements in the back of *Famous Monsters of Filmland* and other magazines, these often skillfully edited condensations featured original box art and could be projected at home. Usually released in black and white with superimposed subtitles, later innovations included the enhanced "Super 8" format and the addition of color and synchronized sound. However, by the mid-1980s, the advent of home video had brought an end to the industry, which once had an annual gross of more than $130 million.

TOP MIDDLE: "Spook Shows" were a popular entertainment across America from the 1940s until the late 1960s. These predominantly midnight stage performances often combined magic tricks with actors dressed-up in monster costumes and screenings of old horror movies.

TOP RIGHT: In 1947, Bela Lugosi appeared in his agent Don Marlowe's touring 45-minute stage production of Edgar Allan Poe's *The Tell-Tale Heart*, paired with screenings of *Dracula* (1931). This Michigan performance was cancelled when the actor became ill.

BOTTOM MIDDLE: Bela Lugosi's ill-fated "Big Horror and Magic" revue ran from December 1950 until March 1951 in the towns of Trenton and Camden, New Jersey, and included a screening of *The Ape Man* (1943) under its working title *They Creep in the Dark*.

BOTTOM RIGHT: 68-year-old Bela Lugosi traveled to Britain in 1951 to star in a stage revival of *Dracula*. Although the production was supposed to play the prestigious West End in London, it ended up touring the provinces for six months before closing.

ABOVE LEFT: Australian poster advertising the "Spook Show," *Dr. Dracula's Living Nightmares*, featuring magician and hypnotist Card Mondor (1922–2001) and his wife, Donna Haynes. The midnight road show toured from the late 1940s until the early 1950s.

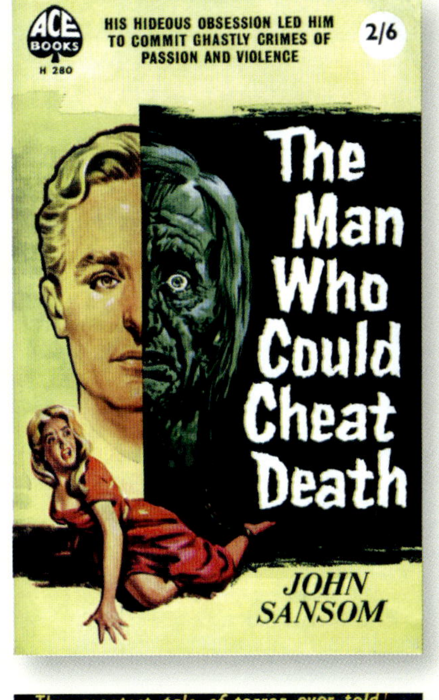

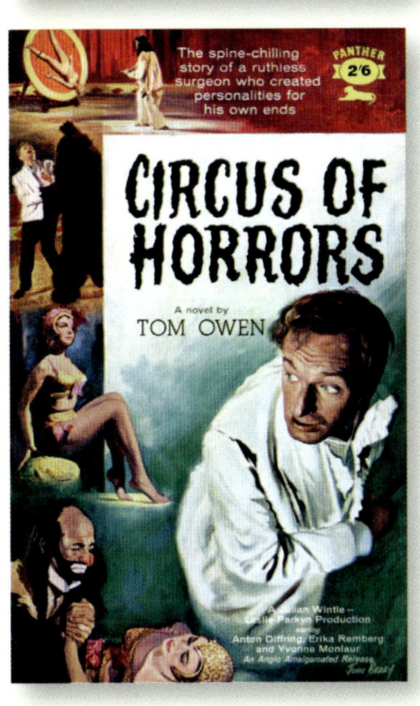

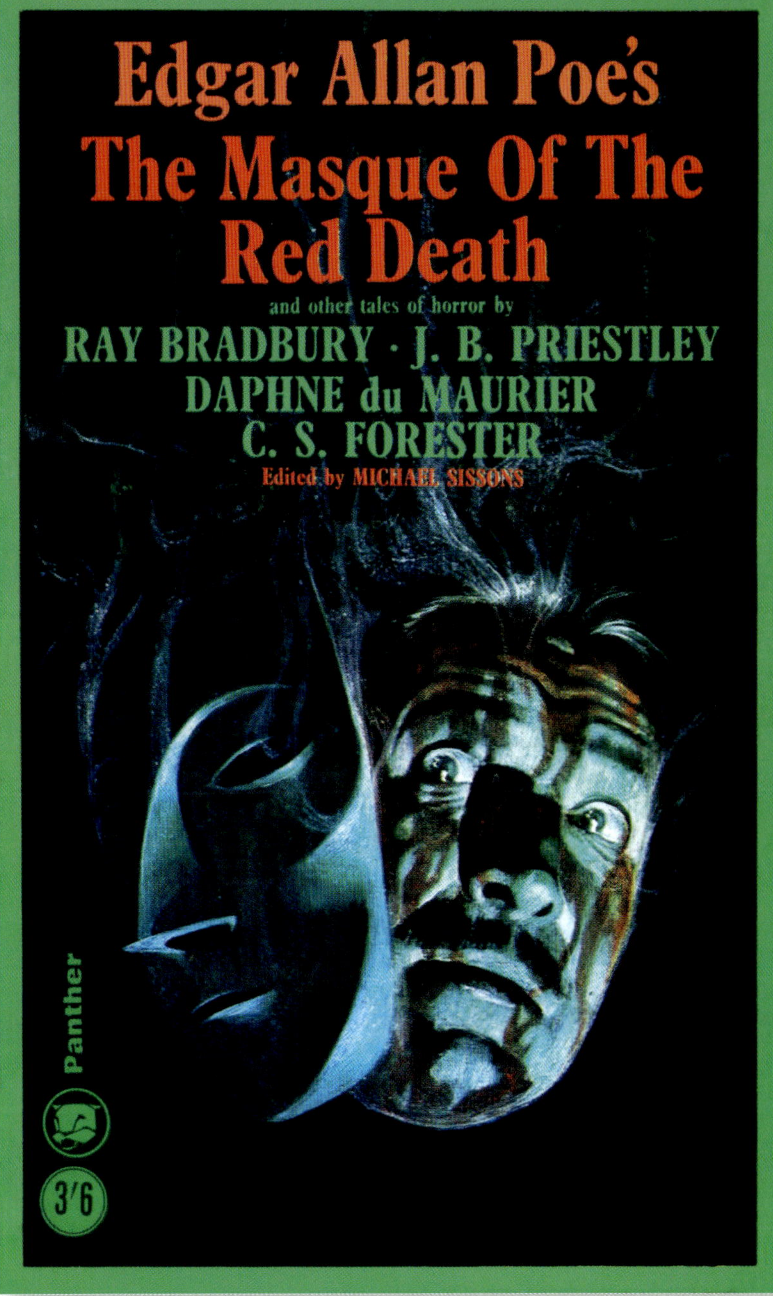

TOP LEFT: The cover to this UK paperback of Hammer's *The Revenge of Frankenstein* (Panther, 1958) is an early work by British artist Josh Kirby (1928–2001). The novelization is only credited to screenwriters Jimmy Sangster (1927–2011) and Hurford Janes (1909–2000).

TOP MIDDLE: The British paperback tie-in to Hammer's *The Man Who Could Cheat Death* (Ace Books, 1959) is credited to screenwriter Jimmy Sangster's pseudonym "John Sansom" but copyrighted by Sangster and playwright "Barré Lyndon" (Alfred Edgar).

BOTTOM LEFT: The two 1960 Panther UK paperback printings of the *Circus of Horrors* tie-in by "Tom Owen" (Peter Watts, 1919–83) featured this cover by future Royal portrait painter John Leslie Berry (1920–2009) and art previously used on *The Haunted Strangler*.

BOTTOM MIDDLE: The cover art for the UK paperback edition of the Edgar Allan Poe collection *The Pit and the Pendulum* (Digit Books, 1962) was based on Reynold Brown's movie poster for the 1961 Roger Corman movie for American International Pictures starring Vincent Price.

ABOVE RIGHT: *The Masque of the Red Death and Other Tales of Horror* (Panther 1964) was an unusual UK paperback tie-in to the Roger Corman movie as it was actually an anthology of classic horror stories edited by Michael Sissons (1934–2018).

7

PULP FICTION

JUSTIN MARRIOTT

"One is always considered mad when one says or does something which others cannot comprehend." He laughed, and the sound was the rattling of skeletons and the thunder of the tomb.

ORGY OF THE DEAD (1966) BY EDWARD D. WOOD, JR.

> "The Penguin books are splendid value for sixpence, so splendid that if other publishers had any sense they would combine against them and suppress them."
>
> George Orwell

DURING THE LATE 1940s, following World War II, the paperback format became increasingly popular with the public in America and the UK, and the pulp magazines—already beset by paper shortages and rising production costs—went from a position of market dominance to the way of the dinosaurs by the middle of the following decade.

Perhaps the most significant event in signaling this decline was the shutdown in 1949 of all the pulp titles from Street & Smith, who had been one of the largest and most successful publishers in the field. Paperbacks—and to a lesser extent the digest magazines, which were miniaturized versions of the pulps—became the go-to format for readers in search of thrills and chills.

The paperback had already established itself in the UK in the late 1930s, as Penguin Books enjoyed success by following a model trailblazed by pioneering German publisher Tauchnitz. Penguin's growing operation of exporting titles to America had been halted by the vigilance of German U-boats during the war, and this led them to setting up an American office.

By the time Penguin took flight, an innovative businessman by the name of Robert de Graff had beaten them to the American shelves with his own softcover line, Pocket Books, based on an ambitious model that offered paperbacks at just 25 cents apiece (thus undercutting traditional hardcover prices) and sold books outside the traditional distribution channels. Dependent upon large print runs to secure a cheap cost per unit, the gamble paid off and was a huge success, to the extent that what we now call paperbacks were known as "pocket books" for many years.

Sensing there was a new game in town, figures from the pulp magazine industry also launched their own paperback imprints. Ned Pines of Thrilling Publications started Popular Library, recruiting science fiction pulp editors Leo Margulies and Charles Heckleman onto his staff. Dell, which had enjoyed a successful couple of decades in comics and magazines, launched a paperback line in 1942. The Dell "mapbacks," with their cover icon of a keyhole and back-cover maps illustrating key scenes from the book, are now part of vintage paperback folklore.

One hugely significant recruit from the pulp magazines was Donald A. Wollheim, who was welcomed by the newly formed Avon Publications, which had been created by a distributor in response to losing their lucrative contract to supply Pocket Books to stores. Wollheim reprinted prime material from the pulps in *Avon Fantasy Reader* and edited *The Girl with the Hungry Eyes*, which was probably the first all-original horror collection in paperback. He left Avon in 1952 to play a key role in the formation of the now legendary Ace Books.

In addition to these early paperback houses, another significant development during the '40s was the series of Armed Services Editions that were distributed for free to serving GIs as part of the war effort. With over 1,200 titles released, they were mainly reprints of hardcovers (with some originals mixed in for the short story collections), including the works of noted authors of the macabre such as H.P. Lovecraft, Algernon Blackwood, and August Derleth.

> Claiming to be based on real events, the luridly painted covers often utilized horror motifs, such as grisly scenes of animals attacking explorers or sexually sadistic images of half-naked women being tortured.

In the 1950s a new generation of paperback publishers emerged, evolving and building on the work of Pocket, Avon, Penguin, and the Armed Services Editions. One of the most significant of the new breed was Gold Medal, an imprint set up by Fawcett, which had been around since 1919 with a long line of magazines and comics. Fawcett had been successfully distributing New American Library (NAL) books (the rebranded American arm of Penguin), and were hungry for a slice of the paperback action but bound by a contract not to directly compete with NAL.

Fawcett's way of navigating this restriction was to launch an imprint that, rather than reprint hardbacks, which NAL and other publishers had done until now, exclusively published paperback originals. With an unashamedly populist stance in their packaging and content, the Gold Medals were a phenomenon and started a trend toward paperback originals.

Another innovation was from the newly formed Ace Books, set up by A.A. Wynn, an experienced publisher in the comics and magazine field. Bolstered by the recruitment of Donald Wollheim, they pioneered the "Ace Double," which ran two novels back-to-back in one binding.

PREVIOUS SPREAD: ***Zacherley's Midnight Snacks*** **(1960), acrylic cover by American artist Richard M. Powers for the Ballantine Books anthology of the same title, edited by TV horror host John Zacherle (1918–2016). Powers would often "crop" his paintings to improve the composition before he sold the originals, which was the case with this one.**

TOP MIDDLE & RIGHT: Movie director Alfred Hitchcock "edited" numerous anthologies over the years. The 1946 mapback *Bar the Doors: Terror Stories* from Dell Publishing Company was actually ghost-edited by Don Ward. It featured a cover by Gerald Gregg and the map on the back cover was based on the Sierra Leone jungle setting from the 1895 story "Pollock and the Porroh Man" by H.G. Wells. Other tales were by F. Marion Crawford, Ambrose Bierce, and August Derleth.

ABOVE LEFT: Published in 1947 by Pocket Books, *The Pocket Book of Ghost Stories* was edited by American author and Civil War historian Philip Van Doren Stern, who wrote the story that inspired the movie *It's a Wonderful Life* (1946).

BOTTOM MIDDLE: In 1949 Dell Books published H.G. Wells's 1897 novel *The Invisible Man* in its series of mapbacks, with a map of the Sussex village of Iping on the back cover. The story was originally serialized in *Pearson's Weekly*.

BOTTOM RIGHT: Ann Cantor's cover for *The Girl with the Hungry Eyes and Other Stories* (Avon Publishing Co., Inc., 1949), edited by an uncredited Donald A. Wollheim, which took its title from a story by Fritz Leiber, Jr., the son of the Hollywood actor.

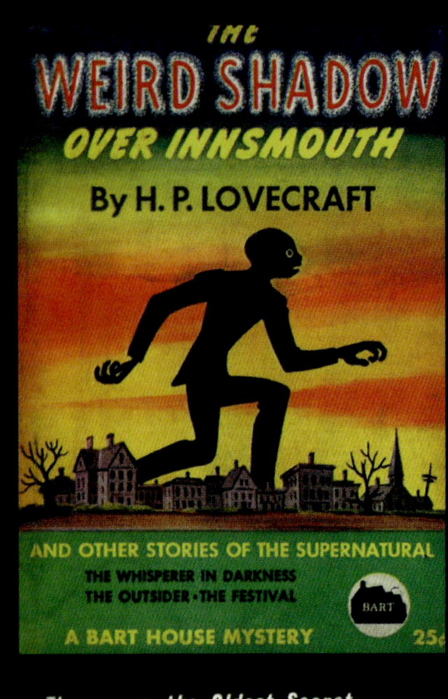

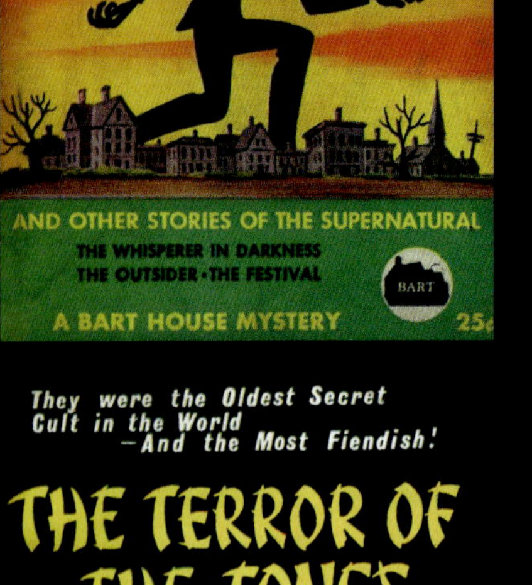

TOP LEFT: Published in 1944 by Bart House, *The Weird Shadow Over Innsmouth and Other Stories of the Supernatural* contained a retitling of the novella "The Shadow Over Innsmouth" (1936) and four other stories by H.P. Lovecraft.

TOP MIDDLE: The first paperback of Fritz Leiber's *Conjure Wife*, from Lion Books in 1953, featured an early cover by an uncredited Robert A. Maguire. The novel was first published in the pulp magazine *Unknown Worlds* (April, 1943).

ABOVE RIGHT: The September 1954 digest edition of *Weird Tales* was the final issue of the original run, which had started in March 1923. The cover artwork by Virgil Finlay was a reprint from the August 1939 issue of the magazine.

BOTTOM LEFT: British artist Robert A. Osborne expertly captured star Christopher Lee for the cover of the anonymous Hammer Film tie-in, *The Terror of the Tongs* (Digit Books, 1962), "Based on the Screenplay by Jimmy Sangster."

BOTTOM MIDDLE: A cover artist who signed himself "Green" was obviously inspired by Hammer's *The Revenge of Frankenstein* for his paperback cover of H.P. Lovecraft's *The Haunter of the Dark and Other Tales of Terror* (Panther Books, 1963).

Throughout the march of the paperbacks during the 1940s and '50s, the newly dominant medium offered slim pickings for US fans of horror fiction, who still had to rely upon the venerable *Weird Tales*, which inevitably went to digest format before it eventually folded in 1954. Other digest magazines featuring, but not dedicated to, horror fiction included the earliest issues of *Fantastic* (1952–80) from Ziff-Davis, the ten issues of *Beyond Fantasy Fiction* (1953–55) from Galaxy Publishing, the cheesecake *Imaginative Tales* (1954–58) from William Hamling, who would soon form sleaze paperback giant Greenleaf, and four issues of *Fantasy Magazine/Fantasy Fiction* (1953) from Future Publications.

Readers in search of horror-tinged material were also served to an extent by the "Men's Adventure Magazine" market, also known as the "sweats." Claiming to be based on real events, the luridly painted covers often utilized horror motifs, such as grisly scenes of animals attacking explorers or sexually sadistic images of half-naked women being tortured. These were tremendously popular, with an estimated 130 titles being published each month at their peak in the 1950s.

Now celebrated due to the kitschy nature of their contents, which received little editorial guidance, their position as the most prolific publisher of traditional horror during that era through their *Supernatural Stories* series (1954–67) is often overlooked.

All was not lost for the connoisseur of dark fantasy, as a number of classics did appear in paperback during this fallow period, including Fritz Leiber's *Conjure Wife*, Shirley Jackson's *The Lottery*, Guy Endore's *The Werewolf of Paris*, H.P. Lovecraft's *The Weird Shadow Over Innsmouth*, *The Dunwich Horror* and *The Lurking Fear*, and Richard Matheson's *I Am Legend*.

The term "classic" is not often applied to Badger Books, the shoestring UK operation that grew in the fertile garden of "the mushroom publishers" that bloomed in post-war Britain. Now celebrated due to the kitschy nature of its titles' contents, which received little editorial guidance, Badger's position as the most prolific publisher of traditional horror during that era through their *Supernatural Stories* series (1954–67) is often overlooked.

Another penny-pinching UK operation of note from the 1950s was Digit Books, which published a series of interesting horror tie-ins and SF/horror mash-ups. Pedigree, Consul and WDL also published horror fiction.

In the 1960s there was an explosion in horror paperbacks, initially influenced by the growing power of the movies, with *Psycho* (1960) terrifying cinema audiences and popular TV shows such as the Boris Karloff-hosted *Thriller* (1960–62) looking to *Weird Tales* for inspiration.

Movie tie-ins became big business, with Lancer linking in with Roger Corman's Edgar Allan Poe adaptations, semi-sleaze publisher Monarch Books sexing-up monster movies such as *Gorgo* and *Konga* (both 1961), and from obscure Chicago-based Novel Books came four Herschell Gordon Lewis tie-ins that are now impossibly rare.

The paperback houses were quick to respond, including a number of new entrants into the market. Ballantine launched its "Chamber of Horror" line characterized by Richard Powers-painted covers and including classic works by Sarban, Manly Wade Wellman, and Theodore Sturgeon, as well as top-quality anthologies. Belmont issued a series of collections from two of *Weird Tales*'s finest in the form of Robert Bloch and Frank Belknap Long.

In the UK, Panther began a program of reprinting the *Weird Tales* school of authors, promoting the likes of H.P. Lovecraft and Clark Ashton Smith to a whole new audience. Pan took a turn for the nasty with their long-running anthology series *The Pan Book of Horror Stories* (1959–89), which was hugely successful and widely imitated on both sides of the Atlantic, while Fontana launched the most sustained rival to Pan with 20 volumes of *The Fontana Book of Great Ghost Stories* (1964–84) and 17 volumes of *The Fontana Book of Great Horror Stories* (1966–84).

New English Library curated the UK's most interesting and original series of horror titles, with inventively themed anthologies and an invaluable program of bringing classic Gothics back into print. Corgi was an underappreciated publisher of horror paperbacks, primarily reprints of US titles that were otherwise unseen in the UK, with a focus on Robert Bloch, Shirley Jackson, and Richard Matheson.

Australia enjoyed the best of both worlds, importing UK and US titles while also producing their own paperbacks. Horwitz was the biggest and most successful, issuing horror anthologies as early as 1961.

The pulps were revived in the pages of the Acme Publishing digest magazines edited by Robert A.W. Lowndes—titles such as *Magazine of Horror* (1963–71) and *Startling Mystery Stories* (1966–71), whose miniscule budgets forced him to raid the pages of lesser-known pulps such as *Strange Tales* and a catalogue of authors like David H. Keller and Seabury Quinn. When the purse strings were loosened to allow the purchase of new material, Lowndes showed exquisite taste, publishing an early story by Ramsey Campbell as well as debuts by F. Paul Wilson and a certain Stephen King.

The pulps may have turned to dust and many of the fledgling paperback houses closed, but during the 1970s and '80s, King would come to dominate the bestseller lists, as horror fiction continued its growth as a literary form and as a commercially successful genre.

TOP LEFT: This Armed Services, Inc. edition of editor August Derleth's 1944 anthology *Sleep No More* dropped the interior illustrations by Lee Brown Coye. These pocket-sized paperbacks were issued free to members of the American Armed Forces serving overseas between 1943–47.

TOP RIGHT: Striking *trompe-l'œil* cover for an illustrated edition of *The Best of Edgar Allan Poe* (1945), one of 48 titles in Royce Publishers' Quick Readers series of miniature paperbacks issued between 1943–45 for distribution to American troops serving overseas.

BOTTOM LEFT: George Mayers's bizarre cover for the early Avon Book Company paperback anthology *Terror at Night: 13 Tales of Mystery and Imagination* (1947) edited by Herbert Williams. It included stories by H.P. Lovecraft, Bram Stoker, M.R. James, and Algernon Blackwood.

BOTTOM MIDDLE: Ronald Searle did the cover for this second, expanded 1947 printing of the Pan Books anthology *Tales of the Supernatural*, first published two years earlier. The uncredited editor included classic stories by M.R. James, Hugh Walpole, and Edward Bulwer Lytton.

BOTTOM RIGHT: Herman E. Bischoff produced the striking cover for the Bantam Books anthology *Shot in the Dark* (1950) edited by science fiction writer Judith Merril. An eclectic mix of genre fiction, it featured writers such as Edgar Allan Poe, Ray Bradbury, Leigh Brackett, and Gerald Kersh.

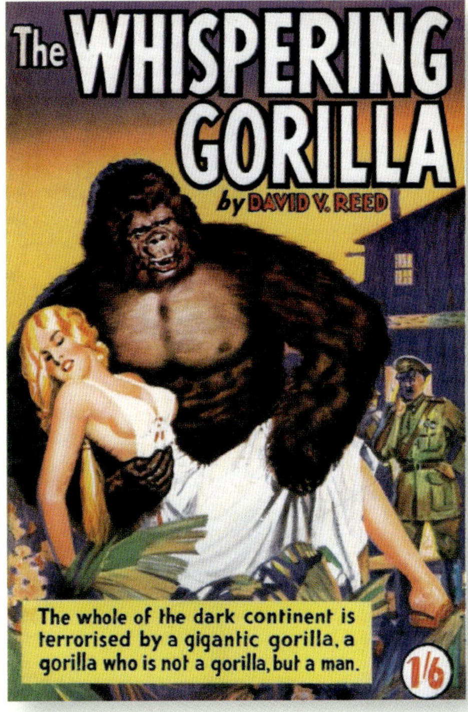

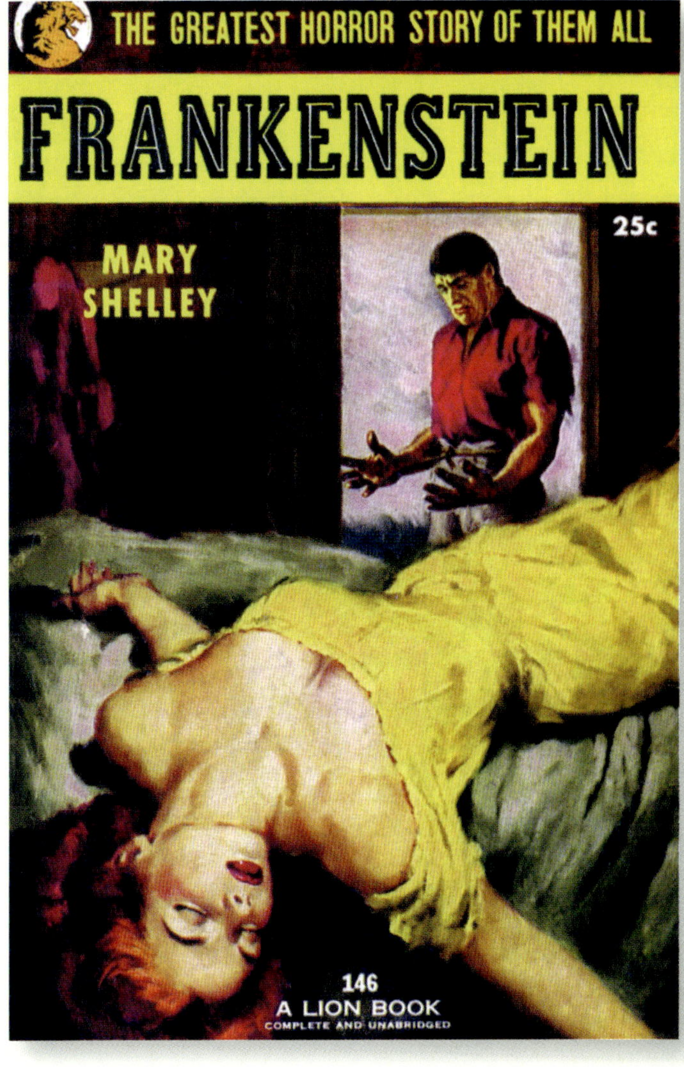

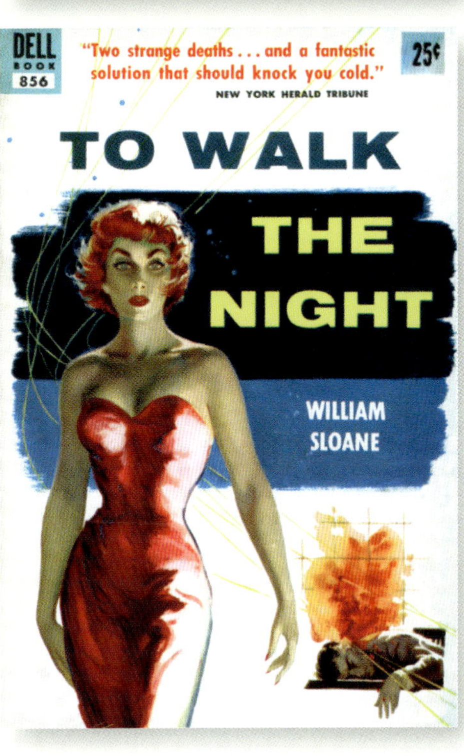

TOP LEFT: Artist William Shoyer aimed his saucy cover at a more contemporary readership for Bantam Books' 1949 paperback of Sir Arthur Conan Doyle's Sherlock Holmes novel *The Hound of the Baskervilles*, originally serialized in *The Strand Magazine* (August 1901–April 1902).

TOP MIDDLE: Originally published as "Return of the Whispering Gorilla" in the February 1943 edition of *Fantastic Adventures*, David V. Reed's sequel to a 1940 story by Don Wilcox in the same American pulp magazine was issued as a paperback in the UK by World Distributors in 1950.

BOTTOM LEFT: The 1933 historical horror novel *The Werewolf of Paris* by "Guy Endore" (Samuel Goldstein) was one of 14 paperback titles published (circa 1952) in Canada by Toronto's Studio Publications, with nary a lycanthrope to be glimpsed on the cover.

ABOVE RIGHT: Following an Armed Services edition in 1946, Lion Books issued the first true paperback of Mary Shelley's *Frankenstein* in 1953, with a decidedly pulp-ish cover painting that was actually a contemporary interpretation of a similar image on the dust jacket of the 1931 photoplay edition.

BOTTOM MIDDLE: William Rose's sexy cover for Dell Publishing Company, Inc.'s paperback edition of *To Walk the Night* (1954) depicted the mysterious *femme fatale* of William M. Sloane's 1937 cross-genre novel, now with an Introduction by literary critic and anthologist Basil Davenport.

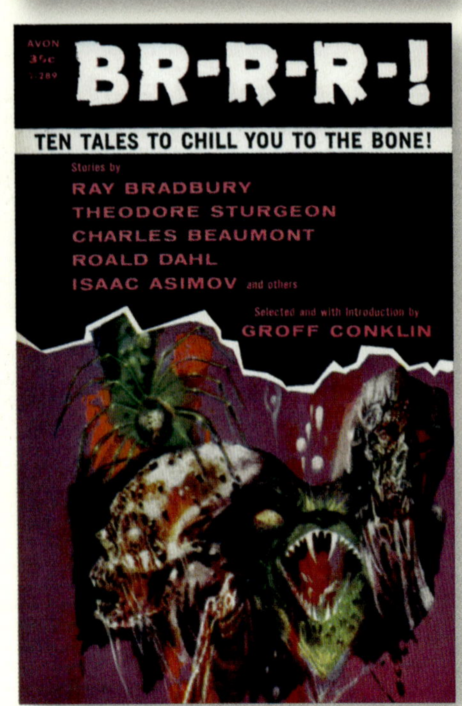

ABOVE RIGHT: The Avon Book Company reused Paul Stahr's unrelated cover for the May 10, 1930 issue of *Argosy Weekly* (see p74) for *Murder Mystery Monthly* (1945), a digest-sized paperback that reprinted *The Ship of Ishtar* by A. (Abraham) Merritt, which was originally serialized over six installments in the *Argosy All-Story Weekly* in 1924.

TOP LEFT: Atmospheric cover for the *Avon Ghost Reader* (Avon Book Company, 1946), an early paperback anthology edited by an uncredited Herbert Williams and featuring 12 reprinted stories by H.P. Lovecraft, August Derleth, M.R. James, Bram Stoker, A. Merritt, F. Scott Fitzgerald, Stephen Vincent Benét, and other literary writers.

BOTTOM LEFT: Edited by Groff Conklin, *Br-r-r-!* (Avon Publications, Inc., 1959) had a cover by Richard Powers and contained ten stories drawn from often more contemporary sources by, among others, Theodore Sturgeon, Charles Beaumont, Ray Bradbury, Roald Dahl, and a collaboration between Isaac Asimov and Frederik Pohl from *Weird Tales*.

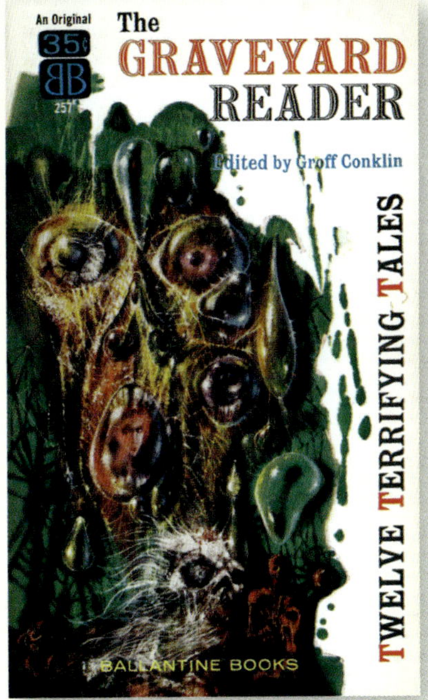

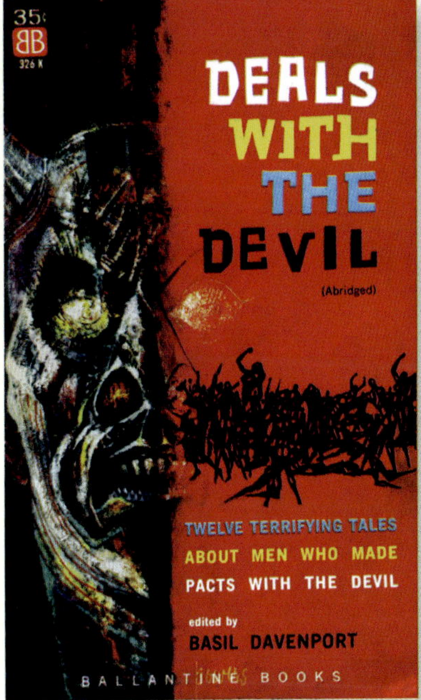

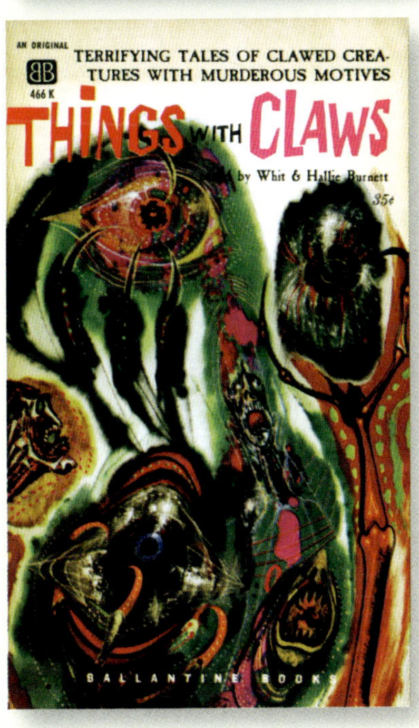

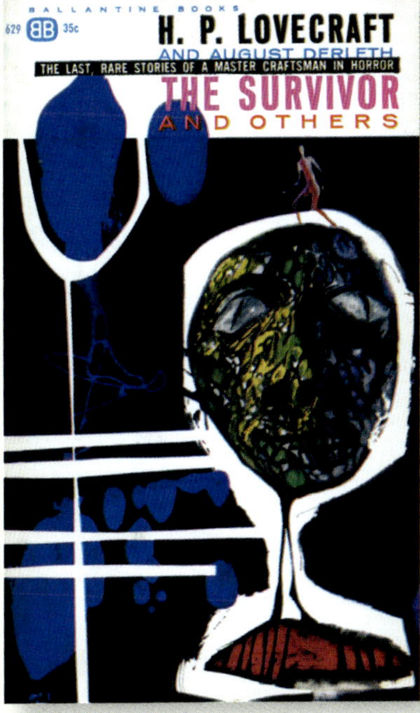

Powers of Darkness

Chicago-born Richard M. Powers (1921–96) was one of the most influential science fiction artists of all time. During the 1950s and '60s he worked as an unofficial art director for Ballantine Books, the innovative American publishing company founded in 1952 by married couple Ian and Betty Ballantine. Inspired by visits to New York's Museum of Modern Art and the surrealist and cubist movements (especially the work of Pablo Picasso and Yves Tanguy), Powers's instantly recognizable abstract expressionist and avant-garde style graced the covers of literally hundreds of SF and horror titles from Ballantine and elevated the look of mass-market paperbacks to the realm of fine art.

TOP LEFT: Groff Conklin's *The Graveyard Reader* (Ballantine Books, 1958) took its title from an original story by Theodore Sturgeon.

TOP MIDDLE: Credited to Basil Davenport, *Twelve Stories from Deals with the Devil* (Ballantine Books, 1959) was ghost-edited by Albert P. Blaustein (aka Allen DeGraeff).

TOP RIGHT: *Stories from The Other Passenger* (Ballantine Books, 1961) collected half the tales Scottish writer John Keir Cross first published in hardcover in 1944.

BOTTOM LEFT: *Things with Claws* (Ballantine Books, 1961) was the second of two anthologies co-edited by Whit and Hallie Burnett.

BOTTOM MIDDLE: *The Survivor and Others* (Ballantine Books, 1962) featured seven "posthumous collaborations" between H.P. Lovecraft and August Derleth.

BOTTOM RIGHT: *The Fiend in You* (Ballantine Books, 1962) was edited by Charles Beaumont and an uncredited William F. Nolan.

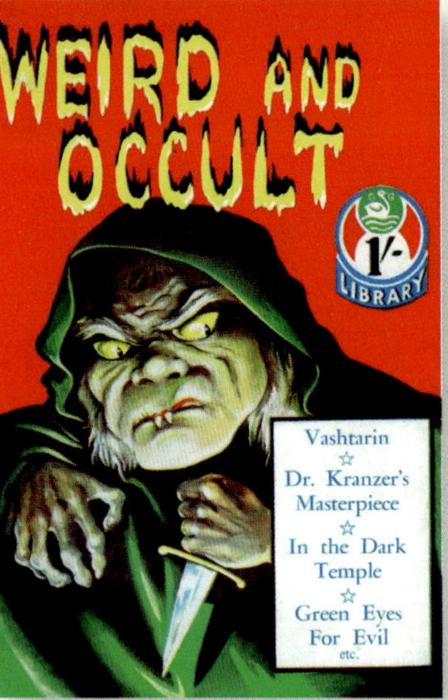

TOP MIDDLE: Cover by Alva Rogers for the British chapbook *Romance in Black* by "Gans T. Field" (Manly Wade Wellman), issued by Utopian Publications Ltd. in 1946. It was first published as "The Black Drama" in *Weird Tales* (June 1938).

TOP RIGHT: The first British paperback of Richard Matheson's 1954 dystopian vampire novel *I Am Legend* (Corgi Books, 1956) was the only edition of the book to feature this striking cover artwork by Corgi's art director, John Richards.

ABOVE LEFT: Dennis Wheatley's classic 1934 novel *The Devil Rides Out* received its second British paperback publication in 1958 from Arrow Books. The volume included an author's warning to the reader against practicing Satanism!

BOTTOM MIDDLE: A garish cover by the prolific S. (Stephen) R. (Richard) Boldero for the 1960 UK paperback edition of Gerald Verner's 1946 witchcraft and sorcery anthology *Prince of Darkness*, published by Pedigree Books.

BOTTOM RIGHT: The first issue of *Weird and Occult Library* (1960), one of four 64-page pocket-sized booklets featuring mostly unpublished fiction that prolific UK imprint Gerald G. Swan, Ltd. had acquired in the 1940s and stockpiled.

Badger's Set of Books

Following the demise of the pulp magazines in the 1950s, Samuel Assael's British shoestring imprint John Spencer & Co. switched to pocket books, producing numerous titles in most of the popular fiction genres. Between 1954–67 the company published 109 monthly issues of the paperback magazine *Supernatural Stories* using a small stable of writers—most notably John S. Glasby (1928–2011) and R.L. Fanthorpe (b. 1935)—hiding behind multiple pseudonyms. Originally having started out as anthologies of short stories, with issue No. 29, the series also began to include novels as "Supernatural Specials."

TOP LEFT: Ray Theobald's cover for *Out of This World: Supernatural Stories* No. 17 (Badger Books, 1958) illustrated Robert Lionel Fanthorpe's novelette "Call of the Werwolf" [*sic*]. The other four stories were also by him under pseudonyms.

BOTTOM LEFT: The possibly pseudonymous artist Ray Theobald's cover for *Supernatural Stories* No. 28 (1959) was clearly inspired by the Creature from the Black Lagoon. The entire issue was written by John S. Glasby under five names.

ABOVE RIGHT: Artist D. Rainey obviously used Christopher Lee from the 1960 movie *The City of the Dead* as the inspiration for his cover on *Supernatural Stories* No. 43 (1961). R.L. Fanthorpe wrote four of the five stories in this issue.

ABOVE: *The Third Pan Book of Horror Stories* edited by Herbert van Thal (Pan Books Ltd., 1962) featured the first of four covers that enigmatic British artist William Francis Phillips contributed to the series.

LEFT: *The Pan Book of Horror Stories* (2015), oils on board by Les Edwards (b. 1949). "This was painted as a nostalgic tribute to *The Pan Book of Horror Stories*," explains the British artist, "a seminal influence on so many of us. Other publishers created their own lines of horror stories, but none achieved the iconic status or were as long-running as the Pan series."

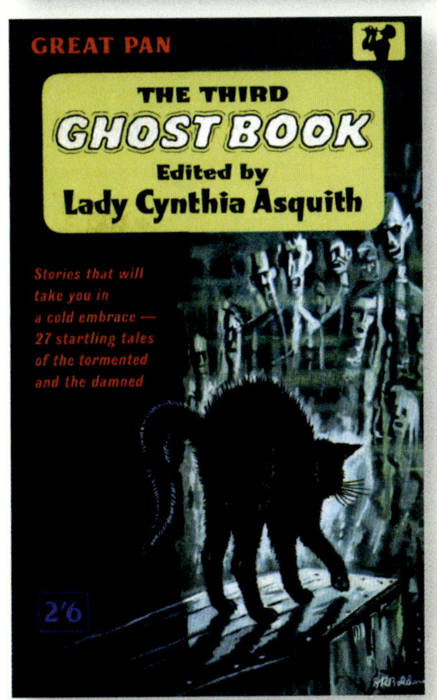

TOP LEFT: British editor and publisher Herbert "Bertie" van Thal (1904–83) edited the paperback *A Book of Strange Stories* for Pan Books Ltd. in 1954. It featured a cover by Prussian-born artist "Sax" (Rudolph Michael Sachs, 1897–1969).

TOP MIDDLE: The first volume of *The Pan Book of Horror Stories*, edited by Herbert van Thal and published as a "Pan Giant" in 1959. He went on to edit a further 24 volumes of the popular horror anthology series, until 1984.

ABOVE RIGHT: Arrow Books' 1960 British paperback of Christine Campbell Thomson's *Not at Night* was not a reprint of the editor's 1925 anthology of the same name, but contained different stories selected from the original hardcover series.

BOTTOM LEFT: S. (Stephen) R. (Richard) Boldero (1898–1987) supplied the cover art for the early 1960s "Great Pan" paperback reprintings of *The Third Ghost Book* (1955), edited by Lady Cynthia Asquith (1887–1960).

BOTTOM MIDDLE: The 1965 British paperback edition of August Derleth's 1952 anthology *Night's Yawning Peal* was published by Consul Books but omitted H.P. Lovecraft's posthumous novella "The Case of Charles Dexter Ward."

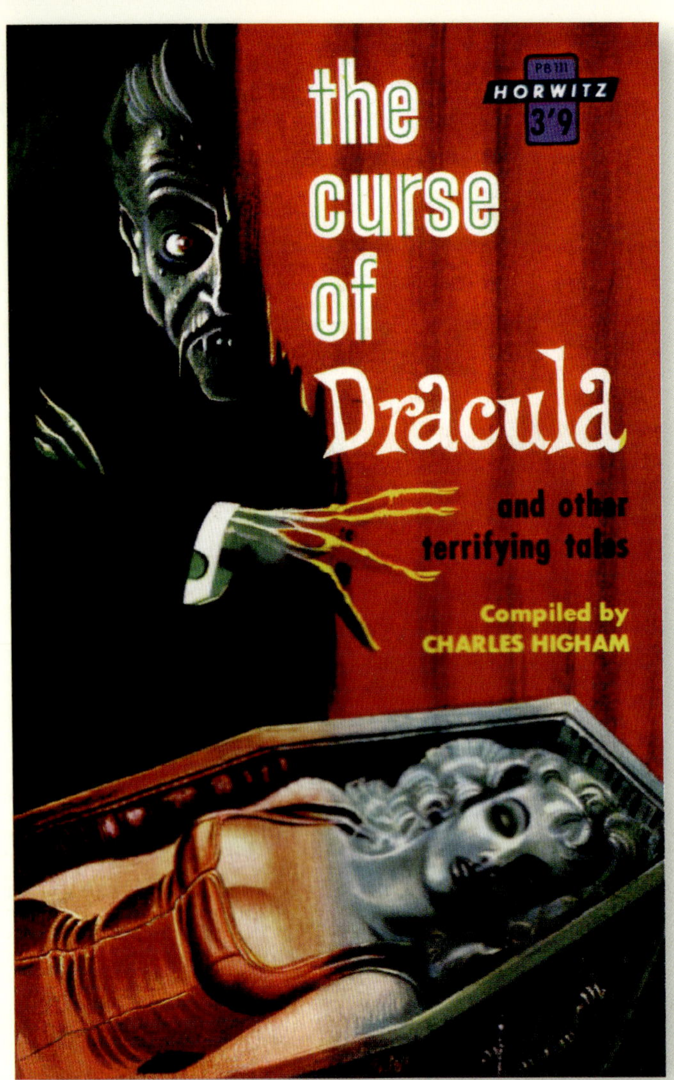

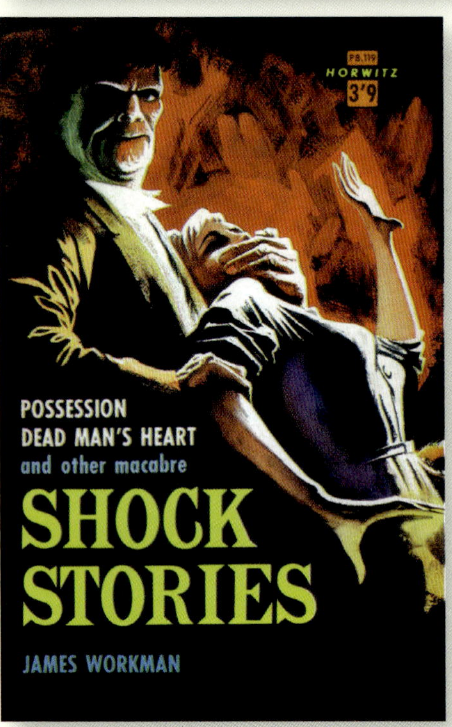

Higham's Horwitz Horrors

Thanks to strict censorship laws, horror was never as big in Australia as it was in America and the UK. British-born author and poet Charles Higham (1931–2012) immigrated to Sydney in 1954, where he became a journalist. In the early 1960s he compiled a series of paperback horror anthologies for Horwitz Publications with covers by cartoonist Frank Benier (1919–98). These were *Tales of Terror* (1961), *Weird Stories* (1961), *Nightmare Stories* (1962), *The Curse of Dracula and Other Terrifying Tales* (1962) [ABOVE LEFT], *Spine-Tingling Tales* (1962, reprinted 1965), and *Tales of Horror* (1962). After moving to the United States in 1969, Higham authored a number of sometimes controversial celebrity biographies.

TOP MIDDLE: Published by the New South Wales Bookstall Company in 1945 with a cover by Brodie Mack, *The Shudder Show* was the only weird collection by Australian mystery writer A. (Archibald) E. (Edward) Martin (1885–1955).

TOP RIGHT: Along with the short zombie novels *The Living Dead* and *Back from the Dead*, *Fangs of the Vampire* was the third in a series of booklets by Michael Waugh, issued in 1954–55 by Cleveland Publishing, Sydney.

BOTTOM MIDDLE: Frank Benier did the cover for *Shock Stories* (1962), a collection of short stories by Scottish-born author, actor, and scriptwriter James Workman (1912–2001) from Australia's Horwitz Publications.

BOTTOM RIGHT: "James Dark" was a house name for James Workman (and possibly other authors) from Horwitz that included novels and collections such as *Terrifying Tales* (1963), which again boasted cover art by Frank Benier.

Horler's Fanged Fiends

Best-selling British novelist Sydney Horler (1888–1954) wrote more than 150 books, many of them pseudo-Gothic thrillers involving apparent ghosts and vampires. Famed comics artist "Ami" (Aimo Hauhio) did the cover for *Kamppailu Keksinnöstä* (Ilmarisen Kirja, 1942) [TOP LEFT], a Finnish edition of the 1928 novel *The Curse of Doone*, while Lopez Rubio's cover of the Spanish *El Hombre de la Media Cara* (Ediciones Marisal, "Colección Aventuras Diamante Amarillo" No. 56, 1942) [TOP MIDDLE] featured yet another vampire. Both editions managed to misspell the author's name.

BOTTOM LEFT: Credited to "Femenía Jr.," the cover to this reprint of *Un dans trois* by Belgian crime writer Stanislas-André Steeman (Editions Hymsa, "La Novela Aventura Serie Detectivesca" No. 9) owed more than a little to *WereWolf of London*.

BOTTOM MIDDLE: Givalt Levin's cover for the Spanish *Los vampiros del Támesis* (Editorial Triunfo, circa 1950), which reprinted six stories about the gentleman thief John C. Raffles/Lord Edward Lister from 1930 issues of the story paper.

ABOVE RIGHT: Michel Gourdon's cover for *La Nuit de Frankenstein* ("Angoisse" Editions Fleuve Noir, 1957) the third of six sequels to Mary Shelley's novel by French author Jean-Claude Carrière writing under the house name "Benoît Becker."

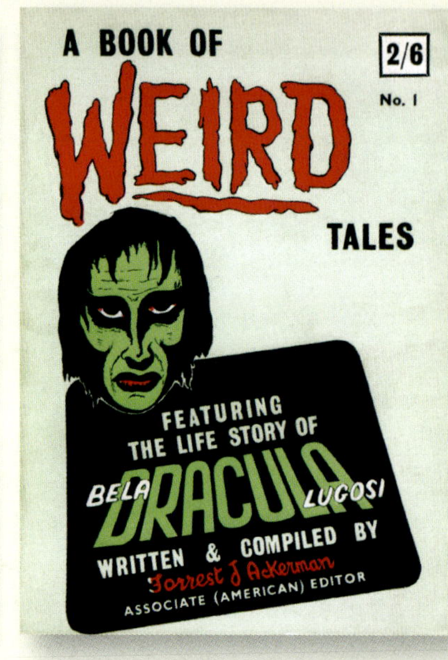

THIS PAGE: With the collapse of the pulp magazine market in post-World War II America and the growing popularity of paperbacks, slick magazines, and TV, many periodical publishers moved to a smaller digest size in an attempt to survive.

TOP LEFT: Barye W. Phillips's cover for the third issue of Ziff-Davis's digest *Fantastic* (Nov.–Dec. 1952).

TOP, MIDDLE LEFT: Rudy Nappi's cover for the first issue of *Tales of the Frightened* (Spring 1957).

TOP, MIDDLE RIGHT: An August Derleth story was illustrated on the cover of the August 1957 *Phantom*.

TOP RIGHT: Forrest J Ackerman was the US editor of one-off British digest *A Book of Weird Tales* (1960).

BOTTOM LEFT: EC's Jack Davis did the cover for the first issue of *Shock Magazine* (May 1960).

BOTTOM, MIDDLE LEFT: Lee Brown Coye's macabre cover for *Fantastic Stories of Imagination* (June 1963).

BOTTOM, MIDDLE RIGHT: The first of three issues of the digest *Bizarre! Mystery Magazine* (October 1965).

BOTTOM RIGHT: As usual, a Virgil Finlay reprint graced the cover of *Magazine of Horror* No. 27 (May 1969).

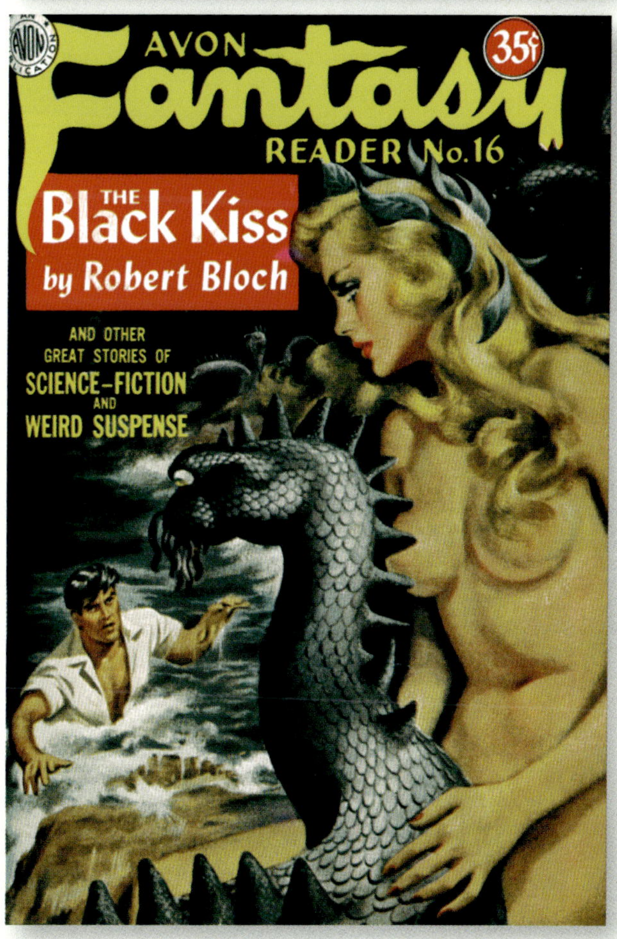

ABOVE LEFT: The gouache on board original cover painting for *Avon Fantasy Reader* No. 9 (1949) illustrated Clark Ashton Smith's story "The Flower-Women," which originally appeared in the May 1935 issue of *Weird Tales*.

TOP RIGHT: *Avon Fantasy Reader* was edited by Donald A. Wollheim and published by Avon Book Co., Inc. Issue No. 6 (1948) featured four reprints from *Weird Tales* along with other stories, including two obscure tales by H.P. Lovecraft.

BOTTOM RIGHT: *Avon Fantasy Reader* ran for 18 digest issues between 1947–52. The cover of issue No. 16 by R. Crowl illustrated "The Back Kiss," which had been credited to both Robert Bloch and Henry Kuttner in the June 1937 *Weird Tales*.

PAPERBACK PIONEER

"In the last analysis no editor can function unless it's by his own taste. Now, I've been an editor since 1941, and it's just my good fortune that apparently what I like at least 80 percent of the readers are going to like."

Donald A. Wollheim

DONALD A. WOLLHEIM (1914–90) did it all: he was a fan who produced his own fanzines full of famous names, edited pulp and digest magazines, and pioneered the rise of the paperback at various publishing houses before founding his own groundbreaking imprint, DAW Books, in 1971.

Wollheim's first love was the science fiction pulps, and he was a leading agitator in nascent fan culture, most notably as part of an influential group known as "The Futurians." He was instrumental in setting up the first fan convention and published multiple fanzines, including the one-shot *Fanciful Tales of Time and Space* (1936), which featured such important authors as H.P. Lovecraft and Robert E. Howard, and *The Phantagraph* (1935–46), which added Robert Bloch and Clark Ashton Smith to the roster. Wollheim may have been an amateur, but was already flexing his editorial judgment.

He was also vociferous in his view that SF should be used as a genre to discuss social issues, but the editors of the major pulps disagreed and consistently rejected his story submissions. Wollheim already felt like an outsider due to being socially awkward, and from physical challenges brought on by a bout of childhood polio, but with admirable tenacity he tackled these rejections by shaping the publishing world to accommodate his vision.

After editing the short-lived SF pulps *Cosmic Stories* and *Stirring Science Stories* (1941–42), Wollheim, who had a finely developed commercial sense, persuaded Pocket Books to publish his selection of short stories as *The Pocket Book of Science Fiction* (1943), the first paperback to include "science fiction" in its title. Later, for Avon Books, he edited what is regarded as the first all-original horror paperback, *The Girl with the Hungry Eyes* (1949), featuring contributions from Fritz Leiber, William Tenn, August Derleth, Frank Belknap Long, and Manly Wade Wellman.

Wollheim worked at Avon from 1947–52, where he oversaw a number of other anthologies and 18 issues of *Avon Fantasy Reader*, which reprinted stories from the pulps in digest format. In 1952 he pitched to successful magazine publisher A.A. Wynn the idea of diversifying into paperbacks. Although initially uncertain, Wynn took the plunge and employed Wollheim to assist him with the launch of Ace Books. Perhaps best known for their

The *Year's Best Horror Stories* series can now be regarded as setting the highest benchmark of any ongoing horror anthology of that era, especially the volumes edited by Karl Edward Wagner.

format of the "Ace Double"—two SF novels back-to-back in one binding—Ace also played a pivotal role in demonstrating the market for fantasy fiction, which led to new reprints of Edgar Rice Burroughs, Robert E. Howard, and H.P. Lovecraft.

By the end of the 1960s, Wollheim had grown disenchanted with life at Ace Books. Founder Wynn had passed away, and the new owners were running the company into the ground while gaining an unwanted reputation for late payments to authors. Wollheim quit in 1971 and the next year he launched DAW Books (rather immodestly named after himself), the first mass-market paperback imprint devoted solely to SF and fantasy.

DAW focused on nurturing female talent, both in editorial positions and as authors, with the likes of Tanith Lee, Marion Zimmer Bradley, and C.J. Cherryh benefiting from Wollheim's ingenuity and forward thinking. He also created three "Year's Best" anthologies for SF (1972–90), fantasy (1975–88), and horror (1974–94). The *Year's Best Horror Stories* series can now be regarded as setting the highest benchmark of any ongoing horror anthology of that era, especially the volumes edited by Karl Edward Wagner, who cast his net far and wide to draw in contributions.

Donald Allen Wollheim retired from DAW in 1985 and left behind a legacy that was not only crucial in establishing the paperback market for fantastical fiction, but also creating the foundation which many have built upon since. *JM*

ABOVE LEFT: Portrait sketch of Donald A. Wollheim by prolific American artist Jack Gaughan (1930–85), originally published in the paperback anthology *World's Best Science Fiction: 1965* edited by Wollheim and Terry Carr (Ace Books, 1965).

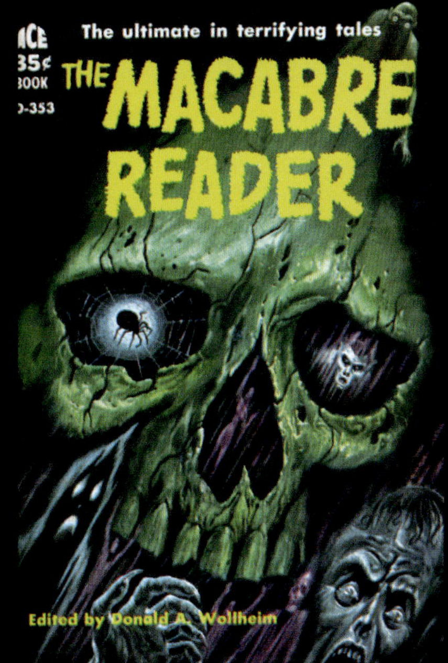

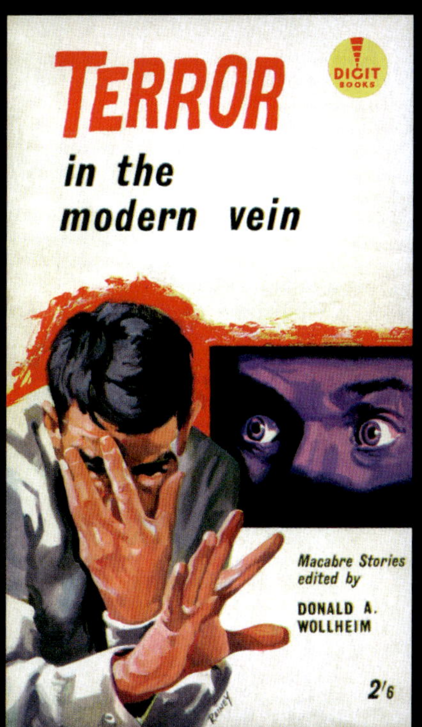

ABOVE LEFT: Clay Ferguson, Jr.'s cover for *Fanciful Tales of Time and Space* (Fall 1936), a one-off semi-prozine published by Wilson Shepherd and editor Donald A. Wollheim in an edition of 200 copies that featured contributions from H.P. Lovecraft, Robert E. Howard, and others.

TOP MIDDLE: Ed Emshwiller ("Emsh") did the cover for editor Donald A. Wollheim's original anthology *The Macabre Reader* (Ace Books, Inc., 1959), which included ten stories mostly drawn from the pulps by Lovecraft, Howard, Robert Bloch, Clark Ashton Smith, and others.

TOP RIGHT: John Schoenherr painted the cover for Donald A. Wollheim's follow-up anthology, *More Macabre* (Ace Books, Inc., 1961). This more eclectic collection featured eight stories by Richard Matheson, Philip K. Dick, Charlotte Perkins Gilman, and Hanns Heinz Ewers, among others.

BOTTOM MIDDLE: Wollheim's 1955 anthology *Terror in the Modern Vein* received a UK paperback reprint in 1961 from Digit Books/Brown, Watson Limited with a cover by D. Rainey. The eight stories included one by Wollheim himself under the pseudonym "David Grinnell."

BOTTOM RIGHT: Donald A. Wollheim's companion volume, *More Terror in the Modern Vein* (Digit Books/Brown, Watson Limited, 1961) featured a cover by Arthur Holmes and another story by the editor, written under the pseudonym "Martin Pearson," along with six other tales.

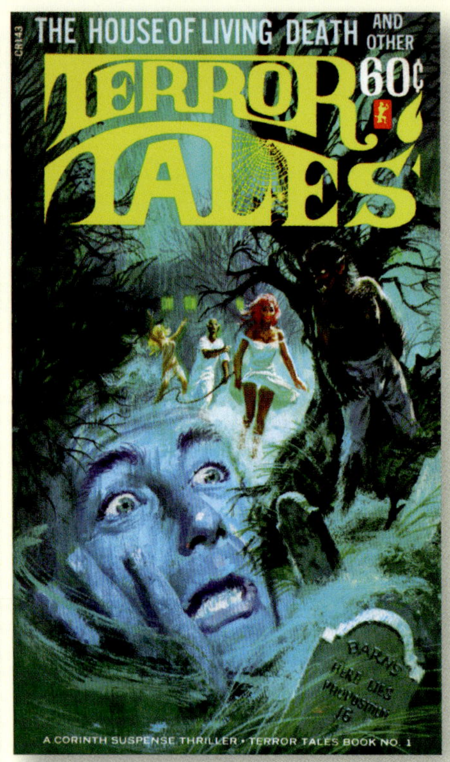

ABOVE LEFT: Although credited to Leo Margulies, the reprint anthology *Weird Tales: Stories of Fantasy* (Pyramid Books, 1964) was most probably ghost-edited by Sam Moskowitz. It boasted a new cover painting by the great Virgil Finlay.

TOP RIGHT: The gravestone depicted a political statement on Robert Bonfils's cover for *The House of Living Death & Other... Terror Tales* (Corinth Publications, Inc., 1966) edited by "Jon Hanlon" (Earl Kemp). The book featured three pulp reprints.

BOTTOM RIGHT: Earl Kemp also edited *Stories from... Dr. Death and Other Terror Tales* (Corinth Publications, Inc., 1966) under his "Jon Hanlon" alias. It featured another cover by Robert Bonfils and reprints from the pulp magazines.

ABOVE RIGHT: Original oil painting by Frank Frazetta (1928–2010) for the cover of the Ballantine Books, Inc. paperback *Tales from the Crypt* (1964), which reprinted eight strips in black and white from the 1950s EC horror comics.

TOP LEFT: Frank Frazetta did the covers for all five of Ballantine Books' EC comics reprints, including *Tales of the Incredible* (1965), which reprinted eight strips selected from the science fiction titles, including the classic "Judgment Day."

BOTTOM LEFT: Having originally had his material swiped by EC without credit, Ray Bradbury ended up working for them and contributed a new Foreword to Ballantine's *The Autumn People* (1965), featuring eight of his favorite adaptations.

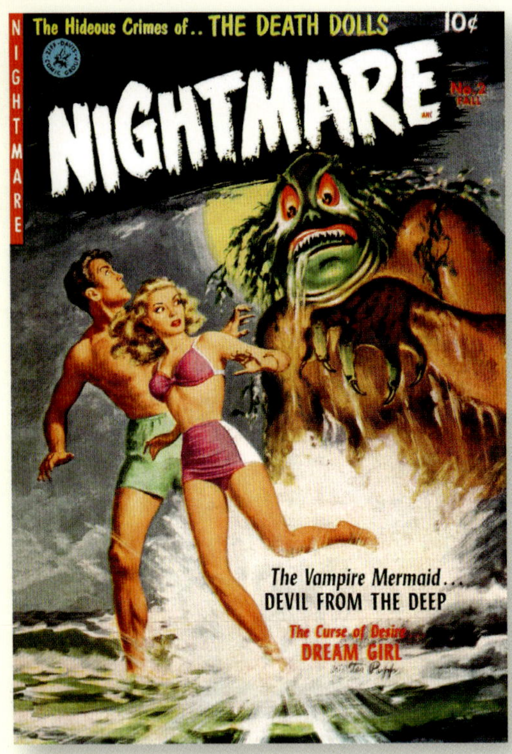

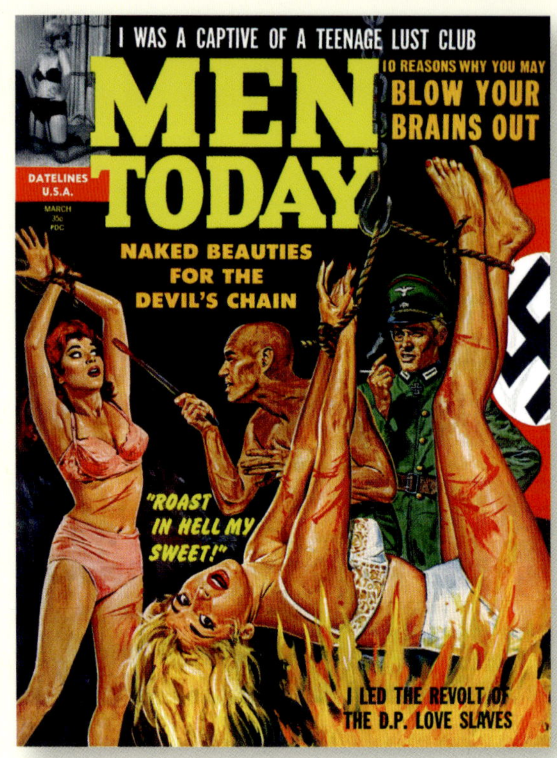

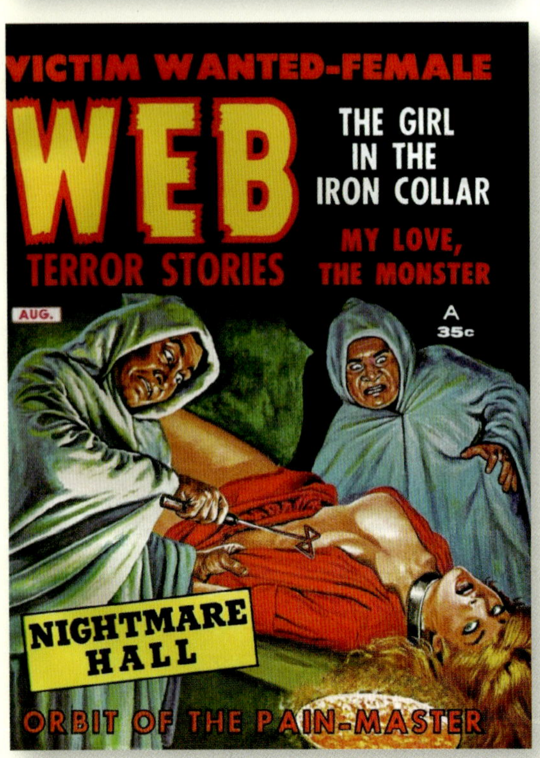

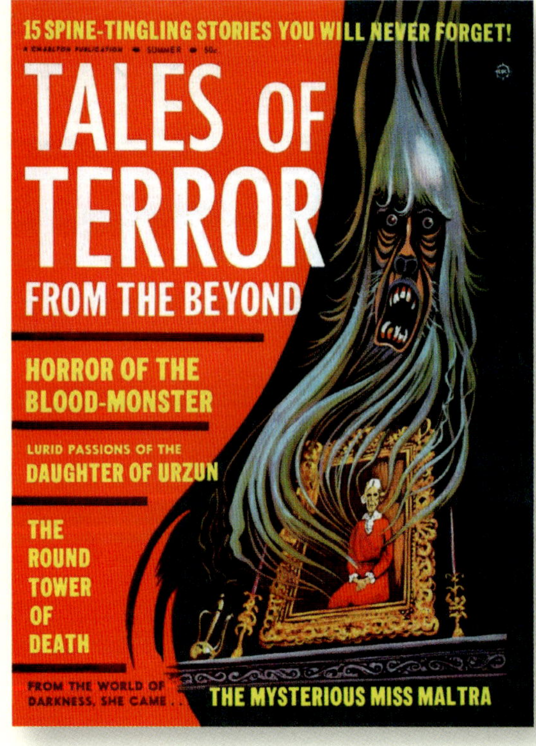

TOP LEFT: Pulp and paperback artist Walter Popp illustrated the cover for the second and final issue of Ziff-Davis's comics magazine *Nightmare* (Fall 1952). It also contained a five-page Edgar Allan Poe adaptation by Everett Raymond Kinstler.

TOP MIDDLE: Clarence Doore's piscine cover for the debut issue of Weider Periodicals, Inc.'s *True Weird* (November 1955). This bizarre mix of men's adventure magazine and tabloid-like newspaper only lasted for three issues.

TOP RIGHT: Recalling the excesses of the "shudder pulps," the men's adventure magazines of the 1950s–70s featured misogynist Nazi torture covers, such as this one on the second issue of Emtee Publishing Company's *Men Today* (March 1962).

BOTTOM LEFT: Cover of the first issue of Candar Publishing Company's digest *Web Terror Stories* (August 1962), which started out as a science fiction magazine in 1957. It lasted for just eight issues under its new "weird menace" title.

BOTTOM MIDDLE: This lurid February 1963 issue of *Shock Mystery Tales* (Pontiac Publishing Company) was the tenth and final edition of the magazine that had started out in 1960 as the three-issue digest *Shock Magazine* from a different publisher.

OPPOSITE, BOTTOM RIGHT: Ralph Brillhart's 1962 paperback cover for Evangeline Walton's *Witch House* was reused on Charlton Publications' one-shot *Tales of Terror from Beyond* (Summer 1964), most of which was written by Stanton A. Coblentz.

TOP LEFT: American fetish/bondage artist "Eric Stanton" (Ernest Stanzoni, Jr., 1926–99) did the cover for the sleaze paperback *Pay the Devil* by Peter Willow (1965), published by Stanley Malkin's "Adult Reading" imprint, After Hours.

BOTTOM LEFT: Eric Stanton's cover for another one of Stanley Malkin's sleaze paperbacks, *Mask of Evil* (First Niter Books, Inc., 1966). Author "Charlene White" may have been a pseudonym of filmmaker Edward D. Wood, Jr.

ABOVE RIGHT: Original gouache on board painting by Robert Bonfils (1922–2018) for the cover of *Orgy of the Dead* by Edward D. Wood, Jr. (Greenleaf Classics, 1966), who was paid just $500 for this novelization of the 1965 nudie movie.

FOLLOWING SPREAD: Acrylics on board wraparound cover painting by British artist Bruce Pennington (b. 1944) for *Dracula Returns* (New English Library, 1973), the first in a nine-book series by American author "Robert Lory" (Robert Edward Lore).

8

EXPLOITATION EXPLOSION

CHRISTOPHER FOWLER

"We have such sights to show you!"

LEAD CENOBITE (DOUG BRADLEY) IN *HELLRAISER* (1987)

"From my own personal point of view, I don't think just blood and guts is enough. At least, it isn't for me. Maybe it will turn someone's stomach; but, I'm not sure that is literature or even entertainment."

Stephen King

"Horror is the future. And you cannot be afraid. You must push everything to the absolute limit or else life will be boring. People will be boring. Horror is like a serpent; always shedding its skin, always changing. And it will always come back. It can't be hidden away like the guilty secrets we try to keep in our subconscious."

Dario Argento

DECADES RARELY START on time. The new horror boom had been kick-started by *Rosemary's Baby* in 1968, but by the 1970s audiences were steeped in disillusionment. After student riots, Watergate, and Vietnam, no one could accept Vincent Price and Christopher Lee as the tasteful avatars of horror. The Hammer and Corman/Poe movie cycles were played out, and cinema was looking to adapt fresh stories with young appeal.

Thanks to *The Exorcist* (1973), *The Omen* (1976), and *Carrie* (1976), horror turned its attention away from Gothic castles to the homes of modern dysfunctional families. Appropriately, the rebirth brought a rash of films and books about abominable births and deranged kiddies, from the lightbulb-headed killer baby of Larry Cohen's *It's Alive!* (1974) to creepy Catholic Brooke Shields in the sleazy, smart *Communion* (1976).

Suddenly, no one was safe. The enemy was inside the house and horror was no longer a monster in a turret—it had come home, and it looked like us. *The Texas Chain Saw Massacre* (1974), *Deranged* (1974), and *The Hills Have Eyes* (1977) inverted the protective embrace of family, turning it into something you have to escape from. Don't look in the basement, don't go in the house, don't open the window were more than just instructions—they were also movie titles. *Burnt Offerings* (1976) disturbed both as a novel and a film, and not just because Bette Davis had to star opposite Oliver Reed. Here was a house that restored itself by feeding on the misery of its occupying family. In the source novel and TV movie *The Dark Secret of Harvest Home* (1978)—also starring veteran Davis—former actor-turned-novelist Thomas Tryon made life in a small rural community seem idyllic until suddenly, as in the world of *The Wicker Man* (1973), there was a price to pay for all those fine harvests.

Hollywood execs made full use of relaxed censorship laws to up the ante on cinematic fear. What had liberated them most were the ten Academy Award nominations for *The Exorcist* (although it won only two), which finally legitimized the drive-in B-movie world of the horror film. Overnight, parents were prepared to sit through a grueling tale of possession and crucifix-misuse. The same year's *Don't Look Now* was another sophisticated supernatural thriller with adult appeal, but it's worth remembering that *The Texas Chain Saw Massacre* also terrified without the use of excessive gore, thanks to its eerie true-life tone. It's as if director Tobe Hooper was daring those newcomers lured in by *The Exorcist* to cope with Leatherface in the most extreme family inversion of all. In a way, his debut horror film was his parting shot; there was nowhere darker for him—or anyone else—to go. Hooper's final image of an enraged madman swinging a chainsaw at the sky said everything. It also limited the audience demographic, which had been broadening and becoming more profitable.

While he sometimes succumbed to sentimentality, King cast a long shadow over other writers and single-handedly sent the genre spinning off in a new direction, thanks to an astute choice of good directors for the film versions.

Stephen King's arrival was therefore extraordinarily timely. His novel *Carrie* (1974) felt fresh and different, and was somehow friendlier. When consignments of King paperbacks arrived, the excitement was palpable. King became the first multimedia horror star, with movie-friendly plots that were just what Hollywood needed. While he sometimes succumbed to sentimentality, King cast a long shadow over other writers and single-handedly sent the genre spinning off in a new direction, thanks to an astute choice of good directors for the film versions. Several of his early books dismembered the nuclear family,

PREVIOUS SPREAD: *Cry of the Banshee* (2018), marker and pencil on Bristol board by American artist Frederick Cooper. "Vincent Price has long been a favorite genre actor of mine," reveals Cooper, "so I jumped at the chance to depict him in all his glory. After Boris Karloff passed, Price became 'The King.' Long Live the King!"

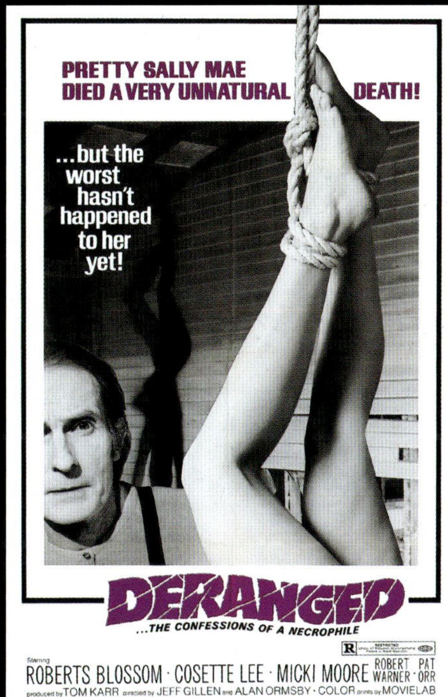

BOTTOM MIDDLE: *Deranged* (Dir: Jeff Gillen and Alan Ormsby, 1974) was based on the same source material as *Psycho* and *The Texas Chain Saw Massacre*, as Roberts Blossom basically portrayed Wisconsin serial killer and necrophile Ed Gein.

BOTTOM RIGHT: The real-life Gein case was also the inspiration for Tobe Hooper's genre-changing *The Texas Chain Saw Massacre* (1974), which expanded its maniac killer to an entire family of cannibals and introduced the world to "Leatherface."

ABOVE LEFT: In *Profondo rosso* (aka *Deep Red*, 1975), which marked director Dario Argento's ongoing revival of the *giallo* genre, David Hemmings's pianist finds himself involved in a series of brutal murders in Rome. It was banned in the UK.

TOP RIGHT: Dan Curtis's *Burnt Offerings* (1976) was based on a 1973 novel by Robert Marasco and starred veteran Bette Davis as the matriarch of a family that moves into a haunted house. Stephen King has cited it as one of his favorite movies.

BOTTOM MIDDLE: Director Brian De Palma began channeling his inner Hitchcock with *Sisters* (1972), as nobody believes Jennifer Salt's journalist when she claims she has witnessed a brutal murder in the next-door apartment.

BOTTOM LEFT: French designers Guy Jouineau and Guy Bourduge created this Spanish poster for *Carrie* (1976), Brian De Palma's version of Stephen King's 1974 debut novel, about a teenage girl (Sissy Spacek) with telekinetic powers.

ABOVE RIGHT: The infamous "scalp" poster for William Lustig's brutal *Maniac* (1980), in which Joe Spinell's psychotic loner stalks and murders young women in New York City and then takes their scalps as a macabre trophy.

TOP LEFT: Graham Humphreys's iconic poster for the British release of *The Evil Dead* (1981), widely regarded as helping to make Sam Raimi's low-budget horror movie the biggest-selling home video of the year in the UK.

but he also poured new wine into old bottles and brought back vampires, werewolves, ghosts, monsters, aliens, and the supernatural—a grand grab-bag filled with Judeo-Christian predestination and sin that had something to offer everyone.

Others sensed that King was onto something big. Their books started bidding wars, but although George R.R. Martin brought us vampires aboard a Mississippi side-wheeler in *Fevre Dream* and Whitley Strieber found werewolves working above the city in *Wolfen*, only the latter became a movie. Boundary-breaking splatter-exploiters like *Cannibal Holocaust* (1980) and *Cannibal Ferox* (1981) tried to return us to gross-out horror and went a step too far. The successful horror entertainment of the 1970s and '80s was often brash and bloody, but it wasn't too keen on subtlety.

While John Landis was busy with the witty *An American Werewolf in London* (1981) and Stanley Kubrick made horror look classy at the Overlook Hotel, down in the cheap seats they started screaming to Sam Raimi's *The Evil Dead* (1981). Britain banned it and Sam went to London to enjoy the show. He loved the idea that his film caused controversy.

Stephen King had brought gate-folded glamour to once-tawdry paperbacks, and helped the sales of many who might not have found success. Among them was Michael McDowell, hailed by King as "a writer for the ages." His sensational *Blackwater* saga ran to six volumes and centered on a Southern family whose women become lethal around water. What differentiated McDowell from the rest was his ability to create mystifying patterns beneath the surface of everyday life that erupted into acts of horror.

Into this new arena came two further game-changers, *Eraserhead* (1977) and *Halloween* (1978). David Lynch's surrealist debut showed us something Europeans had known for decades—it's more upsetting if you can't make sense of it. For Lynch this was a step-off point that would lead to head-scratchers like *Lost Highway* (1997) and international critical acclaim. John Carpenter's thrilling but woodenly scripted slasher began a stalk-and-stab boom that refused to go away, lingering so long that even enjoyable minor entries like *My Bloody Valentine* (1981) were considered successful enough to warrant remakes. Horror-meisters from Lucio Fulci to George A. Romero had realized something fundamental about their chosen genre: a precinct movie with a single main set, a handful of unknown actors, and a killer hook could out-gross the biggest, starriest studio product. Clive Barker's very British *Hellraiser* (1987) hit big despite its garbled transatlantic re-dub, and Dario Argento proved that lurid, deafening set pieces could carry a movie without a script, but it was Brian De Palma who went full Hitchcock, bringing us two decades' worth of blackly comic suspense, although he never topped his earliest Hitch homage, *Sisters* (1973), which used split-screen and an eerie monochrome dream sequence to fine effect. Way down at the other end of the scale (and here we're going as low as 1978's *I Spit on Your Grave*), directors discovered that getting their films banned somewhere merely added to their appeal. They didn't realize they were sowing the seeds of future troubles.

In 1980 a line was crossed with *Maniac*, whose poster depicted a man holding a woman's bloody scalp and a dripping knife. Subliminally emphasized between them was the maniac's swollen crotch, enough to suggest he was sexually excited by killing women. The film was so relentlessly grubby that it felt as if the negative had been dropped in the toilet.

While John Landis was busy with the witty *An American Werewolf in London* (1981) and Stanley Kubrick made horror look classy at the Overlook Hotel, down in the cheap seats they started screaming to Sam Raimi's *The Evil Dead* (1981). Britain banned it and Sam went to London to enjoy the show. He loved the idea that his film caused controversy, but the uncontrolled selling of cheap videos led to the now-infamous banned list of 72 films, and the UK's so-called "Video Nasties" act. *The Evil Dead* was finally released when the glum-faced guardians of public morality realized they'd been exercised over a cartoon comedy filmed with a camera on a rope, not a subversive threat to a nation's way of life.

The tone of films had to be changed. The next great horror wave took a less serious turn. *A Nightmare on Elm Street* (1984), *Re-Animator* (1985), and *Return of the Living Dead* (1985) were knowing and cartoonish, and only David Cronenberg's *The Fly* (1986) acknowledged the present by drawing a parallel to the AIDS crisis then engulfing America. Barker and Argento disappointingly headed off into subsections of the irrelevant baroque, and it took a small Dutch movie, *Spoorloos* (aka *The Vanishing*, 1988) to bring us back into the real world. Here was a film so upsetting that to this day fans still can't drive into a sunlit gas station without shivering. A Hollywood remake eventually followed, draining away everything that had been miraculous and replacing it with bombast.

Looking back, it's hard not to feel that the entire 20-year boom-bust cycle had been created by some kind of fantastical accident. If the lush fairytales of Hammer and Corman had not worn themselves threadbare, if William Peter Blatty had not penned *The Exorcist*, if a new generation of writers and filmmakers had not been ushered in by Stephen King, we might never have been treated to the sight of murderous yogurt in *The Stuff* (1985) or Keenan Wynn having his legs gnawed off in *Piranha* (1978).

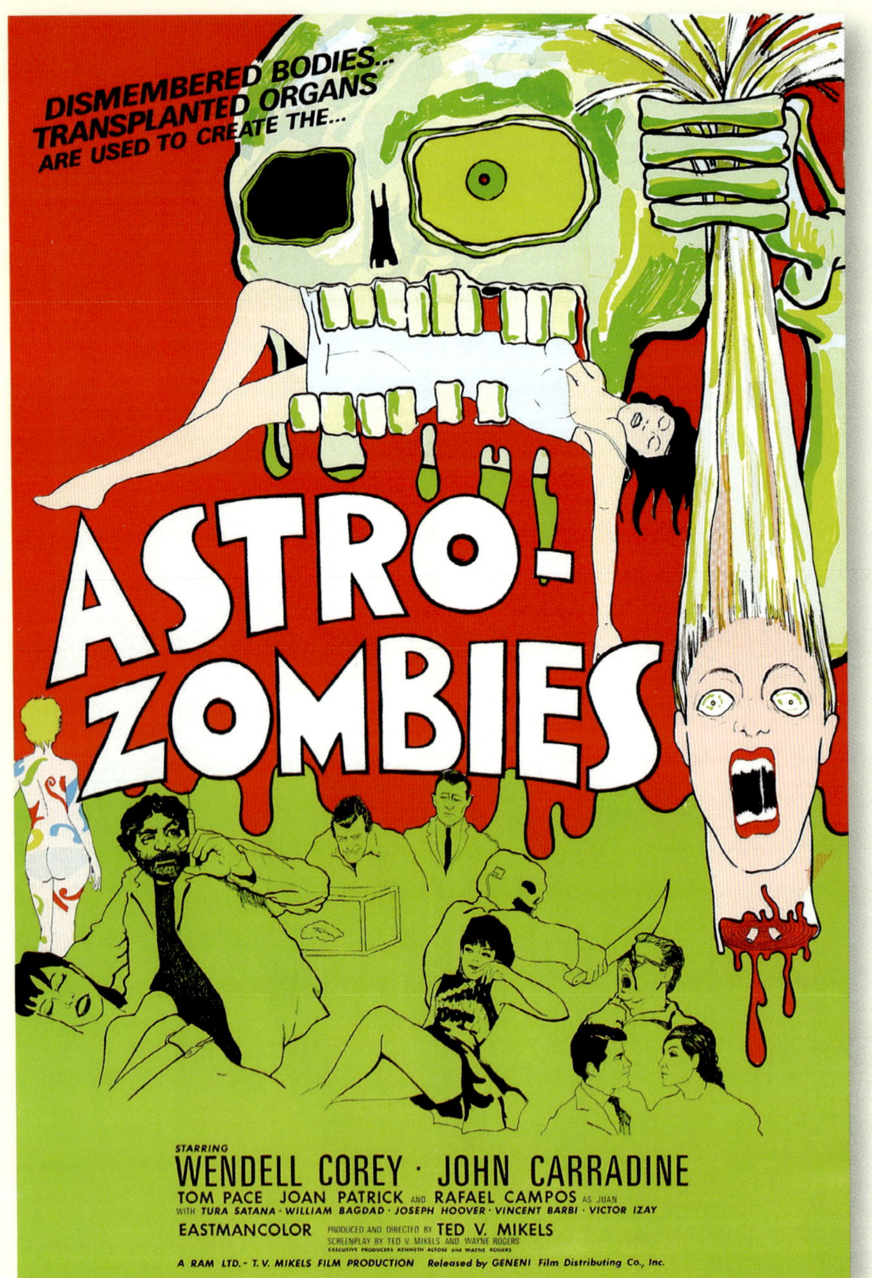

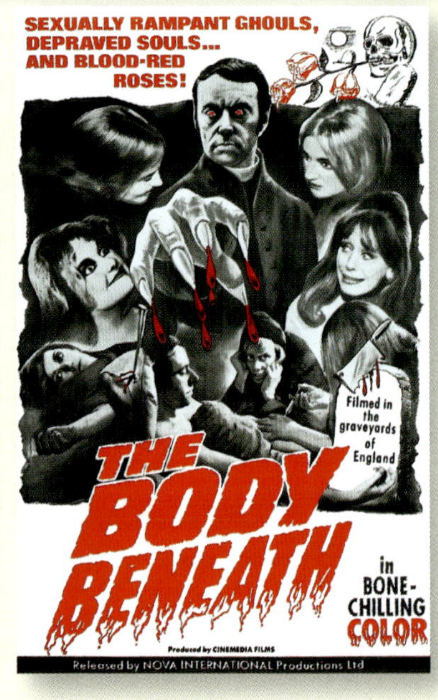

ABOVE LEFT: *The Astro-Zombies* (Dir: Ted V. Mikels, 1968) was co-scripted by actor Wayne Rogers and starred veteran actors Wendell Corey and John Carradine in a story of a mad scientist, his zombie creation, and a ring of spies. A sequel followed 33 years later.

TOP RIGHT: John Carradine also portrayed a demented butler in *Blood of Dracula's Castle* (Dir: Al Adamson, 1969), which starred movie veterans Alex D'Arcy as Count Dracula and Paula Raymond as his wife, Countess Townsend. It was apparently shot in 1966.

BOTTOM MIDDLE: Filmed in early 1969 as a biker movie before new scenes were added, *Dracula vs. Frankenstein* (aka *Blood of Frankenstein*; Dir: Al Adamson, 1971) marked a tragic end to the careers of veteran actors J. Carrol Naish and Lon Chaney, Jr.

BOTTOM RIGHT: *The Body Beneath* (Dir: Andy Milligan, 1970) was filmed in 16mm on location in London's Highgate Cemetery for an estimated budget of $20,000. Gavin Reed headed a mostly amateur cast as the 400-year-old leader of a cult of nineteenth-century bloodsuckers.

ABOVE RIGHT: American comics artist Neal Adams created this poster for *Horror of the Blood Monsters* (aka *Space Mission to the Lost Planet*; Dir: Al Adamson, 1970). Apparently shot in 1966, it featured John Carradine and tinted stock footage from other movies.

TOP LEFT: When a cat-food company uses meat from the local graveyard to save money, fiendish felines soon develop a taste for human flesh in *The Corpse Grinders* (Dir: Ted V. Mikels, 1971). Belated sequels followed in 2000 (again directed by Mikels) and 2012.

BOTTOM LEFT: *The Man with 2 Heads* (Dir: Andy Milligan, 1972), a low-budget version of *Dr. Jekyll and Mr. Hyde*, managed to misspell Robert Louis Stevenson's credit. British actor Denis DeMarne starred as both Dr. William Jekyll and his alter ego, Danny Blood.

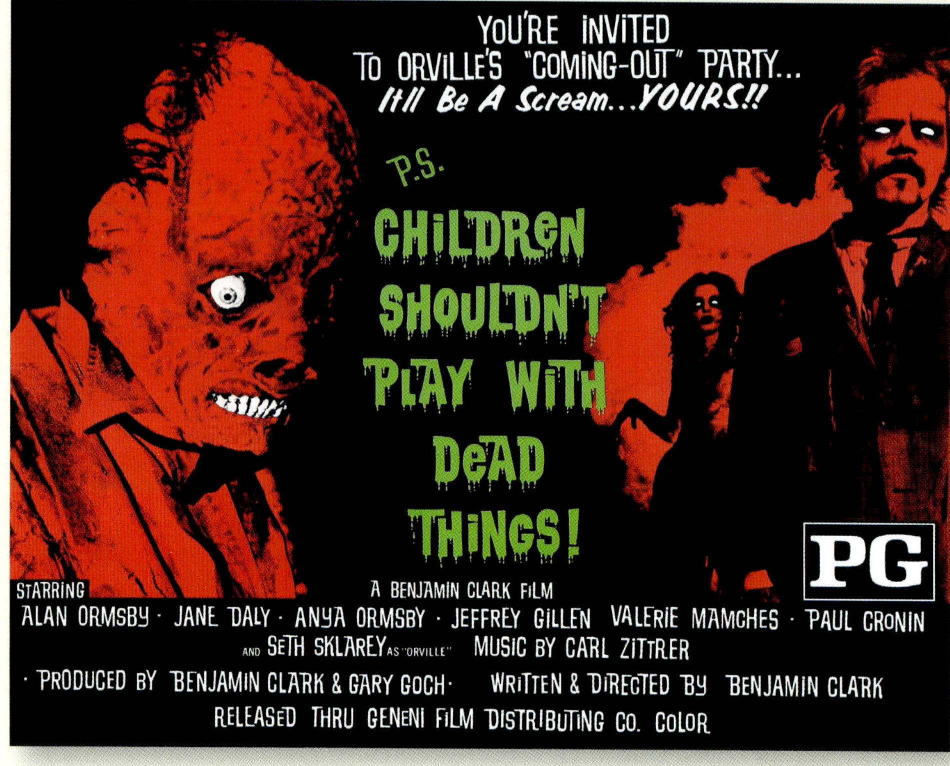

TOP LEFT: Half-sheet poster for *Guess What Happened to Count Dracula?* (Dir: Laurence Merrick and Mario d'Alcala, 1971). Originally released in 1969 as a XXX gay porn film, it was later re-cut into a horror comedy!

BOTTOM LEFT: One-sheet poster for *Invasion of the Blood Farmers* (Dir: Ed Adlum, 1972), which featured a mostly amateur cast. A crazed Druid cult attempts to revive its ancient queen with human blood.

BOTTOM RIGHT: Half-sheet poster for *Children Shouldn't Play with Dead Things* (Dir: Benjamin [Bob] Clark, 1972), which starred co-writer Alan Ormsby as an actor who raises the dead with a Satanic ritual.

TOP RIGHT: Bob Larkin's terrific poster for *Shock Waves* (aka *Almost Human*; Dir: Ken Wiederhorn, 1976). Peter Cushing starred as a Nazi zombie-master, and John Carradine had a cameo as a crusty ship's captain.

TOP LEFT: Filmed in just two weeks and featuring a furry family of Sasquatch that kidnap two nubile young women, *Bigfoot* (Dir: Robert F. Slatzer, 1970) starred John Carradine and several other veteran movie actors.

TOP RIGHT: *John Carradine* (2019), Les Edwards's oil on board portrait of the classically trained actor as wily traveling salesman Jasper B. Hawks in *Bigfoot* (1970). "John Carradine had a long and distinguished career both in film and on the stage," explains the British artist, "but I can't help but feel that he had a face that was made to be in horror movies. A bit like Peter Cushing, you feel you can see the skull beneath the skin."

BOTTOM LEFT: John Carradine was one of the imported American stars battling an intelligent swarm of South American killer bees in the Mexican-made *The Bees* (Dir: Alfredo Zacarias, 1978).

BOTTOM RIGHT: John Carradine was just one of a veteran all-star cast, that included Ray Milland, Elsa Lanchester, Maurice Evans, and Broderick Crawford, in *Terror in the Wax Museum* (Dir: Georg Fenady, 1973).

BOTTOM LEFT: Spanish poster by artist Josep Martí Ripoll (1916–2011) for Hemisphere Pictures' *Brides of Blood* (Dir: Gerardo de Leon and Eddie Romero, 1968) which kicked off a brief trend for low-budget American co-productions to be filmed in the Philippines with American stars.

BOTTOM, MIDDLE LEFT: American double-bill poster for Hemisphere Pictures' release of the Filipino-made *Mad Doctor of Blood Island* (Dir: Gerardo de Leon and Eddie Romero, 1969) and the West German Edgar Allan Poe movie *Die Schlangengrube und das Pendel* (Dir: Harald Reinl, 1967).

TOP LEFT & RIGHT: Original ink wash and white paint over graphite on illustration board poster art for *Superbeast* (Dir: George Schenck, 1972), which United Artists released on a double-bill with another Philippines-shot movie, *Daughters of Satan* (Dir: Hollingsworth Morse, 1972).

BOTTOM, MIDDLE RIGHT: One-sheet poster by Chet [Chester] Collom (b. 1927) for Wargay Corporation's *The Deathhead Virgin* (1974), an underwater horror movie filmed in the Philippines. It was the final movie credit for old-time Hollywood director Norman Foster (1903–76).

BOTTOM RIGHT: Veteran actor John Carradine traveled to the Philippines to film Caprican Three's horror-comedy *Vampire Hookers* (Dir: Cirio H. Santiago, 1978). He portrayed a white-suited vampire who uses a trio of beautiful bloodsuckers to lure victims back to their graveyard crypt.

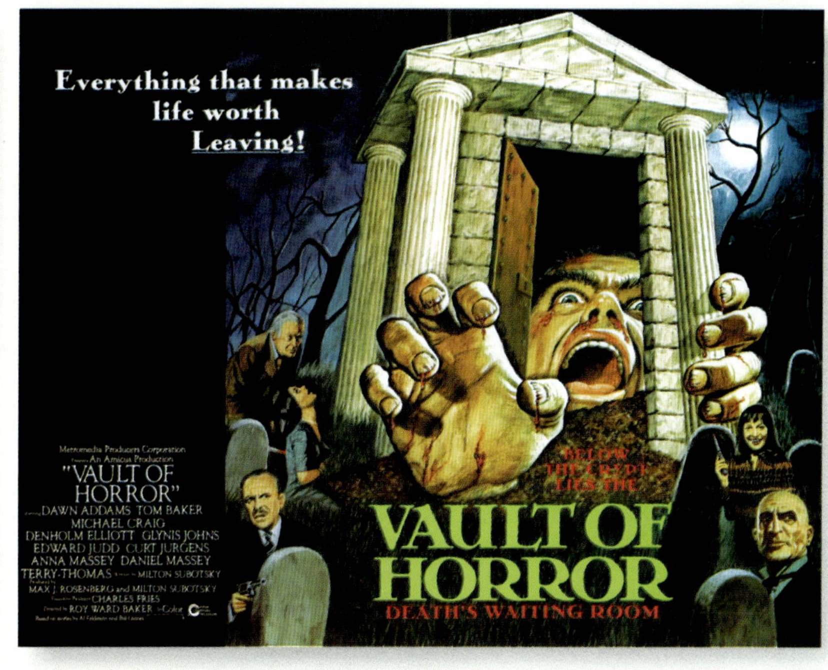

BOTTOM LEFT: Based on the 1966 novel by Ronald Bassett, Tigon Pictures' *Witchfinder General* (Dir: Michael Reeves, 1968) was re-titled *The Conqueror Worm* in the US by American International Pictures (AIP), who added Vincent Price's recitation of Edgar Allan Poe's poem over the credits.

TOP LEFT: Loosely based on a story by H.P. Lovecraft, Tigon Pictures' *Curse of the Crimson Altar* (Dir: Vernon Sewell, 1968) co-starred Boris Karloff, Christopher Lee, Barbara Steele, and Michael Gough. For the 1970 American release, AIP changed the title to *The Crimson Cult*.

BOTTOM, MIDDLE LEFT: Bruce Dern was the mad scientist in American International's *The Incredible 2-Headed Transplant* (Dir: Anthony M. Lanza, 1971).

BOTTOM, MIDDLE RIGHT: Ray Milland was the victim in AIP's *The Thing with Two Heads* (Dir: Lee Frost, 1972).

TOP RIGHT: The British-made *The Vault of Horror* (Dir: Roy Ward Baker, 1973) featured an all-star cast and, following on from *Tales from the Crypt* (1972), was the second portmanteau movie from Amicus Productions to be based on strips from the 1950s EC horror comics.

BOTTOM RIGHT: Boasting another all-star cast, Amicus Productions' *From Beyond the Grave* (Dir: Kevin Connor, 1973) revolved around a mysterious antiques shop run by Peter Cushing's creepy Proprietor. It was based on four short stories by British author R. Chetwynd-Hayes.

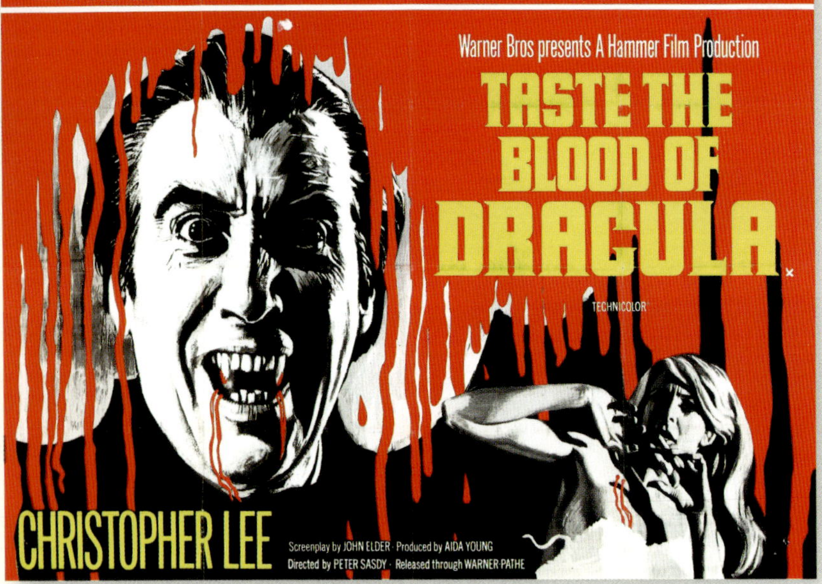

TOP LEFT: Tom Chantrell's British quad poster for *Taste the Blood of Dracula* (Dir: Peter Sasdy, 1970), the fourth in the Hammer Films series to star Christopher Lee as Count Dracula after the actor was convinced to reprise the role.

BOTTOM LEFT: Ezio Tarantelli's Italian *duo-foglio* for Hammer Films' *Scars of Dracula* (Dir: Roy Ward Baker, 1970). Christopher Lee again had to be coaxed back to star in this fifth, low-budget, stand-alone entry in the series.

TOP & BOTTOM RIGHT: Japanese poster for Hammer Films' *Dracula A.D. 1972* (Dir: Alan Gibson, 1972). In the US, some moviegoers received a "HorroRitual" card that gave them honorary membership of The Count Dracula Society.

BOTTOM MIDDLE: Japanese poster for *The Satanic Rights of Dracula* (aka *Count Dracula and His Vampire Bride*; Dir: Alan Gibson, 1973), the seventh and final film in Hammer's series to star Christopher Lee as the Count.

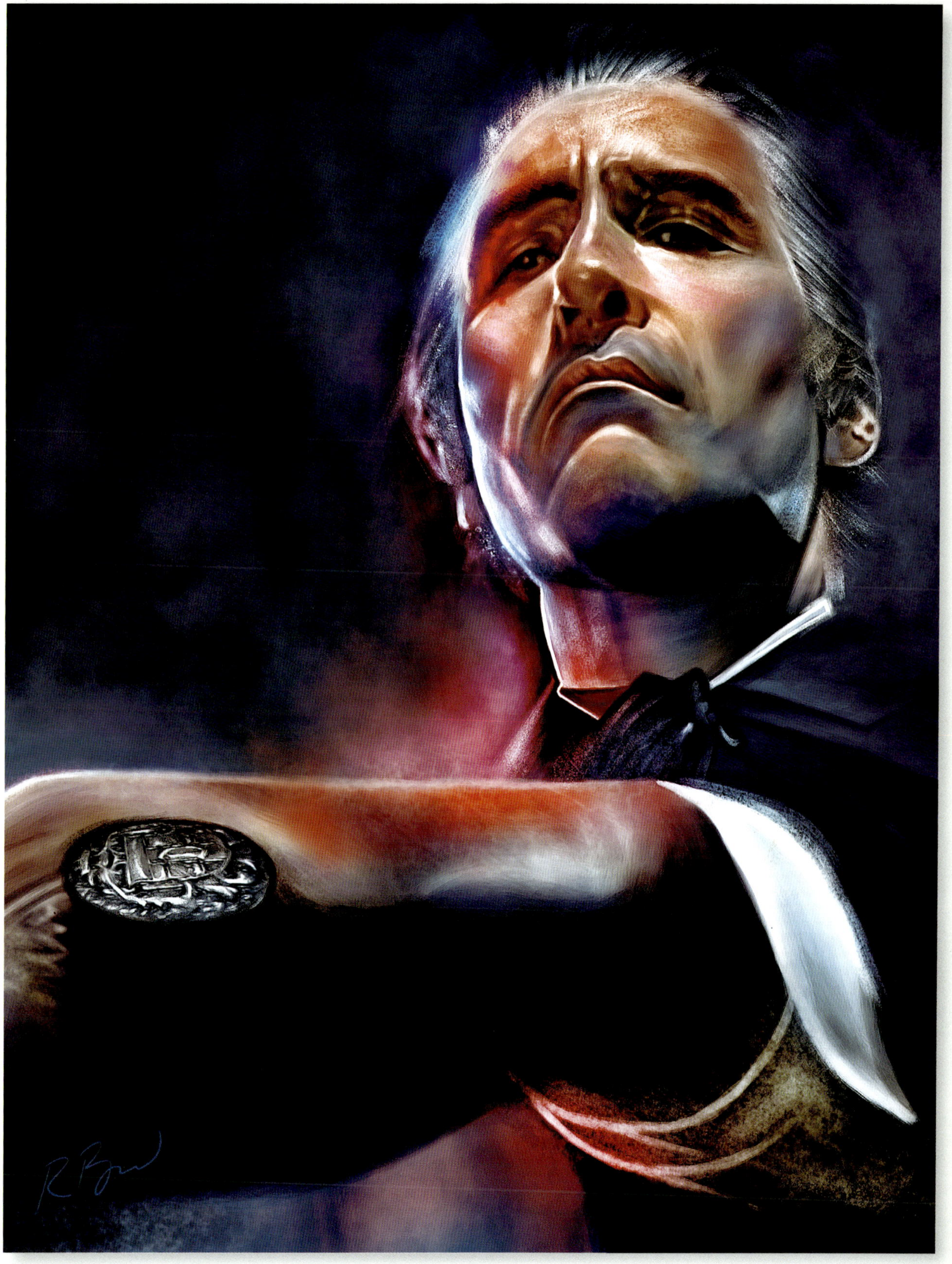

ABOVE LEFT: Japanese *speed* (an equivalent to the US insert) for Hammer Films' *Dracula Has Risen from the Grave* (Dir: Freddie Francis, 1968).

ABOVE RIGHT: *It Was My Will* (2016) by American digital and tattoo artist Rob Birchfield, who explains: "Christopher Lee is my favorite on-screen Dracula. He's got that icy, cold-blooded stare thing going on that can't be matched."

TOP MIDDLE: Stylish Italian *foglio* for the West German Edgar Allan Poe movie *Die Schlangengrube und das Pendel* (aka *The Torture Chamber of Dr. Sadism/The Blood Demon*, 1967). German co-star Karin Dor (Kätherose Derr, 1938–2017) was married at the time to director Harald Reinl.

ABOVE LEFT: Luca (Luciano) Crovato's *locandina* for the Italian *La figlia di Frankenstein* (aka *Lady Frankenstein*; Dir: Mel Welles, 1971). Italian actress Rosalba Neri (b. 1938)—billed as "Sara Bay" on the American print—portrayed the daughter of Joseph Cotten's Baron Frankenstein.

TOP RIGHT: Belgian poster for the Spanish/West German movie *La noche de Walpurgis* (aka *The Werewolf vs. the Vampire Woman/Shadow of the Werewolf*; Dir: León Klimovsky, 1971). American-born Patty Shepard (1945–2013) played the vampire Countess Wandesa Dárvula de Nadasdy.

BOTTOM MIDDLE: Italian *foglio* for the Belgian/Italian production *La plus longue nuit du diable* (aka *The Devil's Nightmare/Vampire Playgirls*; Dir: Jean Brismée, 1971), which starred the striking Italian actress Erika Blanc (Enrica Bianchi Colombatto, b. 1942) as a sexy succubus.

BOTTOM RIGHT: Spanish poster signed "Hermida" for *La saga de los Drácula* (aka *The Dracula Saga*; Dir: León Klimovsky, 1972) which co-starred German-born actress Helga Liné (Helga Lina Stern, b. 1932) as a member of Count Dracula's (Narciso Ibañez Menta) extended undead family.

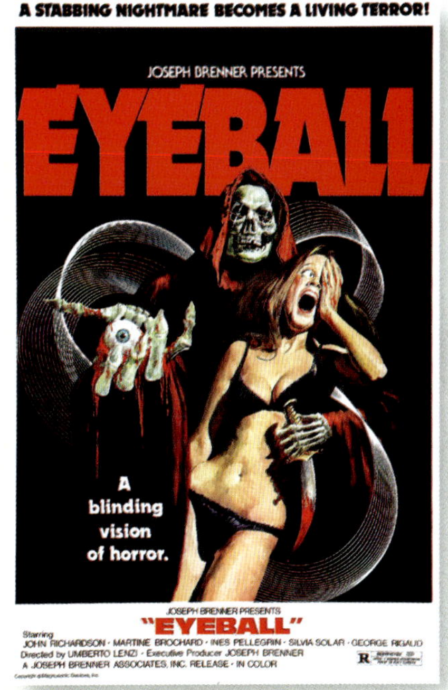

TOP LEFT & RIGHT: Belgian poster for the West German movie *Hexen bis aufs Blut gequält* (Dir: Michael Armstrong, 1970). When distributed in America by Hallmark Releasing Corp. in 1972 as *Mark of the Devil*, theater patrons were handed a vomit bag upon admission.

BOTTOM LEFT: Italian *foglio* for the French-made *Le Frisson des vampires* (aka *The Shiver of the Vampires*, 1971), director Jean Rollin's hallucinatory art-house film in which Jean-Marie Durand and Sandra Julien's newlyweds discover they are honeymooning in a castle full of vampires.

BOTTOM MIDDLE: American International Pictures' one-sheet poster for the Italian/West German/Austrian co-production *Baron Blood* (aka *Gli orrori del castello di Norimberga*; Dir: Mario Bava, 1972), which starred Hollywood veteran Joseph Cotten in a dual role.

BOTTOM RIGHT: Eye-catching one-sheet for Joseph Brenner Associates' American release of the Italian/Spanish *Eyeball* (aka *Gatti rossi in un labirinto di vetro*, 1975), director Umberto Lenzi's *giallo* about a red-coated killer murdering American tourists and removing their eyeballs.

THE CURSE OF THE CRIMSON AUTEUR

"I don't think I've done anything important or magnificent. I'm a worker, and the thing I prefer in my life is cinema."

Jesús Franco

"I've always thought he was very underrated."

Christopher Lee

IN *BARBED WIRE DOLLS* (1976) there's a scene of attempted incestuous rape that always brings the house down. It's played out in slow motion, not by speeding up the camera (such tricks were too expensive), but by making the performers move very slowly. The prolific Spanish exploitation filmmaker Jesús Franco Manera (1930–2013, aka Jess Franco) didn't care if it looked ridiculous. In *Sadisterotica* (1969) a bride dressed only in white stockings and a trousseau is attacked by a werewolf. Such moments define the Franco style.

Few directors could film blood-smeared naked females with such respect that it doesn't feel *entirely* uncomfortable. Franco loved his women, and gore sold seats, so it seemed natural to combine them. He made more than 200 films in 56 years (in 1973 alone he managed almost a film a month) and was more concerned with getting the next one into production than studying critical reception.

Franco's films are best seen collectively, because individually most of them are pretty terrible. These random, ludicrous, sexually provocative sado-masochistic horrors offer bad lighting, Moog synthesizers, and horrible fashions. Many contain sequences of such gauzy soft-focus that you start wondering if you have glaucoma.

When we express admiration for directors we term cult or edgy, we don't usually mean this rough. Franco thought nothing of slipping sexually explicit shots into films without telling his above-the-title stars, and made nine films with a British producer who ran a prostitution ring. He'd impatiently shift scenes from one film to another or squeeze an extra movie out of off-cuts; volume was everything, but as a true *naïf* he left us with some startling images.

Few critics and fans could have seen all of Franco's films, but they reveal obsessions with lesbianism and voyeurism, body exploitation, sexual violence, religion, blood, and "the essence of evil," plus a willingness to jump on any passing genre bandwagon.

It's notable that Franco's works proceed from monochromatic elegance backwards to lurid crudity, and that these dates coincide with the demise of his namesake. Franco the Spanish military dictator kept the censor's

---

Few critics and fans could have seen all of Franco's films, but they reveal obsessions with lesbianism and voyeurism, body exploitation, sexual violence, religion, blood, and "the essence of evil," plus a willingness to jump on any passing genre bandwagon.

---

scissors busy for 40 years, and the constraints proved beneficial to a director whose tasteless excesses were kept in check until 1977, when film was freed of state control. Audiences were shocked by his set pieces, which played out like sexy, violent nightclub acts and were haphazardly distributed through his films.

Franco had switched to horror exploitation after seeing Hammer's *The Brides of Dracula* (1960) at a cinema in Nice. As a result, his more tightly plotted films occur early with *The Awful Dr. Orlof* (1962) and *The Diabolical Dr. Z* (1966). Cinéastes may rhapsodize about his "non-linear deconstructed narratives," but even the director described himself as an amateur. By the time we get to *Sadomania* (1981) there's little differentiation from one film to the next, and less tolerant critics see nothing but a collection of smutty, violent images randomly tacked together.

But consider this: the director wrote his own scripts and shot everywhere under different credits and titles, operating beyond any industry system, with almost total freedom. He wanted to "make a good show" rather than have audiences worrying whether a story made sense. In doing so, he became Spain's most prolific director of Grand Guignol and opened a perverse path for today's Spanish horror masters. *CF*

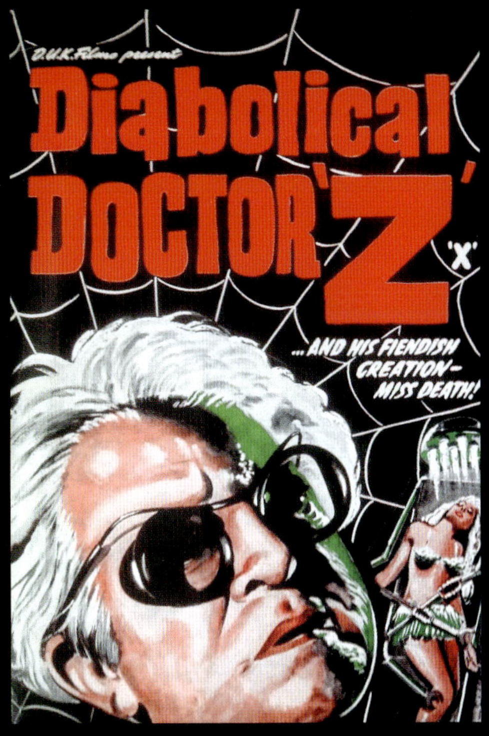

TOP LEFT: British poster for Jesús Franco's Spanish-French *Miss Muerte* (aka *The Diabolical Dr. Z*, 1966), in which a female mad scientist (Mabel Karr) turns an erotic dancer (Estella Blain) into a murderous assassin so that she can revenge the death of her father.

TOP MIDDLE: Egyptian poster for the Spanish/West German/UK production *El conde Drácula* (aka *Count Dracula*, 1970), Jesús Franco's supposedly "faithful" adaptation of Bram Stoker's novel starring Christopher Lee as the mustachioed vampire.

ABOVE RIGHT: Italian *locandina* for the Italian/Spanish/West German/Liechtenstein production *Il trono di fuoco* (aka *The Bloody Judge/Night of the Blood Monster*; Dir: Jesús Franco, 1970), which starred Christopher Lee as a sadistic, witch-torturing judge.

BOTTOM LEFT: Rodolfo Gasparri's Italian poster for Franco's Spanish monster mash-up *Drácula contra Frankenstein* (aka *Dracula, Prisoner of Frankenstein*, 1972), which starred British actor Dennis Price as Doctor Frankenstein and Howard Vernon as Count Dracula.

BOTTOM MIDDLE: Spanish poster for Jesús Franco's obscure stab at the *giallo* genre, *Un silencio de tumba* (1976), by iconic artist "Jano" (Francisco Fernández-Zarza Pérez, 1922–92). Guests on a private island owned by a movie star are murdered one-by-one.

TOP LEFT: *The Monster Club* (1981), surviving portion of gouache on watercolor paper poster by British artist Graham Humphreys. "My very first film poster, done shortly after leaving art college," he remembers. "A very tight agency brief gave me little scope to inject anything other than my preferred color scheme and paint technique. On delivery it was decided the colors were too 'horror.'"

LEFT: Graham Humphreys's final British quad for Chips Productions/Sword and Sorcery's *The Monster Club* (Dir: Roy Ward Baker, 1981). As the artist recalls: "I was given the option to repaint the illustration within two days—the original had taken four—with a child-friendly palette. I struggled to meet the deadline (I was still a novice), but managed to deliver a painting that embarrasses me to this day."

ABOVE RIGHT: *The Monster Club* (1981) by American artist Walter Velez (1939–2018), who was best known for his humorous paperback covers. This portrait of stars Vincent Price and John Carradine was done for the front cover of a glossy pre-release flyer that ITC Entertainment used to sell rights in the children's movie based on the stories of British author R. Chetwynd-Hayes (1919–2001).

THIS PAGE: Thailand, especially during the 1980s and '90s, created some of the most colorful, lurid, gory, and bizarre horror movie posters ever seen, using the talents of local artists. These were often quite variable in quality and technique but, at their best, they offered a hallucinatory snapshot of both locally produced movies and foreign imports unlike anything else seen in the rest of the world.

TOP LEFT: A mad scientist kidnaps his victims, removes their eyes, and attempts to transplant them into his blind wife in *Phi Ti Bo* (The Sunken-Eyed Ghost, 1981).

TOP MIDDLE: A young woman (Thida Teerarat) is possessed by a Krause (a floating witch's head with dangling entrails) in *Krause krahai liveat* (Bloody Filth-Eating Spirit; Dir: Sang-Tawan, 1985).

ABOVE RIGHT: *Mnusy hmapa* (Wolf; Dir: Sommai Khamsorn, 1987) was a werewolf thriller from Thailand featuring Sorapong Chatree, Niranut Atiphon, Phairoj Jaising, and a surprising amount of nudity. The hand-painted poster art is by the prolific Tongdee Panumas, who reigned supreme among Thai movie poster artists for three decades, from the 1970s through to the 1990s.

BOTTOM LEFT: *Mon khun ma jak long* (It Came Out of the Coffin; aka *The Thai Ghost*, 1991) was another Thai horror movie.

BOTTOM MIDDLE: *Ngoo geng gong* (The Snake Woman/ Devil Medusa; Dir: Charint Phromrangsi, 1995) also had a poster by Tongdee Panumas and was based on a popular South East Asian legend about the offspring of a snake-god and a human.

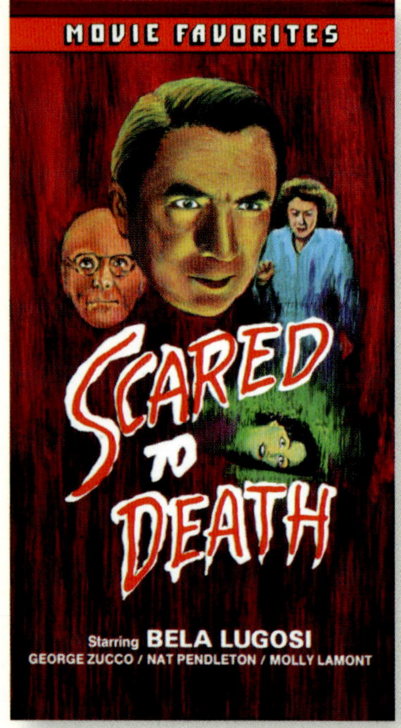

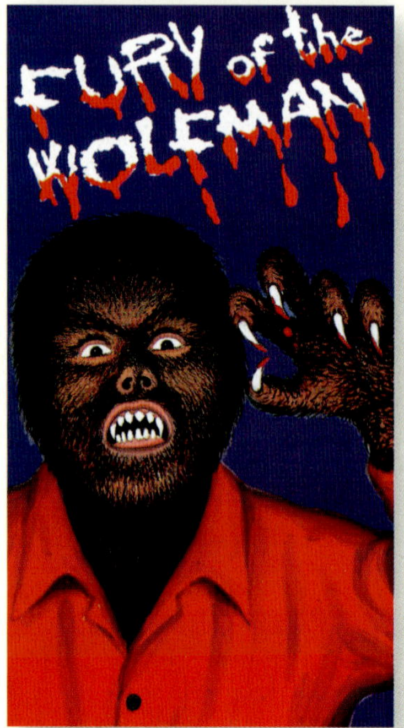

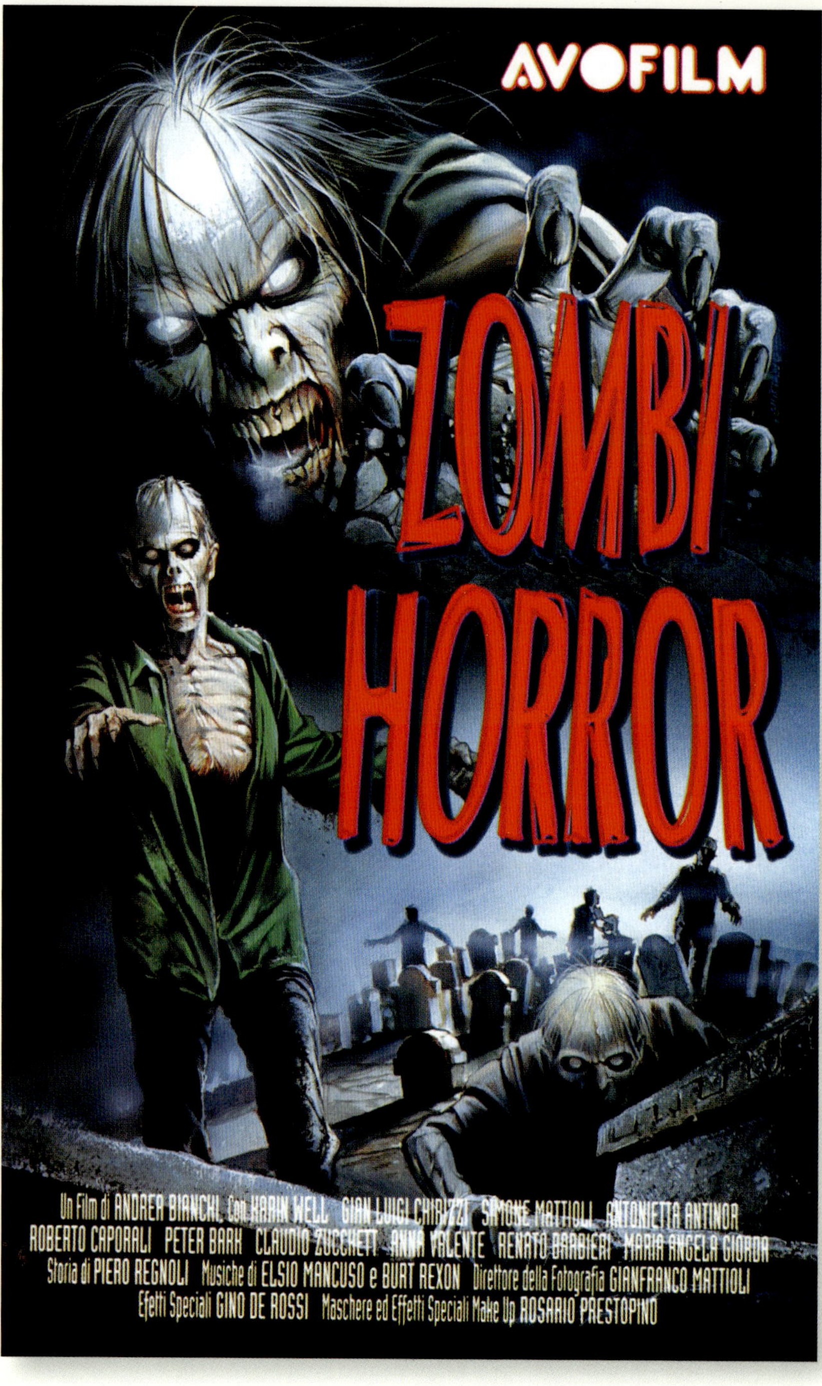

TOP LEFT: Despite having been shot in the inexpensive Cinecolor process, the box for Diamond Entertainment Corporation's 1991 VHS video of *Scared to Death* (Dir: Christy Cabanne, 1947) claimed it was in black and white.

TOP MIDDLE: The 1980s British video box for Al Adamson's *Dracula vs. Frankenstein* (aka *Blood of Frankenstein*, 1971) carried the title *Revenge of Dracula* and advised potential buyers: "It looks good and only lacks humor."

BOTTOM LEFT: Spanish star Paul Naschy wasn't even mentioned on the packaging for *Fury of the Wolfman* (aka *La furia del Hombre Lobo*; Dir: J.M. Zabalza, 1972), which was released on VHS video in America in 1994 by Alpha Video Distributors.

BOTTOM MIDDLE: John Newland's *The Legend of Hillbilly John* (aka *Who Fears the Devil*, 1972), based on stories by pulp author Manly Wade Wellman, premiered in the UK on the Rainbow Video label in 1982.

ABOVE RIGHT: In 1995, Italy's Avofilm released a cut version of Andrea Bianchi's *Le notti del terrore* (aka *Burial Ground/The Nights of Terror*, 1981) on VHS videocassette under the title *Zombi Horror* with box cover art by "Giordano."

ABOVE LEFT: The March 1971 issue of New Edigraf's monthly Italian magazine *Suspense* (1970–71) presented a photo-strip ("*cineromanzo*") adaptation of Tigon's *Curse of the Crimson Altar* (aka *The Crimson Cult*, 1968).

TOP MIDDLE: Paperback novelization (Corgi Books, 1971) of Tigon's 1971 sex-horror movie *Virgin Witch* with eight pages of photos. Author/scriptwriter "Klaus Vogel" was reportedly a pseudonym of British TV writer Hazel Adair.

TOP RIGHT: Paperback novelization of *The Werewolf vs. Vampire Woman* (Guild-Hartford Publishing, 1972) by prolific American writer Leo Guild, who is credited as "Arthur N. Scarm" on the cover and "Scram" on the title page.

BOTTOM MIDDLE: Former EC comics writer Jack Olek (1914–81) novelized Amicus's 1973 film *The Vault of Horror* (Bantam Books, 1973). It featured cover art by Lou Feck and adapted five EC stories by Al Feldstein and Bill Gaines.

BOTTOM RIGHT: French paperback of *Vidéodrome* (Éditions J'ai Lu, 1984) by "Jack Martin" (Dennis Etchsion, 1943–2019), featuring Laurent Melki's *affiche* on the cover and interior photos from David Cronenberg's 1983 movie.

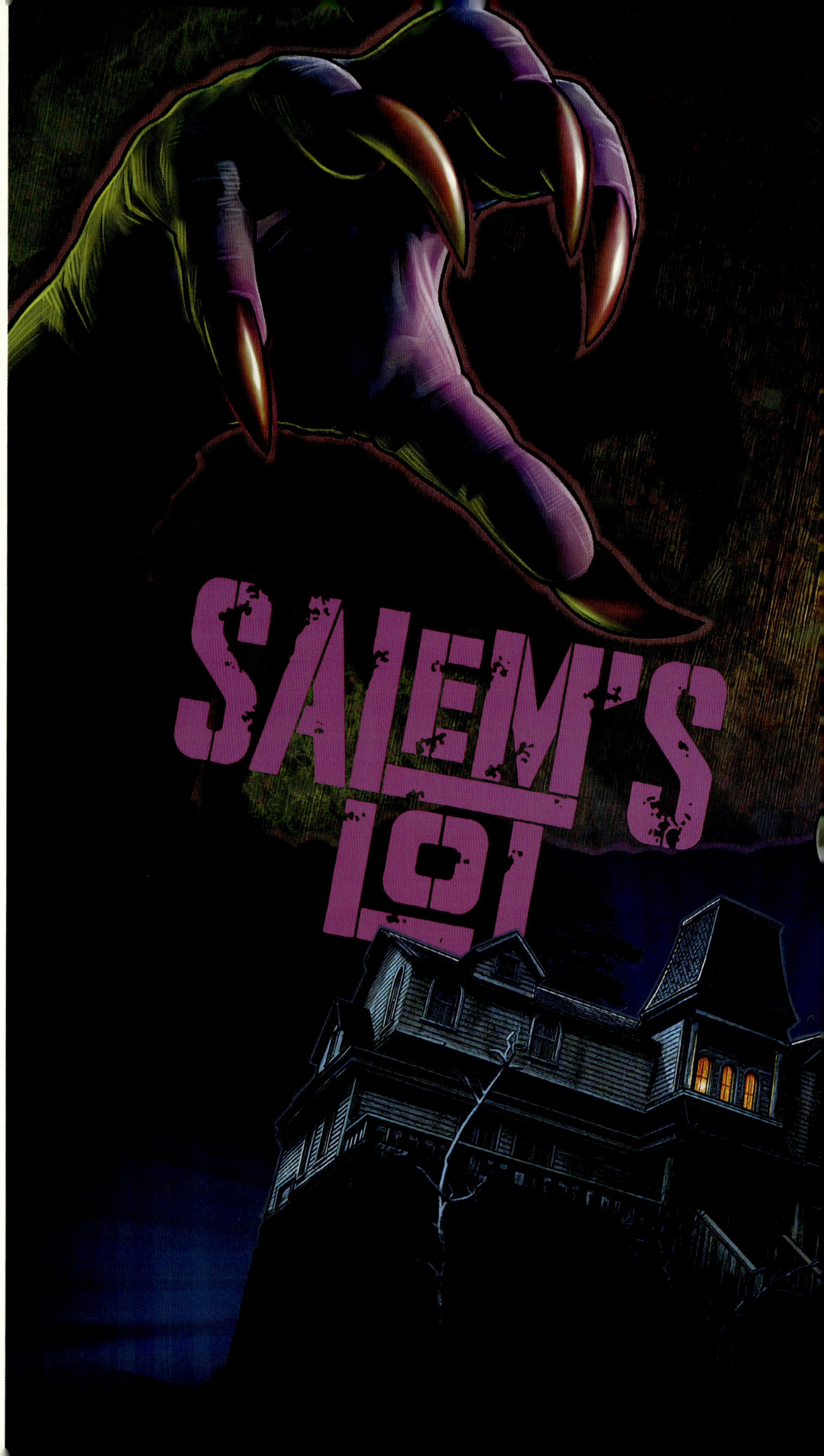

RIGHT: *Salem's Lot* (2019), detail of pencil, acrylics, gouache, Prismacolor pencils, and Photoshop poster by Christopher Franchi, created to celebrate the 40th anniversary of the made-for-TV movie [ABOVE]. "As a 13-year-old monster kid, this film by Tobe Hooper scared me to death," remembers the artist. "Ever since, the film left a stain on me that normal soap and water can't wash off."

9

BOOM AND BUST

STEFAN DZIEMIANOWICZ

"Everybody is a book of blood;
Wherever we're opened, we're red."

BOOKS OF BLOOD (1984–85) BY CLIVE BARKER

"Good taste is the enemy of art."

John Waters channeling Pablo Picasso

"I have seen the future of horror, and his name is Clive Barker."

Stephen King, World Fantasy Convention 1984, Ottawa, Canada

IN THE EARLY 1970s horror did not exist as a category of popular fiction—at least as far as most commercial book trade publishers were concerned. The cover of Ira Levin's *Rosemary's Baby* (1967), generally regarded as the novel that laid the charges for the late-twentieth-century horror boom, sported an adulatory quote from Truman Capote comparing it to Henry James's *The Turn of the Screw*.

The covers of William Peter Blatty's *The Exorcist* (1971) and Thomas Tryon's *The Other* (1971) both featured images of human faces that indicated little about their content, and their paperback reprints simply duplicated the cover art of those editions with lines superimposed above their titles that called out the number of months each book had spent on the bestseller list. The cover of the hardcover first printing of Stephen King's *Carrie* (1974) was similarly non-dramatic and ambiguous.

However, the year before the publication of King's first novel, William Friedkin had memorably adapted Blatty's tale of a demonically possessed young girl as a visceral and shocking film that successfully reached an audience much larger than that of mere horror devotees. King's novel would also be adapted in graphic fashion in 1976 as another immensely popular film by Brian De Palma, released a year after its paperback reprint became a million-copy national bestseller and launched King's career as one of the most popular authors of all time. Both films would garner major Academy Award nominations that helped to fix horror in the general public's mind as a legitimate category of contemporary entertainment.

King's novel was the culmination of a career that, up until then, had developed primarily in the pages of *Cavalier* and similar men's magazines through a string of stories on gritty horror themes—among them "Graveyard Shift," about a nest of overgrown, voracious rats that overwhelms a crew sent in to clean up the basement of a rundown mill. King's counterpart in England, James Herbert, saw his first work of fiction, the novel *The Rats*, published the same year as *Carrie*. Reviewers criticized its disconcertingly vivid descriptions of outsized rats preying on the residents of the slums of modern London, but sales soared, and the explicitness of Herbert's approach to his horror themes became integral to his writing, and to horror fiction released subsequent to his and King's novels in general.

The popularity of King's and Herbert's books heralded what might be called a new candor in the writing of contemporary horror fiction: modern writers were increasingly willing to challenge taboos that had hitherto been considered off-limits, and publishers were increasingly willing to publish fiction that pushed the envelope of what had previously been deemed acceptable. As King famously expressed in *Danse Macabre* (1981), "I recognize terror as the finest emotion . . . and so I will try to terrorize the reader. But if I find I cannot terrify him/her, I will try to horrify; and if I find I cannot horrify, I'll go for the gross-out."

Modern writers were increasingly willing to challenge taboos that had hitherto been considered off-limits, and publishers were increasingly willing to publish fiction that pushed the envelope of what had previously been deemed acceptable.

The very fact that *Danse Macabre*, King's non-fiction study of horror in popular entertainment, found a home with a trade publishing house in 1981 indicates that publishers accepted that horror was a phenomenon in popular culture worth paying attention to. Indeed, the years 1974 to 1984 saw the emergence of several writers whose best-selling books were embraced by an apparently growing readership for horror, among them Anne Rice, Peter Straub, Robert R. McCammon, Dean Koontz, and eventually Clive Barker. Barker's six-volume *Books of Blood* short-fiction collections were published between 1984 and 1985 and they both raised and lowered the bar for the artistic extremes for which a horror writer might deploy violent, gory, and sexually explicit imagery.

The *Books of Blood* were first published as paperback originals, and by the 1980s horror was firmly entrenched in the paperback mass market. Trade publishers, acting on the belief that sales in the millions of titles by Stephen King and other best-selling writers of horror indicated an audience of millions of readers ravenous for that type of fiction, launched horror lines—not only genre publishers such as Tor, Zebra, and Leisure, but long-established paperback imprints of trade houses, including Bantam and Pocket. Each began releasing one, two, or sometimes more horror titles per month to fulfill the perceived market need.

PREVIOUS SPREAD: *Terror by Night* (1974), designer's gouache on board cover by British artist Les Edwards for the collection of the same title by R. Chetwynd-Hayes (Universal-Tandem Publishing Co. Ltd., 1974). "An early painting," recalls the artist. "I was quite pleased with the way it turned out, but I can't remember what, if anything, the image had to do with the book. I've got a feeling she's a werewolf."

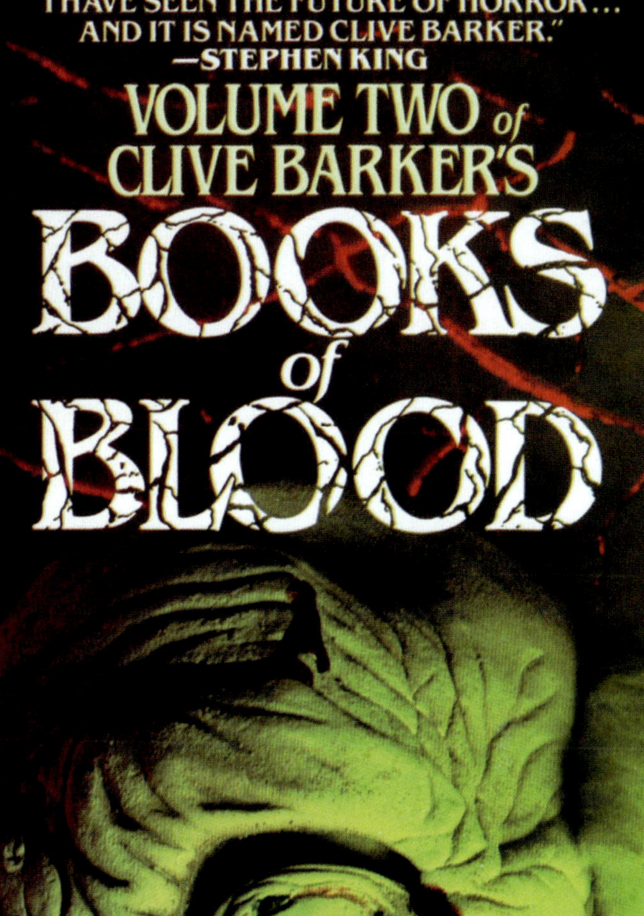

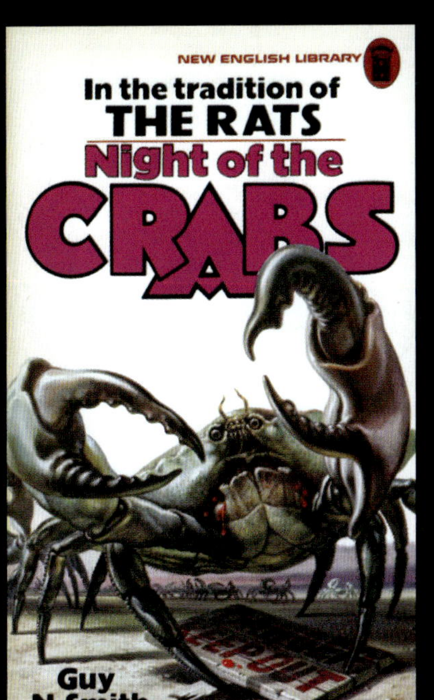

TOP LEFT: Later paperback reissues of Stephen King's 1974 debut novel *Carrie* from Signet/New American Library not only added the title and author's byline to James Barkley's original artwork, but also a running total of sales.

TOP MIDDLE: W. Francis Phillips's cover for *The Rats*, which James Herbert (1943–2013) wrote in secret while working at an advertising agency. When published by New English Library in 1974 it created a whole new subgenre of horror "nasties."

BOTTOM LEFT: Looking to repeat their success with James Herbert, in 1976 New English Library published *Night of the Crabs* by Guy N. Smith, the first of seven novels and a short story collection in the author's "Killer Crabs" series.

BOTTOM MIDDLE: *Slugs* (Star/W.H. Allen & Co. Ltd., 1982) was the second horror novel by British author Shaun Hutson, who went on to rival James Herbert with a string of gruesome books, including a sequel, *Breeding Ground* (1985).

ABOVE RIGHT: In Britain, Sphere Books published all six volumes of *Clive Barker's Books of Blood* (1984–85) with photographs on the front. In America, Berkley Books gave the first three paperback volumes much more striking covers in 1986.

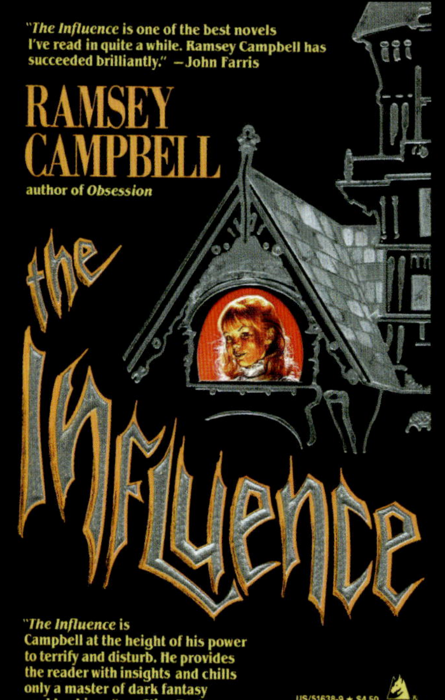

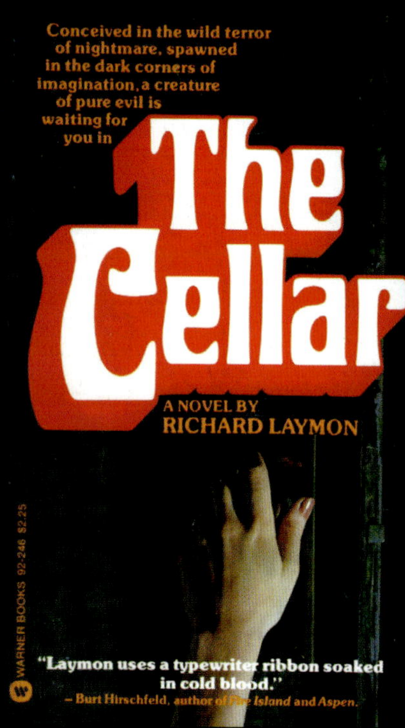

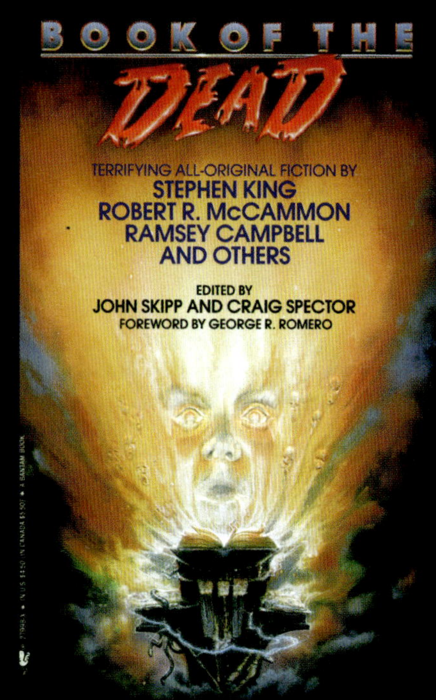

TOP RIGHT: Ballantine Books' 1979 paperback reissue of Anne Rice's groundbreaking 1976 novel *Interview with the Vampire* featured a suitably atmospheric cover painting by historical romance artist H. Tom Hall (1932–2010).

BOTTOM MIDDLE: Following the publication of his controversial first novel, *The Cellar* (Warner Books, 1980), American writer Richard Laymon (1947–2001) was better known in Europe for his graphically explicit horror novels.

ABOVE LEFT & TOP MIDDLE: When Ramsey Campbell's 1988 novel *The Influence* was published in America the following year in paperback by Tor Books as part of the popular child-horror genre, it featured a die-cut cover.

BOTTOM RIGHT: Edited by proto-splatterpunks John Skipp and Craig Spector, *Book of the Dead* (Bantam Books, 1989) was the first of two influential anthologies set in the world of George A. Romero's 1968 movie *Night of the Living Dead*.

In response, booksellers created dedicated horror sections in their stores to separate out horror titles from the mainstream fiction and fantasy sections where books had been stocked previously. Writers—some of whom had been channeling their fondness for horror themes into stories published in crime, fantasy, and science fiction publications of the day, but many of whom were completely new to the genre—rushed in to seize the opportunity that the burgeoning market for horror fiction represented.

While the expanding opportunities for publishing horror fiction benefited many writers, the downside of the genre's market saturation soon became evident. There was often a marked contrast in quality between the fiction published by the paperback imprints of established trade houses and the fiction published by down-market genre publishers. Furthermore, mass-market publishers faced the same problem that publishers of pulp magazines a half-century before faced: there was simply not enough quality fiction to release on a regular basis in a market driven by the publisher's need to fill monthly slots in its schedule.

Consequently, a lot of formulaic, generic, and imitative fiction was released. The popularity of the novels *Rosemary's Baby* and *The Exorcist* and their film adaptations, and movie series such as *The Omen* (1976), inspired scores of novels about demonic children and satanic cults. Likewise the best-selling success of Anne Rice's chronicles of the Vampire Lestat prompted such a flood of derivative stories that vampire fiction virtually became a genre in its own right in the 1980s and '90s, with its own subgenres and secondary and tertiary themes.

Like the pulp magazine publishers of the early twentieth century, many publishers of pulp horror in the '80s relied on packaging gimmicks to distinguish their titles from those of competitors or identify them as horror with instantly familiar imagery. Images of skeletons dressed in human garb, dolls with cracked faces, and children with demonic features became *de rigueur* on paperback book covers, even when there was no reference to them in the stories they illustrated. Covers with holographic effects that transformed the features of ordinary-looking people into fright masks, and die cuts and see-through apertures that gave dimension to horrific scenes obscured by superficial cover images were common as well. These gaudy visual effects screamed "horror!" but they often masked stories that were as pedestrian and predictable as most generic pulp fiction.

These gaudy visual effects screamed "horror!" but they often masked stories that were as pedestrian and predictable as most generic pulp fiction.

By the late '80s, horror's mass market was imploding under the weight of so much mediocre (or at the very least, unremarkable) fiction. Publishers acknowledged that they had miscalculated in their gamble that sales for horror's best-selling writers indicated a vast audience for horror fiction in general, and they began to streamline their horror lines—or discontinue them altogether. But horror didn't go down without a fight and there were several efforts by writers and publishers to take the genre in a viable new direction.

The decade's end saw the rise of splatterpunk, a type of fiction that emphasized physical horrors described in brutal, visceral detail. Although proponents of splatterpunk lauded it as an approach with the potential to revitalize a genre that had become conventional and lethargic, critics of its extremism saw it as little more than a fad that promoted gore for gore's sake and a hallmark of horror's descent into decadence.

Self-described splatterpunks John Skipp and Craig Spector cited George A. Romero's low-budget zombie film *Night of the Living Dead* (1968), with its scenes of gruesome gore and zombie mayhem, as formative influences on their work, and their two anthologies of original zombie fiction, *Book of the Dead* (1989) and *Still Dead: Book of the Dead 2* (1992), spurred a glut of new (and mostly formulaic) stories and novels featuring rampaging hordes of Romeroesque zombies ravenous for human brains.

The late 1980s and early '90s also saw the rise of serial-killer fiction, a crossover from, and into, crime fiction that was partly a response to the popularity of Jonathan Demme's 1991 film adaptation of Thomas Harris's novel *The Silence of the Lambs* (1988), and the revels of its now-iconic cannibalistic killer, Dr. Hannibal Lecter.

Well before the start of the twenty-first century, the '80s horror boom had gone bust and the fiction still being published had pretty much become the province of the genre's specialty presses—which, ironically, had come into being and flourished at the same time that horror was making its mark in the mass market. Publishers such as Scream/Dream Press and Dark Harvest, and later Cemetery Dance Publications, Subterranean Press, and PS Publishing, brought out attractive and collectible hardcover editions of most of horror's best writers—not unlike the handful of specialty fantasy and science fiction presses that had sprung up in the years immediately following World War II. Their print runs, considerably smaller than those for the average mass-market paperbacks, were considered a more realistic gauge of the size of horror's core audience.

Today, horror's boom years in the 1980s are the stuff of nostalgia, and the tide of novels that flooded the market, along with the outrageous cover art they bore, a time capsule commemorating one of the genre's most profligately pulpy moments.

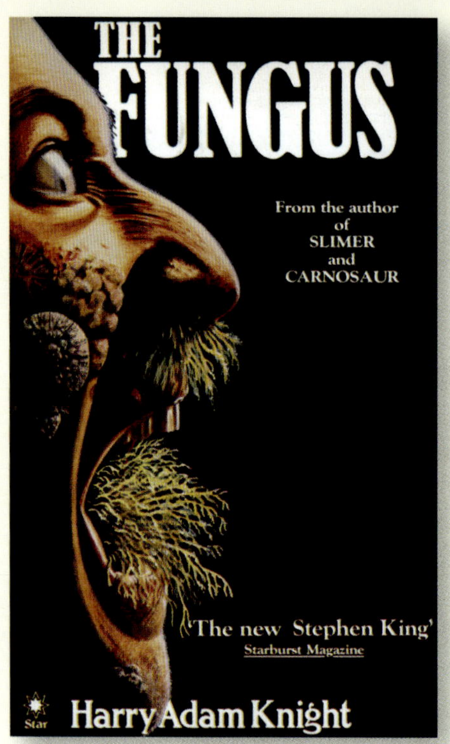

THIS PAGE: In Britain, the success of James Herbert's *The Rats* (1974) led to a grisly and graphic subgenre of bats, cats, crabs, and other "nasties," while some authors returned to the classic tropes of horror and reinvented their themes for a whole new generation of readers.

The first publication of R. (Ronald) Chetwynd-Hayes's episodic novel *The Monster Club* (New English Library, 1976), filmed in 1981.

The Son of the Werewolf (New English Library, 1978) was the third volume in the lycanthropic trilogy by Guy N. (Newman) Smith.

Terry Oakes's cover for the 1980 paperback of Basil Copper's 1974 Lovecraftian novel *The Great White Space* (Sphere Books Ltd.).

Steve Crisp's grisly cover for *Angelus!* (Panther Books, 1985), a "slasher" novel by Peter Tremayne (Peter Berresford Ellis).

The Fungus (Star/W.H. Allen & Co., 1985), a gory paperback original by the acronymous "Harry Adam Knight" (John Brosnan and Leroy Kettle).

Bob Larkin's die-cut cover for Graham Masterton's *Feast* (Pinnacle Books, 1988), originally published in the UK as *Ritual*.

THIS PAGE: In the USA, the success of Stephen King's *Carrie* (1974) led to the creation of a whole new publishing genre that heaped its horrors upon small-town communities, urban cities, and All-American families with devil-children, and would shape the future of modern horror.

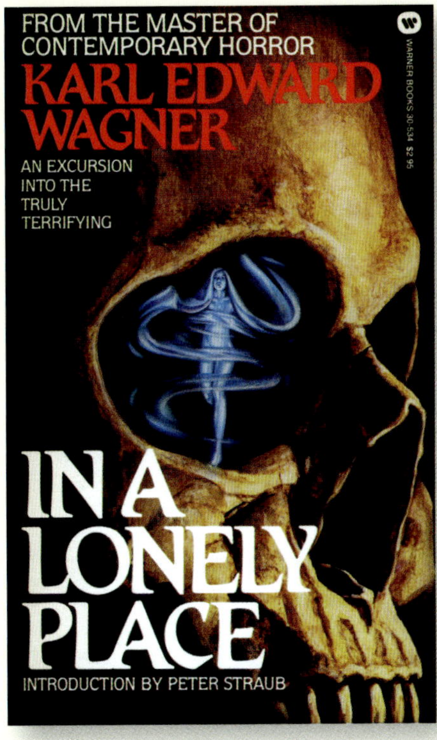

Barclay Shaw's cover for Karl Edward Wagner's collection *In a Lonely Place* (Warner Books, Inc., 1983), introduced by Peter Straub.

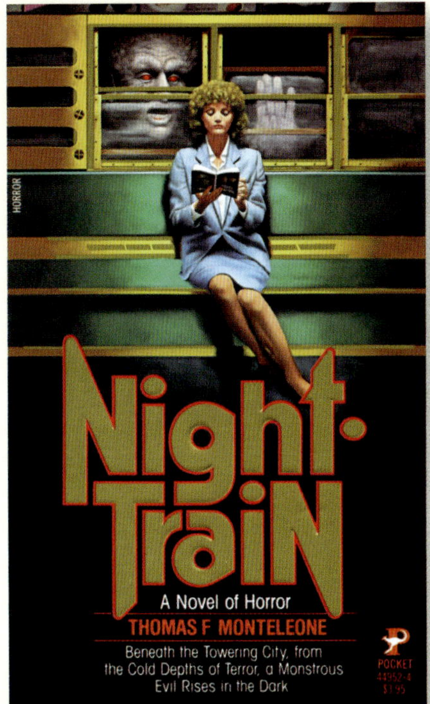

Lisa Falkenstern's cover for Thomas F. (Francis) Monteleone's urban horror novel, *Night Train* (Pocket Books, 1984).

Chris Moore's cover for the UK paperback original *Finishing Touches* (Grafton Books, 1987) by American author Thomas Tessier.

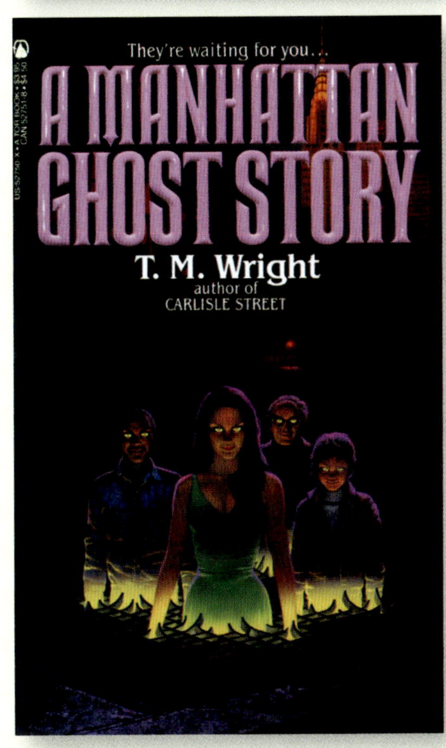

A Manhattan Ghost Story (Tor, 1984) by T. (Terrance) M. (Michael) Wright, one of a new breed of American horror authors.

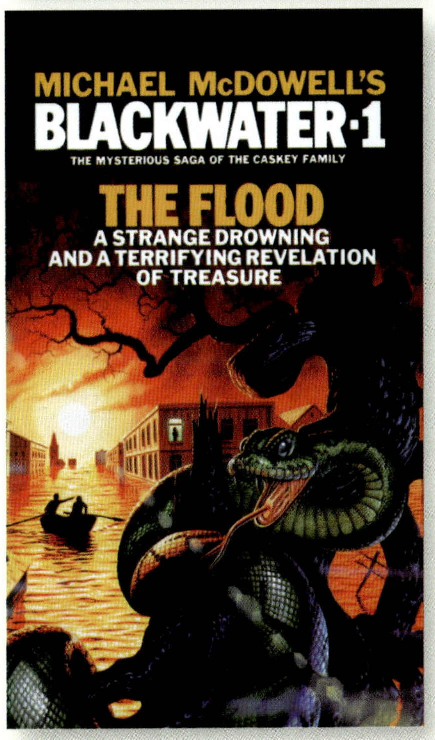

The British paperback of *The Flood* (Corgi/Avon, 1985), the first book in Michael McDowell's six-volume "Blackwater" series.

Reborn (Jove Books, 1990) was actually the third book in the series by F. (Francis) Paul Wilson that began with *The Keep* (1981).

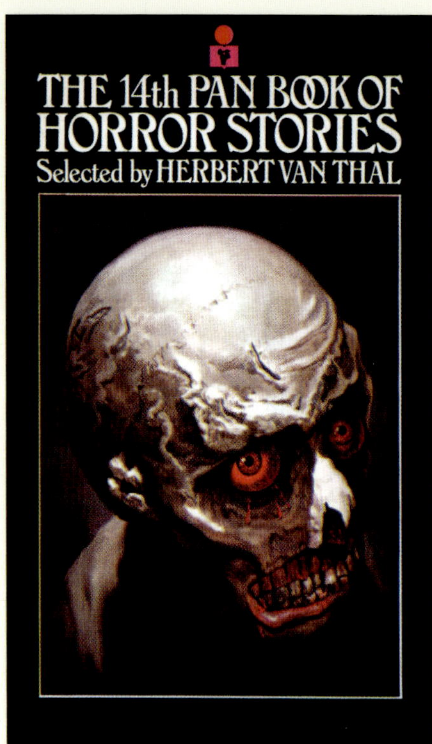

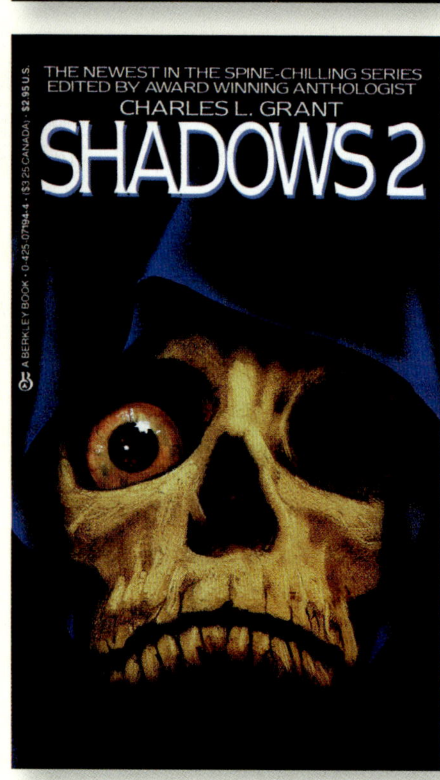

TOP LEFT: Josh Kirby's atypical cover for *The Fourteenth Pan Book of Horror Stories* (Pan Books, 1973) edited by Herbert van Thal. The UK anthology series ran for 30 volumes from 1959–1989, the first 25 edited by van Thal.

TOP MIDDLE: Michael Whelan's cover for Gerald W. Page's *The Year's Best Horror Stories: Series VI* (DAW Books, Inc., 1978). Richard Davis edited the first three volumes (1972–75) and Karl Edward Wagner edited VIII–XXII (1980–94).

BOTTOM LEFT: *The Thirteenth Fontana Book of Great Horror Stories* (Fontana Books, 1980) edited by Mary Danby.

BOTTOM MIDDLE: *Shadows 2* (Berkley Books, 1984), the second in editor Charles L. Grant's 11-volume anthology series (1978–91).

ABOVE RIGHT: *Hotter Blood: More Tales of Erotic Horror* (Pocket Books, 1991) was the second book in a 13-volume series of anthologies created by Jeff Gelb and Lonn Friend in 1989 and continued by Gelb and Michael Garrett until 2007.

OPPOSITE: *Terror by Gaslight* (1977), watercolor on paper cover for the Hugh Lamb anthology by British artist Alan Lee, who explains, "One of the many pleasures of doing covers for horror and ghost-story anthologies is trying to create an image summing up the cumulative effect of the stories."

Rowena

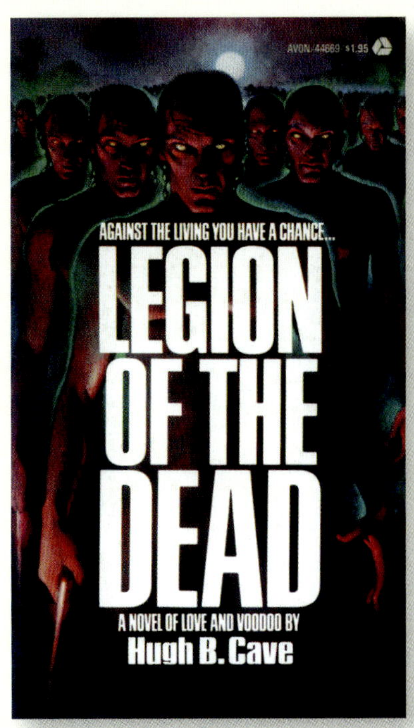

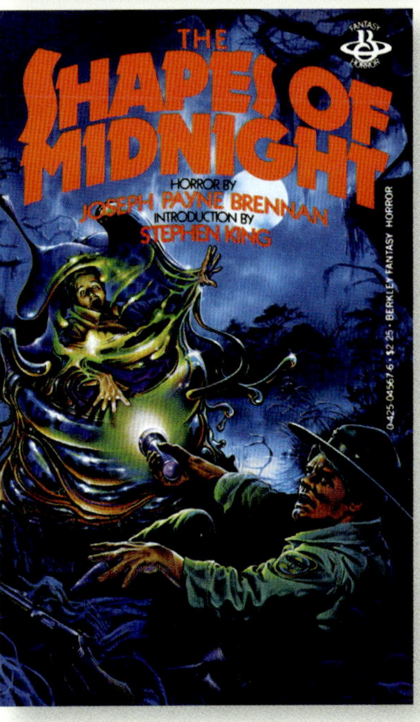

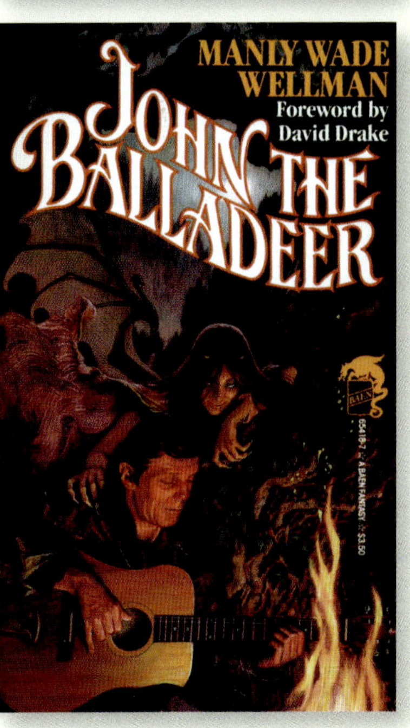

OPPOSITE: *The Dunwich Horror* (1978), airbrush cover by American artist Rowena Morrill for the abridged paperback reprint collection *The Dunwich Horror and Others* from Jove/HBJ. "I find H.P. Lovecraft's monsters so imaginative," reveals the artist, "and I had the most wonderful time putting together all the different textures and colors to depict this one."

ABOVE LEFT: As a teenager, Frank Belknap Long began corresponding with H.P. Lovecraft, and the two remained friends until the latter's death in 1937. Long sold his first story to *Weird Tales* in 1924, and he was still publishing new fiction throughout the 1970s, including the novel *The Night of the Wolf* (Popular Library, 1972). Artist Gray Morrow obviously based his cover on *The Wolf Man* (1941).

TOP MIDDLE: Fritz Leiber had finally dropped the "Jr." from his name long before this British paperback of his final novel, *Our Lady of Darkness*, came out in 1978 from Fontana/Collins with a suitably expressionistic cover by Roy Ellsworth. A shorter version of the literary horror story had been serialized as "The Pale Brown Thing" in *The Magazine of Fantasy and Science Fiction* the year before.

TOP RIGHT: British-born author Hugh B. (Barnett) Cave published his first story in 1929 and was still being published in 2004, the year of his death. Thanks to Karl Edward Wagner, who had issued a collection of his pulp stories, Cave's work enjoyed a renaissance in the 1970s, and *Legion of the Dead* (Avon Books, 1979) was the first in a new series of novels from the veteran writer, who was an expert on voodoo.

BOTTOM MIDDLE: Kirk Reinert illustrated Joseph Payne Brennan's 1953 *Weird Tales* story "Slime" for the cover of the collection *The Shapes of Midnight* (Berkley Books, 1980).

BOTTOM RIGHT: Steve Hickman's cover for *John the Balladeer* (Baen Books, 1988), which collected all Manly Wade Wellman's "Silver John" stories from 1951–1987.

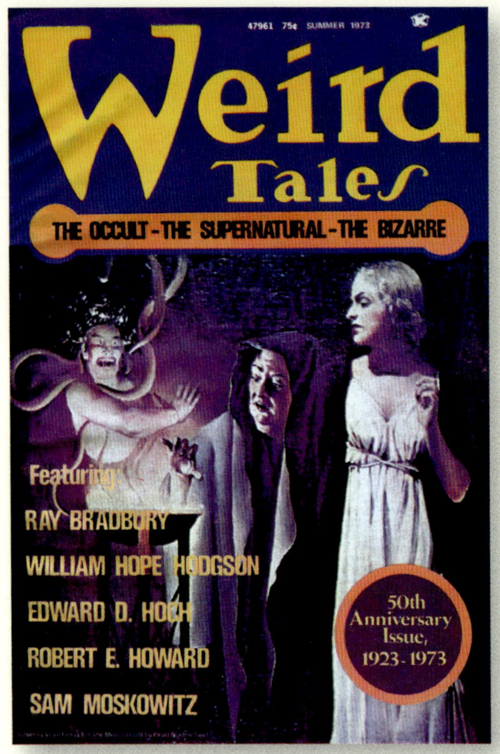

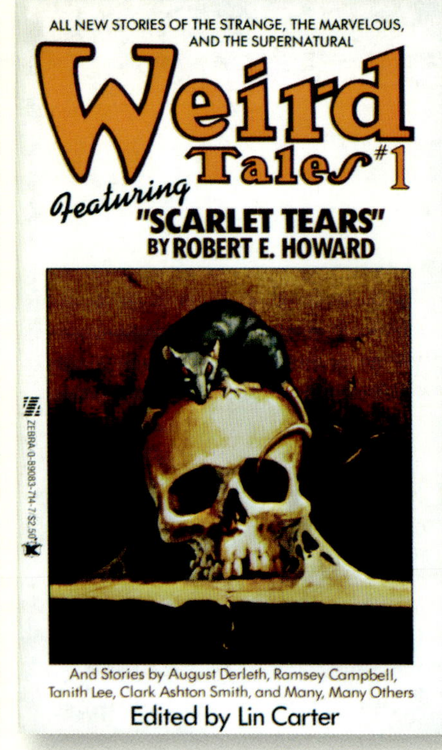

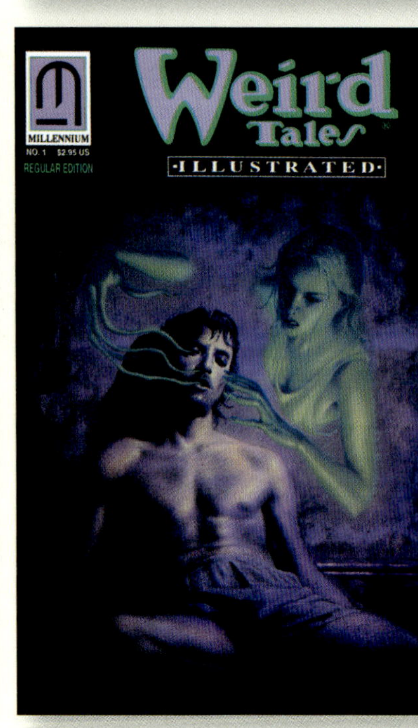

TOP LEFT: After *Weird Tales* ended its 31-year publishing history with the September 1954 issue, this was the first of four issues published by Leo Margulies between 1973–74. Editor Sam Moskowitz used a previously unpublished painting by Virgil Finlay on the cover.

TOP MIDDLE: Between 1980–84 Lin Carter took over the editorship of *Weird Tales* for four paperback volumes from low-rent imprint Zebra Books/Kensington Publishing Corp. Tom Barber did the cover to the first book, which featured a newly discovered novella by Robert E. Howard.

BOTTOM LEFT: Rare proof cover with art by Korean-American artist "Ro H. Kim" (Hyang Ro Kim) for the first of just two magazine issues of *Weird Tales* (1984–85) from California publisher Brian L. Forbes/The Bellerophon Network, Inc. that omitted contributor Stephen King's name.

ABOVE RIGHT: Gahan Wilson contributed the cover and some interior art to the Spring 1991 issue of *Weird Tales* from Terminus Publishing Co., Inc., which published the pulp-sized periodical from 1988–94 before it returned to a magazine format in 1998.

BOTTOM MIDDLE: In 1992, Millennium Publications, Inc. issued the first and only issue of the comic *Weird Tales Illustrated*. With a cover by British artist John Bolton, the Deluxe Edition included an extra story by Les Daniels. A planned second issue never appeared.

TOP LEFT: John Stewart's cover for *Whispers* No. 15–16 (March 1982) was based on Ramsey Campbell's award-winning story "Mackintosh Willy." Editor Stuart David Schiff's influential semi-prozine ran for 24 issues (1973–87) and seven hardcover book anthologies (1977–94).

BOTTOM LEFT: J.K. Potter's surreal photo-art cover for Night Cry No. 6 (Summer 1986), edited by Alan Rodgers. The digest-sized periodical was an all-fiction companion to *Rod Serling's The Twilight Zone Magazine* from the same publisher. It lasted for only 11 issues, from 1984–87.

ABOVE RIGHT: Alan M. Clark's cover for the first of three issues (1990–91) of the glossy semi-prozine *Iniquities: The Magazine of Great Wickedness and Wonder*. Edited by Buddy Martinez, Bill Furtado, and J.F. Gonzalez, the publication expertly tapped into the new generation of horror writers.

FOLLOWING PAGE: *After Midnight* (1985), acrylic on stretched canvas by American artist Jill Bauman. "In 1984," remembers Bauman, "Tor Books assigned me the cover of an anthology entitled *Midnight*, edited by Charles L. Grant. The following year they asked me to do the cover for Charlie's follow-up book, *After Midnight*. I used an old Barnum & Bailey clown doll as the model for the painting, and I am still haunted by that doll as he sits on my dresser. I went back to my original records, and I finished it August 1985 and it was published in April. They turned it around quickly."

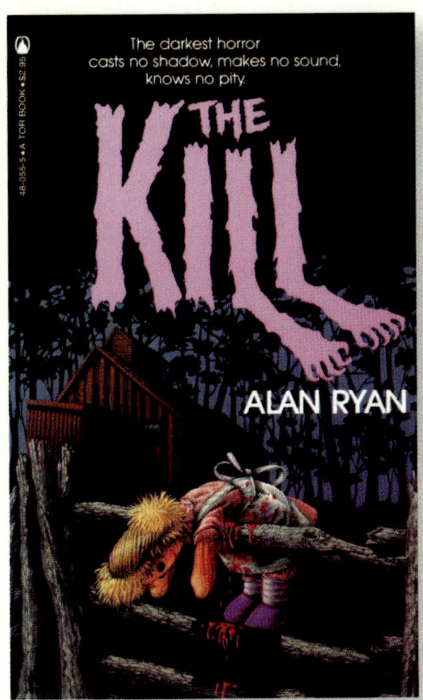

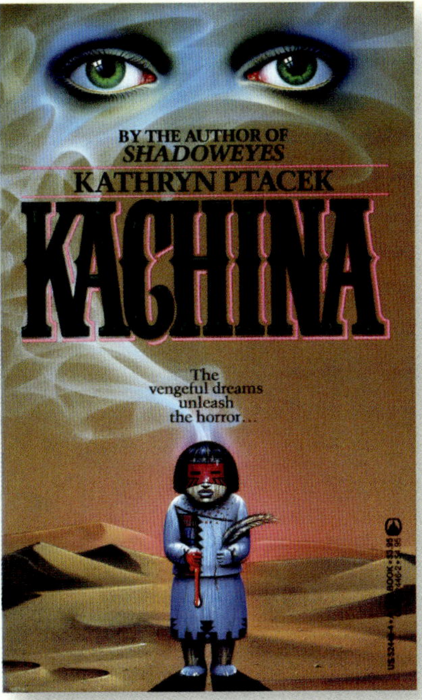

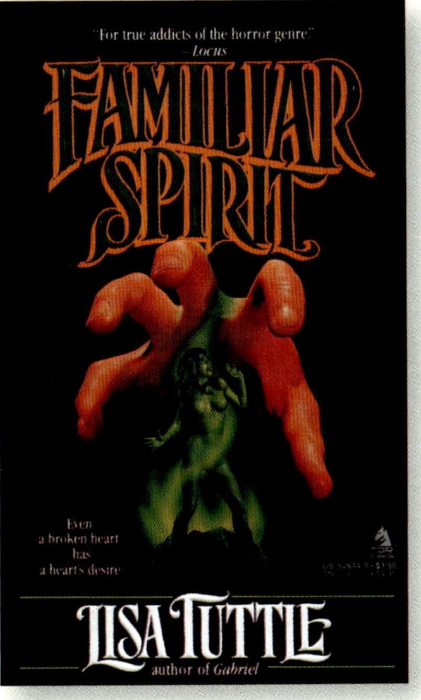

The Peak of Success

Founded in 1980 by former book salesman Tom Doherty (b. 1935), the eponymous Tom Doherty Associates, Inc. revolutionized the way horror books were published in America with its new imprint Tor (named after the kind of mountain peak depicted in its logo). Using modern printing methods such as foiling, embossing, and complicated die-cut patterns, Tor's books stood out from the other paperbacks in bookstores simply by their covers, and it was not long before other publishers started following suit. By the mid-1980s, the Tor Horror imprint was the market leader, and it continued to attract both new and older writers until the horror boom finally imploded in the early 1990s.

TOP LEFT: Jill Bauman used another doll for reference on her cover for Alan Ryan's second horror novel, *The Kill* (Tor, 1982).

TOP MIDDLE: Kathryn Ptacek was married to fellow author Charles Grant, and Tor published her novel *Kachina* in 1986 with cover art by Paul Stinson.

BOTTOM LEFT: American-born author Lisa Tuttle had her 1983 novel *Familiar Spirit* reprinted under the Tor Horror imprint in 1989.

BOTTOM MIDDLE: Tor also supported older writers like Robert Bloch, publishing his new horror novel *Lori* in paperback in 1990 with cover art by Jim Thiesen.

ABOVE RIGHT: Originally published in Britain by Grafton, Brian Lumley's transgressive "Necroscope" vampire series only really took off after Tor Horror used Bob Eggleton to do the covers, as he did on the fourth volume in the best-selling sequence, *Deadspeak*, which was published first in America in 1990.

ABOVE LEFT: *Necroscope* (1988), acrylics on canvas cover by American artist Bob Eggleton for Tor's first American edition of Brian Lumley's best-selling 1986 vampire novel of the same name. Eggleton's fanged skull went on to set the visual tone for the 17-book series and influenced many other artists. "Horror books are very hard to do in a 'narrative' way," explains the artist, "often it is best to sum up the story with an iconic image. In this case: skulls. This was the skull that launched 1,000 screams and many more skulls to come."

TOP RIGHT: With cover art by Spanish artist "Maren," (Mariano Pérez Clemente), the paperback edition of *Yellow Fog* (Tor, 1988) was the fourth book in a five-volume series by Les Daniels (1943–2011) featuring historical vampire Don Sebastian de Villanueva.

BOTTOM RIGHT: Michel Gurfinkel's photo-montage cover for the French paperback (Éditions J'ai lu, 1998) of Kim Newman's postmodern 1992 vampire novel *Anno Dracula*, which imagined an alternate history in which Count Dracula married Queen Victoria.

RIGHT: The first UK edition (Penguin Books, 1988) of Alan Ryan's seminal anthology *The Penguin Book of Vampire Stories* used a re-designed version of the cover illustration by Edward Gorey that had originally appeared on the 1987 American hardcover from Doubleday.

ABOVE: *The Penguin Book of Vampire Stories* (1991), acrylic ink and airbrush on board by British artist Steve Crisp for the 1991 hardcover reprint from Bloomsbury Books. "This illustration was part of a series," recalls the artist, "which were great fun to do and in a larger wraparound format than the usual paperback size. I wanted to use a more realistic vampire than the usual 'Christopher Lee' portrayal, with the teeth at the front. The background is very simple, colorful but dramatic, and I believe makes an eye-catching book cover."

THE STRANGE CASES OF JOHN SINCLAIR

"In the 1970s you needed an English pseudonym as a scary author. I got 'Jason' from a TV series—*Jason King*. My wife could not stand that. I wanted to annoy her a bit, so I named myself after him."

Helmut Rellergerd

JASON DARK'S PULP horror series *Geisterjäger* (Ghosthunter) *John Sinclair* is the most popular horror-detective series of all time—although readers outside of German-speaking countries may not be familiar with it. Dark is a house name for German publisher Bastei-Lübbe, and the pseudonym used primarily by Helmut Rellergerd (b. 1945), who is credited with having written over 2,000 of the more than 2,200 novellas in the series to date.

John Sinclair made his debut in 1973 in Bastei's *Gespenster-Krimi* (Ghost Thriller) magazine. The stories, each of which range from 20,000 to 30,000 words in length, have been published in their own weekly series since 1978 and account for an estimated circulation of 400 million copies—making Rellergerd, by his publisher's calculations, the most widely read novelist in his country.

Sinclair works as an inspector for New Scotland Yard and his assignments frequently pit him against formidable opponents with supernatural endowments. These experiences have given him an accommodating perspective on the uncanny. As he reflects in *Die Nacht des Hexers* (The Night of the Necromancer, 1973), "To be sure, he was a realist, but he also knew there are things which conventional learning cannot explain." Mortal and of Scottish descent, Sinclair is purportedly the reincarnation of King Solomon and Knight Templar Hector de Valois. He arms himself with a Beretta handgun loaded with silver bullets, and he also carries a blessed cross bearing the initials of four archangels whose divine bestowal of it on him has earned him the appellation "Son of the Light."

Like most pulp heroes, Sinclair has gathered a cohort of sidekicks and colleagues about him, including fellow Inspector Suko (a Shaolin martial artist who wields a whip made from the skin of a demon), and their superior, Sir James Powell. Sinclair's closest personal friend is investigative reporter Bill Conolly, his first roommate after he moved away from home. Counterbalancing these comrades in arms is a cast of colorful recurring evildoers, who are sometimes destroyed at the end of one story only to be revived in another. These include Doctor Death, whose soul was transferred into the body of a gangster after a fatal encounter with Sinclair, the demons Asmodina and The Black Death, and Will Mallmann, a former personal friend of Sinclair's turned vampire.

Sinclair's escapades run the gamut of macabre encounters. The first book in his own series, *Im Nachtclub der Vampire* (In the Vampire Nightclub, 1978), pits him against a cabal of gamine bloodsuckers. From just that same year, *Die Totenkopf-Insel* (The Skull Island) features zombie pirates, *Achterbahn ins Jenseits* (Roller Coaster into the Afterlife) a haunted carnival, *Der endlose Tod* (The Endless Death) an undead Viking warrior, *Lebendig begraben* (Buried Alive) a premature burial, *Geister-Roulett* (Ghost Roulette) a satanic casino, and so on. He even travels to America for several of his exploits, among them *Das Horror-Taxi von New York* (The Horror Taxi of New York, also 1978). Most of the John Sinclair stories are distinguished by intensive, sustained encounters with supernatural menaces, as in the adventure *Mein erster Fall* (My First Case, 1999), in which Sinclair and Conolly fend off, at great length, the deadly assaults of their psychotic landlady and her zombie husband.

Sinclair works as an inspector for New Scotland Yard and his assignments frequently pit him against formidable opponents with supernatural endowments. These experiences have given him an accommodating perspective on the uncanny.

The cover art for the John Sinclair series—much of it drawn by Spanish artist "Vincente Ballestar" (Vicenç Badalona Ballestar, 1929–2014), and some of it featuring art repurposed from the work of such well-known artists of the macabre as Les Edwards and J.K. Potter—is integral to the experience of the adventures. Its depictions of supernatural horrors, imperiled victims, and horrific set pieces, often in explicit images and luridly vibrant colors, is very redolent of the ethos of the American pulp fiction magazines of the early twentieth century. *SD*

TOP RIGHT: British artist Eddie Jones (1935–99) contributed cover art to the first issue of Bastei-Verlag's weekly horror magazine *Gespenster-Krimi* (Ghost Thriller, 1973), which introduced readers to the occult detective series by the prolific German author "Jason Dark" (Helmut Rellergerd).

ABOVE LEFT: From 1978, "Geisterjäger John Sinclair" appeared in his own weekly magazine from Bastei-Verlag. Regular Spanish artist Vincente Ballestar contributed the cover to *Der Monster-Club* (1982) which, despite having the same title, had nothing to do with the book by R. Chetwynd-Hayes.

BOTTOM RIGHT: Manuel Sanjulián's cover for Jason Dark's "Geisterjäger John Sinclair" paperback novel *Die Maske* (Bastei Lübe, 1990) was based on the movie *Mystery of the Wax Museum* (1933) and first appeared on the cover of *Famous Monsters of Filmland* No. 113 (January 1975).

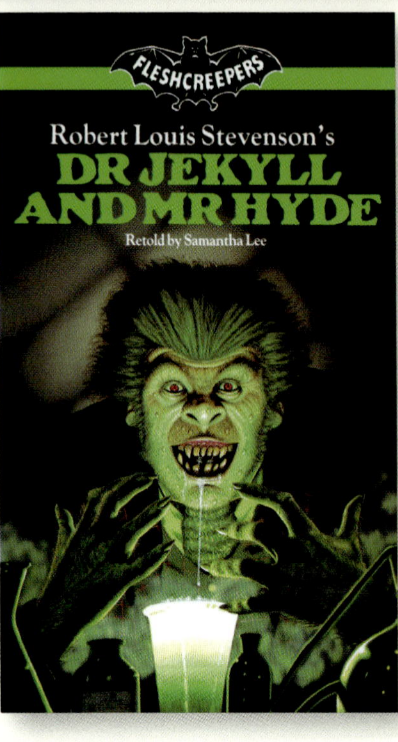

TOP LEFT: Ivan Lapper created the cover and interior illustrations for the children's anthology *The Gruesome Book* (Piccolo Books, 1983), edited by Ramsey Campbell and featuring nine classic horror stories by Nigel Kneale, Robert Bloch, Donald A. Wollheim, and others.

TOP MIDDLE: During the early 1980s, British children's imprint Ladybird Books retold a number of classic novels as part of the "Ladybird Horror Classics" series of pocket hardcovers. Bram Stoker's *Dracula* (1984) was re-written by Joan Cameron and illustrated by Angus McBride.

BOTTOM LEFT: In 1987, India's Poompatta Publications used Nestor Redondo's 1973 comic-strip version of *Dracula*, adapted by Naunerle Farr and originally published by Pendulum Press, to present Bram Stoker's story to a younger audience as part of the "Paico Classics" reading series.

BOTTOM MIDDLE: Robert Louis Stevenson's *Dr. Jekyll and Mr. Hyde* was retold for children by Samantha Lee as part of the "Fleshcreepers" paperback series (Barron's Educational Series, Inc., 1988), which was edited by John Halkin and originally appeared in the UK the previous year.

ABOVE RIGHT: Tim Jacobus's cover for *Welcome to Dead House* (Scholastic Inc., 1992), the first of 62 volumes in the hugely popular *Goosebumps* children's horror series created by R. (Robert) L. (Lawrence) Stine. To date, the series has sold more than 400 million copies worldwide.

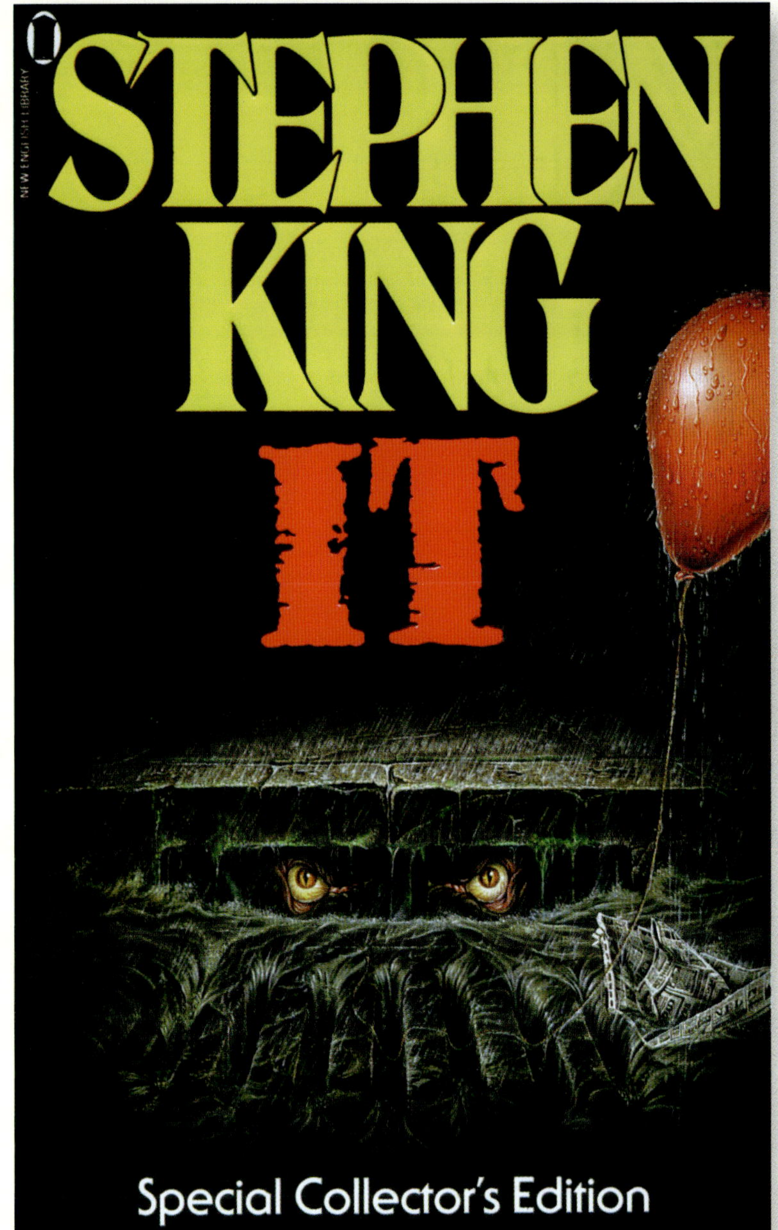

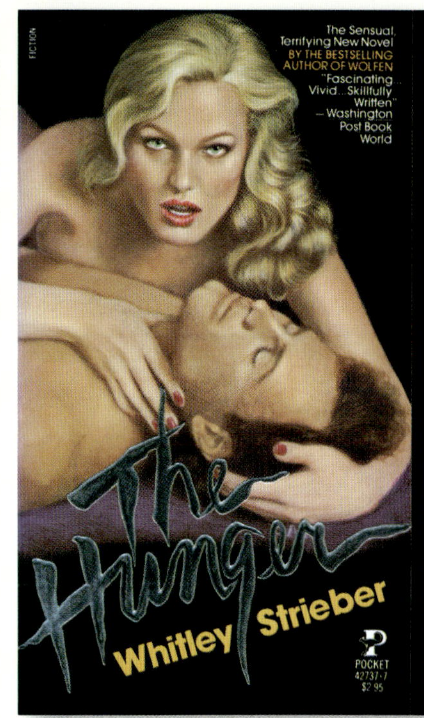

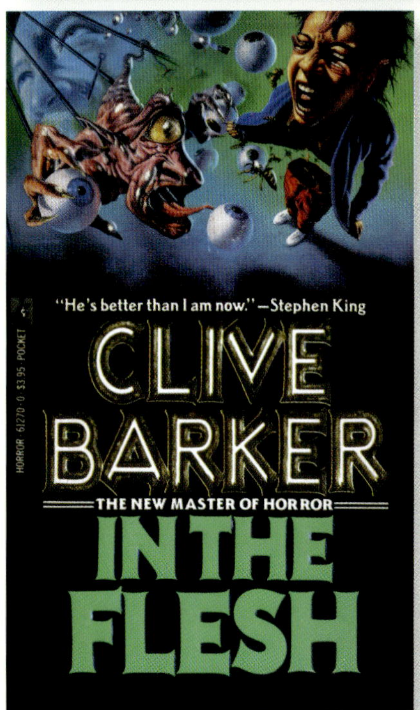

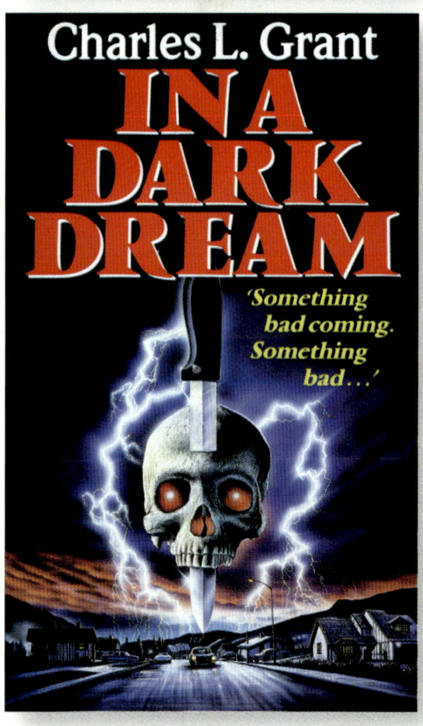

TOP MIDDLE: Berkley Books gave the cover of Peter Straub's literary horror novel *Shadowland* (1981) the full silver-foil treatment. "I thought it was creepy from page one!" exclaimed Stephen King in one of his countless cover blurbs during the 1980s, going on to add: "I loved it!"

TOP RIGHT: Before he became synonymous with aliens, Whitley Strieber tackled vampires in *The Hunger* (Pocket Books, 1982). "*The Hunger* has a lot of power, the kind of muscle that comes from pure and original invention . . . It hooked me," enthused Peter Straub.

BOTTOM MIDDLE: Jim Warren's cover for *In the Flesh* (1988), which was actually the fifth and penultimate volume in Clive Barker's *Books of Blood* collections after Pocket Books changed the titles on the last three. "He's better than I am now," admitted a gracious Stephen King.

ABOVE LEFT: Stephen King blurbed his own book with New English Library's "Special Collector's Edition" of *IT* (1987): "I am thrilled that you are able to obtain the special collector's edition, and hope it will have pride of position on your bookshelf, as it has on mine."

BOTTOM RIGHT: Steve Crisp's cover for Charles L. Grant's novel *In a Dark Dream* (New English Library, 1990). "There are few pleasures as delightful or rare as an exciting and well-written horror novel," stated Whitley Strieber. "Charles L. Grant always provides that pleasure."

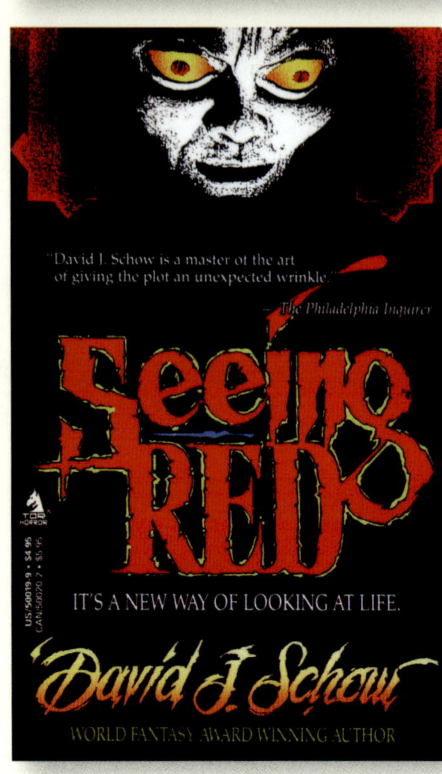

TOP LEFT: Nobody embodied the "splatterpunk" movement of the 1980s more than authors John Skipp and Craig Spector, whose first original novel *The Light at the End* (1986) was promoted by Bantam Books with this advance reading paperback.

ABOVE RIGHT: British journalist Philip Nutman championed the splatterpunk movement in the article "Inside the New Horror" in the October 1988 issue of *Rod Serling's The Twilight Zone Magazine*. Cover art by Richard Newton.

TOP MIDDLE: The British paperback of Joe R. Lansdale's 1988 novel *The Drive-In (A "B" Movie with Blood and Popcorn, Made in Texas)* (New English Library, 1989), which was followed by a pair of sequels and an omnibus edition.

BOTTOM LEFT: Mel Odom's stylish and transgressive design for Nancy A. Collins's debut vampire novel *Sunglasses After Dark* (Onyx/ New American Library, 1989) eschewed cluttering up the front cover and put the lettering on the back.

BOTTOM MIDDLE: Thomas Canty's cover for *Seeing Red* (Tor Horror, 1990), the debut short story collection from David J. Schow, who fellow author Richard Christian Matheson called "The father of splatterpunk" after Schow had coined the term in 1986.

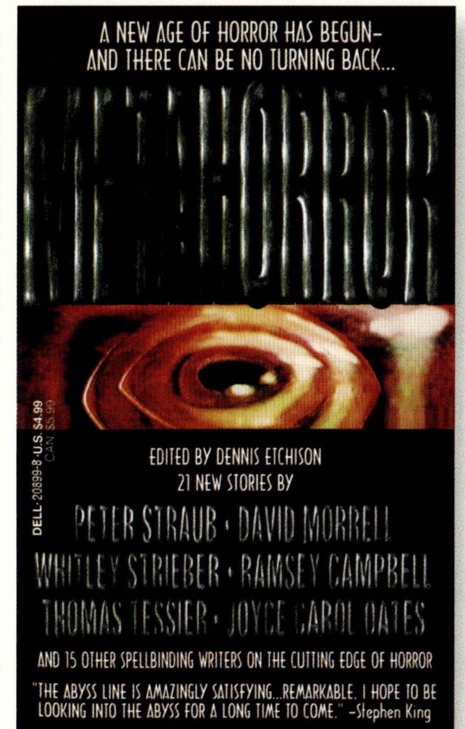

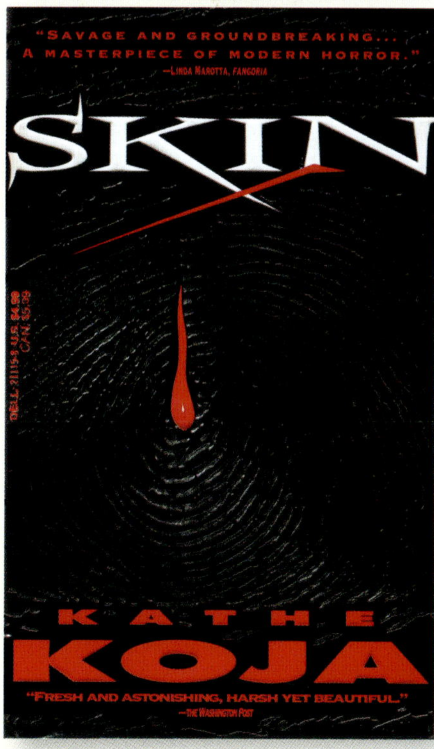

Staring Into the Abyss

Just as the horror boom of the 1970s and '80s—fueled by the success of Stephen King and specialist imprints such as Tor Horror—was finally beginning to decline, so in 1991 (the same year Tor Horror ceased publishing) Dell Publishing decided to launch its own dedicated paperback horror line, under the guidance of editor Jeanne Cavelos (b. 1960). Committed to promoting cutting-edge psychological themes and emerging writers, the Abyss imprint replaced the skulls and moons usually found on covers with impressionistic photomontages combined with the prerequisite foil, embossing, and die-cuts. However, despite huge critical acclaim and multiple award recognition, the line did not perform well commercially, and after publishing 43 titles, the Abyss imprint was discontinued in 1998.

TOP MIDDLE: Editor Dennis Etchison's original anthology *MetaHorror* (1992) was one of the most "traditional" horror books published under Dell's Abyss imprint, due to its mix of emerging and already established authors.

TOP RIGHT: Lisa Tuttle's novel *Lost Futures* (1992) received the full Dell–Abyss cover treatment . . .

ABOVE LEFT: . . . As did Dennis Etchison's die-cut *Shadowman: A Novel of Menace* (1993).

BOTTOM MIDDLE: Poppy Z. Brite's novel *Lost Souls* (1993) only carried the Abyss logo on the spine . . .

BOTTOM RIGHT: . . . While Kathe Koja's *Skin* (1994) actually dispensed with the Abyss logo altogether.

LEFT: *Lovecraft's Nightmare B* (1981), one half of an acrylic on masonite panel diptych by American artist Michael Whelan. "I launched into the Lovecraft panels armed only with my airbrush and my feelings for the 'horrific,'" recalls the artist. Publisher Ballantine/Del Rey used different portions of both artworks on the covers of six paperback collections of H.P. Lovecraft's stories (1981–82), and the complete work appeared on a 1982 "best of" volume [ABOVE].

CONTRIBUTOR BIOS

Bill Alexander
With Gene Bilbrew, Bill Alexander co-created arguably the first black superhero strip, *The Bronze Bomber*. His art appeared on softcore sex paperbacks and bondage periodicals, but he is best known for his covers for Myron Fass's Eerie Publications magazines.

Mike Ashley (b. 1948)
Mike Ashley is a British bibliographer, author, and editor of science fiction, fantasy, horror, and mystery. He has edited numerous anthologies and written such reference books as *Who's Who in Horror and Fantasy Fiction* and *The Supernatural Index* (with William G. Contento).

Al Avison (1920–1984)
"Golden Age" American comic book artist Al Avison worked for Timely Comics during the 1940s before freelancing at Harvey, where he illustrated such titles as *Tomb of Terror*, *Chamber of Chills*, and *Witches Tales*.

Jill Bauman
Jill Bauman is an American freelance illustrator and designer. She has produced hundreds of covers for horror, mystery, fantasy, and science fiction books, and has been nominated for the World Fantasy Award five times.
www.jillbauman.com

Rob Birchfield (b. 1966)
American illustrator Rob Birchfield is a formally trained tattoo artist and "Monster Kid" whose work has appeared in *Rue Morgue* and *Scary Monsters* magazines.
www.horrormovieart.com

Robert Bonfils (1922–2018)
American artist Robert Bonfils began his career as a commercial artist. During the 1960s he was Art Director at Greenleaf Publishing and found himself painting hundreds of paperback covers for the softcore sex publishing industry.

Randy Broecker (b. 1951)
For nearly 40 years Randy Broecker has provided numerous illustrations for horror and fantasy books and magazines on both sides of the Atlantic.
www.randybroecker.com

Hablot K. (Knight) **Browne** (1815–1882)
British artist and illustrator Hablot K. Brown often signed his work "Phiz." Best known for his illustrations for Charles Dickens's books, he also illustrated works by J. Sheridan Le Fanu and Sir Walter Scott.

Margaret Brundage (1900–1976)
American illustrator Margaret Brundage is remembered for her delicate pastel drawings that graced the covers of *Weird Tales*. Between June 1933 and August 1936 her art appeared on 39 consecutive covers of the pulp magazine.

Harry Clarke (1889–1931)
Irish illustrator and stained glass artist "Harry" (Henry Patrick) Clarke illustrated two editions of Edgar Allan Poe's *Tales of Mystery and Imagination* (1919 and 1923).

Sarah Cleary
Dr. Sarah Cleary has published on a wide variety of horror and pop culture subjects and is the Creative Director of Horror Expo Ireland.

Joseph Clement Coll (1881–1921)
American book and magazine illustrator Joseph Clement Coll is known for his pen and ink work for such books as Talbot Mundy's *King of the Khyber Rifles* and Sax Rohmer's *The Insidious Dr. Fu Manchu*.

Frederick Cooper (b. 1961)
American freelance artist and designer Frederick Cooper has collaborated with numerous brands and companies, including Walt Disney and Universal Studios, as well as having been featured in numerous publications and graphic novels.
www.artstation.com/frederickcooper

Steve Crisp (b. 1955)
Having graduated from St. Martins School of Art in London, Steve Crisp has spent nearly 40 years illustrating books, film posters, and video covers. His work now combines traditional and digital techniques.
www.crispart.co.uk

Cyrus ("Ciro") **Cuneo** (1879–1916)
Italian-American artist Cyrus Cincinato Cuneo, known as "Ciro," moved from San Francisco to Paris, where he studied with James McNeill Whistler. He then lived in London, where he painted and worked on book and magazine illustrations.

Sara Deck (b. 1977)
Sara Deck studied Editorial Illustration at Ontario's Sheridan College, and now works as a freelance artist focusing on pop culture and surrealist art.
www.saradeck.com

Vincent Di Fate (b. 1945)
American artist Vincent Di Fate won the Hugo Award for Best Professional Artist in 1978 and was inducted into the Science Fiction Hall of Fame in 2011.
www.vincentdifate.com

Stefan Dziemianowicz (b. 1957)
American book editor, critic, and author Stefan Richard Dziemianowicz has edited numerous horror anthologies (often in collaboration with Martin H. Greenberg and Robert E. Weinberg). He has also published a number of acclaimed bibliographical works.

Reginald Easton (1807–1893)
British painter Reginald Easton was a self-taught artist whose miniature portraiture brought him much favor and popularity among the fashionable and elite of Victorian London, including the Royal Family.

Les Edwards (b. 1949)
Les Edwards began his illustration career immediately upon leaving the Hornsey College of Art. Since then he has become a stalwart of the British illustration scene, working in a variety of genres.
www.lesedwards.com

Bob Eggleton (b. 1960)
Bob Eggleton has won multiple Hugo Awards, Locus Awards, Chesley Awards, and The Mangled Skyscraper Award from The Godzilla Society of North America. He has worked in publishing and as a motion picture conceptual artist.
www.bobeggleton.com

Lee Elias (1920–1998)
British-born American "Golden Age" comic artist Lee Elias illustrated such titles as *Chamber of Chills*, *Tomb of Terror*, *Witches Tales*, and *Black Cat Mystery* for Harvey Comics, and later worked for Warren Publishing's *Eerie*.

Ed ("Emsh") **Emshwiller** (1925–1990)
American SF artist Edward Alexander Emshwiller, who signed much of his work "Emsh," worked for numerous book and magazine publishers during his career. He was inducted into the Science Fiction Hall of Fame in 2007.

Virgil Finlay (1914–1971)
Virgil Warden Finlay was perhaps America's premier fantasy, science fiction, and horror pulp magazine illustrator. Famous for his incredibly detailed pen and ink drawings, he created more than 2,600 pieces of art in his 35-year career.

John Richard Flanagan (1895–1964)
Australian-born illustrator and cartoonist John Richard Flanagan moved to America in 1916, where he began illustrating for books and magazines. He later worked for the comic books.

Barry Forshaw (b. 1950)
British writer Barry Forshaw is an authority on genre fiction and film. He writes for various newspapers, broadcasts, and is the author of *British Gothic Cinema*.
www.barryforshaw.co.uk

Christopher Fowler (b. 1953)
Christopher Fowler is the award-winning British author of many novels and short story collections, and the Bryant & May mystery novels. His memoirs *Paperboy* and *Film Freak* have been published to critical acclaim.
www.christopherfowler.co.uk

Christopher Franchi (b. 1966)
American artist Christopher Franchi grew up on a steady diet of Saturday afternoon Creature Features. He's still a creepy little "Monster Kid" at heart, and he wouldn't have it any other way.
Facebook: Metaluna 5 Media

Frank Frazetta (1928–2010)
Frank Frazetta was the premier American comic book artist of his generation. He went on to illustrate books, movie posters, and much more. His painting *Egyptian Queen* sold for a world record $5.4 million on May 16, 2019.
www.frazettamuseum.com

David Henry Friston (1820–1906)
British illustrator and portrait painter David Henry Friston was the creator of the first illustrations of Sherlock Holmes in *A Study in Scarlet* (1887).

Jack Gaughan (1930–1985)
Hugo Award–winning American SF artist Jack Gaughan was posthumously inducted into the Science Fiction and Fantasy Hall of Fame in 2015.

Gary Gianni (b. 1954)
Gary Gianni is an American comics artist and a fantasy illustrator. He created the *MonsterMen* comic book series.
Twitter: @GaryGianniArt

Thomas Gianni (1960–2020)
Thomas Gianni's artwork was influenced by the pulp magazines. Since childhood he was enamored of the Universal and Hammer horror films, and *film noir*. More recently, he illustrated a series of Robert E. Howard books for the REH Foundation.
Twitter: @thomasfgianni

Karl Godwin (1893–1962)
Canadian-born Karl Godwin was an illustrator and landscape painter who received his art training in America. His work appeared widely on advertising and movie posters, and in popular magazines.

Basil Gogos (1929–2017)
To a whole generation of American "Monster Kids," Egyptian-born Basil Gogos was the acknowledged master of film monster portrait art. Famous for his amazing use of color and bold brushwork, his paintings are as iconic as his subjects.

Edmond Good (1910–1991)
American-born artist Edmond Good wrote and illustrated for the "Golden Age" comic books and produced a number of Canadian pulp magazine covers.

Károly Grósz
As the advertising art director at Universal Studios, Károly Grósz created some of the most iconic movie posters of the 1930s. For some years, his poster for *The Mummy* (1932) was the most expensive film poster of all time, selling for $435,500 at a Sotheby's auction in 1997.

HagCult (b. 1985)
"HagCult" (M. Fersner) is a traditional illustrator who specializes in the spooky and macabre. The shadowy spaces that make life fun.
www.hagcult.com

Graham Humphreys (b. 1960)
Graham Humphreys's style has been forged through Punk Rock in the late 1970s, VHS in the 1980s, and all things horror. With more than 35 years experience in the field, he continues to produce illustration and design for a wide range of subjects.
www.grahamhumphreys.com

Stephen Jones (b. 1953)
Multiple award-winning British writer and editor Stephen Jones has published more than 150 books, including the previous two volumes in this series, *The Art of Horror* and *The Art of Horror Movies*.
www.stephenjoneseditor.com

Richard Wynn Keene (1809–1887)
Richard Wynn Keene was a British theater designer of the Victorian period who was better known under the name "Dykwynkyn." Despite his acclaim, he died in poverty.

Warren Kremer (1921–2003)
American comic book artist Warren Kremer was an art director at Harvey Comics, where he worked on the company's horror titles and also created the characters Hot Stuff the Little Devil and Richie Rich.

Alan Lee (b. 1947)
Academy Award-winner Alan Lee's watercolor paintings are inspired by the great turn-of-the-century Romantic illustrators. He has enjoyed a long association with the work of J.R.R. Tolkien, both as book illustrator, and conceptual designer on Peter Jackson's film adaptations.

Mark Maddox (b. 1961)
Mark Maddox was inspired by artists like Jack Kirby, James Bama, and many others. He is an award-winning American artist whose illustrations have appeared on books and in a wide variety of periodicals.
www.maddoxplanet.com

Gregory William Mank (b. 1950)
Author and film historian Gregory William Mank's sizeable body of work includes the recent books *Laird Cregar: A Hollywood Tragedy* and *One Man Crazy! The Life and Death of Colin Clive*.
www.gregorymank.com

Justin Marriott (b. 1969)
British writer Justin Marriott is the editor and self-publisher of such magazines as *The Paperback Fanatic*, *Pulp Horror*, and *Monster Maniacs*. *The Collected Pulp Horror: Volume One* appeared in 2019.

Fortunino Matania (1881–1963)
Italian-born artist Chevalier Fortunino Matania moved to Paris in the early 1900s, and then to London. With the outbreak of the First World War he became a war artist and later illustrated for a wide range of magazines.

Paul McCaffrey (b. 1966)
British artist Paul McCaffrey's obsession with horror is probably inextricably linked with his obsessions with comic books and drawing. He has worked for IDW, DC, Marvel, and Titan.
www.coroflot.com/paul_mccaffrey

Dave McKean (b. 1963)
In 2014, Dave McKean was chosen by Apple as one of their 30 key creatives representing 30 years since the launch of the Apple Mac. He has illustrated over 80 books, several graphic novels, and directed three feature films.
www.davemckean.com

Mike Mignola (b. 1960)
American artist Mike Mignola's fascination with ghosts and monsters began at an early age. In 1993 he created *Hellboy*—a half-demon occult detective who may or may not be the Beast of the Apocalypse.
www.artofmikemignola.com

Rowena Morrill (1944–2021)
American artist Rowena Morrill is credited as one of the first women artists to have a major impact on genre paperback covers during the 1970s and '80s. *The Art of Rowena* was published in 2000.

Lisa Morton (b. 1958)
American author Lisa Morton is an award-winning prose and non-fiction writer, and a recognized expert on Halloween. Her 2012 study *Trick or Treat: The History of Halloween* won the Bram Stoker Award.
www.lisamorton.com

Lee Moyer (b. 1964)
Rooted in his knowledge of design history, Lee Moyer's work blends classic painting, pop culture, and naturalist illustration, evoking intensity and impish humor.
www.leemoyer.com

Rudy Palais (1912–2014)
American "Golden Age" comic book artist Rudy Palais worked for most of the New York publishers. He is best remembered for his 20 years with *Classics Illustrated* and Harvey Comics' horror titles.

Bruce Pennington (b. 1944)
British artist Bruce Pennington's first book cover appeared in 1967. This led to him becoming one of the foremost cover artists for publisher New English Library. In the late 1980s he moved away from commercial illustration in favor of more personal work.
www.brucepennington.co.uk

Richard M. Powers (1921–1996)
The surrealist paintings of American artist Richard M. Powers graced numerous SF, fantasy, and horror books and magazines from the 1950s to the 1990s. He was inducted into the Science Fiction Hall of Fame in 2008.
www.richardmpowers.com

Sanjulián (b. 1941)
Spanish artist Manuel Pérez Clemente "Sanjulián" is best known for his work in *Heavy Metal* and the Warren Publishing magazines *Creepy*, *Eerie*, and *Vampirella*.
www.sanjulian.info

Norman Saunders (1907–1989)
Prolific American artist Norman Blaine Saunders's work was used on the pulps, men's adventure magazines, paperbacks, comic books, and trading cards.
www.normansaunders.com

Robert Silverberg (b. 1935)
Prolific and multiple award-winning American author Robert Silverberg has been published (under numerous pseudonyms) in most of the fiction genres.
www.robert-silverberg.com

E.F. Skinner (1865–1924)
British painter Edward Frederick Skinner was best known for his patriotic paintings of factories and workers during the early twentieth century.

Richard Harland Smith (b. 1961)
Richard Harland Smith is a film historian living in Los Angeles. He is a former writer for *Video Watchdog* magazine and Turner Classic Movies.

Walter Velez (1939–2018)
American artist Walter Velez's illustrations appeared on book covers, games, and trading cards.
www.jillbauman.com/walter-velez/

H.J. Ward (1909–1945)
American artist Hugh Joseph Ward was known for his often *risqué* covers for Trojan Publications' line of "Spicy" pulp magazines during the 1930s and '40s.

Michael Whelan (b. 1950)
Michael Whelan's art is intentionally imbued with a strong sense of the mystical or dreamlike, and is suffused with symbolic content.
www.michaelwhelan.com

Lawson Wood (1878–1957)
British painter, illustrator, and designer Clarence Lawson Wood was best known for his humorous depictions of dinosaurs and cavemen.

Bernie Wrightson (1948–2017)
American artist Bernie Wrightson's influences were Frank Frazetta and "Ghastly" Graham Ingels of EC comics. He began working for DC, Marvel, and Warren's horror titles in the late 1960s and early '70s, and in 1971 he co-created "Swamp Thing" with writer Len Wein.
www.berniewrightson.com

INDEX

ACKNOWLEDGMENTS

Thanks to all the following who helped with the compilation of this volume: Mike Ashley, Jean-Daniel Brèque, Randy and Sara Broecker, Peter Crowther (PS Publishing), John A. Davis, Alex Eisenstein, Doug Ellis, Brian Emrich, Susan Emshwiller, Lail M. Finlay, Barry and Judith Forshaw, Jane Frank, Frank Frazetta, Jr., Heritage Auctions, Lisa Morton, Frank Motler, Bob Murawski, Neil Pettigrew, Darrell C. Richardson, David Saunders, Mike Smith (PS Publishing), The Steam Man of the West, Mike Stephenson (White Box Studios), Philip Stephenson-Payne, Phil and Sarah Stokes, Bill Wallace, and, especially, to all the writers, artists, and everyone else who contributed their time and talent to this book. *SJ*

ART CREDITS

Key: b=bottom; c=center; l=left; r=right; t=top; br=bottom right; bl=bottom left; tr=top right; tl=top left.

Jill Bauman: p238; © Rob Birchfield: p48l, p213r; Randy Broecker copyright 2019: p19, p41, p69, p95, p121, p147, p175, p201, p225; © Frederick Cooper: p161r, p200; Steve Crisp: p241t; Sara Deck: p108tl: Vincent Di Fate: p101tr; © Les Edwards: p117tr, p186l, p209tr, p224; Art © Bob Eggleton: p51tr, p240tl; Ed Emshwiller "Emsh", courtesy of Susan Emshwiller: p11; Copyright permission by Lail M. Finlay: p77tr, p77br; © Christopher Franchi: p153; p222–223r; Frazetta Jr. Enterprises, LLC: p2; p195tr; © Gary Gianni: p1; © Thomas Gianni: p18; © Basil Gogos: p94; © HAGCULT: p167r; © 2014 Graham Humphreys: p17–18, p56–57r, p218tl; © 2019 Graham Humphreys Ltd/Vintage Movie Posters/ Excalibur Auctions: p162l, p163r; © Alan Lee: p233; Artwork copyright Mark Maddox: p146; © Paul McCaffrey: p46; Dave McKean: p47tr, p61r; Art by Mike Mignola, courtesy of the artist, inspired by the Warren characters currently published by New Comic Company, LLC/Dark Horse (*Creepy* and *Eerie*) and Dynamite (*Vampirella*): p141; © Lee Moyer: p24; © Bruce Pennington: p198–199; Copyright © The Estate of Richard M. Powers: p174; © Rowena: p234; Sanjulián (Manuel Pérez Clemente): p40; Norman Saunders, courtesy of David Saunders: Front cover, p120; Walter Velez: p218tr; © Michael Whelan: p248–249l; © Bernie Wrightson: p25tr. Every effort has been made to trace the copyright holders of artworks in this book. Elephant Book Company would be happy if contacted to correct any errors or omissions in future editions.

FRONT COVER: Norman Saunders's original cover painting for *Unknown World* No. 1 (Fawcett, June 1952).

CHAPTER HEADINGS: Original pen and ink illustrations by American artist Randy Broecker.

SPINE: Detail from Lee Elias's cover for Harvey Comics' *Chamber of Chills* No. 18 (July 1953).

THIS PAGE: Detail from the back cover of the British EC reprint of *The Haunt of Fear* No. 1 (circa 1954).

BACK ENDPAPERS: Splash panel detail by Rudy Palais from *Witches Tales Magazine* No. 5 (September 1951).

BACK COVER: Detail from a "Spook Show" poster for *Dr. Dracula's Living Nightmares* (circa 1950s).